THE MEMORY CURSE

THE LOST GOD BOOK TWO

SHEILA MASTERSON

THE MEMORY CURSE

THE LOST GOD BOOK TWO

SHEILA MASTERSON

Ebook: 978-1-960416-05-6

Paperback: 978-1-960416-06-3

Hardcover: 978-1-960416-07-0

Cover Design: Andrea Laguer

Hardback Case and Map Design: Mike Sisak

Editing: Erin at EKB Books

Proofreading: Mike Sisak

For every tender-hearted soul who has ever been called "too sensitive."

May you find your own spell for the courage to remain brave with your hand and brave with your heart.

A NOTE FROM THE AUTHOR

Dear Reader,

THE MEMORY CURSE deals with mental health struggles (including grief, depression, and anxiety), fertility issues, war, violence, death, profanity, and explicit sex. I have attempted to treat all sensitive topics with the utmost care, but I recognize that this content might still be challenging for some readers.

This book is about many things, but mostly about love, especially self-love, so please take care of yourself above all else.

Happy Reading,

Sheila

THE G☾DS

Olney Gods

Clastor - God of All Matter

Adira - Goddess of the Sea

Aelish - Goddess of Truth

Desiree - Goddess of Love and Beauty

Sayla - Goddess of the Hunt

Devlin - God of Wisdom and Reason

*Cecilia - Goddess of Mind and Memory

Neutral Gods

Grimon - God of Death

Samson - God of Lust

Aurelia - Goddess of Fertility and Harvest

Argarian Gods

Endros - God of War and Discord

*Cato - God of Manipulation and Influence

*Living Gods

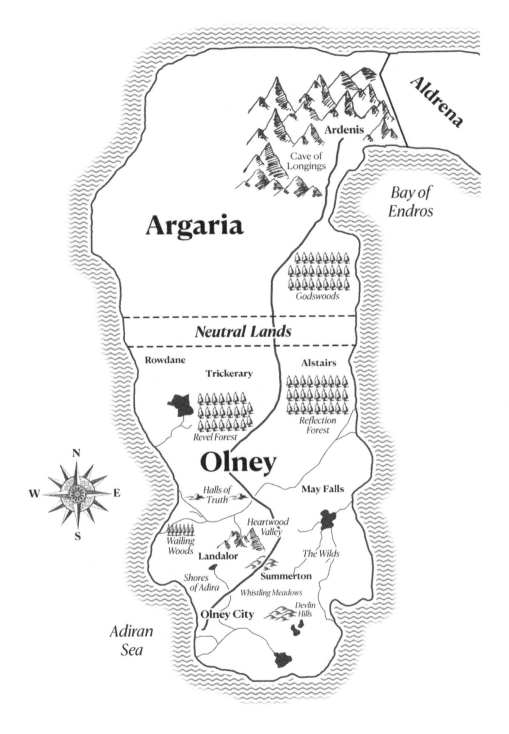

PART I:
THE LAST LIVING GODDESS

1

CECILIA

A ll Cecilia wanted was to take her morning walk on the beach in peace, but the god of death couldn't even let her have that.

Grimon was waiting for her the moment her feet hit the sand.

"What do you want, Grim? I don't have time for gods stuff right now. There's a war coming," she said, brushing past him.

He grabbed her arm and spun her to face him. "You're talking about the war out there. What about the war in here?" He tapped a finger on her chest.

She rolled her eyes so hard it hurt. "I don't know what you're talking about."

She walked toward the water, and Grimon fell into step beside her. He knew how to weaponize a silence until she was anxious to spill her guts. This was the third morning in a row he'd ruined her solitude with his expectant presence.

Cecilia ignored him, focusing instead on the cool sand beneath her feet and the salty breeze ruffling her hair. The world had suddenly become much too loud and unruly and she struggled to adjust to her heightened senses. She had taken to hiding in her cottage with Xander, her body full of restless energy she could never fully spend despite Xander's enthusiastic efforts.

Cecilia's magic had always been about remembering—as if some vibrational pulse in the universe had been whispering to her since she was a child. *Remember.* Even the lessons in school seemed to awaken some wisdom that existed in the back of her mind. *Remember.* And when her brain felt too full, she could always make room for more. *Remember.*

The fates had a sense of humor since her new power was to make people forget. Forget themselves. Forget their purpose. Forget the very things that made them who they were. All while she was doomed to remember.

Memory strung the world together. It sustained the fairy tales and stories that she loved so much. It wound people into and through her life in beautiful, heart-opening ways. Memory was the foundation of personality. It was the roots through which family and friendships grew. It tethered people to reality.

Memory was life, and she its destroyer.

Cecilia, goddess of mind and memory, breaker of minds, ruination of identity, plague on memory. She never dreamed she'd be such a destructive force in the world.

In the quiet, she felt the power climbing through her bones like vines. *Remember.* She felt the call to vengeance, to bring the world to her feet. *Remember.* She felt the darkness clawing its way out of her chest like a rabid beast. *Remember.*

Long ago the Seer had said, *"Only you can decide who fear will make you."*

Cecilia was foolish to think she could anticipate all the things there might be to fear in the world. A lifetime of fairy tales with monsters and dragons and demons, but she couldn't have expected that she would become the thing she feared most.

Grimon finally spoke. "You know, you're being selfish."

She scoffed. "Selfish?"

"You didn't get what you wanted and now you're refusing to integrate your abilities fully."

Cecilia shrugged. "I integrated them just fine when I fought Endros."

"You got lucky. And you had help," Grimon said.

"From who?" Cecilia asked.

"From me." The voice sounded like it came directly from the crashing waves.

A goddess stepped out of the surf, her cerulean gown blending with the sea. Perfectly dry blonde curls spilled over her shoulders and her blue eyes—eyes that looked exactly like Cecilia's—narrowed on her.

"Sister," the goddess said with a nod.

It had to be—

"Adira," the goddess of the sea said.

A lump formed in Cecilia's throat. She was choked by a sudden, intense desire to know this stranger—to have the same kind of intimacy with her that Sylvie did with her sisters. Cecilia hadn't the first idea how someone should act when meeting family they didn't know existed, but she could do little more than gawk, searching for herself in the goddess's mannerisms.

"You were there when I fought Endros?" Cecilia asked.

"You just assumed that you could suddenly control the tides perfectly?" Adira asked.

Cecilia sighed. Apparently sarcasm ran in the family.

"Adira, it's been too long. You look good," Grimon said with a seductive smile.

"Don't even give me that look," Adira snapped. "What happened twenty years ago won't be happening again, even if it was the best sex of your long, miserable life. You ghosted me."

"Ghosted?" Grimon's lips tilted into a smirk.

"Yes, you slept with me and then poof! You were gone—like an apparition," Adira said.

Grimon laughed. "It's a bit on the nose for the god of death, don't you think?"

"Okay, this is getting weird," Cecilia said, looking between her half-sister and the god of death. The last thing she needed was a lover's quarrel between gods.

"Which part? The part where you're meeting your sister for the first time, or finding out you aren't the first of us that Grimon has taken an interest in?" Adira asked, glaring at Grimon.

"I think your guardian is worried you're losing your mind." Grimon looked over Cecilia's shoulder. She turned to find Rainer standing at the bottom of the cliff trail, watching her.

"Why?" she asked.

"He can't see us," Adira answered.

"Of course not." Cecilia cupped her hands around her mouth. "Rain, it's fine. I'll meet you at the stables at lunchtime. Gods stuff."

Rainer nodded and disappeared around a curve in the trail that led up to her cottage.

"I need to learn how to do this invisibility thing," she said.

"Living gods can't do it. Those of us ascended can choose to be invisible when we want," Adira said. "It's so we can move among mortals unseen if we wish. Only other gods can see us in this form unless we choose to make ourselves known."

"Is that how you knew who I was when I was young?" Cecilia asked.

Grimon nodded.

Adira's eyes went wide. "You met him when you were a child?"

"I was summoned by prayers, waiting right here on the beach, expecting an adult. Instead, this tiny little girl—couldn't have been much older than six—walks up and asks if I'm lost," Grimon said. "You can imagine my surprise that she could see me. She told me to call her Lady Cece and asked what I was, since she could tell I wasn't human. When I told her, she wasn't the least bit fazed. She just took my hand and walked with me and talked to me about her mother and the other spirits she met. I started coming back a few days a week and walking with her in the morning until she got older and was too busy with her training."

Adira looked astonished. "All this time, you knew she was the Lost Goddess, and you kept it to yourself?"

Cecilia was hit with a wave of delayed panic. So much could have gone wrong when she was so young and it would have been entirely her fault. She owed Grimon a debt.

Grimon shrugged. "Why would I share it with anyone? She was young and sweet, and I have never had love for Endros and Cato."

Cecilia tugged on her dress. "Thanks for the lovely trip down memory lane, Grim, but can you get to the point? Why are you both here interrupting my morning walk?"

"Because you haven't integrated," Adira said. "You're still trying to push your abilities away, thinking of the goddess as a separate entity when she's a part of you. The only reason you feel different now is because you won't let the transformation fully settle in. It can't be undone now. Accept it. It will be easier if you do. You'll feel more like yourself."

Cecilia blew out an angry breath. "I don't want or need your help. I don't need to be managed and I hate riddles. I'm not the place for the lot of you to hang your hopes. You don't know what it's like to grow up without this kind of power and then learn how to use it right away."

"Lady Cece, what did I tell you about anger at our picnic in the woods?" Grimon asked.

"That I should hold on to it until I knew where to direct it."

"And do you?"

She glared at Grimon. "Yes."

"So it's simple then. Integrate your powers, figure out what Cato is up to, and take him out." Grimon said it as if murdering a living god would be easy—something she could do in an afternoon.

"If it's so simple, why haven't any of the rest of you done it?" she asked.

Adira sighed, twisting a golden curl around her finger. "The rest of us have been outsmarted."

"Or unable to interfere," Grimon said.

That was sobering. Cecilia's stomach twisted in knots. "Just because I'm the goddess of mind and memory doesn't mean that I'm smarter than him. He's been ahead of me this whole time. I'm sure he's still ahead of me now, but Cato also has some of Endros's strength and fighting ability, which negates my last advantage."

"You can't think that way, little sister," Adira said, her face softening ever so slightly. "We're all here to help you in our own ways. We can't give you all the answers because it's against the rules of nature, but we can each give you pieces. You will have to put them together."

Cecilia threw her hands up. "I'm tired of puzzles."

Adira's face pinched in disdain. "Yes, well. You'd have less to solve if you hadn't made a deal with Cato."

Cecilia kicked a shell into the sea. "I didn't know he was pulling the strings."

"Was it worth it?" Adira asked.

Cecilia swallowed thickly. Just the memory of Rainer nearly dying was enough to chill her down to the bone, freezing her body in terror that felt as fresh now as it had then. "It was."

Adira laughed. "Oh, you silly girl. You don't know that yet."

"I do." Cecilia's glare challenged Adira to say otherwise. There was no point trying to pretend that her feelings were a secret.

Cecilia had written it on the beach once when she was younger and more hopeful. A wish in the sand swept away on the lips of the sea. A secret passed back and forth between old friends. *I love Rainer McKay.* The sea lapped it up in waves, murmuring like a gossip along the shore.

Some mornings she'd cried over it, the salt of her tears blending into ocean waves. Other times it was an angry shout, scoring her throat on the way out. *Why can't he just love me back?* Always she returned home feeling like she'd shared what was forbidden everywhere else.

The problem was that everyone knew then. Even if she never said it, it was written all over her face. And now her husband knew it, too.

The goddess of the sea studied Cecilia as if seeing her for the first time. The set of her jaw, her eyes, and her stony face softened. "Well then, I suppose it was."

"What will Cato want for it?" Cecilia tried to keep her voice from trembling.

"He never wants what we think he wants. He is a master of misdirection," Adira said with a shrug.

"If you had to guess?"

Adira shrugged. "Probably the use of your power. You are the last two living gods. The most powerful gods in this realm."

Cecilia frowned. "Isn't Clastor the most powerful?"

"Clastor is ascended like the rest of us," Adira said. "His home is in the Otherworld, the Realm of the Gods. He's weaker in this realm than you are. We ascended gods can pull strings, but we don't have full access to all our powers here. Why do you think so many prayers go unanswered? I may change the tides but I cannot flood the earth. You and Cato can change the minds of men, in your own unique ways. You can make the world forget there was even a time before you. Cato can manipulate people, and mortals are so easily swayed."

"Perhaps I can make him forget me." Cecilia laughed bitterly.

Adira's eyes blazed momentarily brighter. "I'd like to see you try. Unfortunately, your power won't work on him and his won't work on you. But he doesn't need his power to manipulate you. He can use those around you. He's been doing it to the rest of us for centuries. The moves are too many. Only the fates know for sure."

Cecilia swallowed a lump in her throat. "I don't believe in fate."

"Why should you?" Adira asked. "A goddess can make her own fate."

"So what should I do?"

Adira stepped close enough that Cecilia could smell the salt on her skin. She twirled one of Cecilia's curls around her fingers. "Our sisters are trying to figure it out. They are watching Cato closely, but it's a challenge to read his moves. Some he makes just to throw us off."

"Our sisters?" The concept of siblings was still so foreign to Cecilia.

"Did you not read any of your mythology texts, Cecilia? I'm talking about Desiree, goddess of love and beauty. Aelish, goddess of truth, and Sayla, goddess of the hunt. Who knows, perhaps even our brother, Devlin, god of wisdom and reason, might throw some of his considerable knowledge behind us, if he can be bothered to look up from his stupid books."

When Cecilia was young she had desperately wanted siblings, but now they seemed more trouble than they were worth.

"I can trust them?" Cecilia asked.

Adira grinned. "As much as you can trust anyone."

"How comforting." Cecilia plopped down into the sand and flopped onto her back, staring at the clouds streaking the sky.

Adira looked down at her. "Integrate your powers. It will help you control them and learn what exactly they are. We have hints, but we won't know for sure until you surrender to the power that already lives inside you."

Cecilia blinked away tears. It wasn't that easy. Every time she thought about that power, she thought about what she'd lost, the grief cresting like a great wave every time she considered testing the limits of her new magic.

Adira cleared her throat. "I know what you've lost. I'm sorry for it. The world thinks that it's a great boon to have such power. Those of us who have it, however, know that it always requires impossible sacrifice. I wouldn't wish your pain on anyone. Still, wars don't wait for us to be ready to fight them."

Cecilia said nothing.

"I must go, but I'll be monitoring you and Cato. I will help if I can." The warmth that crept into Adira's expression hardened to perfect porcelain coldness and, with the crash of a wave, she was gone.

Grimon sat in the sand next to Cecilia. Silence stretched between them, heavy as the humid air on the unseasonably hot autumn day.

"I'm sorry about your father," Grimon said quietly.

She sat and squinted at the bright sunlight reflecting off the sea, trying to calm the storm churning inside of her. She could not think of her father without seeing his wide eyes as Endros's knife plunged into his neck.

"Thank you," she said, finally turning to look at Grimon again.

"For what it's worth, he's happily reunited with your mother and Selene Carrick."

The reminder that her father had sacrificed his life for hers only added to the growing pressure she felt. Everyone was counting on her and she was barely holding herself together.

"You're still with the prince." There was a hint of surprise in Grimon's voice.

"He's my husband and I love him."

Grimon searched her face like he was expecting her to say more. He shook his head. "Love is the fastest path to madness. You should ask him if there's more to his story."

Cecilia clasped her hands, rubbing her thumb over her inner wrist. "There hasn't exactly been much time. Things kind of devolved into chaos since our last chat. Why don't you butt out and tell me what the hell this does?" She held out her wrist, where she still bore the iridescent mark of Grimon's kiss.

"You carry my favor. It means you can visit my realm for extended periods of time without trouble. It also means you can call me easily if you need help and I'll do what I can. That way, you don't need to make any more deals with Cato."

"As if I would," she huffed.

"You still owe him a favor. I'd advise not letting him know the full depth of your abilities. The less he knows, the better."

Cecilia gave him a sardonic smile. "I was planning to send out a declaration to the entire world. You know how I enjoy being a goddess and all."

Grimon frowned. "I know you've lost a lot, but if you continue to focus on that, this fight is already over, and everything you and those around you have sacrificed will be for nothing. I wish you'd stop sulking and channel your stubbornness into something worthwhile, like defeating Cato. Didn't you wish for the power to make your own choices during that meteor shower months ago?"

Cecilia bristled. "How do you know what I wished?"

"Gods can hear wishes, Cece. Who else would?"

Heat rushed into her cheeks. "Does that mean Cato could have heard it?"

"No, living gods don't have that privilege. The point is, you wanted freedom and time and you got it. You were obsessed with having the power to change things until it was handed to you. Now all you want is to give it back."

Guilt churned in her stomach. It seemed a lifetime ago that she sat in the garden telling Xander what she would do if she had more power. She thought that freedom would look different, but it didn't change the fact that she had more freedom and magic now than ever before. She was terrified of making the wrong choice. Teddy and her father had sacrificed themselves for her. The least she could do to honor their memory was fight back.

"Your people need you. It might not be fair, but it doesn't make it less true. There's a method to the madness of this, I promise. It's time to grow up and release the things you can't change and start focusing on the things you can."

Easy for him to say. "How has no one ever mentioned that the god of death is kind of an asshole?"

Grimon chuckled darkly. "If it helps, I think you might discover that you have some additional powers."

"Like what?"

"People know me as the god of death, shepherd of souls, but that isn't my only power. I can command the dead. I can dampen and quiet sound. But I can also see the truth in souls—what fears, worries, grief, and joy live inside them."

"What does mine look like?" she asked without thinking. She wasn't sure she wanted to know. What if it was ugly—full of the darkness she felt every time she closed her eyes? Still, it was better to know and not be forced to weather more surprises.

Grimon hesitated. "Most people think they want to know until they hear it." His face was solemn, but she noticed his gaze went unfocused, like he was looking through her already.

"I still want to know."

"Always so brave." Grimon's eyes narrowed. "Right now you're holding a lot of grief, which is understandable, and also a lot of rage. It's dimming your soul. You're not as radiant as you usually are."

"I'm usually radiant?" she asked, bewildered.

"Yes, you have a certain radiance, like most gods do, but there's much more," he said. "There's such a warmth to your soul, like standing in the sun on a warm day. You also have some bitterness for your suffering, and hidden underneath everything else, a deep loneliness that you feel all the time. If you let it, it could block out everything else."

Cecilia swallowed hard. "That doesn't sound good."

"It doesn't, but hope threads through the dark and it's a huge part of your essence. It's really beautiful. I gave you my favor because I have faith in you."

Cecilia arched a brow. "Do you have a choice other than having faith in me?"

"I'd put my faith in the little girl I met on the beach all those years ago over pretty much anyone else, because she didn't let fear stop her from facing challenging and scary situations. She's still part of you, Cece," Grimon said.

Cecilia was unsure how to process the contents of her soul.

Grimon placed a hand on her shoulder. "It's time. Integrate. I promise you'll feel more like yourself instead of feeling divided. I know you think it's protecting you, but it's just delaying your healing."

She nodded. "How do I do it?"

"Right now it feels like you're divided, right?"

"Yes."

"Imagine those two halves of you blending. The goddess is another part of you. Close your eyes. I'll stay here with you," Grimon said, taking both of her hands in his.

Cecilia looked into his pale blue eyes. She wanted to cry because it felt like giving up—like a surrender to the loss, to the finality of her exchange, to living an immortal life.

She imagined it exactly as he explained, and after a moment

there was a rush of heat through her body so intense she felt faint. Grimon steadied her.

Everything tingled and the warmth went to her head. She leaned into him more heavily.

"Take a deep breath and let go. Don't fight it," he whispered.

She let it consume her and when the rushing sensation finally stopped, she was surprised to find herself crying against Grimon's shoulder. He held her, stroking firm circles on her back with the heel of his hand.

When the tears abated, she couldn't sense the goddess as a separate part of her anymore. She was alone again.

"It's done." There was no triumph in it.

"You're in the game now." Grimon squeezed her shoulder. "I know it doesn't seem like it's going to be okay, and it might not for a while, but it will. For now, you need to focus on the coming war."

War was inevitable. That was the whisper on every tongue in court, but Cecilia wasn't certain. If she'd known who she was from the beginning. If she chose not to claim this power. If powerful men could be satisfied with ruling half the continent. If. If. If. *If* was a word for the foolish girl who set out for her final Gauntlet run months before and took people at their word. *If* was not for the woman she'd become. She felt as though she'd aged a great deal since she'd set out on that journey.

Maybe war would come no matter what, but she knew that the reckoning of power-hungry men had a much greater impact on the people around them than on the men themselves. The groundwork had been laid before she was even born, but she couldn't help feeling that she may have provoked things by killing Endros.

You're also foolish to be so brave. He's in your life already, Endros had said of Cato. *In ways you haven't begun to comprehend. He will ruin you and he will enjoy doing it. He will bend you to his will and the longer you fight him, the more he will enjoy it. There's no beating him. You will beg for it to end when he is done with you.*

The words still sent a shiver through her. She didn't feel prepared. Cecilia hoped she could help when the time came, but she worried about what that help might look like. She worried about letting her people down as much as she worried about hurting them.

When she was a witch, she'd always considered her memory magic a tremendous blessing. Now her magic felt like a curse. A curse of memory; of how much death she reaped; of all those she'd lost.

If she really was to blame, then maybe carrying the weight of it all in her perfect memory was her reckoning.

"What if I can't control my power? What if I accidentally wipe the mind of one of my friends with a simple touch?" Cecilia asked.

The day she'd killed the battalion of Argarian hunters on the beach might not have left a mark on her body, but it did on her mind.

All of her worst hurts had left no visible scars. She had no scar from the loss of Teddy or the loss of her father. She had no scar from the loss of her ability to have children. Still, she felt each cut so sharply she wondered, were she able to see into her own chest, if she would find a mark from each on her heart.

Grimon patted her shoulder. "It's okay to have a healthy fear of it, but if you listen, your power will tell you how to use it. I've already been in this realm too long and I'm fading. I have to go, but summon me if you need me."

"How?"

Grimon tapped the iridescent kiss mark he'd left on her wrist. "Just kiss here."

A laugh bubbled up from her chest. "Are all the gods perverts?"

"Now that you're integrated, maybe you'll understand. The urges are much stronger and more frequent, and the euphoria they bring intoxicating." He winked. "Be well, Lady Cece. I'll see you soon."

"Thanks, Grim."

Grimon faded into smoke and Cecilia was left alone on the beach with nothing but grief to keep her company.

2

CECILIA

Cecilia stretched out in the sunlight like a sleepy cat, the bedsheet pooling around her waist. The mornings had grown crisper, the chill in the air too much for open windows, though the cottage would be stifling again by midday. Autumn threatened more and more each day, time sliding by like clouds on the horizon.

"Try again," she said, trying not to laugh at the pinched look of intense concentration on Xander's face as he tried to summon a memory.

He sighed and slumped against the headboard, his olive skin burnished in the golden morning light that highlighted the dips and planes of his torso and the savage-looking scar on his left side.

From a time when I was too cocky, he'd said when she asked him about it.

About what? she'd asked.

He'd smiled, but his hazel eyes were full of grief. *About whether Teddy was too pure of heart to play dirty and beat me in a fight. Clearly he wasn't and then I was too proud to go to the healer until it was infected.*

The dark, purplish scar was raised and cut just beneath his ribs.

She wondered if Xander thought of their late friend every time he looked in the mirror.

Cecilia propped herself on an elbow and brushed Xander's messy hair back from his forehead, smoothing her thumb over his jawline. Though his body bore his history as a warrior, he had the face of a prince. His nose was straight, his jawline sharp, and his skin unmarred but for a pale white notch from an old split lip that she loved to kiss.

"My love, you cannot bend magic to your will with brute force," she said. "This is not some swordplay attack that you can master with single-minded focus. You don't need to force it. You already have this ability, just like every other witch in the kingdom. It's about allowing it to flow. It's about remembering."

The news that so many witches had been thrust into memory magic to prop up the myth of the Gauntlet had given way to a rush of witches in the kingdom learning to summon new elements. It was especially tricky for witches like Xander who'd come of age thinking they didn't have an affinity, only to be forced to start over with the basics.

"Easy for you to say. You're a goddess, not a grown man working at the same level as twelve-year-olds," Xander said, playfully nipping at the tips of her fingers.

"I had to work to get where I am now and you know it. You're not usually so thrown by being bad at something."

Xander looked away, the reason for his fierce commitment to memory suspended in the silence between them. He wanted to access this power so he could preserve what he had left of his parents and Teddy.

Cecilia pushed up and swung her leg over his hips, seating herself in his lap. The strap of her silk nightgown slipped down her arm and Xander slid it back into place as she cupped his face in her hands.

"Close your eyes," she said.

He reluctantly closed them and she let go of the reins on her goddess magic. While her memory magic had always been sharp and easy to wield, her new goddess power was even more precise, able to map the topography of the mind through a series of emotional strings or chronological stories. She felt it clearly in her mind, so it stood to reason that it would be the same if she used it on him.

"Just breathe for a minute and don't tell yourself that you can't do it because you're not doing it alone. I'm right here to help."

There was always a moment of hesitation when she reached for the new power, as if she felt herself on a cliff's edge about to tip over. The only thing saving her from the stomach-plunging fear was that it was the tiniest hint of her new magic and Xander needed her help. It was as close to her regular summoning powers as she could get, so it felt safe to try it.

She brushed a kiss to Xander's lips and he smiled. "I thought you wanted me to concentrate."

"I want you to be calm. Now bring to mind a person or an emotion."

She pressed gently against Xander's mind and he immediately let her in. It was her face she saw, though she could tell by the roundness of it that she was younger.

"What are you thinking of?" she asked.

"Love."

She kissed the corner of his mouth. "Now, what do you want to see? How can you build a thread between this memory and other memories of me?"

The scene in his mind sharpened; Cecilia was speaking animatedly with the huntmaster, arguing about assessments. He'd kept the written feedback from her despite how badly she wanted to read it.

"Why this memory?" she asked.

"It was right after your father assigned me to watch you and was the first time I ever saw your fight."

"You hadn't seen me before that?"

He chuckled. "Of course I had. But that was the first time I knew there was more to you. I watched you—"

The scene shifted. Cecilia crossed her arms before giving her father a begrudging kiss on the cheek. As she drew back, she snatched her written skills assessment from his back pocket.

"I watched you steal from him without him noticing," Xander said.

Grief knotted in her chest. Though her father had taught her sleight of hand, he loathed when she used it on him—but nothing rivaled the intense satisfaction of stealing from him and teasing him about it later.

She swallowed hard. "See if you can go back to the first time you ever saw me. Follow the feeling." She pressed her power deeper, the thread glowing golden in his mind. "For me it's usually a vibration. Every person and relationship has an emotional signature and that's what I use to sort and call up old memories. But you usually feel things like a pulse of a storm."

Xander tried a few times, dropping the thread before he found what he wanted, finally calling up the first time he ever saw her. His eyes snapped open and he pulled her into a fierce kiss.

"Thank you," he whispered. "I thought I'd lost everything."

She shook her head. "It's all in there even if that magic is dormant. You can learn to wake it. It might not be as sharp as if you'd learned when you were young, but you won't lose everything."

Xander leaned his forehead against hers and squeezed his eyes shut, his hands sliding up her thighs.

"Xander," she scolded as his lips brushed hers and trailed down her neck.

Loathe as Cecilia was to admit it, Grimon was right. She finally understood why all the gods had such scandalous sex lives.

Now that she was no longer fighting an internal war with her own power, she could focus on her heightened goddess senses, which made Xander's touch twice as intense. There was no end to her stamina or desire for him. Xander could barely keep up.

"Who do you like best?" she asked. "Cece? The princess? Or the goddess?"

Xander drew his finger over her collarbone. "This feels like a trick question. I like them all for different reasons. I like the princess because she's my wife. I like the goddess because there's something hot about seeing a deity helpless and screaming beneath me. But

Cece will always be my favorite because she's half as powerful but twice as brave and she's the one I fell for."

What a relief to be seen exactly as she was and wanted so badly. "Good answer."

"There's also something very sexy about a naked goddess straddling me, although, as you'll recall, I thought you were a goddess long before it was official. And I've always enjoyed worshipping you." He laid back as he slid his hands further up her thighs.

"And how would you like to worship your goddess this morning?" she asked, rolling her hips.

He bit his lip as if it took a great deal of effort to decide. Then he brought his hands to her bottom and shifted her up so that she was poised over his mouth. He wrapped his arms around her legs, holding her in place as he worked her. She braced her hands on the headboard, struggling to balance on trembling thighs. He took his time, until she was wavering on the precipice of release, unable to control the mindless roll of her hips. He was so attuned to her body, holding her steady as he flicked his tongue against her and she cried out, flying over the edge.

She waited for him to let her go, but he held her there, continuing to tease.

"Xander," she panted. "I want you."

He moaned against her and it sent a jolt through her body, but he released her hips and rolled so she was beneath him.

His devilish smile made her heart skip. "I think we should start every morning like this."

He teased her, sliding his hard length back and forth against her. His eyes roamed her face like she was a puzzle he was trying to solve. She wrapped her legs around his back and lifted her hips to meet him as he pushed into her.

Her head fell back and she moaned, tugging him closer. He studied her face with an intensity that both scared and excited her.

It was possible he'd always been so intensely focused on her and she was just noticing now, though it seemed there was a new determination in his eyes. He moved slowly at first, hips finding a steady rhythm, before picking up his pace when he felt the tension building in her.

Xander was everywhere, and she was happy to be caught up in the torrent of him. She'd spent too long numb with grief. Every touch of his hands on her skin, every kiss, every thrust of his hips made her feel alive, grounded, *loved*. She didn't even remember what sex felt like before inhabiting such a powerful body, and her fierce love for him only made things more intense.

Cecilia moaned his name as she fell apart. The familiar lightning sensation whipped through her body, and he groaned into her neck as he followed her over the edge.

"Fuck," he sighed as he flopped down next to her. "One of these days, this is going to kill me."

She giggled as he kissed her shoulder.

"You laugh, but you're wearing me out, love. In the best possible way."

She shrugged. "I could stop—"

"Let's not get carried away. I'm not dead yet." Xander's eyes drifted to the painting above the fireplace. Sunlight cut through the cliffside cottage window, illuminating dust motes that glimmered around the frame.

The first morning after they returned from Argaria, Cecilia had found Xander staring at that painting, her favorite of her mother's works. It depicted a little girl on the beach staring out into the roaring sea, a swirl of color around and above her.

"It's you," he'd said. Xander had known, even though the piece didn't resemble her. Even though it had no label. He looked at the painting and he saw Cecilia, the same way he always had.

"How did you know?" she'd asked.

"Because it looks like how you feel. What's it called?" he'd asked.

"Little Storm. *It's my favorite thing she ever painted."*

"It's very good. It captures you well. I've always thought you were a little stormy. I think that's why I liked you so much, so fast. Your emotions tear through you like a wild, passionate storm. I can always feel those shifts in you, just like when a storm rolls in off the sea."

His simple words brought up so much. Longing for her mother. Relief to be seen. Love for her husband.

In truth, the goddess she was now was much more suited to her husband than Rainer. Rainer had always been the person who knew her best. She had always wanted him to see her, but the thought of Rainer looking into the darkness that lived inside her—the part of her that killed a battalion of hunters without a second thought— scared her to death. He was all that was good and kind in her world. He still looked at her like she hung the stars in the night sky, and she couldn't stomach the thought of him looking at her any other way.

It made keeping her distance easier and highlighted how suited she was to Xander. Her darkness did not faze Xander. He practically begged her to show him her new power. He thrilled in the intensity of her anger. After years of hiding so much emotion away, it was a relief to have someone eager to see it all. She was astonished she could love him so fiercely after so little time.

Cecilia ran her fingers down Xander's chest, tracing the scars whose stories she now knew, trailing down the deep vee of muscles at his hip. Xander's body was sculpted by years of vigorous training, and over the past few weeks, she'd learned every place she could touch, kiss, and lick to bring him the same pleasure he so easily brought her.

"You want something, love?" he asked. "Or are you content just to stare at me? Not that I blame you."

She rolled her eyes. "Could you be more pompous?"

His lips quirked up, dimple flashing. "I'm not sure, but you looking at me like you're ready to eat me is certainly a way to find out."

"Honestly, do you even need all of these?" she asked, brushing her hand across his stomach.

His breath caught, the muscles rippling like a wave under her hand. She was delighted that her touch had the same effect on him as his did on her.

"Feels like I need them right now," he gasped.

She grinned in triumph. Though she was uncomfortable with

most of her power, this was a power she enjoyed immensely, even if she never held it long. They were constantly trading it back and forth.

Cecilia poked his stomach. "I think if you tried, you could probably fit one more ab—"

She squealed as Xander pinned her beneath him. His face grew serious. If she didn't change the subject, he would ask about her father or something else she could not stomach. The grief jammed up beneath her ribs, rattling its cage like a feral animal, always searching for a way out.

Better not to set it free. Better to deflect.

"Love, is there anything else I should know about you?" she asked.

Xander's lusty smile tugged into a frown. "What do you mean?" His anxiety spiked, swirling around them like a tornado.

"I was just thinking about that time that you lied to me about being an Olney hunter when you were actually the Storm Prince who knew I was the Lost Goddess, and I thought there might be something else I should know as well," she said.

He winced. "Why would you think there's more?" He wound his fingers around a loose curl that fell into her eyes.

"I have friends in high places." She wanted to shake it out of him.

She'd always felt the edges where his truth ended and a lie began —like the skip in a heartbeat, his emotions jumping then righting themselves. Always she wondered not just what he was keeping from her but if he would ever trust her with the truth.

"I can't think of anything I left out...unless you're just fishing for compliments, in which case I must say how lovely you look this morning."

She reached her hand up to run her fingers through his hair, but he caught her wrist and placed a kiss on her palm.

"Xan, be serious."

"I am being serious. I don't know what you're fishing for."

The buzz of his anxiety grew like a swarm of bees.

"Then why do you feel so anxious?" she asked.

He frowned. "We agreed you wouldn't read my emotions without permission."

"You're projecting them all around us like a godsdamned storm. I can't help it." Cecilia sighed, raking a hand through her knotted hair. "Look, if you're not ready to tell me, just say so, but don't lie to me more. This is a clean slate. You get to choose who you want to be now and you can't blame who you are on someone else's plan anymore. What happened before might have been to serve the people you love, and I can forgive you for that. What happens now is up to you entirely."

Xander stared at her for a moment, as if trying to decide something. He opened his mouth to speak, but a knock on the door cut him off.

"I assume that's Rainer." He said the name like it was a curse, but it was an improvement over ignoring Rainer's existence altogether.

Cecilia dropped her legs over the side of the bed. "Yes, we're helping at the Little School again today. We will be for a while."

"Cece, I'm a little early but wanted to be on time since you've made us late almost every day this week," Rainer said through the door.

She kissed Xander's cheek. "Rain, bug off. I'm busy. I'll meet you there."

"I'm going to stay right here until you come out."

"Well then, you're probably going to hear some interesting things," she said.

Xander's face lit up. He took her words as an invitation to yank her back into bed and kiss every inch of skin he could find as she giggled.

"I guess Megara is going to be disappointed not to see you before class. You know how she's been bullied lately," Rainer called.

Cecilia cursed her friend for knowing how talking about that sweet little witch would play on her heartstrings. Rainer could wield guilt trips as effectively as a sword.

"Fine! I'll wash up. I'll be ready in a few minutes." She shrugged out of Xander's grip. "Will you let him in?"

Xander frowned as she went into the washroom.

When she emerged a few minutes later, she found Xander and Rainer glaring at each other over steaming cups of tea on the kitchen table. The open hostility between them sent her stomach tumbling as she knocked back her tea and stuffed a piece of toast in her mouth.

"Ready?" she asked.

Rainer nodded.

Xander pinned her against the wall and made a very aggressive show of kissing her before she squirmed away. She ignored the frustrated look on Rainer's face as she brushed by him and walked out into the sunlight.

She didn't want to be cruel and flaunt her relationship in front of Rainer. Navigating their new reality felt a bit like being the rope in a constant tug-of-war between her husband and Rainer. If she declined Xander's advances in front of Rainer, it sent a clear message that she was more concerned with not hurting Rainer than showing Xander affection.

Truthfully, Cecilia loved the way her husband shamelessly flirted with her. After a lifetime of receiving so little genuine attention from men, she was ravenous for it. The fact that he'd already won her over made it that much sweeter. He was constantly trying to one-up himself, make her smile bigger, blush harder, laugh longer. It thrilled her to be the subject of such intense focus. She didn't want him to tone it down.

A more vindictive part of her felt that Rainer had not been nearly as thoughtful with her feelings when he flaunted his conquests in front of her for years.

It was a strange thing to navigate. Her heart was bound to one man by marriage, and her soul bound to another by magic. Those bonds were as different as the men they connected to. One love always grating painfully against the other.

Rainer started down the trail. "It's my turn for the story today."

Since they no longer had evening hours together, they'd taken to spinning stories on the walk to and from the Little School. It wasn't the same, but it was the only compromise she could think of to keep the peace.

She fell into step with Rainer. So much had changed in the weeks since she'd come into her full goddess powers, seen her father killed before her eyes, and killed the god of war, Endros, along with an entire battalion of Argarian hunters.

Given her sway and attitude toward King Hector, a lot of adjustments had already been made in the training of young witches and guardians. That was one benefit of being a living goddess. Even the king didn't want to piss her off.

The changes were part of the reason she and Rainer were such a constant presence at the school where all Olney's youth were trained. Though most witches' magical gifts didn't show until they were in adolescence, the Little School sought to teach all children of Olney— witches, guardians, hunters, and ladies alike—about magic theory, history, combat basics, and strategy before they fully developed their gifts. Those whose magical gifts never showed up became scholars and teachers or potion and spell casters, and those whose did develop became witches who were matched with and bound to guardians.

Cecilia and Rainer were asked to offer advice and guidance on how to continue teaching witches and guardians to work together since many of them were already bonded. Cecilia was helping the school design a new curriculum that would allow young witches to learn how to summon all elements instead of just their primary one or two. Although she suspected those with certain affinities would gravitate toward those elements, she still wanted them to feel like they had a choice.

Her involvement at the school had been Rainer's idea. She knew he was trying to distract her from her grief. She had to admit that the freedom to help healed some part of her that had always felt trapped by her abilities.

In her mind, just giving people the choice to focus on what they wanted felt like a huge win. It didn't make up for the years and lives lost hunting down something that was ultimately just a cruel trick, but it helped ease some of the brutal grief she wore like a second skin.

"You know, for the number of mornings I walk up to your cottage and hear the two of you in the throes, I would expect *His Highness* to be in a better mood," Rainer said. He tried for a smirk, but it looked more like a frown.

"I wonder why he's so sour toward you. All you did was profess your undying love to his wife and kiss her right in front of him," she said sarcastically.

"I said I was sorry."

"To me, not to him, and you didn't even mean it."

He laughed. "I didn't."

They walked quietly, the tension between them too heavy to break.

"You're doing okay, though? You don't talk about what happened."

Cecilia shrugged, trying to ignore the grief that tugged at her. "What is there to say? We've all lost something."

He looked like he didn't believe her, but the bell rang and they hustled into the school.

———

When Rainer and Cecilia arrived at the cottage after school, Xander was waiting outside, looking pleased with himself. Two large rose-bushes that looked shockingly like the queen's roses bracketed the door.

Cecilia eyed her husband suspiciously. "How?"

"Do you like them?" Xander asked. His eyes were a luminous gold in the sunlight.

Cecilia looked from him to the bushes and back. "Xan, how?"

"I know what you're thinking. I didn't steal them. I simply explained to Her Majesty, Queen Elena, that I had yet to get my beautiful wife a wedding gift, and that she loved those roses, and would Elena consider sharing them with her dear friend's daughter? Sylvie was kind enough to lend me some of her earth magic talents to help the cutting grow. Do you like them?"

Sylvie, Cal, and Evan stood off to the side. All of them looked at her expectantly, but Cecilia was speechless.

"Queen Elena told me an interesting story, one I'd never heard before," Xander said. "She said that Lady Rosalee Reznik gifted her those rosebushes as a birthday present many years ago. She had some earth witches help them thrive in the summer heat. It was a beacon of her enduring friendship with the queen. They had tea there once a week until the queen became too busy with Prince Marcos. Then, two years later, Cecilia Reznik entered the picture. According to Queen Elena, every Saturday morning for the next six years, the Reznik ladies came and sat in front of the roses and talked about their week."

Cecilia blinked back tears. The catalogue of memories in her mind pulled up those few days she could remember sitting on that bench with her mother. It was before her gifts were fully available, so unlike the rest of her memories, the quality of them was imperfect and fuzzy, but they were still some of her most precious and private memories.

Xander stepped behind her, wrapping his arms around her waist. "Why didn't you ever say anything, love? I wondered why you sat there alone every Saturday morning. You never told me when I asked."

Cecilia had told no one about it. She continued to go every Saturday morning, even after Rosalee died, because it was where she felt most connected to her. She sat on that bench in the rose garden for hours imagining what her mother might say if she was there. Occasionally, when she was certain no one else was around, she even spoke out loud.

Xander's gift was more romantic than he realized. He'd brought a part of her mother home again, to the cottage that had been the art studio she loved so much. Now she was right there whenever Cecilia wanted to talk.

"Do you like them?" Xander tucked a kiss into her neck.

"I love them." She swallowed thickly as she tried to collect herself. "I love them." She turned to kiss him. Triumph brightened his face. She turned back to Sylvie. "Thank you."

Sylvie nodded, looking pleased with herself.

Cecilia was overwhelmed. It was one of the most thoughtful gifts she'd ever received, but she was completely unprepared for even her close friends to witness that kind of raw emotion.

"I'll be right back." She pushed into the cabin and took a deep breath. She was just beginning to steady herself when something scurried by her feet. She jumped up on a kitchen chair with a squeal.

"Cece?" Xander burst into the cottage.

Rainer was right behind him. He took one look at her on the chair and started laughing.

"It's not funny!" she said.

"What is going on?" Xander asked, looking back and forth between the two of them.

Cal and Evan appeared in the doorway.

"That squeal, combined with Cece standing on a chair, can only mean one thing." Rainer muffled another laugh. "A mouse."

She clamped a hand over her mouth to dampen her hysterical giggles. The quick shift in emotion threw her for a loop.

"Love, you're afraid of mice?" Xander bit his lip. "Cece, who walks into dark, magical caves, and faces off with the god of war?"

"I just don't like them. They're gross," she said.

Xander rooted around for the mouse.

"Wait! Don't hurt it. It's just a baby."

"Then what do you want me to do?"

"Catch it and then release it in the stable," Rainer said as he crouched down, searching for the mouse as he had so many times before.

Evan leaned against the doorframe, laughing. It was the first time she'd seen the stoic hunter do more than half-smile. "This is the best thing I've seen in weeks."

"Happy I could finally get you to laugh, Evan," she said dryly from her perch. "I'm glad everyone is enjoying this, but let me just remind you all that I'm a goddess and I could smite every one of you without lifting a finger."

"Give me your best shot," Xander challenged.

29

"Or I could just wipe this memory from your minds." They all quieted. "Gods, I'm kidding. What fun is it being an accidental goddess if I can't even joke about it?"

The only one who didn't look uncomfortable was Xander, whose gaze heated as it met hers. He may have been a prince, but he still had the competitive spirit of a hunter.

She made light of it and everyone else continued looking for the mouse, but there was some truth in what she said. Although she'd integrated her power, she was afraid of the darkness that now inhabited her. Before, she could feel the pendulum swing from her to the goddess. She knew when to expect it. Now she was both, and even though they had both been aspects of her all along, she was uncomfortable with the blurred lines between the two.

The problem with all of her suffering and loss was that the darkness had grown. It stretched wide, nestling in her bones like it belonged there. It took up residence in the space where hope used to live. After what Grimon said about her soul, she wondered what that meant for her and her future happiness.

She'd lost so many things that used to anchor her. Her father was gone. Her magic had transformed from a comfort to a terrifying, powerful wildcard. Perhaps she should have felt grateful to finally understand why she'd felt so strange her whole life, but she felt no better. The truth hadn't set her free. It had only created more confusion and more loneliness.

The distance that bloomed between her and Rainer, while necessary, only made her feel more restless. She wondered if he could feel the icy creep of grief squeezing the breath from her lungs in moments when she least expected it.

Cecilia felt foolish for ever feeling lonely before. Loneliness was seeing that uneasiness on her friends' faces when she made a dark joke about her power. Loneliness was the way the people of Olney looked at her now as something both to be praised and feared. Loneliness was being trapped in a body that vibrated with power and still feeling powerless to protect the people she loved.

3

XANDER

Xander Savero had a secret. The weight of it was like a boulder on his chest as he settled into his chair in King Hector Teripin's war room. Light streamed through the windows, illuminating the drab stone walls and shining directly in his eyes as if trying to highlight his guilt.

The problem with this particular secret was the longer he kept it, the more damage it would do. The timing was never quite right.

Maybe it was the fact that Cece had just lost her father. Maybe it was the impending war. Or maybe it was the somewhat tenuous hold he had on his relationship after Rainer professed his love to Cece.

The reasons shifted like smoke, never fully forming something he could grasp, though he suspected the truth was that he didn't want Cece to stop looking at him with so much love and trust in her eyes.

Xander found himself repeating a mistake he should have learned from. The truth felt more threatening than the lie. The rational part of his brain insisted that was the wrong way to think of things, but there was no reasoning with his heart, and the only thing that his heart wanted was his wife.

So he busied himself with morning workouts and the king's

tedious war councils. He spent every moment in between trying to make his wife laugh and relieve the grief that had swallowed her joy.

He knew better than to hide anything from her. It was a lesson he'd learned the hard way when he almost lost her.

"Cecilia has a good heart and a forgiving nature. The world will look at her like that makes her weak. They will take advantage of it, but you should never take it for granted."

They were some of his mother's last words to him.

Xander worried he was doing just that—taking Cece's heart for granted—but not enough to compel his honesty. He just needed a little more time. A little more time to figure out how to stop Cato. A little more time to win Cece over from Rainer for certain. A little more time to convince himself that she really loved him; that she would have married him even if she didn't have to at that moment.

The only thing he kept locked away as carefully as his secret was the grief for his parents and Teddy.

"How many shipments are they going to skip out on?" King Hector grumbled.

Xander settled back in his seat, wishing his cup was full of whiskey instead of coffee as King Hector continued his tirade.

Evan caught Xander's eye across the table. At least he didn't have to suffer through the meeting alone.

Hector was in a dreadful mood after his morning session with his trade advisors. The impending war made their foreign trade partners nervous. Nearby kingdoms, like Novum and Aldrena, preferred to stay neutral in the Olney-Argaria conflict so they could keep diplomatic ties with both countries.

It used to drive Xander's father crazy the way other kingdoms hedged their bets, in case one of the two warring kingdoms eventually won out. They didn't want to lose the chance to trade with either in the meantime, but the more intense the conflict, the harder it was to get them to risk sending ships and goods when they weren't sure they would be paid for or received by the intended kingdom.

Xander absently reached into his pocket, his fingers skimming a small piece of paper. He stifled a laugh. If Cece hadn't been born into court life, she would have been an excellent thief. Her impressive sleight of hand allowed her to sneak notes into his pockets daily.

The impulse to pull the note out and read it was overwhelming, but he forced it down. This daily ritual of love notes thrilled him, but he was already certain what the note would say. Some version of *come back to bed immediately.* They were a little different every day, but Xander knew if he read it as the king was winding himself up, he ran too high a risk of simply leaving and doing exactly what her note bid him.

King Hector was proud, exactly how Xander expected him to be, and he had the same restraint as Xander's father. Though Xander could read a simmering rage that welled beneath the king's skin, he did nothing to tip his hand.

Xander's gaze raked over Prince Marcos. His quiet, appraising manner mirrored Queen Elena's. The prince of Olney clearly learned a thing or two from his mother. Xander could respect it. A good king needed to realize that his first impulse wasn't always the best. It was the reason Xander would make a terrible king.

"I'm telling you, I have it from very reliable sources that Davide and parts of his army have been seen in all three locations." Evan's voice was so calm. Years of working with King Damian helped Evan curb his temper, but Xander could still see flashes of it in his friend.

Hector slammed his fist on the table. "That's impossible! They cannot be spread that thin." He stared at the map before him as if his gaze could burn right through it.

"Your Grace," Evan started, "with respect, it might not be. There are stories about Cato that suggest—"

"I don't want to hear another fairy tale about your trickster god. I need facts." Hector turned his scrutinizing gaze on Xander. "Savero, what is your wife going to do to help us? This war is coming whether she's ready or not, and dallying all day with schoolchildren won't save this kingdom from war."

Quiet rage seeped through Xander. "My wife—who is a human being, and a princess, and not a pawn for you to use how you would like—is still grieving the loss of her father."

Among other losses.

The thought sent a bitter chill through him. Xander never ceased to feel the same devastation every time he thought of what Cece sacrificed to save him and Rainer. He wore the guilt of it like an old, familiar cloak. It was easier to focus on the guilt than the grief of knowing that it was also his loss.

He wanted to save Cece from ever feeling pain, but so far he'd failed on all accounts, and the failure tasted much more bitter than it ever had before. It wasn't fair that everyone hung all their hopes on her when she was still terrified and learning how her powers worked.

Hector stared at Xander, disdain apparent on his face.

Marcos broke the silence. "Perhaps we're approaching this the wrong way. Xander is married to Princess Cecilia. All we need to focus on is eliminating Davide. Am I correct that you have no stomach for war, Your Grace?" Marcos's dark eyes bore into Xander in a silent plea.

This was why he was invited to these meetings. Months ago, Xander would have killed for this kind of access to the Olney royal family, but now he found the politics of it all tedious. His father had taught him enough about compromising with political rivals. King Damian hadn't blindly thrown his weight around. He'd collected favors and information, invented fake weaknesses for his opponents to pick apart, and had taught his sons to do the same. Xander had no desire to be king, but that was a weakness he'd rather not air in front of the opposition. Men who craved power distrusted those who didn't, and with that distrust came questions about why he might not want the scrutiny of the throne. Best to keep Hector in the dark about family scandals and old Argarian rumors.

"I have no appetite for senseless death," Xander said finally. "I only wish to maintain peace between our kingdoms, but I would need a guarantee."

"I should think the Goddess would be enough," Hector said. "We'd be fools to attack you while you're married to her, even if we don't understand her power."

Marrying one of his sons to the Lost Goddess had been Damian

Savero's last good plan, even if he'd done it with the intention of invading Olney. Xander could just as easily use the sway of her power to protect his people. He knew Cece would want the same. She'd already witnessed more death than she ever should have.

He thumbed the note in his pocket again, impatient to read it, impatient for her words, impatient to see her face again. He wondered if he'd used up all his patience over his years as a spy, or if it was just the unrelenting way he felt drawn to Cece.

"You'd let us kill your brother?" Hector asked.

The words were jarring, but Xander schooled his face into an indifferent frown. Though Davide had grown cold and distant in recent years, he'd looked out for Xander when they were young. Xander tried to give him the benefit of the doubt, but since Davide had broken Cece's hand, he only saw his brother as an enemy. Still, Xander didn't want his brother killed for the simple reason that he didn't want to be king.

He hadn't been raised for it, nor did he have a desire to rule Argaria, and Cece would hate to be queen. He assumed Hector would prefer to rule both kingdoms, but he wouldn't allow another power-hungry asshole to rule his people.

Xander lacked the temperament of a martyr. His survival instincts were too strong to sacrifice himself in all the ways a king was expected to. But if Xander took the throne, he would make choices that were in his people's best interest, not Olney's.

He cleared his throat. "I'd prefer Davide be banished to the Fallen Islands or come back to live out his days in a cell in Argaria."

Evan gave him a warning look. Xander was reaching beyond his ability to negotiate, but the thought of losing his brother after losing both of his parents was too much.

Hector shook his head violently. "You'd be weak and foolish to let him live."

"He's my brother."

"If you want to be king, you will have to make hard choices."

"I won't be a person who murders my way to the throne," Xander said curtly.

A smug smile spread across Hector's face. "We will be happy to dispatch him for you."

Only a man who'd never dirtied his hands would talk about murder in such a way, and only a king would dirty another's and then say "we" while carrying none of the burden of it. Not everyone had the stomach for cold-blooded murder, but plenty of men had convinced themselves they did. Everyone was brave until the moment they had to follow through. That's what separated the hunters from everyone else. There could be no hesitation.

For the moment, Hector needed him, but Xander knew that the king of Olney would be just as happy to be rid of him. After all, Prince Marcos had yet to make a match, and with Xander out of the way, the king could solidify the Olney empire with a goddess for a daughter-in-law.

The thought made Xander uneasy. Wise not to let anything slip about the exchange Cece made for her power, and wiser to make sure the king knew she wasn't so easily managed.

"I think my wife would be happy to do it. She owes him and she loves to show those who threaten us how she'd easily slay them. After all, there's no bigger threat to me right now than Davide," Xander said plainly.

Marcos hiked his shoulders slightly, letting Xander know he understood the subtext of his words. The king kept his face placid. The only sign of his displeasure was his racing heart.

Evan nodded in approval, and Xander knew not to push further.

The king dismissed them with a wave of his hand.

Xander nearly leapt out of his seat and out the door. Evan fell into step beside him as they left the castle grounds.

"What would you do if you were Cato?" Xander asked.

Evan sighed heavily. "I'd do exactly what he's doing. I'd distract us with a million minor battles in different spots so that I can hit where it hurts."

Xander bristled. "You think he'll come directly here? To Olney City?"

"He has to. Davide is single-minded. Having the rest of Olney won't be enough and Cato needs the Teripins gone in order to ensure that Davide can rule over both kingdoms," Evan said.

"How is he doing it? Are you certain he has soldiers in all those places? To divide the Argarian army like that would be dangerous. Olney has long had us outmatched in sheer size."

"It's possible that the rumors about Cato's abilities are true," Evan said.

"Those are just stories."

Stories about tricking space and time and traveling great distances in the blink of an eye. It was legend in Argaria when Xander was growing up that you should never speak ill of the trickster god, lest he appear next to you to strike you down. The son of Endros was considered the lesser of two evils, but Xander suspected that Cato was much worse.

Evan cocked an eyebrow. "Stories like the Storm Prince?"

"Fair enough," Xander sighed. "You trust the spies who are feeding you this information? Cato could have compromised them."

"I trust them with my life, and you would, too."

Xander scrubbed a hand through his hair, squinting into the midday sun.

"How is Cece?" Evan asked. "I know you hate to think of it, but we'll need her, Xander. She slayed a battalion with barely a flick of her hand."

"She's not ready."

"She needs to get ready." Evan fixed his lips into a thin line. "I care about her too. I was there when you and Rainer and her father were taken and she agonized about reaching out to that power. I was the one who talked her out of it about four times while we waited to trade her for you. The last thing I want to do is to put her in another situation where she has to do something that she can't live with, but do you think she will find it easier to live with so many of her people dying? Give her the choice, Xan. If you take that away, you're no better than everyone else in her life."

Xander hated that his best friend was right, and he hated being faced with his mistake. He shoved down the guilt that stalked him day and night.

"I want to protect her."

"From a god? That's pompous even for you."

Xander shrugged. "Cato has a deal with our family, you know that. He cannot use his magic on a Savero."

Evan narrowed his eyes. "You know very well he doesn't need to use it on you to manipulate you, and if that's the case, do you really think Davide's transformation isn't courtesy of his magic?" He grew quiet. "You know she's stronger than even you give her credit for."

Xander shook his head. "You didn't see her that night."

"What does Rainer say?"

Xander blew out a slow breath. "Fucking Rainer McKay."

If Xander could get through just one full day without hearing that name or seeing his face, he would praise the gods.

Before his mission and attention narrowed to Cece, Xander actually liked Rainer. The guardian trained with hunters, even though it wasn't required, because he thought it would help him protect his charge. Most guardians thought themselves above hunters because that's where their social stature placed them, but Rainer was a willing student. Xander would still like the guardian if he could free himself of the sight of him kissing Cece.

Evan patted his shoulder. "Rainer's smart and he's her best friend. He's a good place to get advice. You might not like it, but she's going to need both of you."

Xander narrowed his eyes at Evan—the only person bold enough to cross him on issues like this. Teddy wouldn't have dared.

Teddy. His late friend's name was still a gut punch. It wove into the grief for his late parents and his brother, who was alive but still just as lost to him as the rest.

"Are you okay?" Evan asked. "I've been on board this whole time. I know you love Cece, but you seem a little more intense and protective of her every day."

"What do you mean?"

"You've always been extreme and single-minded when you set

your sights on something, but you just seem a little—" Evan blew out a breath. "Obsessed."

"Weren't you the one who used to have to drag me from Nessa's apartment after days? I didn't even love her. Things are different with Cece."

Evan tilted his head and pursed his lips, studying his friend's face as if searching for secrets.

"Let's chalk it up to love," Xander said.

"You used to say you'd never bother with love."

"That was before I met Cece."

For years, Xander had waged a private war against the entire concept of love, knowing his duty as the younger prince of Argaria would require he marry a princess of some distant kingdom to help bolster Argaria's power. He thought he could avenge himself against the concept of love by fucking his way through the two kingdoms without ever feeling a thing for the women he bedded.

Love was a complication Xander didn't need, so he'd tried to be content to fuck and flee. His family told him his heart was expendable, and he'd believed it.

But all of that changed when Leo Reznik assigned Xander to monitor his daughter. Cece had been on Xander's radar because of her success in the Gauntlet, but it was different to follow her from afar, to observe her in the moments she thought no one was watching. She drew him in with her quiet observation, the longing on her face when she looked at her guardian, the deep and apparent loneliness she felt even in a room full of people.

In his wildest dreams, he never imagined Cece would be thoughtful, compassionate, and forgiving, all while being so sexy and free. The world they lived in was not one that cultivated those qualities in women, and he marveled at her.

Xander didn't care if Evan, Grimon, and even Rainer thought he was intense in his borderline obsession with his wife. Nothing seemed extreme to him when it came to Cece, because she was the one thing he'd never allowed himself to dream of. He'd nearly bought into the idea that he was too much—too cocky, too reckless, too single-minded. But Cece's intensity matched his, and that healed a wound he hadn't realized had festered for so long.

If there were words for what he felt, they'd been left out of his lessons. Love seemed too small a word for what bubbled up inside him every time his wife shared a secret smile that was only for him. When she looked at him, she really saw him, and for the first time in his life, he felt like enough.

Evan tapped the tip of each finger to his thumb, an old exercise in patience that he used when a situation or person was wearing on him. "I know there's something going on with you. This is your chance to tell me what it is before it catches up with you. I can't quite tell what it's about, but I know something is off. You used to have the same look on your face when we were kids and I caught you in the midst of a bad idea."

"I don't know what you're talking about." Xander feigned nonchalance, but he knew his friend would catch the skip in his heartbeat. Evan's magically heightened hunter senses were as attuned to lying as Xander's.

Evan nodded, casting a quick glance at the cottage doors. "Let me know when you change your mind. The lines may have blurred, but I'm always on your side."

Evan peeled away and left Xander to walk the rest of the way home with only his guilt as company. He'd tell Evan soon. He just needed a little more time to tell Cece first.

He cracked the cottage door.

Cece lounged on the window seat with a book propped on her knees. She snapped her fingers, conjuring flame before swirling her fingers again and extinguishing it, over and over, the magic that drained him in simplest use second nature to her.

She must have heard him. Her enhanced goddess senses were even sharper than his magically enhanced hunter senses, but she didn't acknowledge him. He loved watching her in those quiet moments, loved the glimpse of something no one else got to see.

"Just going to gawk, or are you going to come give me a kiss?" she asked without looking up.

"I was simply waiting for a greeting appropriate for a prince."

A smile broke over her face like dawn over the ocean. "My prince!" She skipped across the room and threw herself into his arms as if he'd been away for months.

Xander had always been prone to extremes, and seeing those same extremes reflected in his wife thrilled him. She kissed him for a long time before pulling away and running her fingers through his hair.

"Is that sufficient, *Your Highness*?"

"It's never enough. I always want more of you."

"Did you get my note?" she asked. "You're back earlier than expected. I suppose you found it compelling."

"I didn't get a chance to read it."

He finally pulled the scrap of paper out of his pocket.

———

I love being your wife. Even if it means I'll never get a good night's sleep again.

———

The words wrapped around his heart and squeezed. Gods, he loved her, even if he was obnoxious in showing it by waking her up multiple times a night to make love, at least until her nightmares ripped her from sleep and summoned Rainer to ruin his fun.

"How are you feeling today, my love?"

She regarded his concern with wariness. "I'm fine."

Behind the words was a hint of something more, an abyss of grief that she hid away for fear it would swallow her. Since the first night that he and Rainer found her under a mountain of blankets in her bed, she'd hardly said a word about her father's death, the men she'd killed, or losing her ability to have children.

Grief was an unwelcome houseguest that lived in every silence. Neither of them knew how to address or banish it. Instead, they allowed each other the dignity of passing it back and forth wordlessly when it was too much to hold alone. She kissed it into him when she was close to breaking—breathless sobs turning to soft gasps on his lips. He squeezed it into her in hugs when he got home each day—the tremors in his body turning into shivers as she ran her hands through his hair.

They were both satisfied to ignore the ghosts in the room and focus on lighter things. Silence was a mercy. The problem with their relationship was that she was so exceedingly good at distracting him, and he was just as talented at distracting her. With neither of them eager to face the reality of their grief, they simply enabled each other's avoidance. Eventually, they would deal with it all. They had time. Now that they were back in Olney and safe, they had time to get to know each other better—to build a life.

Even the threat of war didn't seem as overwhelming when Xander came home to Cece every day. There was a part of him, one he would never admit to outwardly, that was relieved at her new immortal status. He'd never known fear like watching her nearly die from poison. When she was fighting off the goddess power, exhausted and frustrated, she'd seemed so terribly small and fragile to him. As much as she'd lost the moment she relented to that power, she'd gained immense strength, an immortal lifespan, and truly terrifying magic.

She refused to talk about or experiment with her magic, but she made a point of kicking his ass any time she convinced him to spar with her. She was now faster and stronger than him, and delighted by that fact. To Rainer's horror, she'd convinced Xander to try tossing a dagger at her to see if she could catch it in mid-air like he did. It thrilled her that she could.

She enjoyed finally being able to fight the same way he and Rainer did now that she had the same strength advantages as her opponents, though she was frustrated that her status as a princess meant only he or Rainer would test her. She claimed they were both still holding back, and she might have had a point. Xander couldn't bring himself to fight his wife full force. Rainer was good enough to give it his all, and it was worth it to see the absolute delight on Cece's face when she took him to the ground.

"How was King Blowhard today?" Cece asked, pouring Xander a cup of coffee.

"Pissed. Irrational. Dying to kill my brother. So, much like every other day."

Cece studied him. "We won't let him do that."

"I didn't think you were a fan of Davide."

"I'm not, but he's your brother. I owe him some broken bones, but I have to believe that the brother you knew is in there somewhere."

"And if he's not?" Xander asked.

"If he's not, I will make sure that you're not the one who has to deal with it."

Something dark flashed in her eyes. They turned from their bright blue to a glowing, deep ocean blue. "Let's talk about something else." She broke off a piece of the lemon cake sitting on the table and popped it in her mouth. "Gods, this is the best lemon cake I've ever had. You must try it."

He fought a smile as he took a bite. She'd said the same thing thirty-two times—every time she ate a lemon cake. They all tasted the same to him, but he loved the way she savored them, loved how he turned her pockets out every night to find them full of crumbs. Xander didn't know how something so small could make him feel like his chest was going to collapse. With every little intimacy, she hollowed him out and filled him up all at once—like he'd never truly felt sunlight but there she was shining it on him with a smile like the dawn breaking through a storm.

Xander glanced around the cottage, which was a bit of a mess. In Argaria, it hadn't been obvious with servants cleaning up after Cece, but now in their space, her messy nature amused him. Her clothes were in little piles all over the cottage in whatever place she'd been standing when she shed them—or, more frequently, where he tore them off of her.

"Love, I did not know that you were such a slob."

Cece grinned. "Well, now you know. And you're aware that I can't cook, so I guess it's a good thing I signed up for this whole princess thing, huh? But it's too late now. No taking it back. You're mine for life. You already promised."

Xander laughed, nearly spraying his coffee everywhere.

She shrugged. "What? I hardly think it's my fault that you insist on leaving my clothes all over the place every time you decide to take them off of me."

"Perhaps it would help if you just didn't bother getting dressed at all."

She laughed, her dark hair falling in front of her face like a curtain. "Of course that would be your suggestion. And what happens when Evan shows up unannounced? Or Sylvie? Or Rainer?" She giggled at the scowl on his face. "Are you ever going to stop hating him? He's not going anywhere."

"Don't remind me."

Her tone grew soft, a clear fondness on her face that he wasn't sure was for him or Rainer. "Xander, he's my best friend."

"And how would you feel if Evan were in love with me?"

"I'd invite him to our bed," Cece teased. Xander's eyes went wide, and she collapsed onto the bed in a fit of giggles. "Gods! Your face! What? He's very handsome."

"I did not know you were so adventurous, love. I'll have to keep that in mind. Personally, I'd prefer to invite another woman to our bed first."

Cece froze, the smile on her face dissipating like smoke in the breeze. "That will not happen."

"Why not?"

"I would prefer not to share your affections with any other ladies." She winced as if realizing the trap she'd stepped into.

"And I'd prefer not to share your affections with any other man."

"You don't," she said flatly. A lie neither of them believed.

"Don't I?" He crossed his arms.

She could lie and deny it, or agree and admit that she still loved Rainer. Xander still wished that she would. In the past, he had thought it impractical to expect to have all needs met by one person.

He was open because he didn't believe in lying or manipulating women into bed. Honesty served him best.

But his views on monogamy had changed since meeting Cece. He hated the thought of sharing her with anyone, especially someone she loved.

Cece met his eyes, the corner of her mouth kicking up. "Fine. Another lady it is—"

The taunt broke through his frustration.

"Don't make promises your jealous heart can't follow through on, love," he said as he closed the distance between them.

"Okay then, we will leave it as is with just you and me in this bed."

"I think I can live with that." He tugged her into the bed with him, kissing her as he pulled off his shirt.

Xander had a secret and he would hold on to it just a little longer. Once the dust of this war settled—once they survived this—there would be plenty of time to explain.

4

CECILIA

Cecilia woke with a harsh scream scraping her throat raw. Xander had already gathered her into his arms, but she couldn't stop shaking as tears streamed down her cheeks. She'd thought integrating her power would make things easier, but now that she was fully back in her body, all of her unprocessed emotions were eager to make themselves known.

Her dreams were vicious, muddled, and always threaded through with her reliving Rainer's near-death.

Xander's lips brushed her bare shoulder, his breath warm on her skin. "It's okay, love. It was just a dream."

Cecilia leaned into him, trying to orient herself with reality.

Everything had felt so real: the metallic scent of blood, the pain sharp in her chest, the fear in Rainer's eyes.

A surge in Cecilia's bond sent her to her feet. Rainer was close, woken by her terror once again. Their bond didn't differentiate between real and perceived danger. It summoned Rainer all the same.

Cecilia tugged on her silk nightgown. Xander let out an exaggerated sigh as she crossed the cottage and opened the door, letting in a cool breeze.

Weeks had passed, summer tipping into autumn. The days had lost their humidity, and the evenings held a chilly reminder of how quickly the urgent fear of war in Olney dissipated into subtle agitation as attention shifted to the harvest.

Argaria's random attacks on Olney's outskirts continued. There were reports of Davide's army appearing in different places all over Olney's borders. King Hector and the new huntmaster were frustrated and baffled by conflicting reports. Each time they settled on a course of action, they would have to change it again as Davide's troops appeared elsewhere. Xander spent long hours in the war room, attempting to break down what appeared to be chaos and not strategy at all.

They'd expected retribution would be quick and vicious, but it never really came. Instead, the threat hung over the entire court, an anxious haze that made the people short and jumpy. Cecilia wondered if waiting was worse punishment than battle itself. It was as if they were bleeding out from hundreds of shallow wounds instead of one great killing blow.

She squinted into the darkness outside the cottage.

Rainer strode down the trail from his apartment on her family's estate in a sweater and loose pajama pants, his hair mussed with sleep, his arms already open as he stepped into the doorway. She broke into a fresh sob as he tucked her against his chest. Tension bled from her body, relief a reflex of Rainer's closeness, their bond buzzing pleasantly in her chest.

"I'm right here. I'm not going anywhere," Rainer murmured into her hair.

Needing him was so weak, but she could never seem to settle after those visceral nightmares until she saw him whole and healthy. He felt like the only solid thing in the world as she brushed her fingers over the scars on his neck and chest.

Xander's gaze burned into her back like a jealous brand.

Guiding her back into the cottage, Rainer closed the door behind him. He walked her back to bed, kissing the scars on her hand and inner wrist before tucking her under the blankets.

"Can you go back to sleep?" Rainer asked.

She pointed to the couch, a silent plea for him to stay the night. Several nights in the past few weeks, he'd still been there in the morning because he'd been too tired to wake up and walk back to his apartment.

"I'll wake you up when you need to worry," Rainer said with a smile.

It was something she'd once said to him when his mother was dying—words that she'd only learned later had meant the world to him.

The words anchored her even more than Xander's arm around her waist. By the time she fell asleep, she could almost forget the nightmare altogether.

———

In the morning, Rainer was gone, and Cecilia was glad for it. Xander was all over her before her eyes were even fully open. He took his time waking her up with strategically placed kisses and caresses until her heart thundered in her ears and she was more awake than any cup of tea could get her.

When they were finished, Xander milled about the room as Cecilia got dressed for her day at the Little School. She pinned her hair back carefully, turning to investigate Xander's uncommon silence.

He sat on the edge of their bed with a book in his hands. Cecilia froze. It was the book of fairy tales Rainer had written for her.

"He wrote you a book?" Xander said without looking up.

Jealousy slithered through the air around them. It was an emotion she read on him whenever Rainer was around, but it had never been so prickly.

"It's not a big deal," she said quickly, wishing she could snatch it from his hands. "I haven't even read it."

She didn't know why she felt territorial about the book. It wasn't like it had been hidden away. It was just sitting on her bookshelf, untouched since a few days after she'd arrived home. Seeing it then was enough to send her back to the night she had laid out in the field with Rainer watching the meteor shower. It still bothered her that Rainer had never revealed the wish he'd made. Her wish had come true, just not in the way she expected. She'd wished for the power to make her own choices, and now she was constantly terrified of making the wrong one.

The hurt must have shown on her face, because Xander snapped the book closed.

"You're upset I looked at it."

"I'm *not* upset," she said, but her voice was tight and there were suddenly tears in her eyes.

The hard set of Xander's jaw softened. "Really?"

Cecilia wiped a stray tear. "Fine, I'm upset. I think it just feels like another lifetime ago and I don't even feel like that person anymore. The girl who loved those stories so much was a fool. I'm done with the fairy tales."

Cecilia missed that version of her. She missed falling asleep with Rainer every night, listening to his animated voice as he wove stories and the way he taunted her for making every story romantic. She just missed *him*. They spent little time together other than when he comforted her from her nightmares, and after spending every day together most of her life, it felt a bit like missing a limb. Her whole life had changed, and she'd lost so much that it seemed silly to mourn little things like his constant presence, the way he reached for her hand when he was nervous, or the soothing smell of his skin.

She felt a bit like an addict trying to break a habit. The problem was that he wasn't bad for her. Rainer had been a shelter for her for most of her life, and even though he was still there, everything had shifted.

Navigating a soul bond with him while she was married to Xander felt like walking along a cliff trail, feeling it crumble under her feet, knowing at some point it might give out and she'd lose everything.

She tried to convince herself that her love for Rainer was entirely a product of their magical soul bond. There was no way to know for sure, but it absolved some of her guilt to think of it as just one more way she'd been stripped of her free will.

Xander tugged her closer. "My love, I'm not sure you need to give up on fairy tales yet. After all, you married a charming, handsome prince. I think you might be living one."

Cecilia barked out a laugh. "If your ego gets any bigger, it won't fit in this cottage." She closed the distance between them. "Maybe you're the one who is living the fairy tale. You married a goddess."

"I most certainly am. Perhaps I should write it down, so I never forget how incredibly lucky I am." Xander toyed with a curl that had escaped her bun. "Can we please stop having nightly visits from Rainer? I know it makes you feel better, but these dreams aren't going anywhere and I don't love having him as a permanent roommate."

Cecilia sighed, guilt twisting her stomach in knots. "I know. I'm sorry."

"Unless, of course, you want him to watch us, in which case he's welcome to stay and see how I would like to make you feel better when you wake," he said with a devilish smile.

Cecilia shook her head. "I'll talk to him. I promise."

———

Cecilia didn't bring up Xander's request on the way to the Little School in the morning. After school, they made their way to Sylvie's house for a visit with her older sister, Maeve, who was in town with her new baby.

Sylvie met them at the front gate and Cecilia stifled a giggle when she looked past her friend and found Evan lurking in the side yard.

She pulled Sylvie aside as Rainer and Evan started toward the greenhouse at the back of the Brett Estate where the family was taking afternoon tea.

"You've been keeping secrets, Sylvie Brett," Cecilia whispered.

Sylvie blushed. "It's new. I wasn't sure what it was. You know how I am with men, but he's just very persistent, thoughtful...creative. He shows up seemingly out of nowhere to keep me company. He's mysterious and disarming."

Cecilia grinned. "I've never seen you so flustered by someone."

"I know. I don't have the upper hand and that won't do," Sylvie said.

"It seems like he's a bit out of his element too," Cecilia said.

"Here's hoping."

Cecilia glanced at the estate and saw an old man hunched in a plush chair by the garden windows.

"Is your grandfather's memory still failing him?" she asked.

Sylvie sighed heavily. "I use my power to show him memory to remind him, but he keeps getting worse. He can't retain what we show him. I'm not sure how much longer we will have him."

Cecilia squeezed her friend's hand. "I'm sorry, Syl."

"We keep thinking he'll give up, but it seems to be the cruelest, slowest-moving decline." Sylvie turned her attention to the greenhouse. "Let's focus on happier things today."

They crossed the yard to Sylvie's parents, younger sister Vera, and older sister Maeve with her husband, Guardian Mark Fry. Maeve rocked a tiny baby girl with blonde hair and blue eyes, like all the women in the Brett family.

Sylvie's mother startled. "Your Highness, forgive me. I'm still not used to it."

"Oh my gods, me neither. Please stay seated and don't fuss," Cecilia said. "Congratulations, Maeve. How are you doing?"

"I'm exhausted! Luna may look sweet now but she is not very cute when she's up screaming every three hours." Maeve laughed. The fatigue was clear on her face, but so was her joy. Her husband looked at her like she was a goddess. "But tell me about you, Your Highness. Where are you hiding this handsome husband I've heard all about?"

Cecilia smiled. "I expect he'll be along in a little while. They keep him so busy at court all day."

Evan and Rainer broke into easy conversation with Mark about the latest changes to guardian training, and Sylvie's parents took a walk around the garden, leaving the girls with tea.

"How do you like married life, Cece? For a while there, I thought you might never go for it, but it seems you've outdone us all," Maeve teased.

Cecilia nodded. "It certainly caught me by surprise."

"You must show Maeve and Vera the wedding!" Sylvie insisted.

Maeve and Vera each took one of Cecilia's hands. Memory witches were so casual about their power that it was easy to ignore the intimacy of sharing memories. Cecilia obliged, showing Maeve and Vera memories of the ceremony.

"Gods! What a gorgeous dress," Vera said.

Maeve sipped her tea. "Your husband is so handsome. No wonder you look so smitten."

"You don't know the half of it," Cecilia said.

"Oh *really*? Do tell. I take it things are going well." Maeve winked and Cecilia flushed. "I remember the first year or two with Mark. I could not get enough. Having a baby ruins all that fun. So tell us, how is it?"

Cecilia's cheeks heated as she tried to find the words. "It is like nothing else and so much more than I could have imagined. Xander is relentless and incredibly talented, which is equal parts wonderful and upsetting, because he clearly had the practice to get good at it, but I can't complain about being the beneficiary of such talents."

Maeve sprayed her tea, Vera blushed, and Sylvie fell into a fit of giggles.

Cecilia frowned. "I'm sorry, was that inappropriate? I should be more discreet."

"Gods no!" Maeve said. "This is exactly what I need to hear. I haven't spoken to an adult other than my husband in months. Please spare no details."

Cecilia was suddenly glad the men had walked a little farther away. "When we first slept together it was really lovely, but then the next morning he basically acted like a sexual tutor, teaching me to ask for what I wanted and helping me figure out what I liked."

"You're a lucky girl to have someone so concerned with your enjoyment," Maeve said, pouring herself more tea.

"Now he's just very creative. He just gave me a wedding gift of rosebushes and the next morning he made me climax simply by tying me to the bed with a silk scarf and rubbing one of the roses all over my skin."

"What!" Sylvie said it so loud that all three men turned to look and the girls burst into another bout of laughter.

Cecilia shushed them, her cheeks blazing.

"How on earth did that happen?" Sylvie asked, laughing when she took in Vera's wide eyes and bright red cheeks. "Most men seem to struggle to bring a woman to completion even with the tool they're born to use."

"Talent, creativity, and patience. He's never in a rush," Cecilia said.

"I feel like I need a drink after hearing that," Maeve said, fanning herself.

Although Cecilia was embarrassed to share so much, it was nice to have validation from other women that her relationship was normal.

"What are you ladies giggling about?" Mark asked as the men walked back within earshot.

"Darling, we were just saying how we could use something a little stronger than tea. Would you run and get us some wine?" Maeve asked.

He nodded and turned back. Cecilia caught Evan's eye. He was trying not to laugh. She gave him a dirty look, then in a very low whisper said, "No one likes an eavesdropper."

"I'm taking mental notes," he whispered.

Cecilia was about to remind him not to further boost Xander's ego when Mark placed baby Luna in Rainer's arms, and all rational thought abandoned her.

Something Cecilia didn't realize was frozen in her chest thawed. Rainer looked enthralled with the baby, making faces to get her to smile. Cecilia always knew he would be a great father, but never more than at that moment.

She rose to her feet and tentatively touched one of Luna's tiny hands. It was too much, and yet she couldn't stay away.

"You're such a natural, McKay," Mark said as he struggled to open a bottle of wine. "I was a mess the first time I held her. We guardians are raised to hold weapons, not something so delicate."

Cecilia had to disagree. Rainer had always been unbearably gentle with her.

Luna looked so tiny and fragile in his hands. A revelation haunted Cecilia like a ghost she hoped would go away if she refused to look right at it. But watching Rainer, she could no longer ignore it.

It was the one thing that ensured she'd never tie Rainer to her. She couldn't bear the sacrifice he'd be making too—couldn't bear for the world to be without more of him. She couldn't give him a thing he so clearly wanted and she couldn't live knowing that and seeing him try, anyway. It was a blessing and a curse to know someone so well, and while she was accustomed to the ache of longing, this hollowed out her chest.

Rainer had never met anyone related to him. Of course having a family of his own would be important to him.

Rainer mistook the look on her face. "Do you want to hold her, Cece?"

She hesitated, but he placed the baby in her arms. Cecilia was playing with fire and sure to be the only one who got hurt. Luna looked up at her and smiled, stretching out a tiny hand and grabbing a handful of her hair. She gave it a powerful yank.

Cecilia laughed. "She might be a little warrior with that grip."

"Oh, that's her new thing—trying to rip all the hair out of our heads. I should have warned you," Maeve said apologetically.

"It's fine. I can take it," Cecilia said, smiling down at the baby.

Rainer carefully extracted the tiny fingers from her hair and brushed it back over her shoulder, out of reach. "I think she likes you."

"I think I like her back."

Luna's eyes fluttered closed. As Cecilia rocked her, the newborn grew limp with sleep, her little mouth fixed in an adorable pout.

"Oh Cece, you're so good with her. Maybe you'll have one of your own soon," Maeve said.

A sleeping volcano erupted in Cecilia's chest, laying waste to all the ground she'd gained in accepting her future.

If she hadn't heard those words, she might have been able to ignore the intense longing that rose the moment Rainer placed the baby in her arms. Cecilia closed off her connection to Rainer. She didn't want him to know. She'd had weeks to get okay with it.

She slowly handed Luna back to Rainer.

"I'm so sorry. I just remembered I told Xander I would meet him at the cottage because he doesn't know how to get here. You'll have to excuse me." Cecilia nearly ran across the yard, ignoring Rainer calling after her.

She ran back toward the cottage, but instead of going inside, she made her way down the trail to the beach, pacing the sand as she tried to calm the storm blazing through her. It wasn't until she saw the churn of the water and the clouds blotting out the sun that she realized she was conjuring with her emotions. She closed her eyes and took ten deep breaths, trying to release her power back to the ether.

"Bad day?"

She jumped. Grimon stood on the beach in front of her.

Cecilia shrugged.

Grimon approached and fell into step next to her. It reminded her of the walks they'd taken when she was a child.

"I didn't summon you."

"Talk to me, Lady Cece. What plagues you?" the god of death asked.

"Grief."

They were quiet for a moment.

"Sometimes with family members it comes up over and over at the strangest times," Grimon offered.

"No, it's not my father. It's the exchange. The price I didn't want to pay. I thought I made peace with it until someone put a baby in my arms today, and even then I thought I was okay with it. I could feel the hurt, but it was bearable until they suggested I'd have one of my own soon, and then it was just blinding. Why is it still like this?"

Grimon sighed. "Grief isn't linear and you've been going through so much, you're just beginning to heal."

Her chest felt like a collapsing cavern. "I feel like I can't breathe. I'm so angry. How do I get rid of it?"

She'd turned the question over in her mind since her conversation with Clastor in the Godswoods. The exchange she'd made for her powers nagged at her. At the time it made sense, but it wasn't as if she could opt out of it once she walked into the Cave of Longings. That alone seemed to violate the rules of magical exchanges. Why would the witches who created the Gauntlet approve an exchange that robbed her of a choice? Why would her mother be so cruel to require that of her?

"Shouldn't you be an expert on grief?" Cecilia snapped. "I want to be done with it. I want to stop picking it up in every quiet moment and turning it over like it's a puzzle I can solve."

"Some people can sit in the discomfort and welcome the sad feelings for as long as they visit. Some need to rage and scream it out—"

"That one. That sounds good. I want to do that!" Cecilia said.

Grimon nodded. "I'll give you a sound barrier."

"You can do that?"

"It's one of my lesser-known powers. We all have them. I can bend and muffle sound. Turns out death needs to be able to move around undetected. I don't want people to see me coming," Grimon said. The smile on his face made her unsure if he was joking or not.

Cecilia couldn't see the barrier, but she felt it rise and circle them like a bubble. She smelled the smoky cinnamon of Grimon's magic. She'd forgotten that smell from when she was a child. It reminded her of a bakery—not a very intimidating scent for the god of death.

"Let it out, Little Goddess," he said.

Cecilia screamed herself ragged. She reached into the darkness inside her and pulled out every bit of grief, every part of her that mourned the loss of her ability to have children. She mourned the thing she hadn't even known she wanted so badly—seeing Rainer holding Luna like it was second nature, feeling something so tiny and precious that would never be her own, watching Xander light up when he talked about children back in Argaria.

Grief over a person dying was one thing, but grief over a lost possibility wrecked her. There was no public recognition of it. No pyre built to honor it. No bowed heads and whispered prayers. Just the specter of a loss—a ghost only she could see.

She grieved the choice that had been taken from her.

She worked herself into a frenzy until she collapsed in the sand, her limbs heavy and her eyes puffy. It felt good to be empty of anger, to have nothing left but cooling embers in her chest and charred scrapes in her throat.

"Feel better?" Grimon asked.

"I don't know," she whispered.

They sat in silence as Cecilia considered Xander's request from the night before. It was a good idea for her to get some space from Rainer. She had nothing to offer him and even if she did, she couldn't bear not to give him what he wanted most.

From one moment to the next, love morphed from the most potent magic that existed into a millstone waiting to drown her.

Cecilia couldn't stop thinking about the exchange of things. *All good magic requires an exchange.* They were words she lived by for years, and she saw them reflected in her life post-Gauntlet as well.

She exchanged vulnerability for closeness. She exchanged hiding little parts of herself away for being seen. She exchanged doubt for trust.

Despite everything in her life until that point being about the necessity of exchange, it was a fight against her nature every step of the way.

It was easier to look at those smaller exchanges than the one right in front of her. She was exchanging Rainer for Xander. She couldn't have both, at least not in the same way. They were so very different.

Xander, all heat and fire, was prone to extremes and single-minded focus. He loved when she asserted herself. He loved when she challenged him. She loved that he wanted to know every part of her. He wanted her to feel powerful. Still, she felt herself holding back in small ways, unwilling to fully surrender to loving him since it meant giving Rainer up for good; Rainer, whose dying words were still lodged in her heart.

"I was made to love you, and I'll never stop."

The men she loved couldn't have been more different. Rainer was steady and pensive. He overthought every move and action—so rigid and habitual that even when she was immortal, he wanted to stand in front of her, keeping her blind to the things that would hurt her. He meant well, but his lack of faith chipped away at her confidence.

Grimon shifted, startling her with the reminder of his presence beside her. "Your guardian is going to be here soon."

Cecilia turned to see Rainer make his way down the winding cliff trail. When she turned back, Grimon was gone.

"Thank you, Grim," she rasped.

Rainer crossed the sand and sat down beside her. She tried to ignore the relief of having him close. She needed to ensure that comfort was rare going forward.

5

RAINER

Rainer slouched in the sand next to Cecilia, his mind racing.

He swore he was trying to give her space. He'd tried to stay at the Brett Estate, covering for Cecilia's sudden disappearance, but then her grief crashed through their connection and he was so desperate to be needed.

Cecilia was so startlingly beautiful—as if the sun shone more radiant on her, even in her grief. Her cheeks were flushed, her eyes puffy, and her hair had come loose, hanging down to her waist in a mess of windblown ringlets.

His gaze dropped to her lips. Kissing her cleaved his life into a before, when he could function like a normal person with his feelings neatly tucked away, and an after, when not touching her was unbearable.

His love for her was an unsolvable riddle. No matter how he worked it over in his mind, it came out in a tangle of hurt, want, and joy.

"Rain?"

His name drove him from his daze.

"I'm okay," she said.

His gaze settled on her puffy eyes. "You don't look okay."

"Thanks," she muttered.

He scrubbed a hand over his face. "I mean, you look upset."

She stared out at the sea, worrying her lower lip with her teeth.

Rainer wanted to tilt her chin up and press his mouth to hers and take back everything Xander had stolen from him. Cecilia was supposed to be *his*. He'd always felt wildly possessive of her, but now it was practically a compulsion. Rainer needed to hold on to any piece of her he still possessed. His desperation haunted every moment with an unspoken *I love you*.

She knew, of course, but speaking it again would wreck their tentative peace, and she had enough on her mind.

Finally, she turned and met his gaze, clearly unaware of his desperation. "I didn't realize it would be so hard. Everyone is going to ask about children, especially because of who I am—because of who Xander is. Heirs are important to royals. I'm never going to get away from the question."

Rainer took her hand in his tentatively, and when she didn't pull it away, he brushed his thumb back and forth over her inner wrist. The scar from the wound Nessa had dealt her in Argaria was bumpy under his thumb.

Cecilia closed her eyes as her breath slowed, each inhale deepening. At least this hadn't changed. The motion was soothing to them both.

Rainer cleared his throat. "That doesn't mean it isn't hard. You lost something, and it's complicated by so many things. The fact that you didn't know your real parents, and that the ones you had lied to you. The fact that you had to make the decision when you were so young and you didn't want the thing you traded it for."

The fact that I didn't tell you how desperately in love with you I am until you'd married someone else.

The truth of the words did nothing to ease the ache in his chest. Rainer was forever swept away in the riptide of her, waiting to be bashed on the rocks.

"I can't understand why Selene Carrick—" She cleared her throat.

"Why my own birth mother would force me into an exchange that I had no control over. I keep turning it over in my mind but it makes no sense. Exchanges are supposed to be about free will, but once I went into that cave I couldn't back out of it."

Rainer wished he understood—wished he could do more than nod and feel her grief swell in his chest—but the truth was that he had no idea what she was going through. "You're right. It seems strange that she would have allowed such a permanent exchange."

"I know I need to get over it because one of these days Davide is going to attack and we still have Cato to deal with, and I can't lose it every time someone asks when we're going to have children—" she hesitated, meeting his eye, "or wake everyone up every night with my horrible nightmares."

"I don't mind that." Rainer draped a supportive arm across her shoulders.

She shrugged it off, and his stomach plunged.

"I appreciate it," she said. "Really, I do, but we have to stop. I'm married and as much as it's a relief to see you, I shouldn't need that. I need to just deal with it on my own or with my husband. I can't have you sleeping over every night."

Rainer's love for her was well-worn and comfortable, but the new jealousy chafed. Even when she'd married Xander, Rainer had convinced himself it was for the best. But watching her share the intimacy of grief with someone else rubbed him raw with envy.

"Is this your idea or his? Because you seem pretty willing to take the comfort when I'm there." He bit the words out harsher than he meant to. Anger had always been a reflex to someone coming between them, but now Rainer's fury was a life force all its own; better to let that out than give in to the intense panic tucked beneath it.

Cecilia frowned. "It's Xander's, but he's my husband. What you and I have is codependent. If someone touched him the way you touch me, I would be furious. I know you don't like him, but he's shown a lot of restraint."

Her eyes flashed over his face, searching for understanding where she would find none.

Rainer lost Cecilia in little ways as the days went by. He'd spent a lifetime pushing her away. Losing her for real was his reckoning and the knowledge was a knife twisting in his gut, the pain sharp and deserved.

While Cecilia had nightmares of her own, Rainer woke in cold sweats every night, dreaming of the day she married Xander. He dreamed of the moment he saw her in her wedding dress, and the look on her face, the way her eyes pleaded with him. He felt the conflict in her, but he put concern for her safety over concern for her heart. Cecilia had given him so many chances. She coaxed him out, told him outright about the differences in their circumstances, but he had done nothing but betray her trust.

So he sealed his mouth shut when he should have been shouting how much he loved her for anyone who cared to listen.

Rainer let out a bitter laugh. "He does very little to hide his disdain for me."

"And why should he?" Cecilia snapped. "You kissed me and said you're in love with me and you show up to comfort me every night. Should Xander be warm to you?"

Suddenly, it seemed there were miles of thorns between them. The damage rendered too great. The path back to each other unnavigable. Cecilia had never felt out of reach, but now a ravine had formed where their friendship used to be and he could do nothing but look at her longingly from the other side.

Rainer slapped a hand on the sand, unable to curb his frustration. "I feel your terror when you're dreaming the same as if you're actually in danger. If you want me to stop coming to comfort you, you're going to have to stop pulling so hard on our bond." His chest was so tight he could scarcely draw breath. "This is how it starts. Xander starts by telling you we can't spend as much time together, and pretty soon it will be not at all. I rarely see you outside of our walks to and from school. We're supposed to be best friends, and we rarely talk anymore. You have no idea what's going on in my life. I don't want it to be like this."

She threw her hands up, her cheeks flushing as anger surged through their bond. "I told you it would be. We talked about this that day in the woods. We talked about it before we left. I told you things would change when we got back, that it would never be the same between us. You took it for granted. I understand that you don't like Xander, but I love him. I'm committed to him, and he comes first. If he makes a simple request that is completely understandable, who am I to deny him?"

Rainer was stunned. "I guess that's how it is now. Fine. I'll leave you be. I just wanted to make sure you were all right."

"No, Rain, I'm not all right, but don't you think that it's a problem that you're always running to find me when it should be my husband? I know change is hard, but you can't stop it from happening by clinging to the past. Just because you professed something when you thought you were dying doesn't mean you own me."

Rainer opened his mouth and then closed it, shaking his head. He wished poisonous words came to him as easily as they came to Cecilia when she was angry. Sometimes it was exhausting operating under the assumption that she was the only one with big feelings. Sometimes he wanted to be the one that said something that stung just so she could see how it felt. But he never would because the thing that hurt him most was feeling how much she hurt.

"I never thought I owned you, Cece. It's my job to take care of you."

"Well, now it's his too."

There it was laid bare: Rainer and Cecilia's connection was a liability in her marriage. Her commitment to Xander was driving a wedge between her and Rainer when she needed support the most. It was so unfair for her to ask Rainer to ignore it when he was so aware of her pain.

He'd felt it so many times over the years. Every time she tried to make small talk with the ladies of the court, their cruel words sliced into him as they sliced into her. He felt it when Cecilia stepped into a fighting ring, like his heart was outside of his body, taking every blow. He couldn't stand the way she let herself be bloodied and kept going back for more. It was as if the more the world denied her, the more determined she was to prove it wrong. Rainer was equally amazed and terrified by her fortitude because he couldn't take it. He was never more weak, more lost, more in her thrall than when she was hurt. And now she was giving all that delicacy to Xander.

Their bond had gone from being a source of comfort to an agitated buzz in his chest, compelling him to tend to his charge. In the past, she'd let him hold her, silently pass things through their bond, or at the very least tell her a story. Now, Xander's eyes burned into Rainer every time he touched Cecilia, and he'd never felt less welcome in the arms of the person he loved most in the world.

"I suppose that settles it," he whispered.

He stood and walked away without looking back, even when a loud sniffle broke the silence as he reached the foot of the cliff trail.

He stormed up the trail and down the path toward his apartment on the edge of the Reznik Estate. It was once the late Lady Reznik's first studio, before they bought the cottage overlooking the sea.

The apartment had been a place to hide his most precious possessions when Rainer was young and without a space untainted by his father's cruelty. A lump formed in his throat. The huntmaster had willed the space to him. Right before Leo died, he'd told Rainer to fight for Cecilia, but clearly the huntmaster had more faith in Rainer than he did in himself, and certainly more than his own father.

"Show love when you need to, never when you feel it." He no longer heard those words in his father's voice. Now it was his own voice, constantly nagging and belittling. Raymond McKay had been so efficient in his erosion, Rainer could anticipate the criticism, rendering his father's presence unnecessary for further damage.

Rainer took one last glance over his shoulder at the sun melting into the horizon.

What cruelty to still feel Cecilia and know he was losing her all the same. It made him wild with fear. He caught himself, like a poppy addict with a fix, taking deep drags of her scent when she hugged him goodbye each day.

Nothing he did to distract himself helped much. He swam in the Adiran Sea every morning for an hour. He trained constantly with Cal or Anders or anyone who would fight him. He worked himself into exhaustion, but it did little to burn off his relentless uneasiness.

In the evenings, when there was no one left to pummel and everything was quiet, he distracted himself from Cecilia's absence by cooking. He took up residence in Clara Reznik's kitchen. Clara—who'd taught him how to cook years ago when Cecilia proved deeply disinterested—said nothing, though there was a knowing in her eyes as she watched him make fresh pasta almost every night. He had no stomach for it, and instead brought it to Cecilia. It was worth it just to watch her take a bite of his culinary creations. He loved how she tasted everything, so much expression on her face at the first bite, and her approval brought him a pathetic amount of joy.

The worst part of his day was when he tried to go to bed alone. After years of telling stories until they fell asleep together, the silence made him restless. The minutes slogged by, and when he finally fell asleep, he was dragged from the depths of it when he reached out for Cecilia, only to find her absent. Instinct and habit jerked him from sleep until he remembered that Cecilia sleeping in someone else's arms was his new reality.

The only time she still needed him was in the middle of the night. Rainer was so familiar with her fear that even in sleep he recognized the signal to wake and search her out. Surrendering to her then was easy. He'd give her anything she wanted. It was the only time she let him hold her anymore, and it was exquisite torture to not be able to kiss the tears away from her terrified face.

She'd caught him off guard on the beach. The rational part of him recognized it was a completely understandable request for space, but his heart wasn't rational. The part of him that loved her with a fierceness that sometimes took his breath away saw her draw a line in the sand that he couldn't cross and he wanted to fight it.

It wasn't fair of him to want that. Not after she'd given him the chance to fight for her, practically begged him to, and he hadn't taken it. At first it was because he knew what she was, but then he'd been so helpless to protect her and so angry at himself for lying that he encouraged her to be with Xander. He'd thought it was the right thing until the moment she kissed her husband and a fissure had formed in Rainer's heart, so painful and deep he thought it might kill him.

Now, there was a new ache in watching her hide bits of herself from him. Rainer wondered if it was something Xander could see too, or if it was only visible to someone who'd spent his whole life studying her. Her grief came in glimpses. Like a reflection in a lake, he could only see it when she was still, and as soon as it formed fully, she'd move, and he'd lose the glimmer of sadness that she worked so hard to disguise.

He'd been relieved to realize their bond was still intact even after she came into her new power, but Cecilia spent a lot of time shutting him out. Rainer couldn't tell if it was because she didn't want him to know how sad she was, or because she wanted to put distance between them after his confession. He didn't know which was worse.

The large wooden door of his apartment groaned open. For years his private apartment in the old studio space had seemed like an honor, granting him both privacy and proximity to Cecilia. Now the place seemed a sad relic of a different time. The bed pushed against the far wall covered in a blanket his mother had knitted, his clothes neatly hung in the closet alcove in the corner, the bookshelves sparse save for a few of his most prized histories.

He'd practically lived in Cecilia's cottage, and now he felt like a refugee—cast out from the haven he'd built with her. But if she wanted Rainer to keep his distance, he would. There was no way he'd be able to avoid being woken by her terror at night, but as long as she didn't tug on their bond, he could stay put and ride it out, no matter how anxious it made him.

Rainer stoked the fire with one hand and poured himself a drink with the other. When the fire roared back to life, he slumped into his chair and took a long swig of the whiskey. It burned all the way down.

He considered dinner, but he couldn't bring himself to get out of the chair.

His mind was fractured—torn between continuing in the same way and giving Cecilia the space she'd requested. Was this what his life would be like now—waiting for her to need him? Would she ever actually *need* him?

His heart kicked up, sending a flurry of anxious tingles through his limbs.

He reached into his pocket and pulled out the satin ribbon he always carried. While he didn't have memory magic, the day Cecilia gave it to him was burned into his brain forever.

He saw her in his mind, six years old, all short limbs, bouncy curls, and bright eyes. He'd been so awkward as they waited for their fathers to finish speaking after their bonding ceremony. He leaned against the picket fence outside the Seer's cottage, trying desperately to figure out what to say.

Rainer was only eight—as overwhelmed by the possibility of pursuing the Gauntlet as he was by the newly-formed bond that seemed to swell and press against his sternum.

Cecilia was nervous, or maybe he was. Their bond was too new for him to tell.

She'd frowned like she was mulling something over. Finally, she'd tugged the ribbon from the end of her braid. Immediately the plait started to unravel. The green satin shimmered in the sunlight as she handed it to Rainer.

"What's this for?" he'd asked.

"It's my favor. Like in the stories my mother used to read me. When a knight is going into a tournament, a lady gives him her favor. If you're going to be protecting me, you should have something of mine."

He'd wanted to remind her that the Gauntlet wasn't a fairy tale— that it was dangerous. Instead, he'd said, *"I like stories, too."*

She'd smiled. *"Good. It's settled. My ribbon favor will make you brave."*

"But favors were a promise to come back from battle alive."

Cecilia shook her head with such fierce certainty. *"I don't think so."*

"Then why did knights carry them?" he'd asked.

Her eyes had darted warily to Rainer's father like she'd taken one look at him and recognized him for the monster he was. *"I think they just wanted a reminder that they weren't alone when heading into battle."*

The words stripped Rainer of all his defenses—they still did years later. Cecilia had shown him in such a small way that love was making someone else's troubles your own.

The ribbon was a bit faded now but Rainer hoped it had a little magic in it, because he'd never felt more alone.

6

XANDER

Cece crashed through the door with fierce determination on her face. Xander barely had time to take in her puffy eyes and the smell of salt on her skin before she was kissing him.

Her mouth was hungry, salted with tears, searching for comfort.

He pulled back. "Love—"

"Wreck me. Ruin me. Make me forget this wretched day." Desperation laced her voice.

Gods, she could level him with just her words—as if she'd looked into the deepest recesses of his mind and dragged out fantasies he didn't even know existed.

She untied her dress, letting it pool at her feet. The sight of the red lace slip against her pale skin stopped every rational thought in his head.

"What's got you so wound up, love?" he asked.

She arched a brow. "Do you want to ask me questions or do you want to spend the next hour doing whatever you want to me?"

"What I want," he said, tossing off his shirt, "is to hear you screaming my name."

His brain urged him to ask questions, to understand her hurt—

which probably had to do with Rainer—but the rest of him thrilled at the challenge and freedom she offered. When it came to his wife, he always lost out to that part of him. He was addicted to her.

Teacups shattered on the floor as he lifted her onto the table. Tea pooled in the cracks between floorboards as he freed his cock from his pants and pushed into her.

Cece groaned, her thighs trembling around his waist. He moved in long, sensual strokes, kissing her as if he could press all the love she'd lost back into her, holding her body against his until she was moaning his name and digging her nails into his back and telling him how much she loved him.

There was nothing like Cece. No one who made him feel so seen, so loved, so at home in his own skin. She laid herself out first, her vulnerability so welcoming it made room for his own, and he'd been trying to match her ever since.

She gripped Xander's forearms as he drove into her relentlessly, desperately trying not to lose control as she fluttered around him. Gods, she made him crazy when she was like this.

Her back arched, and she moaned his name and fell apart in a flash of ecstasy. He picked her up, and she wrapped her legs around him as he carried her over to the couch, placing her on his lap. She sunk down on him and started to move her hips, the smooth skin of her back warm under his callused hands as he controlled her pace.

He went on and on, trying to obliterate her grief, until finally he gave in to the building pleasure and moaned into her neck as he finished.

They lay together afterward in silence. Xander was desperate to know what was on her mind, but his wife was a bit like a wounded animal. Any false move might make her run. If he wanted to know, he would have to give her time and space. He needed to let her come to him.

It was clear when she woke from her nightmare a short time later why she'd been so upset. Instead of searching for Rainer, she begged Xander to make her forget.

He made love to her until the quaking terror in her body dissipated, replaced by happy, sated tingles, and she fell into a blissful sleep.

As he listened to her gentle breathing in the dark, he longed for the days before the nightmares started, when he woke her up in the middle of the night simply because he couldn't get enough of her. He missed the way her soft whimpers and sighs woke him, and he'd coax more of them out of her by kissing her neck until she woke up, urging him to do more. He dreamed of a day when he could make love to his wife without the specter of Rainer McKay hanging over them.

Sleep was scarce now, with his guilt growing by the day. Usually he just lay there with Cece in his arms. When his restlessness was unbearable, he picked up charcoal and paper and attempted to capture her in black and white—a nearly impossible task. Though sleep was the only time she was still enough to track the light on her face, he lacked the talent to show the way she glowed.

Xander looked around the cottage, lit only by the light of the moon. The night they returned to Olney, it thrilled him to finally see inside her world. The cottage was bursting with his wife's essence. He hadn't realized how desperate he was for that glimpse into her space until he saw it. Sweaters and shawls hung over the backs of nearly every chair, like she was afraid to be more than an arm's reach from warmth, even in Olney's temperate climate. Dried herbs hung from hooks by the kitchen sink along with the roses he'd left her before she left to finish the Gauntlet. Books on magic theory, history, and spells filled the bookshelves, crammed beside volumes of fairy tales and myths with dried flowers pressed between the pages.

His favorite part of the whole place was the dark notches next to the cottage door that documented Rainer and Cece's height at different ages, marking where she'd peaked at thirteen while Rainer had gone on growing.

Xander loved the cottage. He would live there forever if he could. There was no corner of it he hadn't explored. He wanted to know every thought in Cece's head.

She sighed and wiggled against him. The movement and sound

sent a surge of heat through his body. He ground his hips against her, kissing her shoulder.

"Xan," she rasped.

She reached her hand back and pulled his hips toward her, urging him to grind against her again. A soft whimper parted her lips as his hand snaked between her legs.

He dipped his fingers between her thighs. She was already so wet. Her head rolled back against his shoulder.

"What do you want, love?" Xander nipped at her ear.

"You," she moaned.

"Again? So soon?" He loved when she said it.

She pressed her ass into him impatiently, trying to reach for him. He moved his fingers faster.

"Xander," she panted. "Please—"

"Please what, Goddess?"

"Please fuck me," she said impatiently.

He loved her desperation.

He teased her with shallow strokes before thrusting into her. She cursed as her hands balled in the sheets, smothering a string of profanity into the pillow. Anyone who heard the creative strings of obscenities that came out of his wife's mouth while he was inside her would be shocked to hear such words from the lips of a princess, but Xander loved it.

"Such a filthy mouth." His teeth grazed her neck as she shivered. "How do you want it, love?"

"Hard. Make me forget," she moaned as his hips rocked against her.

Forget what? he wanted to ask.

Instead, he pushed her onto her stomach. She spread her legs wider as he drove into her. Her fingers clawed at the sheets and he interlaced his hands with them. The room filled with the sound of their heavy breathing, Cece's soft moaning, and their slick bodies meeting.

His lips rarely left her skin, his tongue gliding over the salty sweetness of her neck as she groaned his name.

How could it always feel like this? The madness that struck him every time he made love to his wife was beyond his comprehension. It was a frenzy. He never knew love could feel so much like magic, but the way he felt for her was beyond reason. She reminded him of early spring in Argaria, when the crocuses pushed through the cold ground and the weather could change in an instant. He never knew what to expect from her, and he loved watching her unfold.

It was a challenge each time to get her as wound up as possible and see what she would do. Constantly in competition with himself, Xander found new, creative ways to surprise her in and out of bed. He knew he should enjoy the journey and let it unfold naturally, but there seemed to be a driving force that compelled him to learn as much as possible about her. He was impatient to know her, to see what made her tick, to understand all her likes and deepest desires.

They were a mess of limbs and teeth and brutal kisses. A static pulse, like a storm, rushed through her. He gritted his teeth as she clenched around him and screamed into her pillow. He moved with her frantically, trying to draw out her release as he found his own.

He panted, trailing kisses down her spine before rolling to the side. Cheeks flushed in the silvery moonlight, she smiled at him as she ran her fingers through his messy hair.

"You can't just let me sleep through the night, can you?" Her eyes fluttered closed as he kissed her palm.

"Perhaps if you didn't insist on wiggling against me and moaning in your sleep. If you didn't beg."

Her eyes shot open and she pursed her lips. "You could just have some self-control."

"Not with you, love. You shred it to bits every day with your smile and your charm and the way you undress me with your eyes."

Cece's laugh rang through the room like a bell. "I do not."

"You do. I like it because it makes me feel less guilty about doing the same to you."

It was a relief to see her as herself. He still expected the goddess to show up. She'd returned from her morning walk weeks before, mumbling about "fucking Grim and integration" and said that she was the goddess now. He didn't question her, just nodded, but she'd been her warm self ever since.

His fingers danced over the curve of her hips, and she shivered at his touch. "My love, do you want to share what has you so upset?"

She froze. "No."

Xander wanted to peel her secrets from her until there was nothing but the truth between them. She was content to hide, still testing him to see if he'd run.

He tried again. "If not that then perhaps you could explain something to me. I know you said you integrated your powers and the goddess won't return, but how do you know?"

She curled closer to him, the tension unwinding from her body. "Grim and Adira told me I had to integrate my power. I was afraid to be this *thing*. Afraid it would somehow corrupt me more. Afraid I wouldn't recognize myself if I fully let it in. Grim said it's just a part of me that I could stop fighting. That I needed to. I've been fighting my whole life. I just didn't know how to stop." Even in the dim light he saw the pain in her eyes.

"Did it hurt?" He took her small hand in his much larger one and placed it over his heart.

"No. I was a little dizzy, but it didn't hurt. It felt like—" She sighed. "Surrender."

"Why were you scared?"

Cece swallowed hard, a few rogue tears cutting tracks down her cheeks. The fierceness with which she brushed them away broke his heart. Xander hated how she fought that vulnerability in front of him when he wanted to see all of her. He hated the world that made her ashamed of her strong feelings and forced her to hide away the very things that made her so unique and lovely in his eyes. She was so careful to reveal herself little by little, a wariness in her eyes as if waiting for him to run.

"Because it was so easy for me to kill all those people," she rasped. "Easy to feel nothing—to ruin a battalion with only a glance. I loved the power. I thought if I touched it again, I could never put it down. Power corrupts. I didn't want to be another brutal god. I was so tired of feeling powerless, but now I'm afraid of how power will corrupt me."

Xander considered her words. "I'm a prince. Has power corrupted me?"

She cocked an eyebrow. "Did you ever really have any?"

The words stung like nettles.

Her face softened. "Oh gods, me and my stupid mouth. I'm sorry, Xan. That didn't come out right. I just meant that what I felt at that moment was like nothing else. It wasn't like summoning. I've been a powerful witch since I was a girl, but this is something far beyond that. I can feel it all the time. A buzzing sensation below my skin. I was afraid it would change me. That moment, when I killed those hunters and then when I turned and killed Endros, I was split in half. I was still in there, but the goddess was running the show. She protected me. I'd already lost too much that I couldn't get back. I couldn't bear the thought of losing more."

He squeezed her hand, silently pleading with her to continue.

"When I was in the Cave of Longings and I knew what it would cost, I was so caught off guard. I almost didn't do it. I almost let the cave have me. I expected that my greatest longing would be about loneliness, so I thought it would be you or Rainer. When I thought of loneliness, I didn't think of being childless, but that's the nature of exchange magic—it's the intersection of free will and fate. It's volatile and you have to make any sacrifice required. It's a choice we make in the moment, but we can't always control the repercussions. There must be a reason that was the price I had to pay. Integration was hard to accept because it meant finally confronting what I—" She swallowed hard. "What *we* lost."

Cece stopped trying to hide the tears. The pain in her eyes was deep, and as much as Xander longed for her vulnerability, it was hard to see her in such agony.

"I'm sorry that I couldn't be stronger for both of us. I've replayed that day on the beach in my head so many times. I feel like I let you down—" Her voice broke.

Xander was devastated that she'd felt that and even more upset that he couldn't undo it. He traced the lines of her face with his fingers. He could do it all night, all day, for the rest of his life. He'd happily wear away his fingerprints touching her. The freedom to do so was his favorite luxury.

He placed her hand over his heart again. "You didn't let me down. You fought so hard for us. Endros was the god of war. You did what you had to and you saved us. You saved so many people. I'm so sorry you had to go through that alone. I love you and hate that you're blaming yourself when I'm the one who got caught."

She shook her head insistently. "I don't blame you." She was quiet for a long moment. "Today I held Sylvie's niece and someone commented what a natural I was and speculated that I'd be having children soon."

Xander pulled her closer. He would stare down any evil for her, face any villain, but there was nothing he could do to make this better. Telling her that his own grief blew through him daily like an icy squall would do nothing but make her feel worse. Instead he held her close and kissed her tears as they fell.

When her crying slowed, he met her eyes. "Are you still afraid of your power?"

"I'm less afraid that I won't be able to control it, more afraid I will like it," she whispered.

Xander frowned. "Why shouldn't you like to hurt those who would harm you without a second thought?"

"Because that's not me. It's never been me. I've defended myself, but I've never enjoyed it. I hate feeling helpless, but I never enjoyed wielding power over other people."

"You never enjoyed seeing Rainer on his ass looking up at you in shock?"

A laugh bubbled through her tears. "That part, yes. But I took no joy in killing, even when I was defending myself. We did what we had to, but I didn't like it. This time I did. I ended a thousand lives with a glance and I felt nothing but boredom."

"I'm not afraid of you."

She chewed her lower lip. "You should be."

"Ask me why I'm not afraid?"

"No."

"Ask me."

She shook her head.

"Stubborn as always." Xander rolled onto his back to look out at the moon over the sea. The quiet stretched between them heavily.

"Why?" she whispered.

"Because you lying awake at night so worried about it means that you aren't the same goddess now that you were then. You lost control over a brand-new power, but you're in charge now. The woman I fell in love with, my beautiful Cece, she is hope itself, and I wish she had the same faith in herself that she does in everyone else."

Her body softened against his as if the words were a balm against all the fears that she kept locked in the depths of her heart. He wished he could always be an antidote to worry the way she was for him, but she was selective in the moments she allowed herself to be cared for that way.

Xander longed to unburden himself from the guilt that haunted him. Her vulnerability drew his forth, but instead of sharing what he truly wanted to—needed to—he filled the impulse with a different guilty secret instead.

"I should have told you this a long time ago, but I think I was afraid to admit it even to myself. The day you found out who I was, when you were so angry and hurt and you said that I preyed on your loneliness, I never hated myself more. Because it wasn't until that moment that I realized how lonely I'd been my whole life."

She was very still, but her eyes were fixed on his face and he knew she was reading his emotions. He didn't mind.

"I know I can be extreme," Xander said. "I spent most of my life behind enemy lines, only home in Argaria two months a year. My mother loved me, and Davide when we were young, but I never fit in with my family. I was a witch, and I wanted to be a hunter. My lack of interest in power or elevating myself above other people was disappointing for so many reasons. I was supposed to be a prince, and that didn't fit their idea of what I should be. My mother tried, but my father didn't encourage my magic. I suspect he didn't like that I had access to a power that he didn't and didn't want the constant reminder. The only person who helped was my grandmother, and those lessons were secret and few and far between. Then they sent me to Olney. I had Evan and Teddy, but I only saw them a couple of months a year. We wrote tons of letters in between, but I had to burn them all for safety. Here in Olney, I had friends among the hunters, but no one knew who I was. I couldn't be my full self anywhere. I was always hiding pieces of myself away. That's what a good spy does."

The pain on Cece's face reflected his own. She looked at him not with pity, but with understanding.

"When I first started talking to you and you were funny and cutting and unimpressed with anything but the truth, I was so thrown. I know you say I was the first person who really saw you, but Cece, you're the first person who really saw me. Not the spare Prince Alexander Savero, or the Storm Prince, or a charming hunter. Just Xander. You wouldn't let me hide, and worse, I didn't want to. You broke through this cage I hadn't realized I'd built around myself. I'd talked myself out of wanting love. I'd convinced myself to be satisfied with less."

Cece ran her fingers through his hair, her eyes glassy with unshed tears.

"You helped me embrace my magic," Xander said. "You've taught me how to summon memory, which has allowed me to hold on to my parents and Teddy longer than I otherwise could have. But even more than that, talking to you was the first time I ever felt that sense of loneliness fade away. So when you told me I'd used that exact thing to manipulate you, I knew you were right, and it killed me. There aren't words for how sorry I am about doing that. I love you so much and I never wanted to hurt you that way."

Tears blurred his vision. When they cleared, Cece looked startled. He was quick to show passion, frustration, and anger, but it was rare that he showed that sensitive side of himself.

She kissed him. "I will not say it's okay, because it wasn't. I hate what you did, but I understand why you did it. You thought you were doing the right thing for your family and your kingdom. We were all just trying to do what was best, and when it counted, you protected me, Xander. I wish you'd been honest with me sooner, but I've forgiven you already. Now you need to figure out how to forgive yourself."

"I would never forgive someone else who did this to you," Xander said.

Her touch was so gentle on his cheek and the love in her eyes was too much. He looked away as the guilt settled like a stone in his stomach.

"As I understand it, I am now a princess and a goddess, so I command you to forgive yourself."

He barked out a laugh and kissed her.

She brushed her fingers over his cheek. "I like you like this."

"Embarrassed?" he asked.

She shook her head. "Unguarded. You really make me work for it."

Love wasn't about the grand, sweeping gestures, as much as he might enjoy the way his wife reacted to them. Love was looking into the darkness inside of another person without judgment, and sometimes seeing your own reflection in that wild dark. What he really needed was to be seen and understood. Cece knew what it was to be wounded in the same way and she wanted to see him.

Xander swallowed his guilt. He wanted to tell her everything— turn himself inside out and bare his soul to her—but he'd spent the past eleven years undercover. *Lying is survival.* That creed had kept him alive for years. Dishonesty never came naturally to him but he'd worn the cloak of it for so long that he didn't know how to reach into the depths of himself and drag out the truth.

7

CECILIA

Rain drummed against the cottage windows and dark clouds smudged out the sun. Fog blanketed everything beyond the shoreline, making it impossible to tell the time of day or how many ships might be waiting beyond.

Cecilia took the day off from the Little School. Facing Rainer would have been too much and she needed time to collect herself. She'd tried to read some old mythology books to see if she could learn anything more about Cato and his abilities, but gave up when she couldn't find a single book she hadn't already scoured.

Her gaze fell on the book Rainer had written for her birthday. It sat on her nightstand where Xander left it the day before. She picked it up, unable to avoid the pull of it any longer, and read Rainer's inscription on the inside cover.

———

Rainer and Cece's Book of Fairy Tales

Happy birthday, Cece! I wish I'd done this since the beginning because our stories are worth telling. I know you're 23 now, but my birthday wish for you is that you never feel too old for a good fairy tale. Thank you for being my best friend for all of these years. Your courage and grace never cease to amaze me. Wishing you many more years of joy and adventure with me by your side.

Love, Rain

———

She bit back the tears that threatened as she paged through the stories. Minutes slid into hours as she read each one, vacillating between laughing and crying. It was easier to ignore their history without seeing it written in front of her. In black and white, it felt impossible to push aside.

Still, she couldn't help feeling like Rainer was in love with who she'd been before. She never quite felt certain that he could love who her new power had made her, or what the coming war might demand she become.

Cecilia wanted to be loved for all that she was, not in spite of her darkness.

She laid back on the bed, lost in the stories and the memories. It felt like just moments, but she was stiff when the cottage door creaked open and startled her.

Xander stepped inside and paused when he saw her sprawled with the book.

"You're finally reading your book," he said as he crossed the room and kissed her cheek.

"It was time," she said.

"What are you doing home so early?" he asked.

"I needed a day off from being stared at."

Xander raised a skeptical eyebrow. "Are you sure this isn't about your fight with Rainer?"

Cecilia narrowed her eyes at him. "How did you know?"

"I didn't know. You just confirmed it." Xander smirked. "You know you can talk to me about it. He's not my favorite person, but I love you. If you need to talk, then I need to listen."

"It's nothing. It will blow over." Her heart plummeted. It most certainly would not blow over. She still felt the heat of Rainer's anger like smoldering embers in her chest.

"What happened?" Xander asked.

"He was trying to comfort me, and I asked him to stop coming over at night. I don't regret asking that, but I shouldn't have done it when I was in a bad mood. I could have handled it much better. He took it poorly." The words tumbled out of her. Xander rubbed her shoulders, trying to release some tension. "It's been years since we had a terrible fight."

"Is that because you didn't need to or because you were a doormat?" Xander asked.

Cecilia flinched. "Excuse me?"

"Don't forget, I watched you for the better part of a year. I watched you grin and bear everything, even though you were in love with him. You forced yourself to take everything in stride so you wouldn't upset him. So I'm wondering, did you not fight because there was nothing to fight about, or did you not fight because you forced yourself not to say anything? You are all fight everywhere else, but with Rainer, it's like you have no backbone."

She hated that he was right. She hated that she'd been a doormat. She hated that he'd seen it. It left her feeling exposed and embarrassed.

For so long she'd taken every scrap of attention Rainer gave her, so afraid that any objections would make him turn away from her. She was angry at herself but it was easier to be angry at Xander for seeing it.

"Like you're one to talk. You let your brother walk all over you. He was so sure he could do whatever he wanted that he broke my fucking hand, Xander."

Xander looked like she'd slapped him. "Clearly I hit a sore spot. I'm not allowed to say anything bad or even honest about perfect Rainer McKay." He shook his head. "Gods forbid I threaten the perfect love story that is Cece and Rainer. What happens when we look at it closely? We start to see the cracks in the perfect veneer, huh?"

Cecilia flinched. She didn't need the reminder. She still felt the humiliation of Rainer's initial rejection and the whiplash of his profession of love when he was at death's door.

"Oh, I'm sorry," she snapped. "Is our love story better? Do you prefer love stories where the prince lies to and traps the princess?"

Xander went completely still.

She knew as soon as she said it that she shouldn't have. Some deep, vicious part of her was always determined to win the fight, but this win felt rotten instead of triumphant. She hated that part of her that lashed out when she was wounded.

It wasn't totally her fault. She'd been taught to fight as soon as she was old enough to hold a weapon. It was a shame no one had ever taught her how to stop.

"Xander, I—"

"Don't." The hard set of his jaw filled her with guilt.

Her big, stupid mouth. Would she forever be cursed to speak before thinking?

"I don't know why I said that. I didn't mean it at all."

"Yes, you did."

"I didn't. I was mad, and when I'm angry I say the meanest thing I can even if it's not true. I'm sorry. If I didn't want to marry you, I would have found another way, and I certainly didn't need to marry you a day early."

She reached for him, and to her immense relief, he let her wrap her arms around him and kiss his cheek.

"I'm working on things with Rainer. I never realized how many boundary issues we had until you. Neither of us has ever been in a serious relationship, and we're just trying to figure this out. He's upset because we hardly spend any time together anymore except for our walks to and from school. He misses his friend. I miss him too. But I also recognize that being a princess means our relationship will be under scrutiny. I want you to know that I'm working on it."

Xander nodded, his hands still balled at his sides. "Have you considered severing your bond?"

The words punched the air out of her lungs. She stumbled away from him, a knot of disbelief in her throat. How could he even suggest that? She knew he was jealous but severing was such an extreme measure.

"You mean have I considered subjecting myself to excruciating pain so you can feel more secure?"

Xander frowned. "I've seen you deal with considerable pain as if it's nothing. I doubt that is holding you back."

She was so angry at him for suggesting something so drastic, and equally furious that he was right about her reasons. The physical pain was temporary. But the emotional pain of losing that connection —the fear of being without the thing that had held her steady her whole life—terrified her beyond comprehension.

They stared at each other, Cecilia's anger burning through her veins like a fever.

Xander's eyes narrowed, and his grimace warped into a smirk. "I hate how good you look when you're angry. I can't even fight with you without being turned on."

Her rage cooled. She wasn't really mad at Xander. He was justifiably insecure, but it was disturbing that he'd see her hurt to make himself feel better. She was torn between pressing on and finishing the fight and ignoring it and hoping it worked itself out.

She took a tentative step toward him and his hand on her hip decided for her. "Do you want to be mad, or do you want to kiss me?"

He smiled, pulling her onto the bed so she straddled his lap. He kissed her softly before leaning his forehead against hers.

"I know it's kind of messed up, because you hurt my feelings, but I'd be lying if I said it doesn't make me a little hot when you're mean," he said, smiling against her lips.

Cecilia laughed. "You are so disturbed."

"I know. I blame the hunter training. It's made me a little too bloodthirsty." He was quiet for a moment, then he pulled back and looked at her seriously. "Love, I have to tell you something. I should have told you quite a while ago. We got interrupted, but then I was a coward and put it off. I really need to be honest with you. Promise you'll hear me out once I say the first thing I'm going to say."

Her heart pounded in her chest. "I promise, but you're making me nervous—"

Cecilia stopped, wincing as a grating sound filled the air like a great chorus.

She hadn't heard it in weeks. Not since the day her father died.

"What is it?" Xander asked.

"Death whispers."

8

CECILIA

"Something is very wrong," Cecilia said.

She hopped up and yanked on her boots, then grabbed her bow and sword from the corner by the door.

Xander was beside her in a moment, strapping on his short swords and picking up his bow. "Let's go."

She stared at him. "You're not going to try to get me to stay behind and be safe?"

"While the idea of you running toward danger scares the shit out of me, I'd much rather have you beside me with a weapon in your hand than sitting back and feeling helpless. I know that isn't in you and there's no one I'd rather fight beside."

She grinned, and he pulled her into a fiery kiss that was over much too quickly.

"Don't make me regret it," Xander whispered, kissing the top of her head. "I know you are immortal, love, but please don't be tempted to test the limits of that particular boundary."

They opened the door and found Rainer standing there, breathless. "Davide's army is here. They're burning everything."

"Let's go," she said.

Rainer frowned. "Please think before you race into the center of the battle—"

"Rainer, I'm not your responsibility anymore. I thought you would relax once I became a living goddess."

"Those vows are for life, Cece," Rainer snapped. "Or did you forget because you're mad? We don't know what we're walking into. They could have Cato with them. Cato undoubtedly has a Godkiller like you."

She shuddered at the mention of the one type of weapon that could kill her. If she had her dagger imbued with the power to kill a living god, she had to assume that Cato had a Godkiller of his own.

She tapped the dagger on her thigh. "We'll be well matched then."

Rainer frowned. "He's the son of the god of war. I'm sure he has extensive combat training."

"And I'm the daughter of the Olney huntmaster who killed his father. So do I."

Rainer stopped arguing when they crested the hill toward town. The world was on fire.

Homes and businesses burned, but even more disturbing, flames shot through the windows of the Little School. Cecilia ran toward it before Xander or Rainer could react. When she got close, she found Cal, Evan, and Sylvie. Sylvie was conjuring earth to smother flames by the doors of the school. The heat and smoke made Cecilia's eyes tear.

"I'm doing my best, but there's so much fire. It went up too fast. There are still kids in there!" Sylvie's voice was panicked. "Can you put it out?"

"If I suck out the oxygen and put out the fire, I could kill anyone who's still alive," Cecilia said. "I got it. I can get through. Just try to keep a path open at the door."

"How do I do it?" Xander asked.

Cecilia took his hand. "Conjure flame, then walk right through. When you conjure fire, you're fireproof. Just be mindful of your clothes."

She reached out to her power, calling to the flame. It lit at her fingertips and they ran through the flames at the entrance. Inside, the sights were horrifying. Sweat broke out on her skin instantly and smoke burned her eyes as she squinted down the hallway. She and Xander kept low as they approached the rear classroom. Little ones no older than six huddled in the corner. Several children had passed out from the smoke. Their teacher was unconscious in another corner, a piece of rafter across her chest.

Xander rushed to the teacher's side and checked for a pulse, grimacing as he turned to Cecilia and shook his head.

"Miss Cece!" a little girl yelled.

"Hey, everyone!" Cecilia tried to sound calm, but the smoke burned her eyes and lungs. "I know you're scared. Guardian McKay is waiting for us outside. I need you all to be really brave and follow me and the prince outside. I know it's hot and there's a lot of smoke. We are going to stay as low as we can and move as fast as we can, and the prince and I will carry your classmates."

She bent low and scooped up two unconscious children, and Xander lifted two others. She took up the lead, guiding the kids out, Xander following behind. The roof only held up long enough for them to dash back inside and grab the last four unconscious children and check that the remaining classrooms were empty.

Cecilia's eyes burned and she gulped in lungfuls of air as they stepped out of the building. Panicked parents hugged their children and water witches frantically tried to douse the flames. Sylvie, Cal, and Evan took the unconscious children and shepherded everyone to the healer's clinic.

Cecilia turned to Xander and the horror hit her. She'd been so focused on solving the problem, she wouldn't let herself feel it inside. Now that they'd saved all the children, the fear hit her like a tidal wave. She broke down, collapsing against Xander in a fit of sobs.

Xander took her face between his hands, wiping soot from her cheeks.

"My love, I wish I could give you the time to process it, but I need you to focus. Look at me. Look at my eyes, Cece."

All she could smell was smoke and blood. She squeezed her eyes closed. She wanted to scream.

"Look at my eyes."

She snapped her eyes open, meeting his gaze again.

"I'm sorry that I have to push you," Xander said. "We're still under attack. Focus that anger on those who deserve it. We have to keep going or they will hurt more people. Can you do that?"

She nodded as he brushed away her tears. "Xan, I'm so sorry about earlier."

Xander shook his head and winked at her. "You can show me how sorry later. Keep an eye out for Cato. Stay close to me, and whatever happens, we do whatever it takes to get back to each other."

Cecilia nodded. "Whatever it takes."

She forced herself to swallow her horror and fear as she, Rainer, and Xander hurried into town where the fighting was heaviest.

It was their worst nightmare, and exactly what Evan suggested might happen. Davide and Cato's attacks on their borders had drawn out most of the Olney army. Only two battalions of hunters remained in Olney, one to protect the city and the other to protect the castle. They were woefully outnumbered.

Olney City sloped down toward the city center to make it easier for farmers and merchants to bring their goods to the central market there. From their vantage point on a side street several blocks away, they could look down at the whole brutal battle. Tide witches and fire witches struggled to smother the flames spreading between homes and businesses.

Cecilia suspected she could end the fighting with very little effort, but her powers frightened her. She hadn't reached for her goddess abilities since the day her father died, and she didn't think she could deal with more blood on her hands. Instead, she shot arrow after arrow into the fray, with Xander and Rainer beside her doing the same thing.

"Can you do something?" Rainer asked.

She met his eyes, shame uncoiling in her stomach. "I'm afraid."

"You don't have to do what you did before. Try something different. There must be more power," Rainer said.

He looked so confident, but all she felt was doubt. How could she use her power of the mind to make them stop fighting and surrender? She closed her eyes and settled her thoughts, trying to listen as Grimon had suggested—to let the power tell her how to use it.

The idea came seemingly out of nowhere. She could implant a false memory of surrender. She conjured the image of Davide's face in her mind, imagined him saying the word, and held it until she felt her memory magic stitch it together.

Then, Cecilia charged down the slope into the center of town. She ran through the fray, planting the memory. One by one the Argarian soldiers laid down their weapons and surrendered. The Olney forces looked confused at first, but Xander followed behind her, instructing them to corral their prisoners.

The shouting died down as she cut through the streets, squinting through dirt and ash.

She made it through the heaviest part of the battle in the city center, urging most of the Argarian hunters to surrender. It was a relief that her power could do more than ruin memory. She kept moving, Rainer and Xander in tow.

Finally, she saw King Davide Savero. Cecilia looked forward to paying him back for breaking her hand. She walked toward him with menace in her heart, the tide of the battle changing in her wake. An arrow arced through the air and lanced her left shoulder. She yelped and fell to a knee, yanking it out before continuing her march toward her brother-in-law.

The wound would heal soon, and thanks to her newfound goddess healing abilities, it wouldn't require her to even use magic.

Only it didn't heal. It continued to hurt like crazy and bled down her shirt. Xander called her name, but she kept walking toward Davide. A rush of dizziness shuddered through her body and she stumbled.

"You're not looking so good, Goddess," Davide taunted.

"What was on that arrow?" she asked.

She felt faint. The buzz of her power beneath her skin faded, and when she tried to reach for it, nothing happened.

"They call it Godsbane, Princess. It takes away your godly powers for a time. You won't be able to heal as fast or use any of those fascinating mind powers of yours."

She summoned earth, relieved to find that her summoning magic still worked even if her goddess power had fled—after all, she was half-witch. Thick roots rose around Davide's legs, and she enjoyed the look of panic on his face.

"I owe you," she said.

"You do," Davide said, righting himself. "But sadly, you won't get to collect. There's someone else much more interested in fighting you today."

As if out of a fold in the air itself, Cato stepped forth next to Davide. Her eyes went wide. If Cato could trick time and space that way for himself, it explained how they moved Davide's army so quickly from place to place.

She stepped back.

"Hey, Little Dove." Cato smirked, drawing his sword.

Xander drew up next to her, his eyes wide as saucers.

"Stay away from Cato," she breathed. "Focus on your brother, and if you can't do that, have Rainer do it. Just make sure he doesn't get hurt. I remember the Reflection Forest. I know fighting Davide is your worst nightmare, but I need both of you away from Cato."

Xander kissed her with a desperation that stole her breath and sent a rush of heat through her whole body. He pulled back and leaned his forehead against hers. "I love you. Please be careful."

"I love you, too," she said, taking one last look at her husband before she turned to face the trickster god.

"How touching," Cato teased. "Why don't we play fair, Cece? I'll put my Godkiller aside if you will. I just want to test your skills today."

The clang of steel startled her. Xander faced off with Davide behind Cato.

Cecilia patted the dagger on her thigh as she drew her sword. "No thanks. You stopped playing fair the moment you set a school on fire."

Cato sighed heavily. "That was not supposed to happen. Davide's men went directly against my orders and they'll be punished for it. Why don't you drop that dagger? Though I must admit you look lovely with a weapon in your hands."

Cecilia blanched. "I'll pass on that. I don't have any godly tele-porting abilities or any godly abilities at all, thanks to Davide. I'll not be surrendering any advantages."

"Very well then. I'll still leave mine away from the fray," Cato said, dropping his dagger and stalking toward her.

He swung down on her with his sword, and she blocked. If she had her goddess strength, she could have matched him blow for blow. Now, she'd have to rely on her huntress wits.

She deflected another blow from Cato in time to see Rainer fighting the Argarian huntmaster, Lukas Ducrane, whom she'd met in passing before she killed his daughter back in Argaria. She spun and whacked Cato on the back of the head with the flat side of her blade. It was a taunting blow and had the desired effect of wiping the annoying smirk off of his face.

Behind Cato, Rainer stumbled. His fatigue and worry slid through their connection. She turned her attention to Lukas Ducrane.

"Hey Ducrane, I killed your daughter, and it wasn't even a good fight," Cecilia shouted.

He turned to her, eyes blazing at the insult. Rainer sliced up the back of his leg, waving Cecilia off. She ducked in time to miss Cato's next blow, but had to spin on her knees through the dirt before hopping back to her feet. She cut a slice up Cato's left side. He stum-bled back, but she knew the wound would heal almost immediately.

She took a swipe at Cato. "So tell me, Cato. How did you trick your father into giving up his most prized possession?"

"I had something he needed more," Cato said as he brought his blade down with another heavy blow.

She blocked it, the shock reverberating down her arms. She

missed her goddess strength already. They traded blows until Cato caught her off guard, giving her an almost identical swipe over her left side. She stumbled back but quickly regained her composure.

"Uh-oh, looks like you distracted your love," Cato said, at the same moment Rainer's fear shot through her chest.

Cecilia's gaze flew to Rainer, who was on his back without his sword, with Ducrane coming for him. She wasn't close enough to throw her dagger and she didn't want to part with it before she could try to end Cato.

"Xander!" she screamed.

Xander turned to look at her as she blocked another blow from Cato. She pointed to Rainer. Xander tossed his dagger into Lukas Ducrane's back. It wasn't a mortal wound, but it was enough to give Rainer time to scramble away and grab his sword.

"Interesting that you looked at your guardian and not your husband," Cato taunted.

"I could feel Rainer's fear. Plus, he felt my pain when you cut me. That's how I knew who you were talking about."

Cato chuckled. "Whatever you need to tell yourself."

She took a heavy swing at Cato, swatting him back before summoning earth, growing roots around Davide's feet to give Xander a chance to recover.

The move cost her. Cato brought his sword down along her left shoulder, slicing into her arrow wound. Instead of slinking away like he expected her to, she pressed into it and slid her blade across his left shoulder. He stumbled back.

"Tricky goddess," he laughed. "That hurt you more than me."

"It was worth it," she said, climbing back to her feet. They circled each other. She looked around, trying to figure out what could give her an advantage.

"I don't know why you're so eager to fight. I am the only one standing between you and war."

Cecilia scoffed. "What do you call this?"

"A taste. You're young. You have no idea what real war looks like and you don't have the stomach for what it will make of you, Little

Dove." Cato cocked his head to the side. "You fight with no fear despite your obvious disadvantage. How did you beat my father? He has centuries of experience on you."

Cecilia shrugged, trying to shake off the burning pain in her shoulder. "Despite those centuries of experience, he's no different from every other warrior. Powerful men all have the same fatal flaw: hubris. They look at someone smaller and see an easy target, but those who are small know you need to run toward the blade instead of away if you want the advantage."

Cato had done her a favor, reminding her of that battle. She conjured fire and heated his blade the way she had with Endros. She kept him engaged by throwing as many blows as she could while it heated. Finally, he felt the searing heat in his hand and cursed, dropping his sword.

"Ouch. That looked like it hurt. That's how I beat him," she said.

The barrage of hits she'd delivered had cost her. Cato's pace and strength were brutal.

"Feeling tired?" Cato grinned.

Cecilia shuddered, her arms aching. "You know I am. You have the advantage. Obviously, you were too afraid to fight me at full power."

"Who says I wanted to fight you at all? Maybe we were just trying to distract all of you."

Cecilia froze, the air rushing out of her lungs at once. Her gaze flashed to Rainer and Xander, still engaged with their respective targets, before turning back to Cato. Two Argarian hunters stood next to him. She spun and found two behind her.

She was in trouble. "Xander!"

It wasn't her fight with Rainer that made her call Xander first, but the recognition that her husband had become the person she trusted most. She knew he would get to her.

Both Xander and Rainer whipped their heads around to look at her as a guard seized her around the waist. She elbowed him in the jaw and the gut, spinning away and slicing him across the throat.

"Don't hurt her any more. I want her healed up immediately when we get back," Cato said.

The other hunter grabbed for her, but she twisted, kneed him in the stomach, and brought an elbow down on the back of his head as he crumpled forward. She sliced down over the back of his neck with her sword.

Xander stalked toward her, slicing through anyone who stood in his way. He smiled at her as he cut through another hunter.

It was mesmerizing to watch him fight. She'd seen a glimpse of it when they were on the run from Argaria months before, but he was so in his element. A storm spun overhead, and she knew he was trying to help both of them. Lightning crackled.

Cecilia was about to pull a bolt to hit Cato when a blow to the back of her head made her whole world go dark.

9

XANDER

The moment Cece yelled his name, Xander's world narrowed to his wife. It was rare to hear genuine fear in her voice. She struggled out of the grip of a huge Argarian hunter.

He would lay waste to the entire battalion if someone hurt her. There was not a man between them he wouldn't strike down with lightning and wind.

He cut through two hunters effortlessly, his short swords slicing through them like a warm knife through butter. All the fatigue he felt from the brutal battle with his brother was gone. He was aware of Rainer beside him and, for once, it didn't annoy him that he was rushing to Cece's aid. Xander easily sliced through two more hunters. It was nothing, because she called for *him*, not Rainer. His wife, who so rarely took help from anyone, needed him.

Xander summoned a storm, and the sky darkened. Cato turned to look at him. He felt like a fool every time he interacted with the trickster god. He should have noticed that Davide was moving their fight farther and farther from Cato and Cece. They wanted *her*.

Cece struggled away from another hunter, sliding her dagger into the gap between his leather breastplate and shoulder guard.

Pride swelled in Xander's chest. He loved her fight. *Just hold on, love.*

He focused on the storm as a huge hunter brought a blade down, narrowly missing him. They traded blows before Xander plunged his sword into the man's side. When he spun back to face Cece, he saw a look in her eyes that he knew well. She was watching him and she was turned on. He almost laughed at how alike they were.

Then a hunter stepped behind her and hit her over the back of her head. She crumpled into his arms.

A dam broke open in Xander. The storm raged as he cut through every single hunter between him and his wife. Rainer was a few yards away, struggling with a surge of hunters that seemed to appear out of nowhere, just as Cato had earlier.

Evan had suspected that this was part of Cato's power, tricking space and the very laws of nature, but now this proved that he could also move others in his army anywhere in the two kingdoms.

The hunter carrying Cece over his shoulder was getting away. Xander charged ahead, striking the man with a bolt of lightning. The hunter went flying and Cece crumpled into the dirt. Xander tried to get close to her, but he was waylaid by five more hunters.

Slowly but surely they fought their way to Cece. She was still unconscious as Xander and Rainer turned back to back, keeping close to her so none of the hunters could drag her away.

Xander cursed in frustration as he pushed two of them back with a swipe of his sword. Metal clanged behind him and he felt Rainer at his back.

"They just keep coming out of nowhere," Rainer said.

Rainer's fatigue was obvious in his stance and his voice. Xander could feel his own energy faltering, along with his storm magic. They needed an escape plan. Cece lay on the ground next to them, unmoving, blood matting the back of her hair. Xander desperately wanted to go to her, but he needed to focus on the fight.

"We're surrounded," Rainer whispered.

"It's just us, then," Xander said resolutely.

"They don't want to hurt her. I heard Cato say that," Rainer said.

The revelation made Xander's blood run cold because it meant that they wanted her for Davide. Xander's marriage to Cece would only be recognized in Olney. Davide could easily take his wife back to Argaria, marry her himself, and do gods know what to her. Bile rose in his throat at the thought of the fate that awaited her if Davide got his hands on her.

Panic made his voice wheeze. "We can't let them have her. Davide is not right. He's obsessed with power. He wants to marry her—"

"She's married to you," Rainer said, swiping his sword to widen the circle.

"But they won't recognize that marriage in Argaria. If they have more Godsbane, they could control her. That and an Unsummoner bracelet would be enough to render her powerless. The brother I knew would never hurt a woman, but—" Xander couldn't speak the words.

Davide was power hungry, a shadow of the brother Xander had once known, ruled by a darkness that seemed never ending. Legacy was incredibly important to royals, and getting his new queen pregnant would be his top priority. Even if Cece told him about the exchange she made for her power, it was unlikely that Davide would believe her.

Nausea rolled through Xander. "Rainer, he could hurt her in ways no healer can fix."

Rainer spun to look at him, his eyes wide with horror as the same revelation set in his mind. For once, Xander was relieved that there was another person who loved Cece as much as he did. Two men desperate to save her from what was sure to be a horrible fate were better than one.

"There's no other battle going on but this one here with us. Why?" Xander asked as he blocked blows from two more hunters, clearing their way.

Rainer turned to him with wide eyes. "They don't just want her. They want both of you."

They stared at each other for a moment.

"Get her out," Xander said.

Rainer shook his head, cutting through a hunter. "She will kill me if I let them take you."

"You kissed my wife right in front of me. You owe me. If you can't get both of us, take her."

The guardian sighed heavily, cutting down another hunter.

"Promise you'll get her out, McKay."

Rainer glanced at Cece and then met Xander's eyes, as if already accepting that he was about to be in a world of hurt either way.

"She's going to kill me if you don't get out, so you better move your ass, but I promise."

"Get ready." Xander took three wild swipes with his sword, sending the hunters by Cece stumbling back as Rainer picked her up and threw her over his shoulder.

Xander knew Cece was going to be furious if he didn't get out, but at that moment, she was his priority. She had called for him, knowing he would save her. If all three of them were captured, their hopes of saving Olney and Argaria were done for. Failure wasn't an option. He had to at least get Rainer and Cece out.

"Now!" Xander yelled as he sent a tremendous gust of air outward, blowing six incoming hunters back.

Rainer raced through and Xander followed behind him just as he lost his grip on the storm and it started to clear. He cursed as he ran after Rainer with hunters on his heels.

If Xander didn't turn and fight, Rainer wouldn't make it and then he'd have a dead guardian and a furious wife to deal with.

"Tell her I love her and not to feel guilty for what she said right before all of this. Tell her I'll do whatever it takes to get back to her. And tell her I said 'Do you want to be mad, or do you want to kiss me?'" Xander said.

Rainer only glanced at him out of the corner of his eye for a second before continuing to run away from the fight. Xander sighed in relief. Rainer knew the town well. He'd be able to escape the Argarian hunters once he got closer to the town center.

Xander fought his heart out to the bitter end of his fading strength. He swung and ducked and sliced into the hunters, but they just kept coming. He waited for Cato to appear and strike him down.

Sweat dripped from his brow, burning in his eyes. His heart raced in his chest and a sinking sensation swelled.

Cece had given him her heart and her fragile trust months ago, but today it felt like she finally chose him first. To lose her right as he finally won her over was brutal, but at least he knew for a moment that he had her. Xander could go to the underworld with that satisfaction.

He should have felt grateful, but he wanted more. He'd never felt greedy until the first time he kissed his wife. It was as if he'd unknowingly lived his whole life in shadow and that kiss was a knife rending him from the dark. It left him squinting into her brilliance. Consumed him with fever. It said: *this is what it means to burn.*

He was so foolish for tempting fate. For thinking he could get so close to someone he'd already been enamored with from afar and not fall into her completely. He wanted to trap her heart under glass, to study it like he could unlock something inside it that he didn't have access to—to know for sure there was no depth that he wasn't aware of. Xander wanted it all.

He'd known he was fighting an impossible uphill battle for her affection, but he finally had it. She'd called for Xander because she trusted him to get to her and because when she was afraid, she didn't want Rainer McKay. She wanted Xander.

His heart soared even as dread crept into his chest.

The air bent in front of him, revealing Cato. The trickster god's mouth kicked up in a half-grin. Xander hated that stupid fucking grin.

"Your Highness, you killed so many of my hunters I'm going to need a new army."

"You tried to take my wife." Xander wanted to sound menacing but he was so tired the words slurred together.

"Your wife owes me a favor," Cato said.

"Cece is not a favor."

Cato rolled his eyes and sighed. "Relax, Savero. No need to wax poetic about your wife. I know you love her. I wanted both of you."

"Why?" Xander wanted to get up off the ground, but he was bone tired. Every muscle in his body ached. His skin and clothes were caked with dirt and blood, and two large gashes on his forearms burned viciously. If he had any energy or Cece's disgusting witch tea, he could heal them, but he was entirely spent.

"I don't know if you've noticed, but your brother isn't exactly the easiest person to control." Cato crouched so he could look Xander in the eyes.

"You wanted both of us so you could use us to control each other." Xander nearly cried with relief that Rainer had escaped with Cece. He hoped they were far away.

"Among other things. She can't keep that power under wraps forever. I want to see what she can do," Cato said. "I suppose I'll have to make do with prying the details out of you."

Xander sent up a silent prayer to Grimon. The god of death may have loathed him, but what waited for Xander was much worse than death.

Cato reached for him and Xander did nothing to resist.

10

CECILIA

Cecilia came to with a massive headache. The first thing she was aware of, other than the pain, was the soothing sensation of someone rubbing the inside of her wrist.

"Rain," she rasped, her throat so dry it was hard to make a sound.

"I'm here. You're okay. You just took a bad hit in the head and you're in the healer's suite. Just open those beautiful eyes for me, Cece," he whispered.

Her eyelids were so heavy but she blinked a few times, trying to focus on him.

He had a smudge of soot around his hairline where he'd missed washing post-battle, and a bruise on his jaw, but he otherwise looked unharmed. "There you are. How do you feel?"

"Like I took a sucker punch to the head. What happened? How much time did I lose?"

"Just a couple hours. It's evening now. Cato and Davide fled with their army."

"Where's Xander?" She turned her head. Dizziness slammed into her, and she settled back into the pillows.

She took in Rainer's grim expression.

"He made me promise, Cece."

"Promise what? Where is he?"

Rainer squeezed her hand. "They wanted both of you. Xander made me swear that if we could only get to one of you, that I would get you. I only had a second to decide. Xander fought like hell, but you were unconscious and basically mortal. I couldn't risk you getting hurt trying to get to him. We were afraid Davide would hurt you—that he might force you into marriage or worse."

The thought sent a sinking feeling into her gut.

"That's why he made me promise. It was just me and Xander. As soon as I got you out, I went back for him, but it was too late. Cal and I rode back out with Evan but they only found a couple of hunters who said they saw Cato disappear with him through a crease in the air."

Cecilia shook her head. "Rain, how? Xander was conjuring the storm. He was cutting through those hunters like butter."

"When he saw you go down, he was like a man possessed. I could barely keep up with him. We were surrounded. Xander said if they had you, they'd be able to control him, anyway." Rainer stumbled over the words. "I'm sorry. I thought it was the right move, but now I see how it might not have been."

Tears stung her eyes. "Because now they can control me by hurting him."

"Yes," Rainer said. "If it's any consolation, he probably wants Xander alive."

"Like that's better," she sighed. Her voice was even, but grief pulsed through their bond.

Rainer hesitated. "He wanted me to tell you not to feel guilty about what you said right before the battle. That he loves you and he'll do what it takes to get back to you, and he said, 'Do you want to be mad at me, or do you want to kiss me?'"

She laughed through a few rogue tears rolling down her cheeks. She could practically read on Rainer's face the recognition that the words echoed what she'd said to him for years. Anytime she'd done something reckless, and he was furious with her, she simply asked, *"Do you want to be mad, or do you want to hug me?"*

"Oh my gods, all those kids—the school. Are they—"

Rainer squeezed her hand. "They're all right. They all got out, except for Miss Divs."

Cecilia shook her head. Miss Divs was a kind woman and a good teacher for the youngest children. Her chest grew tight, the horror of the day washing over her all at once, the panic like a fever. Xander had helped her save all those children. He'd saved her. And now he was in the hands of a god who manipulated people for sport.

She'd done a good job of compartmentalizing, but with the battle over, she couldn't fight it off any longer. Her skin smelled like smoke, blood, and sweat. All the losses stacked on top of each other. It was all too much, and she lay there, crushed by the weight of it.

Rainer reached for her but she flinched.

"If you touch me I will fall apart and I—" Her lower lip quivered.

"I know," he said. "I think maybe you've been holding it together too long already." He climbed into bed next to her and pulled her close. "I know. I know it's too heavy," he whispered into her hair, squeezing her tightly. "I'm here. I'm holding it too."

She felt Rainer's grief as clearly as her own. They clung to each other as she sobbed, and he held on to her for dear life as he whispered words that were little comfort to either of them. They stayed like that for a long time.

"It's going to be okay," Rainer said, stroking the inside of her wrist with his thumb. "I know you think we can't go back or that too much damage has been done, but we will get through this, and now that the goddess is gone—"

She froze, pressing her hands to his chest. "The goddess was just part of me—"

A crease formed in Rainer's brow. "Right, but now that she's—that *you're* figured out, you won't go back to that dark place."

Cecilia pushed further from him. "Rain, I am made of that dark place. The goddess was just another part of me. I'm still—" *Lost. Furious. Broken. Terrified*. She blew out a ragged breath. "I will always be the part of me that fled when things went wrong and the part of me that stood up and fought and didn't care who I hurt."

He shook his head. "It was just—"

"Me! It just was me. *It is me.*"

Rainer had always understood her so innately, but now it felt like she was staring at a stranger who was just noticing how the years and pain had chipped away at her.

Maybe he preferred to miss who she used to be because that was more romantic than loving who she'd become. Easier to love a memory from afar than someone broken up close.

Rainer licked his lips and opened his mouth to speak, but Cecilia was suddenly terrified of what he would say. She didn't want him to prove her right. What did it say if the person she'd always counted on to believe in her had lost his faith?

"Your Highness?" a soft voice called from the doorway, startling both of them.

Cecilia flinched, still not used to her title, but she recognized the healer, though she could not place her name. Her dark hair was swept back from her face with a kerchief, and although she was only a year or two older than Cecilia, the horrors of the day made her look like she'd lived a thousand lifetimes in a few hours.

Rainer beckoned her inside. "I'm sorry about earlier, Lyra."

The healer smiled. "It's quite all right. We've had our fair share of worried guardians around here. Would it be okay if I tend to Her Highness now?"

Cecilia held up a hand. "Please just call me Cece."

Lyra nodded. "*Cece*, if it's okay. I need to look at your head and ask you some questions. I already healed the worst of your other wounds while you were unconscious, but I want to make sure that you don't have a concussion. You still have some more minor cuts and bruises, but we've healed everything major. We know little about Godsbane or how long its effects take to wear off, so we wanted to be sure you didn't have any permanent damage."

Cecilia nodded and Rainer helped her sit up, their argument momentarily forgotten. He moved out of Lyra's way and the healer took Cecilia through a series of reflex tests and healed what she could of the throbbing in her head.

"We'd like to keep you overnight—"

Cecilia shook her head, swinging her legs over the side of the bed and starting toward the door. "I have to go find my husband," she said.

Lyra looked to Rainer for support.

Rainer held up his hands. "It's a long way to Argaria and we don't even know if he's there."

Appeased, Lyra left them alone in the room.

"He's probably closer, in one of Davide's camps." Cecilia tried to calculate how many hours it had been since Xander was taken, how far they could have traveled, but with Cato's power he could have been anywhere by now.

Rainer placed his hands on her shoulders. "Evan can send out his spies and find out for sure. We need to be smart about this. Slow down. It's been a long and terrible day. Let me take you home so you can get some rest. We'll talk with Evan and Cal in the morning and see what we can do. I know you don't want to hear it but you're no good to Xander right now. If I let you go out there and get yourself hurt again, Xander will kill me himself."

Cecilia looked at her best friend, struggling to control the panic and frustration raging through her. She could feel the first buzz of her goddess powers returning just from the way her rage was building. Cato had already hurt so many of their people—if he hurt Xander, she would become wrath itself. She didn't care if he was ancient or strong. She would tear Cato limb from limb, and she'd enjoy it.

Rainer frowned. "You know I'm right." He cupped her face in his hands, ignoring the menace in her eyes. "Cece, you aren't helpless. You never will be again. You saved a lot of innocent people today, and you'll save Xander too. We can fix this. But right now, you need to rest so you can be at your best. I promised him I would take care of you, so will you please just let me?"

"Okay," she sighed. He put an arm around her, guiding her out of the healer's suite.

Outside, the air smelled like ash and salt. The fires in town had all been put out but the remnants of charred furniture filled the streets.

Evan leaned against the wall outside of the healer's clinic. His voice was low but Cecilia sensed his agitation as he spoke to Cal Bennington.

"It's good to see you up and walking, Cece. How are you feeling?" Evan asked.

"Pissed off at my husband for getting captured and insisting that Rainer save me. Pissed off at Cato for being awful. Pissed off at Davide's men for setting a fucking school on fire."

"That's our girl," Evan sighed.

"How are the kids?" she asked Cal.

"Horrified. Traumatized. I wish I could say otherwise. Maybe you could make them forget?" Cal suggested.

Cecilia considered it. "I don't know if that would be a kindness. Xander asked me about that a few weeks ago. If I could heal people's pain by helping them forget scary or traumatic things, but memory lives in the body and emotions and not just the mind. Imagine them seeing fire again and not understanding why they feel so terrified. They'd have no memory of the event, but the fear would still exist. Forgetting isn't the solution everyone thinks it is," she said solemnly. "I wish it were otherwise. I'm not saying no. I'm just not sure it would really help."

Cal looked contemplative. "I guess I never really thought about that."

She shrugged. "We learned about it in memory magic classes. Memory is more than just what we call up in the mind, but also what our body remembers and the emotional signals that make us feel safe. Messing with memory is a dangerous game. When you mess with formative memory and emotions, you mess with personality. I'd worry about someone losing their sense of self." She turned to Evan. "You'll help me get Xander back?"

"Of course. I also know that there's nothing that could keep him away from you for long. I'm sure they're going to have their hands full with him as it is," Evan said.

"I wonder what they want from him. I'm worried Cato is going to call in that favor for something," Cecilia said.

"What deal did you make?" Evan asked.

"I said the favor couldn't be me and it couldn't be used to hurt someone."

Evan nodded. "Wise."

"I'm sure if there's something I didn't think of, he will, and I really dislike the idea of Cato having my husband. Plus, Davide is such an asshole. I cannot believe I still didn't get to shatter his fucking hand," she huffed.

Evan was unfazed. "You should rest, Cece. We'll figure it out in the morning. I have an idea."

"We'll help however we can," Cal said.

"You and Sylvie?" Cecilia tried to hide her surprise.

"You better believe it. Sylvie spent all day with those poor kids. She's mad as can be. Honestly, I might be more afraid of her than you right now, Rez," Cal said with admiration in his voice.

"What's your idea, Evan?" Cecilia asked.

"I have my spies out looking." He hesitated. "I thought maybe your sisters would know how to find Xander."

Cecilia frowned. "My sisters?"

Evan nodded. "The daughters of Clastor. Xander mentioned that you'd met Adira and that your sisters wanted to help, so I thought maybe we could use their resources."

Cecilia couldn't hide her skepticism. "You think getting more gods and goddesses involved is going to *help* the situation?"

He shrugged. "I think that they've known Cato the longest and can probably offer the best insight into how he operates."

After her run-in with Adira, she wasn't exactly eager to meet the rest of her siblings, but Evan had a point. They were an untapped resource, and Adira had said they wanted to help defeat Cato.

"Fine," she sighed. "If I have to deal with an awkward family reunion to get Xander back, it's a small price to pay. I maintain that this is a disaster waiting to happen, but I have no better ideas. How do we find them?"

Evan held up the book he'd had tucked under one arm. Her eyes narrowed on the familiar gilded cover. *Myths and Folklore of Olney*. She and Rainer must have made his mother read that book to them cover to cover at least ten times as children. She had some of the stories memorized.

"You think the answer is in a book of fairy tales?" she asked.

Evan shrugged. "You fought Endros on the Shores of Adira and had her help summoning tides. It seems that maybe there's more truth to these stories than we think. I think we should start with Sayla. Fair to say you'd have most in common with the goddess of the hunt. So we'll head for—"

"The Wailing Woods," Rainer finished. He looked half-exhilarated, half-terrified.

"When can we leave?" Cecilia asked.

"You're in charge, *Your Highness*," Evan said. "I can have the supplies we need by morning."

The tension in Cecilia's chest started to unravel. "We leave then."

Evan nodded as Rainer guided her toward the trail back to her cottage.

Cecilia bathed and climbed into bed, exhausted from the harrowing day. But sleep showed her no mercy, refusing her no matter how desperate she felt to release the horror of the day for just a few hours. When the cabin finally began to brighten, she miserably rolled out of bed and packed a bag for her family reunion.

PART II:
GAMES GODS PLAY

11

RAINER

Orange and red leaves swirled on a breeze, scattering along the trail in the fading daylight. It would have been easy for Rainer to get lost in the hypnotic, percussive beat of horse hooves kicking up desiccated leaf pulp from the forest floor—it would have been, if he could stop staring at his best friend.

To see Cecilia in the wild was to see her come alive. Rainer knew the way she always felt out of place at court. She lacked the traditional elegance that most courtly ladies possessed. But Cecilia had a wild, ethereal beauty that was much rarer and better suited to the forest than a ballroom. Something radiant bloomed in her as she rode with the wind in her hair, her eyes sparkling and her cheeks flushed with the autumn heat.

Their bond had never felt so treacherous. Her warmth wrapped comfortably around his heart and the fierce shifts of her emotions, once overwhelming, felt more like salvation now. Rainer wanted to fight for her, but so far, he'd only succeeded in fighting *with* her.

They'd left Olney City early in the morning and made it into the hills on the way to the Wailing Woods, the alleged home of Sayla, goddess of the hunt, who seemed as safe a place to start as any, given Cecilia's affinity for the bow.

She'd pushed the pace since they left Olney, and now she rode ahead of everyone, her long braid blowing out behind her.

Evan shouted from somewhere behind Rainer, clearly just as disturbed by her reckless riding as Rainer.

"I know Xander told you not to test the limits of that immortality, *Princess*. Can you slow down a bit and let someone else in front?" Evan shouted.

"It's not my fault I ride with inferior riders," she called back.

Evan groaned. "Gods, you are so much like your husband."

Rainer felt a pang of sympathy for the hunter and he slowed his pace slightly, allowing Evan to catch up. Evan was perhaps the only one who could understand the frustration of trying to keep someone so reckless in one piece. The hunter kept glancing from Cecilia at the front of the pack to Sylvie, who trailed a distance behind them with Cal.

"You're leaving Lady Brett in the dust," Evan called.

Cecilia finally slowed her pace. "Fine. Wouldn't want you to lose track of Lady Brett," she teased.

Rainer's eyebrows shot up. He had missed it before, but judging from the hike in Evan's shoulders and the glare he directed toward Cecilia, there was more than met the eye between him and Sylvie. It was so like Cecilia to be in the middle of a disaster and still find time to taunt a friend.

Evan rode beside Cecilia. "I know you want to press on, but we should stop up ahead. The Wailing Woods are hardly a place to camp for the night."

Cecilia shook her head. "You don't strike me as a believer in ghost stories."

"But I am a believer in not taking unnecessary risks," Evan countered. "You should try it sometime."

Cecilia laughed.

"Daylight is fading, and we're only about an hour's ride from the Wailing Woods. We can head out first thing tomorrow," Rainer said.

The mythology surrounding the Wailing Woods was fixed in Rainer's mind from years of intensive study of the gods and goddesses after the huntmaster told him Cecilia's true identity. It was known as a haunted place where hunters and riders often went missing. Sayla also had a particular score to settle with men who harmed women and children. Those who entered her wood reported apparitions and disembodied voices.

Many years ago, a fire had turned most of the trees at the forest's edge bright white and bony. When the harsh northerly winds blew through the barren trees, they created a wailing sound that had given the forest its name. Whether or not one believed the stories, it was their best guess for a place to find the goddess of the hunt.

Evan set up camp while Cecilia helped Rainer start a fire.

After dinner, Cecilia sat staring into the flames. Anxiety swirled through their connection, and for once it wasn't Rainer's. He wanted to reach out to soothe her, but he kept his hands to himself.

He could have punched his younger self for all the times he complained about holding hands with a girl. Cecilia used to reach for his hand mindlessly when she was anxious, and it drove him crazy. He'd been so embarrassed by her affection because of all his teasing peers and would bat her hand away or drop it as soon as other people were around.

As he matured, he found he didn't mind it, and often sought her touch when he was nervous. Sometimes it wasn't even clear which of them had reached out first, as if they both realized they needed support at the same moment. Sometimes he reached out when he was alone, expecting her to be there beside him.

Now, as he watched her rub her thumb across her inner wrist, he wished he'd appreciated what he had in those moments.

It was ridiculous Rainer had ever thought he could be anything other than completely in love with Cecilia. He'd done a laughable job of hiding his feelings. No other guardians fussed over their charges the same way. No one laid in bed with their witch every night telling bedtime stories. No one spent hours writing all those stories down in a book for her birthday. And certainly no one could decipher every look on their witch's face the way Rainer could with Cecilia, like she was a book he was born to read. That kind of attention was only born out of love. Love they were precariously pretending no longer existed.

He sat down next to Cecilia. She kept her gaze fixed on the fire and her hands folded in her lap like she was afraid to get too close.

"Doing okay?" he asked.

She wrung her hands. "Just worried. I can't stop thinking about what Xander might be going through." She shook out her fingers like she could shake loose her fear. "Tell me what's going on with you. We've been very focused on me. What's on your mind, Rain?" She finally looked at him and the weight of her gaze felt too heavy.

He looked away. Cal, Evan, and Sylvie were deep in conversation on the other side of the fire. The pop of the logs covered their conversation and provided the illusion of privacy.

Rainer ran a hand through his hair. "I've been thinking a lot about what my future looks like and, for once, I have no idea. I reached out to my father—"

Cecilia's face darkened. She didn't know the half of Raymond McKay's sins, but Rainer had let enough of his pain slip through their bond over the years for her to make assumptions.

He cleared his throat. "I reached out to my father, but he thought offering to take over the family business was a silly idea. He wants to sell it and be a man of leisure."

"And what does that have to do with you?" she asked.

Rainer shifted uncomfortably. "Everything about my life before this was planned out and scheduled. Now things are chaotic and I'm not sure where I fit anymore. You're a goddess, and while I have no doubt you will test the limits of immortality, I know you don't need me the way you once did."

A faint smile tugged at her lips. "I would argue that I never needed you as much as you wanted me to."

Rainer was only realizing now how little she'd needed him and how much he'd really needed her. "That's fair."

"I wasn't finished. What I meant to say was that I needed you more as a friend than I did as a protector."

"That's a little true, but I also think that most of the time the only person you needed protection from was yourself, Cece."

She laughed and some of the tension left her shoulders.

"I just feel a little lost," Rainer said. "Everyone else has taken this whole thing in stride. They seem unbothered by the entire foundation of the guardian program crumbling. Obviously, it was problematic, and it needed to change, but I feel like I only learned how to be one thing, and I only imagined one future for myself. Now there are endless possibilities. How could I possibly narrow it down? How do I figure out who I am?"

She rubbed her thumb over the crescent scar on the outside of her palm. "I think all you can do is look at your skills and history and try something new. It doesn't have to be *the* thing. It's just an experiment. You're just trying things. You figure out what you like slowly. I'm in the same boat. So are Cal and Sylvie and Evan. We're all figuring it out and it will probably take a while."

Of course she would say that. Cecilia was the only one who'd loved him as much after his failures as she did after his triumphs. He worked so hard, and the approval came, but every hit of it brought a shorter-lived joy. No matter how he chased it, contentment eluded him.

Rainer sighed. "I hate that."

"You hate not knowing how to be the best at something," Cecilia said. "You're going to be bad at things for a while. I know it goes against your nature, but the only way to learn is to try something new. I'll be right beside you. Don't worry. I'll let you know what you're bad at."

He smiled half-heartedly. "I don't even know where to start."

"I think you should start with being a chef. Start selling some of that pasta."

He beamed at her, happy for the light of the fire to hide his warm cheeks. "I don't know about that."

She shook her head. "I do. It's delicious. You have an incredible privilege to not need money. You're looking at this the wrong way.

This is an opportunity to figure out who you would be if this world didn't make you a warrior."

Rainer loved the simplicity of making something in the kitchen, the way he could exert his will on a small piece of the world and know the outcome. For so long his hands had only bloodied opponents, but now they could create something from scratch.

The single-minded goal of being the best guardian and protecting Cecilia had ruled his life for so long. He didn't know how to give it up, or who he would even be without it to anchor him. He had the privilege of family money but it always came with strings attached, and none of that could buy him a new sense of purpose. He could only imagine what his father would have to say about a cooking venture—how he'd find a way to ruin it.

Rainer had always found the world too loud. In town, in training, in striving so hard toward one thing for so long, there was nothing but the clang of swords, shouts from his training captain, and his father's words to remind him how he was falling short. His mind was always scanning the world around him for trouble, poised for any threat, his training and his thoughts tying him in knots. But when Cecilia looked at him with such warmth in her eyes, everything grew quiet and all the restlessness in his heart settled.

Cecilia turned toward him, her face gilded in firelight. "I hope I didn't offend you."

"You didn't. You're right. I'm just anxious."

"I know." Her eyes were bright and understanding. It was a comfort to be seen by her with no judgment.

"I always thought that being a warrior didn't suit you," she said. "You're much too kind. I'm excited to see who you become on your own."

For someone who had a habit of speaking before thinking, her words were surprisingly poignant, soothing him more than he expected.

He didn't want to admit that she was right. He was used to the easy gravity of someone else's orbit. It was less scary than cutting his own path, and it gave him someone else to blame when it all went wrong. But he couldn't keep hiding.

They fell into silence.

"Show me a memory," he said.

"Which one?" She slid her hand into his, laying back in the grass.

"Something significant. Remind me of a time when I was bold. Surprise me."

She closed her eyes and Rainer felt the gentle press of her magic on his mind as she drew him into her memory. He was staring into his own face and he knew right away that she was sharing one of her memories, and not one he'd shared with her. He looked about sixteen.

––––––––

They stood in the grove where they usually trained, surrounded by wisteria and the sweet smell of ever-blooming lilacs.

"Cece, why are you so distracted today?"

Frustration and anger bubbled through her as she looked up at him. He helped her to her feet. She said nothing as she prepared to fight again. Again they fought, again she was sloppy, and again she landed on her back with Rainer standing over her.

"Do you want to tell me what's going on?"

"No," she huffed.

"Again?"

She nodded. He took her down a third time.

"Okay. I think we're done unless you want to tell me why you're so angry. You're going to get hurt if we keep doing this while you're distracted."

She stayed on the grass where he'd taken her down. Her hands scrubbed over her face, and a frustrated sigh escaped her.

A new feeling rose to the surface: humiliation. Tears blurred her eyes as she looked up at him.

"Just tell me what's going on," Rainer said. He sat down next to her and pulled her up to a sitting position. He took her left hand in his and ran a finger over her crescent scar.

She brushed the tears out of her eyes and looked away. "Some of the ladies were talking this morning. It's not a big deal. It shouldn't be a big deal," she started. She was too embarrassed to continue. "Just forget it. I'll talk to Sylvie about it. It's fine."

Rainer shifted uncomfortably. "Is it about, umm, lady things? I don't mind talking about it if you need to. Are you in pain? Do you need a day off from training?"

"Oh my gods." Cecilia buried her face in her hands in pure humiliation. "No! Gods, Rain!"

When she looked back up at him, he blushed, equally embarrassed.

"Now that we're both sufficiently mortified, why don't you just tell me?" he whispered.

"Trust me, it's more embarrassing," she said. "You wouldn't understand."

"I can try, Cece. That's how this works. Have I ever judged you before?"

"No."

Rainer's thumb circled her inner wrist. His eyes pleaded with her.

"At lunch today, all the girls were talking about their first kisses... and I..."

She didn't need to finish. Recognition stole across Rainer's face. They told each other everything, and that would have been something major to leave out.

"And you never have," he finished.

She shook her head, wiping away another rogue tear. "And they asked me and I didn't know what to say. Sylvie interrupted, but I think they all knew. No one has ever liked me enough to even try to kiss me. Anders always says I'm more hunter than lady and all the guardians know it. You wouldn't understand. All the girls like you, Rain. You can kiss whoever you want."

When she met Rainer's eyes again, he blushed. "I've never kissed anyone either."

Her jaw dropped in disbelief. "You haven't? But you flirt with girls. You make it look so easy."

He shook his head.

"Why not?"

He traced a finger over her palm. "It just never felt right, and now I'm a *little afraid I'll seem like I don't know what I'm doing. I understand more than you think."*

She stared at him. "But all the girls like you. You flirt all the time."

Rainer shrugged. "I wanted it to mean something. I didn't want to just kiss someone for the sake of doing it."

"I guess that makes me feel a bit better," Cecilia said.

Rainer's face contorted the way it always did when he was conflicted, waging some internal war with himself. He looked down at her hand in his.

"I could kiss you, Cece."

Her heart kicked against her chest, and her cheeks heated. "I don't want my first kiss to be a pity kiss."

"It's not. I meant—I want to kiss you."

She searched Rainer's face and their connection for a sign that he was lying. There was none. She sensed only warmth and honesty.

"Plus, you'd be doing me a favor so I don't embarrass myself."

She looked away, certain her face was bright red.

"What?"

"I just kind of hoped it would be a little more romantic. I know that's stupid. I just hoped it would be with someone who really liked me."

Rainer scooted closer. His hand brushed her cheek. "I do like you. I know it's not romantic like the fairy tales, but I think you're pretty and you're my best friend."

A breeze stirred the branches of the flowering trees and white petals floated down around them like snow. Cecilia thought it didn't get much more romantic than laying on the grass surrounded by so much natural beauty as the sunset painted the clouds pink, orange, and purple.

Rainer brushed a few of the petals out of her hair. His hand stayed on her cheek.

"Can I?" he asked.

She couldn't speak, so she nodded instead.

His lips brushed hers so lightly. She could hardly breathe as her fingers intertwined with his. The urgency of the kiss intensified as his hand moved from her cheek to wrap around the back of her neck, pressing her closer. She was overcome by a rushing warmth all around her heart, the same that she'd felt years before when they were bonded together. She could have kissed him all day.

Much sooner than she wanted, he pulled away. They stared at each other, wide-eyed.

"Was it okay?" Rainer asked. His face was so earnest that she almost laughed.

"It was really nice... I..." She bit her lip, willing herself to be quiet.

"You what?"

"I didn't want you to stop."

He smiled, and it felt like a reward. She shrugged and looked away, aware of nothing but the tingling on her lips and the heat on her cheeks.

———

The memory cut and Rainer blinked his eyes open. Cecilia still lay next to him with her eyes closed and a smile on her lips, her hair spread out around her head like a dark halo.

"I suppose that was bold and unexpected. I remember that day," he whispered.

"Me too." She laughed, trying to make light of things. It was an old joke between them. He'd ask if she remembered something just to see her roll her eyes or hear her witty reply, since she remembered everything with perfect accuracy.

"I was waiting to kiss you," Rainer whispered. "That's why I never kissed anyone else. I hated the idea of it being anyone else. You were the most beautiful girl I'd ever seen."

Cecilia looked away. "I'm still glad it was you."

"I'm still glad it was you too, Cece. I wish you'd taken my side of that memory at the time so we could see both sides."

"I wanted to, but I was too embarrassed to ask you to share it. I was afraid it meant more to me than it did to you." She shifted away from him. "I'm glad we're still best friends."

Her voice was soft, the tone meant to ease the reminder that they were still just that. *Friends.* It was meant to be a kindness, but every boundary she set felt like a slap in the face.

Don't go where I can't go, Rainer wanted to say, the way she used to say to him. She'd followed him everywhere through his guardian training, including all the training to pass the Guardian Final Exam —three days in the rugged wilderness with no map on a treacherous hike. She'd always hated any distance between them, but now she was the one pulling away.

Cecilia propped herself on an elbow, meeting Rainer's gaze. "Why do you ask to see a memory when you don't care which one I show?"

"Because I love to see the world the way you do."

She swallowed hard. He'd seen her speechless so few times in their history that he almost laughed and ruined the moment.

She gathered her blanket and turned away from him, curling into a ball by the fire. "We should get some rest. We need to be ready for Sayla tomorrow."

Rainer couldn't hide his disappointment, although he did not know what he expected her to say instead. He laid down beside her, though farther away than usual, watching the steady rise and fall of her back as she faded to sleep.

Normally, Rainer fell asleep so quickly next to Cecilia, but unlike the way she found his presence so soothing, hers seemed to wake every nerve in his body. He'd felt electrified the first time he saw her shoot her bow, and then again when they were bonded together, and every time he looked at her since. Like he recognized something that went beyond the face of his best friend that sent a steady hum through his blood. He didn't understand it, and the more he tried to explain it to himself, the more numinous it felt.

"Fight for her."

That's what Leo Reznik told Rainer to do right before he died. Still, he couldn't bring himself to push too hard. The way to Cecilia's heart wasn't through force. It was through gentleness.

Rainer was impatient for every part of her. He was bound by the strings that tied their souls together and no matter how he struggled against them, they always drew him back in.

12

CECILIA

The Wailing Woods were beautiful and terrifying, exactly as the mythology books described. Sharp white branches slashed toward the trail from all directions, like jagged teeth waiting to tear them apart.

Cecilia shivered. She and Rainer had passed by the borders of the woods on a Gauntlet run years earlier, but they felt even more haunting on the inside. Delicate saplings sprang from the ashen ground, and boughs of the larger burnt-out trees groaned in the canopy above. Ivy climbed thick tree trunks and hung like streamers between branches.

So far, the trip had been fruitless. Cecilia had no idea how to summon Sayla or if the goddess was even there.

She and Rainer wandered the east trail while Sylvie, Cal, and Evan took the west, hoping to meet unscathed on the other side of the woods.

They rode in silence, scanning the horizon for any signs of the goddess of the hunt. The farther into the woods they traveled, the more disoriented Cecilia felt, as if they kept passing the same few trees. The hair on the back of her neck stood on end. She had the distinct feeling of being watched. A flock of ravens darted across their path, spooking their horses and setting Cecilia's already fried nerves on edge.

"Sister, you're getting rusty. I've been tracking you for a mile. I thought at least your hunter would notice."

Rainer and Cecilia jumped, craning their necks to find the goddess of the hunt standing several feet behind them on the trail.

"Sayla," Cecilia said.

Rainer turned to Sayla, touching his forehead, lips, and heart in a sign of reverence. Cecilia rolled her eyes as she and Rainer dismounted.

Sayla was close to six feet tall with dark auburn curls draping over her shoulders. She had fair skin, freckles, and eyes that were the same blue as Cecilia's but more narrow and calculating. Even at a glance, Cecilia could pick up on similar mannerisms and movements as if looking at herself in a distorted mirror.

Sayla wore a draping, diaphanous, hunter-green gown that shifted in the breeze and left little to the imagination. Cecilia was grateful her sister hadn't forgone leggings. Clearly modesty was not a priority to goddesses.

"That's not my hunter. That's my guardian, Rainer," Cecilia said.

"So you're saying he's available?" Sayla's gaze raked over Rainer.

Cecilia crossed her arms. "I did not say that."

Sayla pursed her lips and looked Cecilia up and down before undressing Rainer with her eyes again. "Territorial. I like it. How many lovers do you have, sister?" she asked.

"Oh my gods! We're not lovers. He's just my—" Cecilia wasn't sure how to finish. *He's just my best friend I've been in love with my whole life? He's just the person I imagined spending my life with? He's just the man who professed his love to me after I was already married?*

"I'm her best friend," Rainer finished.

"Oh! Samson told me about this. He said you have a soul bond."

Cecilia cringed at the mention of the god of lust. The last time they met, he'd aired everyone's romantic dirty laundry and made for a very uncomfortable lunch guest.

"Yes," she muttered.

Sayla looked as if she was waiting for them to elaborate, but Cecilia was tired of talking about it.

"Surely you must understand, even to us gods, that's a rarity," Sayla said. "It's hard to show us something new. Tell me, Guardian. What does she feel right now?"

Rainer bit back a laugh. "She feels annoyed and also impatient."

Sayla clapped her hands and laughed. "And how does she feel when you touch her? Go on, show me."

She waved her hand at Rainer, who looked at Cecilia, who reluctantly offered permission. He slid his hand into hers and intertwined their fingers. Rainer closed his eyes and the two goddesses studied his face. Cecilia leaned into him involuntarily.

"She feels relieved, but guilty," Rainer answered, blinking his eyes open.

Cecilia pulled her hand away.

"Fascinating." Sayla took Cecilia's face in her hands.

Cecilia braced her hands against her half-sister's hips.

"I thought you'd be taller."

"Why does everyone keep saying that?" Cecilia huffed.

Sayla's face was half-shadowed by the forest canopy. "You have the eyes, though. We all do. At least you're pretty. Though you're such a tiny thing, I'm not sure how you expect to beat Cato."

"I've been fighting men who are much bigger than me my whole life. This is no different," Cecilia said.

Sayla laughed. "I like your courage, tiny goddess. You will need it. What made you seek me out?"

"I thought maybe it was a good time for a family reunion with the impending war and Cato trying to capture me," Cecilia said sarcastically. "I need help finding Cato and my husband."

"Of course. The Storm Prince. Adira says he's very handsome. She said your guardian was too, and now I see with my own eyes that's true."

Cecilia sighed, her impatience growing by the second. "Can you tell us where Xander is?"

Sayla pulled out her bow. "Show me what you've got, little sister, and I'll tell you what I know about Cato and your love."

Rainer passed Cecilia her bow.

"Best of three?" Sayla suggested.

"And if you win?" Cecilia asked.

"I'll still tell you what I know. I owe Cato some payback, but if I win, I want to kiss your guardian, and then I'll consider bargaining for the information."

"Excuse me?" Cecilia choked. "He's not mine to whore out."

"I didn't suggest such a thing. I only suggested a friendly wager that I suspect he wouldn't be opposed to. What man can say he's kissed two goddesses?" Sayla said, winking at Rainer.

"Cece, I don't mind," Rainer said.

"*I* mind," Cecilia said.

Rainer smiled at her. "We do what we have to do in order to save Xander, right? You just told me to try new things. Small price to pay to help you. I don't mind, and you don't really have a right to mind, Cece."

Cecilia covered her hurt with a sigh as she turned back to Sayla. "Fine. Best of three."

Sayla jumped up and down, clapping her hands. "Shall we hunt live game? I found a hunter, a guardian, and a witch on one of the other trails."

Cecilia's eyes went wide. "Oh my gods, no! They're with us. Did you hurt them?"

Sayla waved her hand. "They're fine. I just thought it would be more fun than regular target practice. An oversight. I should have realized they were your friends."

"Do you make a habit of playing target practice with real people in these woods?"

"How do you think the stories of hauntings and disappearances came to be? I come and go, but I try to keep the murdering to a minimum," Sayla said magnanimously.

"How thoughtful," Cecilia said.

"I can only stay corporeal for short periods of time, so that limits my ability to enact vengeance. Come this way," Sayla said, gesturing toward a small trail.

Cecilia walked a step behind, unwilling to give the goddess of the hunt her back.

"So tell me, has Grim tried to fuck you yet?" Sayla asked.

"Excuse me?" Cecilia was so startled she tripped over a root.

"Adira said he's known you a long time. She thinks he's being so helpful because he wants to get up your skirts. Clearly he's invested and now that you're grown and so pretty, I can't imagine him keeping his hands to himself. He's got a thing for goddesses."

"You too?" Cecilia asked, her eyes wide.

Sayla cackled. "Of course not. Adira would have drowned me. She gets very jealous, and she had first claim to him, but that hasn't stopped him from trying with the rest of us. Word in the woods is that he and Goddess Aurelia had a thing going for quite a while, being two of the neutral gods and all. But you know what they say, opposites attract."

"Why is Aurelia neutral?" Cecilia asked.

"Can you imagine if the goddess of harvest and fertility became political?" Sayla clucked her tongue. "What a nightmare it would be! Same as death and lust. If only one kingdom could own those things, it would be a mess."

"Why not love? By that measure, shouldn't Desiree be neutral?" Cecilia asked.

"Oh, she was for centuries." Sayla waved a hand like it was information everyone knew.

"What happened?"

Sayla's knuckles went white on her bow. "Cato saw love as a weakness. He went to war with the concept, and therefore made her an enemy. We gods can be possessive and Cato killed Desiree's favored lover for sport. So she took sides then, but it was so long ago most people forget she was ever neutral," Sayla said. "I know Grim told you none of us can give you the full picture. We have to speak in riddles, but everything we do and say serves a purpose, so pay attention. We are all telling you something with words and actions. Don't forget that."

Cecilia nodded, glancing back at Rainer, who followed behind them.

"So tell me. Why haven't you taken a lover?" Sayla asked.

Cecilia balked. "Because I'm married."

"Surely your husband can't keep up with your newfound appetites. Gods have needs that are too much for most mortals." Sayla smirked, winking at Rainer.

Cecilia felt an unnatural amount of rage. She chalked it up to goddess bloodlust. "It hasn't been a problem so far," she said curtly.

"*Really?*" Sayla's eyebrows shot up. "Good for you. I might have underestimated your prince. Now I'm dying to meet him."

Cecilia wasn't certain it was a great idea introducing her sister—who'd already hit on Rainer so blatantly—to her husband.

"There. Do you see that X on the tree down there?" Sayla asked, pointing to a large pine a great distance away.

Cecilia nodded. Sayla took aim first, letting her arrow fly. Cecilia didn't even need to look to know it would be lodged right in the center of the mark. She stepped forward, aimed, and shot. When they approached the tree, their arrows were pressed against each other, both piercing the dead center of the mark.

"You be the judge, Guardian. What do you think?" Sayla asked, running her fingers over Rainer's broad shoulders. Her hand came to rest on his chest, and Cecilia thought briefly of what it would feel like to break each of her fingers.

Rainer smiled at the goddess of the hunt. "Looks like a tie to me, Goddess."

Sayla shrugged. "Very well. On to shot number two. Tell me, Cecilia, which side of you do you think is most likely to defeat Cato? The huntress? The witch? The goddess? The mortal woman?"

Cecilia followed Sayla, turning the question over in her mind. "Well, I already fought him, but it wasn't really a fair fight because he gave me Godsbane beforehand and I was wounded, but I'd still say probably not the huntress. The goddess also seems unlikely since I can't use my powers on him. It was the witch that beat Endros, so maybe that's my best opportunity."

"Or maybe you're used to that magic and you use it as a crutch. Think strategically. You could have others attack Cato for you," Sayla said.

Cecilia rolled her eyes. "And he could just as easily manipulate them to attack me."

"You have better combat skills."

"He has centuries more combat experience," Cecilia said.

"But you're braver," Sayla offered.

"But he has a greater sense of self-preservation," Rainer interrupted.

Sayla chuckled darkly. "Your handsome guardian has you pegged."

Cecilia rolled her eyes as Sayla came to a stop next to a tree.

"Can you see the tiny wooden hoop attached to that tree down there?"

"Yes." Cecilia's eyes narrowed on the wooden hoop hammered into the bark of an oak tree. She was certain she wouldn't have been able to see it without her newly enhanced eyesight.

Sayla took her shot without hesitation, and once again Cecilia saw it hit the mark. Cecilia took a breath and shook out her tight shoulders. She aimed and shot, and they moved to check the target.

"Guardian?" Sayla asked.

"Another tie," Rainer said, looking at their arrows, once again pressed against each other.

"You're quite good, Cecilia. I'm glad my gift has served you well," Sayla said.

Cecilia frowned. "Your gift?"

Sayla nodded. "I gifted your mother, Selene, her marksmanship at Clastor's request, and bestowed it on you as well when they discovered she was pregnant. I'm glad to see you haven't let it go to waste."

Cecilia stared at the goddess. "You're why I'm so good with a bow?"

Sayla's eyes sparkled. "Natural ability is only useful if you actually practice, which it's clear you have. I can't take all the credit."

Cecilia shook her head. "Can we get back to Cato?"

"Of course. I think you're approaching the problem from the wrong angle. What you really need to think about is which of those sides of you Cato is most likely to *underestimate*," Sayla said meaningfully.

Cecilia considered it. If he wasn't afraid of her goddess abilities, he wouldn't have bothered with the Godsbane. She'd burned him with her fire summoning already, so he knew some of her witch tricks now as well.

"He's most likely to underestimate my human side," she said.

"In that, both gods and men are alike," Sayla said with a wink. "They see a beautiful woman and they see weakness. Dazzle them with your beauty and they'll never see your mind." She slung an arm around Rainer and Cecilia bristled. Sayla watched her, smirking. "You don't like when I touch him."

"I don't know what you're talking about." Cecilia pursed her lips.

"Is she always so territorial with you, Guardian?" Sayla asked Rainer.

"Yes," he said.

Guilt swelled in Cecilia's chest. "I like to think of it as protective, and as you recall, you've always been the same, Rain."

"I have." He smiled.

"Oh really? Did he scare off your suitors?" Sayla asked.

"Yes."

"I was not that bad," Rainer argued.

"Honestly, Guardian. You should have let her have her fun. A girl is only young and beautiful once—well, I suppose that once is forever for you now, lucky girl," Sayla teased. "Why did you scare them off?"

"I didn't want Cece to get hurt," Rainer said.

"You didn't want me to experience anything. You didn't want to be with me, but you also didn't want anyone else to." Cecilia's voice held more venom than she'd intended.

"You love him very much." Sayla said it so casually, as if such a simple sentence wouldn't shake all of Cecilia's guilt loose.

Cecilia and Rainer stared at each other, agitation buzzing across their bond. Saying anything was too risky. Cecilia opened up their connection, sending a rush of peace through. Rainer closed his eyes and brought a hand to his heart.

"So that's how it works. You can communicate without speaking?" Sayla asked.

They both jumped, having forgotten they had an audience.

"I suppose it's a type of communication. One with no words, just feelings," Rainer said.

"Fascinating," Sayla said.

The goddess paused and Cecilia realized the heavy foliage around them had thinned and they were stanging on the edge of a cliff.

Sayla gestured to the edge. "Last shot is a trick shot. On the underside of this cliff lip. Let's see how good you really are."

"But that's a twenty-foot drop," Rainer said, peeking over the edge.

"And she's a goddess. She'll be fine," Sayla said.

With that, Sayla turned and jumped, firing an arrow on her way down. Once she was out of the way, Cecilia prepared her bow.

She jumped and turned. Instead of seeing the bullseye, she got an eyeful of sunshine. Cecilia blinked wildly, shooting at the very last second and landing hard on the ground below. The shock of the impact reverberated through her bones. Not her finest landing, but she was unharmed. She looked up and saw that she'd just missed the bullseye.

"I win!" Sayla sang. She gestured to a rope ladder fixed to the cliff.

They climbed back to the top, and Sayla walked toward Rainer.

"I won. I'm here to collect my reward, Guardian," she said with a smile. She brought a hand to Rainer's chest, pressing him back until he sat on a large boulder and she straddled his lap. His eyes went wide in surprise. He settled his hands on her hips.

"Let's see what you've got, Guardian," Sayla said. She wove her hands through his hair and brought her lips to his.

At first Rainer seemed tentative, but as the kiss deepened, he relaxed into it.

Cecilia didn't want to watch but also couldn't make herself look away. Jealousy hollowed her out and filled her with guilt. She wanted to scream or throw her slutty goddess half-sister across the forest. She wanted to feel nothing at all.

Sayla slid her hands up Rainer's tunic.

Cecilia grabbed Sayla's shoulder and wrenched her back.

"Okay, enough. You said make out, not fuck." Her voice was shrill, not at all the casual taunting tone she was going for.

"I am surprised you let me get that far, Cecilia." Sayla's grin turned feral. "Look how jealous you are!"

"Just tell me what I need to do in exchange for the information about my husband."

"Deals with gods are binding, little sister. Lest you forget."

"I haven't forgotten. I'm just highly motivated. I'll do whatever it takes," Cecilia said.

Sayla arched an eyebrow. "Be careful which gods you make such promises to." She rubbed her chin as if she was thinking, but Cecilia knew from the look in her eye that the goddess had already decided.

Cecilia's uneasiness spread like a fever beneath her skin. What could a god possibly want from her?

"If you want the information I hold, you'll need to kiss the guardian—a real kiss. I want to see how it compares. I sensed he was holding back because you were watching."

Cecilia crossed her arms. "I'm married."

Sayla grinned. "Have you noticed that you can't say that you don't want to?"

"Have you noticed that you're kind of a bitch?"

"Cece!" Rainer scolded, but Sayla laughed at the insult.

Cecilia shook her head. "This is ridiculous."

"Then why are you making such a big deal of it? And none of this quick peck nonsense. I want to see a proper kiss," Sayla said.

What did kissing Rainer have to do with defeating Cato? Was this all a game to them? Perhaps Cecilia was a fool to trust that the gods had any sense of duty or compassion for the living. The gods were ancient and humans were just their toys. Hadn't Sayla just suggested hunting her friends?

Rainer smiled at Cecilia. She loved his easy grin so much it hurt —so much it filled her with bottomless guilt.

"I can't kiss someone else."

Sayla rolled her eyes. "You mortals and your monogamy. It's so tedious."

"Surely there must be worse punishment than kissing me." Rainer's tone teased, but doubt shaded his eyes.

"It's not a punishment, and that's the problem," she rasped.

Rainer sighed. "Didn't you tell him you'd do whatever it took to get back to him?"

She wasn't sure it was the right thing, but what was one kiss to a lifetime of love she'd promised Xander? She'd come clean as soon as he was safe. She'd tell him everything. For now, she was so desperate to get him back that a kiss seemed a small price to pay.

Cecilia knelt, her thighs bracketing Rainer's. He cupped her face in his hands and she balled his shirt in her fists, trying to fight off the nervousness suddenly coursing through her.

"Don't be nervous," Rainer whispered. "I think about this all the time."

He tilted her chin up and brushed his lips to hers so lightly that she almost whimpered from the tenderness. He shattered all of her defenses with his sweetness. Before Rainer touched her that way, she didn't understand how something so gentle could make her feel like she might break into a million pieces. That tenderness unearthed a hidden, fragile part of herself for the first time in a life that forced her to be so hard.

She couldn't have that. Gentleness would break her when she needed to be strong. Her lips parted, taking the kiss deeper. One of Rainer's hands tangled in her hair and the other pressed against her lower back. He pulled her hips flush to his so there was no space between them.

Rainer kissed her as if it was the first and last time he'd ever get to do it and he wanted to put his all into it. It broke through her remaining resistance.

Cecilia gave herself over completely to the ravenous hunger building inside her. She was so thoroughly undone, all she could do was exactly what his lips demanded. Her hands slid up the front of his tunic, brushing over hard planes of muscle and warm skin. She rolled her hips. He groaned into her mouth as he caught her lower lip between his teeth. She let out a gasp, and he pulled her hair gently to tilt her head back, trailing a line of kisses down her jaw and neck.

Chills spread over her skin, and a warm tingling sensation settled in her whole body. Her skin buzzed with the pleasure of his touch. Time and reason slipped away, the bond in her chest serene. She wanted to live inside that moment forever.

She lost herself in Rainer in a way she had never let herself before. Her heart thundered in her ears and her skin felt too hot. She rolled her hips. Her body demanded more, and she forgot everything else. An ache settled in the pit of her stomach. She wanted—

Sayla cleared her throat and Cecilia jumped, struck by a surge of guilt. She pulled her hands back as if she'd been burned. She was supposed to be finding Xander, not kissing Rainer in the woods.

Rainer leaned his forehead against hers, meeting her eyes. "Fuck."

Cecilia nodded as she tried to catch her breath. She sat back to put distance between them despite her body's desperate plea for more. That was too much. That was more than just a kiss. She felt breathless and sick with guilt for liking it.

"My goodness. He certainly did not kiss me like that. That was revelatory," Sayla said with a self-satisfied smirk. "If your husband kisses you better than that, more power to you, because I think if someone kissed me the way your guardian just kissed you, it would bring me to my knees. Lucky goddess."

Cecilia flushed. She thought back to Sayla's words earlier, that every word and action was intentional, but she couldn't possibly see the purpose behind this one. What reason could Sayla have had for kissing Rainer and then forcing Cecilia to?

She tried to put the kiss out of her mind even as she felt the remnants of it sparking through her body.

You're just stressed. The kiss was nothing special. Sometimes a pretty lie was safer than an ugly truth.

"We should head back to the trail. Your friends are waiting," Sayla said. Cecilia imagined slapping the knowing smirk off Sayla's face.

"What about Xander?" Cecilia asked impatiently.

"For information on Xander we need to visit Desiree in Heartwood Valley."

Cecilia crossed her arms. "But you said—"

"I said I would tell you what I know, and what I know is that Desiree has the details on your husband. Did you even pay attention? I told you about Cato. Everything I've said and done has been for your benefit."

"Yes, I paid attention." Frustration burned through Cecilia.

"Then let's go find your friends," Sayla said.

They walked to their horses in silence and rode through the forest, Sayla on their heels. Evan, Sylvie, and Cal were waiting at the trailhead.

"We were getting worried," Evan said.

"Sorry, we were having an archery contest," Cecilia said.

"Hello, I'm Cecilia's sister—"

"Half-sister," Cecilia corrected.

"You probably know me better as Goddess Sayla," Sayla said with a flourish of her hand.

Evan and Cal both went down on a knee and Sylvie curtseyed.

"Oh, that's what you all do for other goddesses?" Cecilia asked.

"Other goddesses seem to be more agreeable so far," Evan said.

"You may rise." The goddess of the hunt looked each of them over carefully, her eyes coming to rest on Evan. "I enjoy this hunter. I'd like to keep him for a while."

"Are you always this much of a predator? He's not available right now. He's helping me search for Xander and also he's a person. You can't just have him." Cecilia rolled her eyes, but Evan looked like he might not be totally opposed to the idea. She almost burst out laughing. "Am I wrong? Do you want to stay, Evan?"

Evan stared at Sayla in such a way that Cecilia's guard went up. She could smell a strange magic in the air, like wet leaves and fresh grass. It wasn't until she looked at Sayla that she realized it was the scent of her magic.

"What are you doing to him?" Cecilia asked.

"Just taking him in. Holding him in my snare for a second as any good huntress would," Sayla said with a wink. Evan blinked and shook his head as she released whatever magic she was using. "I like him."

"Great. Well, we have to go. Will you be riding with us?" Cecilia asked her sister.

"No, unfortunately, I need to take a break and rest in the Otherworld. I'll meet you in Heartwood Valley. There's an old waterfall and swimming hole that Desiree and her minions spend time around. I'll meet you there in two days."

Rainer held out a map. Sayla marked the waterfall, then nodded to Cecilia.

"Remember what I said, little sister. Think it all over."

"I will."

"And Guardian, take care of my sister. Don't let her do anything I wouldn't do." Sayla winked at Rainer. "If you do a good job, maybe I'll kiss you again when I see you next."

Cecilia leveled a murderous glare at Sayla as the goddess turned and disappeared into the woods.

"You kissed Goddess Sayla? What was it like?" Cal asked, smacking Rainer's shoulder.

"Intense." Rainer held Cecilia's gaze and she knew he wasn't talking about Sayla at all.

She shrunk away from him, fixing her face into a grin. "Evan seems like god-bait. Both Samson and Sayla were very interested in you, Evan."

Evan shrugged. "Better to be a trap than a target."

Cecilia rolled her eyes. "Always the strategist."

"She wasn't *that* pretty," Sylvie said. "You know, for being a goddess and all."

Cecilia cocked her head. "And did you make that assessment before or after she flirted with Evan?"

Rainer grinned. "Maybe it will come in handy and we can use him as a diversion with Cato."

"Diversions are only used when a plan is weak," Evan said without a hint of humor.

"We may only have bad plans," Cecilia said plainly.

"I think we all know a thing or two about choosing the best bad option," Rainer said, meeting Cecilia's eyes.

She thought back to their conversation through prison bars in Argaria when she was trying to decide if she should marry Xander. "Let's hope we have the time to find a good one."

13

CECILIA

After a long ride, the group settled in for the night in the hills overlooking Landalor, a small town north of Olney City, keeping to the woods so they wouldn't draw too much attention.

The fire crackled as Sylvie plopped down next to Cecilia. "How are you doing?"

"Terrible," Cecilia sighed. "Sitting still is the worst. At least when we're moving, I have something to focus on. All I can think about is that those monsters have Xander. I know Davide's brand of terrible, but Cato's is still a question mark. All I can hope is that what I imagine in my head isn't as bad as what's actually happening."

Sylvie put an arm around her and Cecilia leaned her head on her friend's shoulder.

"And then when things slow down like this, I think about the school on fire and all of those people back home who were hurt or killed in the attack," Cecilia said, trying to keep her voice even.

"I know exactly what you mean. Every time I close my eyes, I hear the screaming."

"How do people live through this kind of war? How do they endure such cruelty?" Cecilia asked.

"I wish I knew," Sylvie said.

They sat quietly, watching the three men tend to the fire and talk about their route for the next day.

"What was it like meeting Sayla? It must be so strange to have a whole family you didn't know about," Sylvie said.

"She was intense. She would not stop flirting with Rainer, and she was just so forward."

"You must have loved that," Sylvie laughed.

"It's so disorienting. None of the gods can speak directly. So they give me riddles. She took a very roundabout way to suggest that the side of me that Cato is most likely to underestimate is my human side, which makes sense, but she wasn't very helpful outside of that. And then she tricked me and beat me in our archery contest, kissed Rainer, but wouldn't give me the information I needed until I kissed him, too."

Sylvie's eyebrows shot up. "You kissed Rainer?"

"It was the price for information on Xander. It was a trick."

Sylvie narrowed her eyes as she shook out her long blonde hair and ran her fingers through it.

"What?" Cecilia shrugged. "I thought I would win."

"Against the goddess of the hunt?"

"Okay, maybe I overestimated my skill, but I thought she had valuable information."

"How was it?" Sylvie asked.

Cecilia pressed her lips together. "It's probably best not to think about it."

"That good, huh?"

A cold breeze ruffled Cecilia's hair, blowing the words from her lips. She leaned closer to her friend, the log under them creaking as she shifted. "You must think I'm a terrible person. Maybe I am. I'm turning out to be a pretty bad wife."

Sylvie shook her head. "I doubt His Highness would agree with that assessment. Xander is completely besotted with you, which is saying something, because I only ever saw him flirt and fuck anything in a skirt before that. With you, he doesn't even glance at anyone else."

Cecilia buried her head in her hands, guilt gnawing at her.

"Everything changed quickly and you're still getting your legs under you. Maybe I'm the only one who will say this to you, because I understand what it's like to be a lady of the court, but it would have been easy to follow the path laid out for you. We're trained to believe there's no greater thing a lady can be than agreeable. Your resistance to that is why I have always admired you. I always wanted to be like you," Sylvie said.

Cecilia stared at her, unable to hide her shock. "Like *me*? I wanted to be like you. You knew how to play the game."

"Of course I did," Sylvie said, tossing her hair. "But it was someone else's game I was playing. I was the master of it, but it wasn't the game I would have chosen for myself. A lot of women, faced with the choices you were given, would have crumbled. It's difficult to do something different. Change is scary. You finished the Gauntlet and married a prince, but Xander lets you be yourself and loves you for it. You are imperfect, but mistakes are how you learn. I saw what was happening before you left on that last Gauntlet run, Cece. You were giving up."

Cecilia frowned. "I wasn't."

Sylvie held up her hands. "I don't say it with judgment, but I saw your resignation. You really thought you were facing down the first thing you couldn't fight against. You stopped wanting things for yourself and started letting other people tell you what to want. When you came back, it was like you were your old self again."

"I was a mess!" Cecilia laughed.

"But you were *your own mess*. I was so proud of you. I still am."

Rainer and Xander could intellectually understand where Cecilia was coming from, but Sylvie understood through her own experience; she'd been a prisoner to the same societal constraints and watched the same stifling future stretch out in front of her.

"I don't judge you for struggling with the choices you made, or for struggling to move on now, Cece. We all make mistakes. I want the opportunity to be more than someone's pretty wife. I want to choose things instead of hoping someone will choose *me*. Maybe there's still time, but I'd follow your lead and snatch whatever opportunity shows up that will let me decide for myself." Sylvie was quiet as she studied Cecilia's face. "You still haven't told me what exactly happened with Rainer. While I was shocked you came home married to a prince, I was more surprised that Rainer let you go."

A lump formed in Cecilia's throat. "He had every chance. I practically begged him to fight for me. I will always love him, but when I told him how I felt and gave him the chance, he didn't take it. Then I just kind of shut it down in my mind. I fell so hard for Xander. It happened so fast and I just gave myself over to it and, gods, did Xander make it easy. But beyond all of that, he never asks me to stand behind him and stay safe. From the time I met him, he kept asking me what I wanted. He trusts me to decide things for myself."

Sylvie nodded, braiding her blonde hair into a crown wrapped around her head. "That's a big change, although I can also understand why Rainer acts that way. Cal's always been very protective—granted, I don't have as much training as you. But you have to forgive them. It's drilled into guardians from the time they're children to protect their witches. It's hard to fight that instinct."

"It is, and I understand that, but it's just so different with Xander. Once we were married and fled, he knew something was wrong with me, but he gave me the space to figure things out and let me know that he was there to support me. Then, Rainer almost died—"

Cecilia took a deep breath, trying to shake off the chill that swept in with those words. Rainer glanced at her, clearly feeling her fear through their connection. She waved him off.

Sylvie laughed. "Gods, Xander must hate that."

"He does," Cecilia said. "It wasn't until Rain was on death's doorstep that he told me how he felt. And this thing in me I thought was gone just came roaring back." She swallowed the lump in her throat. "But sometimes, I feel like he looks at me and sees who I used to be instead of who I am. Like he's waiting for me to go back to being that sweet, naive person I was before we left to finish the Gauntlet.

And I'm afraid he's in love with someone I can never be again and I—"

I've sacrificed too much to lose him, too. The words died on her lips. Giving voice to that much left her breathless.

Maybe she was just as guilty of wishing she could go back. Why else would she have shown Rainer that memory of their first kiss the night before? All the years of fairy tales and memory magic had trapped her in nostalgia with no strategy for a nightmarish present.

Sylvie was quiet for a moment, then she squeezed Cecilia's hand. "You deserve to be loved exactly as you are. You don't need to be less. If he wants less, he can go find it elsewhere."

Cecilia managed a watery half-smile. Friends had to say things like that. Certainly that was what Sylvie deserved. She'd never killed a battalion of hunters with the wave of a hand.

"We both deserve that," Sylvie continued, her gaze flickering to Evan.

Cecilia cleared her throat. "Enough about me. Let's talk about you and Evan."

Sylvie pretended to stretch, not meeting her eyes. "I don't know what you're talking about."

"I think you do. Come on, I just poured my heart out. Give me something good. Distract me from my own chaos."

"He's very different and I am inconveniently interested."

Cecilia laughed. "Meaning you still don't have the upper hand?"

Sylvie lowered her voice. "I don't know who I am anymore. My parents clearly have no clue what to make of an Argarian hunter lurking about. It's unnerving that I have no desire to play my usual games. He's so sneaky. He found out how much I love raspberry tarts —I don't know how—and he showed up with a bunch of the best ones I've ever tasted. I don't even know what bakery they were from, but they were incredible. He just does all these unexpected sweet things. It's disorienting."

Cecilia grabbed her hand. "Answer a critical question for me. Does Evan talk about his feelings?"

Sylvie tipped her head back and laughed. "He's definitely a man of few words, but he's good at expressing himself in other ways."

"Do tell!"

"A lady never tells," Sylvie countered.

"Bullshit! You owe me some details." Cecilia sighed.

"I don't know. Everything is so different with him and I don't really care about the things I used to. With the Gauntlet over, it feels like I'm freed up from all the games I used to play. I can want what I actually want instead of trying to climb for status. People are actually considering what *I* want and, for the first time, I'm uncertain."

"Well, I really like him," Cecilia said. "He's brave, and you'd have to be a special kind of patient to deal with a lifetime of Xander's nonsense. I'm happy for you, Sylvie. Make sure I'm invited to the wedding."

They both giggled again.

"Don't hold your breath. The man seems allergic to vulnerability." Sylvie sighed, her face filled with longing.

"Ladies, it's getting late. You should quit your giggling and go to sleep," Cal called from the other side of the fire.

"Okay, *Dad*," Sylvie teased.

"We should do dual watch, just in case. Davide's spies are everywhere. Better to be safe than sorry. I'll take first watch," Evan said.

"I can stay up with you," Cecilia offered.

Sylvie gave her a suspicious look, but Cecilia ignored her.

Cal and Sylvie huddled together against the chill in the night air. Cecilia went to sit next to Evan by the dying fire. She shivered, and a moment later Rainer handed her one of his spare sweaters.

"That still weirds me out," Evan whispered as he watched Rainer settle under a blanket near Cal and Sylvie.

Cecilia tugged on the sweater. They sat quietly for a while, listening to the chirp of crickets and the creaking of branches above them. Evan scanned the perimeter in consistent increments.

Finally, when it was clear he thought everyone was asleep, he turned to look at her. "How are you doing?"

Cecilia shrugged. "I've been better. You?"

"About the same."

Cecilia wrung her hands. "I wish I could feel him like I do Rainer. I wish I knew he was okay."

"Xander is a survivor. He's been behind enemy lines his entire adult life. He'll be okay. I keep trying to puzzle out why they wanted to take both of you. I understand what you could offer Cato, but I don't understand why Davide would be on board," Evan said.

"Why?"

"Because if Cato has a prince and princess, all he has to do to run Argaria is kill one king. He'd be able to use you and Xander to manipulate each other into behaving."

Cecilia's eyes went wide. If that was Cato's endgame, Davide's days were numbered. "Maybe Davide doesn't know."

"Davide's pretty clever. I doubt he would miss that. My guess is that he has some sort of deal with Cato that he thinks protects him."

"But with Cato, there's always a trick." She swallowed hard. "Evan, I didn't make my deal to say that he couldn't have someone else. I just said it couldn't be me and that he couldn't hurt anyone. What if Xander is my favor?"

Evan shook his head, frustration breaking through his calm veneer. "I can't help feeling like we're operating blind. Like Cato sees the whole puzzle but we're just fumbling around trying to find one piece."

"I miss him already."

The crease in Evan's brow softened. "We'll get him back. You just have to be patient and we have to have a plan. He will kill me and Rainer if we let you get caught. So you can't let your emotions rule you like you always do. We have to be smart. We are outnumbered and if we don't play this right, Cato could crush all of us easily and use us to manipulate you."

"I'm trying." She hesitated. "Xander and I had a fight right before everything happened and I said something I shouldn't have. I feel terrible."

"I'm sure he's over it already. He's much too quick to forgive you, if you ask me." Evan's tone was teasing, but she sensed the truth underneath.

"If something happens to him, I'll never forgive myself," she said.

"He'll be fine. You'll have plenty of time to make up for it." Evan said it like he was trying to convince himself as well.

"Distract me. Tell me about Sylvie."

Evan pursed his lips. "I don't think so."

"Oh, come on. Give me something. I must have access to some information a spy like yourself would be interested in."

Evan hesitated.

"I command you as your princess."

He laughed. "I like her."

Cecilia waited for him to say more but he stared into the woods silently. "Go on and knock me over with your effusiveness."

Evan rubbed the back of his neck. "Fine. It's possible things could become more serious one day if I was sure that my status didn't matter to her. That stays between us."

The admission surprised Cecilia. "I'm pretty certain she couldn't care less for titles, but obviously you'd have to discuss that with her."

"What's something she loves that no one else would know?" Evan asked.

Cecilia tugged at a loose string on the sweater's hem. "There are these folk dance parties on the outskirts of Olney every full moon. Sylvie loves to learn all the old dances, and party all night. I am almost certain the only two people who know that are Cal and me. You'd probably win her heart forever if you took her to one, though now that I say it, I can't imagine you taking dance lessons and dancing the night away."

"I'll have you know I am a fantastic dancer. I'm no Xander Savero, but I can certainly hold my own." He rubbed the back of his neck. "You told Teddy about her when he was dying. Did you really think of the two of them together?"

Cecilia's stomach sank at the mention of their fallen friend. "No, I suspected the two of you might make a better match. She's a strategist through and through. The trick with her isn't to play games, but to treat her like a normal person. Which isn't to say that she doesn't want compliments. She is as vain as can be, but she wants someone who sees her mind as much as her pretty face. I used to think—" Cecilia cut herself off.

"Yes?" Evan looked so eager for the words.

"Sometimes I can't tell if her act—all the posturing with suitors— is to draw people in or to keep them out."

"Why keep them out?"

Cecilia narrowed her eyes at him. "Don't work me. You're too smart to actually wonder that. I'm sure you have your own suspicions so I assume you want my opinion."

Evan seemed chastened by her tone.

"Something happened when we were teenagers, and before you ask, I don't know what it was. I only know that when she and Cal broke up, something shifted in her. She'd always loved attention but she'd never been so desperate to weaponize it. She was different and she never told me why so I didn't press. But sometimes I felt something like grief and rage swirling around her."

"At Cal?"

Cecilia shook her head. "It was never when he was around. And he was so heartsick at the time it didn't seem likely he was to blame."

Evan picked at a thread on his leather vest.

"I can tell you want to dig, but I wouldn't on this. Sylvie likes to call the shots but I get the impression that is a very closely-guarded secret and she'll tell you if she wants to."

Evan nodded. "Do you want to tell me what happened with Rainer today?"

"Excellent deflection, but I don't know what you mean," Cecilia said smoothly.

Evan smirked. "The two of you both looked like you were dazed when you rode out of that forest with Sayla. You were all flushed and he wouldn't stop staring at you."

Cecilia felt trapped, unsure whether the truth or a deflection would cause more damage.

"I'm not asking to judge you, but you're always very guarded about him."

"I lost my archery contest with Sayla and had to bargain with her for the information we needed. I truly thought I could beat her."

"That's a little stuck up, even for you," Evan laughed.

"Rude." She looked away from Evan's eyes and into the embers of the dying fire. "It's not a big deal. It was just a kiss. I'll tell Xander about it."

"I know you will. You've always been fully transparent with him about Rainer. I guess my question is the same as what it's been in the past. Are you going to walk away?"

"From Xander? Gods, no!" She sighed. "Evan, I love him, though I worry sometimes that I won't be enough for him."

"What do you mean?" Evan asked. "I didn't see it at first but you are remarkably well-suited. The thing about Xander is that everyone treats him like he's too much, but you like it. You like the flirting and the teasing. You like his obsession because you obsess too. How you could think that you wouldn't be enough is puzzling." He frowned, cocking his head to the side.

Cecilia wasn't ready to talk about the exchange for her powers. She had no idea how Evan would react to the news that there would be no children for her and Xander. Legacy hadn't been an issue for Xander before his parents were killed, but now a family of his own might be more important.

"I want to give him everything he wants. He deserves that after all he's been through and I worry what will happen if I can't."

Evan tipped his head to the side. "I think you are all he wants."

"I don't." Even if royal heirs weren't important to Xander, they would be to his people. She didn't know how they would find a way around it.

"And what if Rainer moves on?" Evan asked.

"He has every right to." She swallowed hard around the words.

Evan watched her carefully, as if looking for a crack in her facade. "What if Xander let you take on a consort?"

"What?" She looked at him, shocked.

"It's not unheard of. In fact, it's pretty standard among Argarian royals. The only reason Damian didn't have one was because he wanted to carry on multiple affairs, but Juliana had a long-term consort. Arthur Randal. He was a hunter, not a noble. It caused quite a stir when it came out, although I was too young to remember most of it. He died two years ago but people still whisper about him."

"Why?" Cecilia asked.

Evan shifted uncomfortably. "This stays between us because there's no truth to it, but it's obviously something that could be damaging. There were rumors that Xander was actually his son and not the king's."

Cecilia gasped. Why hadn't Xander ever told her? Perhaps that was the secret Grimon was hinting at—the one Xander had wanted to share before the attack on Olney City.

"But Xander looks like King Damian." Cecilia called up the memory of the late king in her mind and suddenly doubted herself. Xander certainly resembled his mother but she saw more of Damian in Davide than Xander.

Evan held up his hands. "Arthur Randal had hazel eyes and dark hair and was a legendary hunter in Argaria. It's not a leap for people to suspect. I have never found evidence to suggest that was true and I've done my own digging and come up empty-handed. Plus, Arthur did not become Juliana's official consort until Xander was six. That's why I hardly remember it. I was just a kid myself."

"But you think it's possible or you wouldn't have told me," Cecilia said.

Evan frowned. "I think it's possible that it would come up if Davide gets himself killed and Xander becomes king, which is looking more possible daily."

Cecilia leaned back, trying to take it all in. "So you think Xander would go for me having a consort at all, let alone with Rainer?"

Evan shrugged. "Honestly, I think he would do pretty much anything to make you happy, no matter how jealous it made him. With the right boundaries in place, he could do it."

She brushed her thumb over her inner wrist. "I don't think I could do that. Plus, I've got my hands full. Xander's pretty needy."

Evan chuckled and poked at the fire. "Do you ever get the impression that he's hiding something important?"

The words sent a shiver of fear through her. "Grimon suggested that might be the case, and right before the attack, Xander was about to tell me something important that he was certain would upset me. Maybe it was this."

Evan didn't look convinced. "Maybe, but he's never even talked about it to me."

Cecilia shook her head. The silence between them grew and her fear grew along with it. In all the chaos, she'd almost forgotten Xander's interrupted confession.

"If he was telling you before me, it's either bad enough that he wanted your support to tell me, or it's something I already know," Evan said.

Cecilia stared up at the starry sky and made a wish that wherever Xander was, he was safe, and that his secret wouldn't get him hurt.

14

CECILIA

After a day and a half of travel, Cecilia was thrilled to finally dismount her horse in the lush, humid air of Heartwood Valley. The spray from the roaring falls caressed her face, carrying the smell of hibiscus and orchids. Tropical plants flourished around the edge of the pool the waterfall dumped into and five women swam in the bright blue water, their pink dresses swirling around them as they floated.

To the right of the falls, three women in pink dresses sat in meditation outside of a white marble temple. To the left, Samson, the god of lust, was shirtless and sprawled on a rock, his bare feet dipping into the water.

He grinned at Cecilia. "Little Goddess! It's so wonderful to see you again."

"Grim's Gates! What are *you* doing here and why aren't you wearing a shirt?" Cecilia scowled at him.

Samson sat up, gesturing to his tanned skin. "I would be naked if that didn't cause such a frenzy. I hate to have tan lines." He winked. "I'm here because Des told me you were coming. We're old friends, as you can imagine. I didn't want to miss you meeting your big sis. Plus, I had some information I thought you might be interested in."

"About Xander?" she asked hopefully.

He tucked his dark hair behind his ears. "Indeed. You'll have to earn it. Godly bargains and all. You know how these things go."

She tipped her head back, preparing to argue, but a beautiful woman stepped out of the water beyond Samson. Her pale pink dress was almost completely translucent from the water and clung to her ample curves. She unpinned her hair, and it fell around her shoulders in raven curls. Her bright blue eyes stood out against her dark skin, which glowed with a radiant golden aura. Her full crimson lips tipped into a smile as her gaze passed over Cecilia's friends. The goddess of love and beauty certainly lived up to her name.

"You keep such handsome company, little sister," Desiree said, her voice a sultry caress.

All four of Cecilia's friends went rigid. The scent of crushed rose petals filled the air as Desiree's magic swirled around the group.

"Stop whatever you're doing. Don't use magic on my friends," Cecilia said, taking a step toward her sister.

Desiree's lower lip popped into an exaggerated pout, but she released them from her spell. She stepped by Cecilia to get a better look at the group. All three men bowed, touching fingers to lips and hearts, and though Sylvie curtseyed, she narrowed her eyes in suspicion.

Cecilia gave her sister's dress a long look. "We can wait for you to change, if you'd like. Wouldn't want you to get cold."

Desiree laughed as she ran her fingers over Cal's chest. "What's your name, darling?"

Cal had never looked so nervous. "Calvin Bennington, Goddess."

"Are you the one my sister is so smitten with?" Desiree asked.

"I think you're thinking of my husband, who you know is currently in Cato's hands," Cecilia said impatiently.

Cal shook his head, struggling to keep his gaze on Desiree's eyes and not the sheer dress clinging to her breasts. Sylvie gave the goddess a long, skeptical look.

Desiree looked from Sylvie to Cal. "No, I see it now. This blonde witch is your charge. There's old love between you two. Something that was once fiery has cooled to something much more platonic but still lovely."

Desiree moved on to Evan. Ever the soldier, Evan kept his gaze straight ahead, unfazed by the goddess's flimsy attire.

"Oh, I like this one. He has an intensity about him and quite a fervent desire for this blonde. How interesting." She ran her fingers over Evan's shoulder. "Tell me about the witch."

Evan said nothing. Desiree met his eyes as the smell of crushed rose petals again filled the air.

Evan's eyes went glassy. "She's smart and honest—"

"Enough! My friends are not your playthings. You have plenty of toys already." Cecilia let her power strike in a quick, precise swipe, seizing temporary hold of Evan's mind to release him from whatever Desiree was doing.

For a moment, Evan looked utterly betrayed. Cecilia gave him her most apologetic smile.

"Testy, little sister," Desiree chided.

Fury swelled in Cecilia's chest. Her siblings were so flippant she was beginning to wonder if their offer to help was purely for their own entertainment. The more they toyed with her, the more desperate she grew to find Xander.

Cecilia stepped between Desiree and Rainer.

"Now I see." Desiree took a long look at Rainer. She pursed her lips as she walked toward him. Cecilia did not move out of her way. "If you want to know what I know, little sister, you'll let me have some harmless fun."

Cecilia gritted her teeth. "This may be a game to the rest of you, but it's not to me."

"If you don't like it, you can leave," Desiree said plainly. "I'll take good care of him. I only want to know what he feels."

Rainer slid his hand to Cecilia's hip, urging her to move aside.

"Relax, tiny goddess, Desiree likes guardians," Samson offered, his lips quirking into a smirk. "Oh, right, that's what you're afraid of."

If looks could kill, Cecilia would have slain him with her glare. Samson chuckled.

The goddess of love moved around Rainer like a shark circling prey. To his credit, Rainer held perfectly still despite the anxiety spiking through their bond.

"Tell me about my sister. You've known her the longest."

Once again, Desiree's magic filled the air.

"She can be willful and stubborn, but only when she believes in something strongly—which is all the time." Rainer smiled. "She's so naturally talented but she's never used her talent as an excuse not to put in the work. Cece can be extremely reckless at the least opportune moments, but only because she can't stand by and let other people get hurt. She can read people's emotions, but she doesn't unless she has to because she respects people's privacy."

Desiree ran her fingers over his shoulder. "It sounds like you have great respect for her."

Rainer nodded. "I do."

"What do you love most about her?"

He resisted, but Desiree sent another wave of magic into him.

"It will come out. May as well surrender to it."

"That no matter how lonely she feels, she spends all of her time making sure that no one else ever feels that way," Rainer said plainly.

Cecilia swallowed hard. She felt exposed and raw. Her resentment for the gods grew. They didn't just want blood and homage. They wanted to play with people for sport and it was getting old quickly.

Desiree brought her hand to Rainer's cheek and looked into his eyes. It took every bit of self-control for Cecilia not to swat the goddess's hand away and throw her into the water. A moment later, Desiree stepped back, smiling at Rainer.

"Relax, have lunch. We should talk, little sister." Desiree waved her hand, and a picnic appeared. Her friends sat down to eat, Desiree's entourage joining them.

Desiree threaded her arm through Cecilia's, guiding her away from the picnic.

"Now, I haven't met your husband, so I'm only seeing half of the picture here, but how are you not with that guardian?"

"I thought you wanted to talk about getting my husband back," Cecilia said, exasperated.

"You are absolutely no fun at all," Desiree whined. "I can't believe we're related."

"*Half*-related."

"The boring half," Desiree said.

Cecilia threw her hands up. "I'm much more fun when I'm not worried that my husband is being tortured."

Desiree's face softened. "He's well enough. I have a spy with Davide's army. Several, actually. Your husband is unharmed and, apparently, as stubborn as you are."

Cecilia almost fell over from relief. "Can your spy get him out?"

Desiree shook her head. "He's staying there to keep you safe. The situation is complex." She opened her mouth to say more, then shook her head and closed it. Sighing, she met Cecilia's gaze. "I'm sure you've figured out some of the puzzle. Tell me what you know."

"Evan suspects Cato wants me and Xander so that he can use us to manipulate each other. Then, he'll kill Davide so that he has dominion over the Argarian monarchy, and then invade Olney so he rules both kingdoms. Is that true?"

Desiree struggled with the words. *Right, she can't answer directly,* Cecilia reminded herself.

"Cato is always several steps ahead. To assume you can see the full scope of his plan would be foolish."

"So that's only part of it," Cecilia sighed. "How do I get Xander back?"

Desiree placed a hand on her shoulder. "You don't. If you're wise, you go nowhere near the trickster. You are outmatched, Cecilia. We have already warned you about that. You cannot go at him head on and you know it."

Cecilia brushed her thumb over her inner wrist, trying to calm her rising panic. "I cannot just sit here and let them have Xander."

"But you can sit here and let him fight his way out. Do you have no faith in your husband? Was he not behind enemy lines most of his life? Trust that he is the man you fell in love with. Someone nearly as tricky as Cato himself. Have some faith."

Cecilia wanted that to be true. "But he would never leave me on my own."

Desiree stopped abruptly. "If you went to him now, you'd only make things worse. I know you're frustrated, but the best thing that you can do is try to come up with a larger plan. Cato is a problem you cannot avoid forever, but if you play into his game, you will lose." The confidence in Desiree's expression evaporated until only pain remained. "Trust me. You do not want to challenge him directly. Especially when you have so much to lose." Desiree looked to Cecilia's friends enjoying their picnic across the water. "You know what I've lost."

Cecilia nodded, recalling Sayla's story about how Cato had killed Desiree's favored lover years before.

"Then believe that I would not lead you astray," Desiree continued. "I understand that pain. It is hard enough to love as an immortal, knowing you will always eventually lose that which you love, but to have it taken so swiftly? That is an unimaginable pain."

Cecilia had worried before that the gods just faked emotion, but Desiree looked genuinely wounded.

"I'm sorry for what he did to you. I'll pay him back."

Desiree smiled. "I am counting on it. My love, Tallulah, deserved much better than she got. She was kind and gracious, and Cato used her as a pawn in his game. I hope he gets exactly what he deserves."

They walked on. The roar of the waterfall grew faint the farther they moved from their friends.

Desiree patted Cecilia's dagger. "Your dagger is not just a Godkiller. It's spelled."

Cecilia pulled the weapon out and held it up to the light, the silver ivy engraving glinting in the sun. "Yes. For a sacrifice I'm unwilling to make." She shuddered to think what more she could lose. She'd already given up so much. How much more could she lose and still be herself?

Desiree placed a hand on her shoulder. "You'll know your moment if you meet it. Now, do you know what my powers are?"

Cecilia was terrified of that entire line of questioning. She cleared her throat. "Just that you can help with broken hearts, see heart bonds, and link people who are meant for each other."

"That's true, but I see the ties that bind people together. All of us gods see truths in different ways and I can read the lines of love between people—the depths of their love for each other, how love inhabits those lucky enough to let it." Desiree sat on a rock at the water's edge and patted the ground next to her, gesturing for Cecilia to sit. "The guardian—"

"Rainer." Cecilia's heart felt like it would beat out of her chest as she sat.

"I've felt soul bonds before. They are different from what I can do for people in terms of finding true heart matches. I've always been mesmerized by such an intuitive bond."

"Why are you telling me this?" Cecilia asked.

"Because you want to let go of him," Desiree said.

Cecilia really didn't, but she didn't know what else to do. She wrung her hands. "Holding on is too hard."

"Holding on is hard. Letting go is hard, too. Who says you have to choose half of your heart? You are a goddess and a princess. Choose both of them. Let them decide. Too much love is not a problem. It's a gift. You should be mindful not to let go of anything that tethers you at a time like this."

Rainer had a way of making Cecilia feel grounded, but lately their interactions had become treacherous, as if at any moment they might fall from a height they couldn't survive.

"I don't know how to do that," Cecilia said.

"This idea that your love can only belong to one person is so small and mortal. You can love however you choose."

Cecilia considered it. It wouldn't be the first time their culture was wrong about such a thing. "Xander's not one to share."

Desiree looked exasperated. "What do you want?"

Cecilia threw her hands up. "How can I know what I want in a world that's never asked me that question?"

"This is your time to figure it out, and fast. What do you want, Cecilia?"

"I want my husband home and both kingdoms safe. I want things to be simple for the first time in months. I want—" Her voice broke, the grief and fear creeping up on her.

Desiree took her hand. "I know everyone else will tell you to guard your heart, to harden it against the viciousness of the world. It is easy to hide, much easier than it is to walk around as we do. People see us as foolish, but what could be more foolish than spending your life hiding yourself away? You get to stay safe, but the best things in life aren't in the shallow water—they're out in the depths."

Cecilia pulled her hand away. "Can you please just tell me how to win against Cato?"

"*I am.* Love is about who you pull close when things are uncertain. Love is the hands you reach for when you're standing in the heart of the storm and can't see the path forward. Love tethers mortal souls here in this realm." Desiree patted her shoulder. "You're blessed with courage. Use it to dig deeper. The world might tell you that showing your heart makes you weak, but you are strong, sister. You look into the abyss of grief and you don't turn away. You look at the rage, the sadness, the ugliness that people fear most and you meet it with compassion. It's not weakness but strength that allows you to stay soft in a world that would try to make you hard. Remember that when Cato looks at you and sees a weakness, he'll exploit it. There is wisdom in hiding your strength until you need it. Pick your moment, Cecilia."

A rush of peace surged in Cecilia's chest. Rainer must have felt her frustration. She brought her hand to her heart.

"He calls you through your bond."

Cecilia nodded.

Desiree smirked. "We should go back. Your friends have had too much of the amorous wine, anyway."

Cecilia's friends lay strewn about. Sylvie and Evan rested side by side on a rock next to the waterfall, their feet dangling into the cool water. They were locked in a staring contest, faces inches apart, as if they could communicate solely through a gaze. Cal lay nearby on a blanket, his head in the lap of one of Desiree's ladies, who ran her fingers through his hair and smiled down at him.

Rainer sat alone on his own blanket, looking sober and ignorant of the chaos around him. His gaze burned into Cecilia.

"What's wrong with them?" Cecilia asked.

Desiree shrugged. "The wine makes them carefree and affectionate. It will wear off in a few hours." Her gaze darted to Samson, who was whispering to someone in the water.

It wasn't until the woman pushed up onto the rocks that Cecilia recognized her.

"Lovely to see you again," Sayla said, leaning her head on Samson's shoulder.

"Little Goddess, did you learn what you needed?" Samson asked.

Though Samson's power didn't affect Cecilia the same way it had when she was mortal, she still felt its seductive press. It swirled in the air around her, smelling of tobacco and vanilla.

"Care to tell me what you know?" she asked.

He pursed his lips. "I need something from you first. Sayla was telling me about your little contest the other day, and I was jealous I didn't get to see you and your guardian together."

Cecilia rolled her eyes. "I'm not here for your pleasure."

"Nonsense. Everyone is here for my pleasure," Samson said. "Just one good kiss."

Just one kiss. No big deal. Just one kiss that feels like coming home after being away my whole life. Just give this man another piece of my heart, as if he doesn't own way too much of it already.

She turned to Rainer. "You haven't had any of the wine?"

"No. I thought one of us should keep our heads," Rainer said. "I don't mind, Cece."

Samson laughed. "I bet you don't."

Rainer shot him a dirty look. Desiree sat next to Samson and Sayla to watch their game play out.

Cecilia gritted her teeth. *We do whatever it takes to get back to each other.* She could see Xander in her mind and hear the urgency in his voice when he'd said those words.

Rainer guided her into his lap. Cecilia placed her hands on his chest. His heart beat wildly beneath her palms as he ran his fingers through her hair. He leaned closer.

"Wait!" Samson's command made them both jump.

"Now what?" Cecilia huffed.

"I'd like you to just look into each other's eyes."

She shot the god of lust a scathing look. "Why?"

"Humor me—just for a moment." Samson's eyes glowed golden as he watched the two of them.

Cecilia turned back to Rainer. Her hands gripped his tunic like claws. She couldn't decide if she wanted to shove him away or pull him close. Focusing on things she didn't normally see so closely—the freckle under his left eye and the light creases in his skin from smiling—Cecilia settled. Rainer's eyes were a kaleidoscope of greens, some as bright as early spring grass, others dark emerald, and in between, a few flecks of gold, like warm honey. She didn't know if they had always been so beautiful or if her improved senses allowed her to see that which she hadn't before.

She brushed her fingers over his stubble. The love in his eyes burned her with its intensity, made her sick with guilt and fear. She looked away.

Rainer brought his hands to frame her face, guiding her gaze back to his. She looked into the eyes she loved so much, wondering if he could feel her at war with herself through their bond. Tears blurred her vision.

"Cece." His gaze was so tender that she wanted to shrink away from it. "We don't have to," he whispered softly, his fingers tracing down her cheek. She leaned into the touch. He pressed closer, his lips a breath away. "Tell me to stop, Cece."

"No," she murmured as his lips gently brushed hers.

Once again, Rainer's tenderness was her undoing. One hand threaded through her hair, holding her lips to his, and the other pressed into her lower back. Every touch was as reverent as a whispered prayer, his hands leaving a light tingling in their wake. She felt like she was falling, seemingly endlessly, as his teeth grazed her lip and a wave of shivers spread through her body.

Cecilia wrapped an arm around his neck, drawing herself closer until their hips were practically fused together, her chest pressed firmly against his.

She knew he couldn't read her mind, but she felt the words so deeply she thought he might understand. *Don't let me go. Don't stop touching me. Don't ever leave me.*

The kiss unraveled her. Everything tangled in her chest by grief and loss and fear unwound at once. She feared the moment he pulled away, everything would bind back up in a hopeless knot inside her.

She waged a silent battle in her head. Her deep longing for her husband warred with the history, memory, and ever-present love of Rainer. Logic warred with her heart. Her magical bond with Rainer warred with her hard-fought bond with Xander. Guilt was the only clear winner.

Cecilia didn't understand how something could feel like not enough and way too much at the same time. One moment she was yanking Rainer closer, digging her nails into his back; the next, balancing her palms lightly on his shoulders, afraid she might faint from the dizzy, soaring ecstasy in her body. She would have chased that feeling to the ends of the earth.

She shouldn't have been kissing anyone but her husband, but if the gods were going to move her around like a pawn in their chess game, she might as well savor the last chance she had to kiss the man she'd wanted half her life.

Tears streamed down her cheeks, but she clung to him.

Not yet, she silently begged. *If this is the last time I kiss you, don't let it be over yet.*

Rainer groaned into her mouth as if he'd been holding back, waiting for permission to let his true hunger show. He tugged her hair, tilting her head back, and his teeth and lips grazed down her neck. He was unhurried, working his way up the other side of her neck before his lips melted into hers again, softer and more tender.

Finally, he pulled away.

He leaned his forehead against hers, lips still faintly brushing hers as they both tried to catch their breath.

"Don't ever do that again," she whispered.

She hoped he knew what she meant. *Don't ever do that again, because I won't be able to stop. If you do that again, I will never want it to end. If you do that again, I will be completely lost to reason.*

"I suppose that's good enough for me to share what I know. When you two finally come together, I expect the stars will fall. Let me know if you want an audience," Samson said, clapping.

Cecilia would have rolled her eyes if she could tear her gaze away from Rainer's. If she wasn't absolutely wrecked from the kiss. If she didn't feel the absence of his lips like an ache in her bones. Rainer held her face in his hands. Everywhere their skin touched was warm and buzzing.

When Xander was there, it was easy to pretend that what existed between her and Rainer was history, but the moment he touched her, it was as if no time had passed, no ground had been made up. She slid right back into the place she'd always existed.

I am not in love with Rainer. She tried to convince herself, but the pang in her heart at the thought of that being their last kiss suggested otherwise. She tried to pull back and look somewhere else, anywhere else, but she couldn't.

Rainer was just as focused on her, his gaze like a caress. There was so much love and worship in his eyes, but that only hurt worse. He was in love with an echo of who she'd been and it felt like he was looking through her.

Samson cleared his throat, startling them. "I have two things you might find interesting, Cece. The trickster likes to keep his power shrouded in mystery, some of which you've already seen. He can teleport himself and others and can disguise himself or others. Pay attention to what you feel, not just what you see. But there's something else about his power. He's a gardener but not a creator. Do you understand what I'm saying?"

Cecilia thought about it for a moment. She was only starting to grasp the way the gods communicated in riddles, and it was exhausting.

"He can't create. He can only work with that which exists," Rainer said.

Samson was silent, which was as good as confirmation. Cecilia let out a sigh of relief. Cato couldn't just invent something to drive Xander crazy.

"What's the other thing?" she asked.

"Tomorrow, if you head home via the New Road and stop just before noon in the hills north of Summerton, you'll come across someone else who knows more than I do."

"Someone?" Cecilia asked skeptically.

"Someone who owes a painful debt to you," Samson said meaningfully.

"Davide."

Samson said nothing again, but that was all the confirmation she needed. She would find her brother-in-law, the king of Argaria, and she would pay him back for breaking her hand, just as soon as he helped her get Xander back.

15

RAINER

Rainer struggled to focus on the problems laid out in front of them the entire ride to Summerton. His eyes lingered on Cecilia. When they stopped for the night in the hills just north of Summerton, along the New Road, his heart raced as if he'd just kissed her. She would barely look at him. Kissing her twice in three days tore apart the restraint he'd worked so hard to maintain over the past few months.

Banishing the wanting was a constant, tiring action, like keeping a muscle flexed at all times. But the brush of her lips had released that muscle and now desire poured over him.

He could still hear her sigh against his skin, still taste the lemon-sugar sweetness of her mouth, still feel her fingers weaving through his hair. Her touch woke up everything in his body that he hadn't even realized was sleeping. A thrumming pulse beat through him as soon as her skin brushed his, as if every cell in his body knew exactly who she was. *Mine.* Not a claim of ownership so much as a recognition of mutual belonging. *Mine.* He wanted to take her away from everything that hurt her and never let her leave his arms.

Before, he'd been able to convince himself that impulse was all about protecting Cecilia because she was his charge. That was why he scared off suitors before Xander. That was why he slept beside her every night. That was why his eyes were always on her, even when they were safe in Olney. He'd become a master at lying to himself.

With her kiss still lingering on his lips, an understanding settled into Rainer's bones. The familiarity between them wasn't that they were two mirrored halves of a whole as they'd read about in fairy tales. Instead, it felt like their souls were born of the same star, breathed into life by the same wish. Cecilia ignited some fierce desire for more that lived in him, and Rainer grounded the wild, aimless parts of her.

He fumbled through his satchel, trying to act like everything was normal, though he was certain his desperation was written all over his face.

After dinner, Evan and Cal took the first watch while Sylvie settled in to sleep close to them. Twenty feet away, Rainer lay down next to Cecilia. Every accidental brush of her skin was dry kindling in a lightning storm.

The memory of their kiss echoed through every silence. Cecilia orbited Rainer with calculated cautiousness. The unspent desire between them flickered like a flame that needed no tending to burst into a bonfire.

She settled in to sleep a few feet from him, but Rainer was too restless. He moved closer. Her eyes were incandescent in the moonlight. Though there was no sign of it on her face, he felt her fatigue through their connection.

"Go to sleep, Cece. I'll wake you when you need to worry," he whispered.

Her face softened, but still she didn't close her eyes.

Rainer wanted to say something, but what else was there to say?

I love you. I need you. It kills me that I can't have you. How did we get here—a place where I'm so desperate to touch you that I have to keep clenching my fists to stop myself from doing it? There's nothing I fear as much as losing you, and every inch you pull away sends me into a spiral of panic. I dream of you every night and wake up reaching for you every morning. I was the worst kind of fool to not let myself have the only thing I ever wanted. I want to spend every night for the rest of my life watching the stars blur while holding your hand. You are beautiful and infuriating, and I love you with my whole heart.

He'd spent so long keeping all his feelings inside, now they seemed too large to get out.

Cecilia's eyebrows shot up as she read the swirl of emotions he did nothing to suppress. He stopped thinking and brought her hand to his lips, kissing her crescent scar.

She held stark still. He brushed his cheek over the skin inside her wrist and she sighed. Rainer tried to rein in his desire, but it was a wild, feral thing. There would be no controlling it once it was loose.

He pushed the sleeve of her tunic up, his breath dancing over her skin, and goosebumps rose inside her forearm. He brushed his lips back up to her wrist and she let out a soft, strangled sound he could hardly hear over his thundering heartbeat. Cecilia's eyes fluttered closed, her head tipped back, and her chest rose and fell more rapidly. The lightest touch seemed to have equal effect on both of them. When he met her eyes again, he knew the question in them without her speaking.

What do you think you are doing?

The same question screamed through his own mind. He kissed her palm.

"Rain," she rasped.

Rainer desperately wanted to kiss her, but he couldn't. Before, when it was a request of other gods, was one thing, but out in the wild, there was no excuse. It was wrong to want someone else's wife, but impossible not to. The wanting was woven into his soul. There was no way to tear it out without ripping himself to shreds.

His name on her lips nearly broke his last thread of restraint. He leaned closer, so his lips brushed her ear as he spoke. "I love you so much."

Cecilia gasped.

"You're so beautiful that I couldn't stop staring at you all day." His breath danced over the pulse point in her neck. "Could you feel my eyes on you?"

"Yes." Her hands fisted as his nose grazed up and down the column of her neck.

"I can't stand not touching you. You have no idea what you do to me, Cecilia."

She arched into him again, her body tight as a bowstring, her fists pressed against his chest. Her breath came in quick gasps.

"I'd like to spend the rest of my life with my lips on yours," he whispered. The desire to kiss her was a life force of its own. He leaned closer but her hands braced against his chest.

"I can't," she murmured.

Rainer backed away, instantly missing her warmth. Frustration burst through their connection, its intensity unmistakably Cecilia. He loved those extremes so much. He rolled aside and propped himself up on an elbow beside her.

"I'm sorry." He looked away, his passion spoiled by shame.

She shook her head. "I won't make you something I regret."

Rainer only ever regretted not having more of her. He regretted realizing he loved her too late. He regretted acting too late.

"Go to sleep, Cece."

"Will you tell me a story?"

"What kind of story?" Rainer asked.

"Nothing romantic," she said dryly.

Rainer launched into a story about an artist who lost her ability to paint when her heart was broken. Finally, Cecilia's breathing settled into a soft rhythm.

He stared up at the blanket of stars and made the same wish he'd made months ago when they watched the Summer Firestorm meteor shower together. The same wish he'd never share with her unless it came true.

Rainer felt it now the way he had that night under the stars—the wonderful, all-consuming terror of loving someone so completely.

Cecilia slipped away from him a little more daily, but he held out hope that his wish could still come true.

———

Rainer couldn't believe the ease with which Cecilia wielded the power that she'd been afraid of just days before. She was determined to get Xander back by whatever means necessary, and that single-minded focus made Rainer very nervous.

It turned out to be much easier than they'd expected to ambush Davide. Even though he was the king of Argaria traveling in enemy territory, he only had twenty hunters with him to keep his travel party small and agile. Evan had Sylvie grow the forest into the trail, creating a bottleneck in the road so he, Cal, and Rainer could easily subdue Davide's contingent of guards.

Cecilia moved efficiently through the enemy ranks, the air thick with the lavender and lemon scent of her magic. She planted a false memory in Davide's hunters so they'd think the king had been thrown from his horse and they had to stop and rest earlier than expected.

She looked so self-satisfied as she put each of the hunters to sleep, erasing the memory of their presence on the road.

King Davide Savero spat blood into the dirt, wiping his mouth with the back of his hand. "Well played, *Princess*," he said, giving Cecilia a taunting wink.

Rainer held Davide in place as Cecilia made her way back to him with a viciousness in her eyes that made Rainer take a step back.

"I should have known you would find a way, dear sister. You owe me," Davide said.

"Guess you shouldn't have wandered without your benefactor," Cecilia retorted.

Davide shrugged. "I normally prefer his mode of transport, but he has his hands full with my brother at the moment."

"Is he—" Cecilia cut herself off, schooling her face into calm apathy, but her worry slid through the bond in Rainer's chest.

Rainer had seen Davide from a distance during his imprisonment back in Argaria, but seeing him up close for the first time was star-tling. Though he was slightly taller and slimmer than Xander, they looked remarkably alike—only where Xander's eyes held humor and flirtation when he looked at Cecilia, Davide's held murder.

Davide grinned at her. "Will you take your price in blood like the vicious goddess I know you are?"

Cecilia's eyes narrowed. "You could just cooperate and I won't have to."

"How does it work?" Davide asked.

His whole body went rigid as Cecilia pushed into his mind. The air grew thick with her magic. Just as quickly as she dipped in, she released him and his shoulders went slack. Davide groaned.

"That's how it works. I'm getting better at it." She smirked.

Rainer hardly recognized the cold look on Cecilia's face. It wasn't clear how much of it was an act to intimidate Davide and how much of it was really her. He pushed on their bond, but she kept the door between them closed.

Davide frowned. "What do you want?"

"Go back to wherever Cato is keeping Xander and release him."

"Why would I do that?" Davide asked.

"Because you're not as foolish as your pride has made you," Cecilia said. "If Cato gets ahold of me, he doesn't need you anymore. He will have married heirs to the kingdom and we're much easier to control since we love each other. Cato's agenda and your own may not always line up. I can't imagine he'd prefer someone so volatile over Xander."

The truth of Cecilia's words landed, and Davide's eyes narrowed on his sister-in-law. "You're smarter than I gave you credit for—or perhaps Evan is. Makes sense. One doesn't go from being a common whore to a princess without a talent for manipulation."

Cecilia nodded at Evan—a signal neither of them had let Rainer in on. Evan forced Davide's hand flat against a boulder as Cecilia pulled out her dagger. Davide struggled against Evan, but Cecilia quickly took hold of his mind again.

"Stay," she said, her eyes glowing with power.

Davide stopped struggling immediately and held his hand still. Rainer watched in horror as Cecilia brought the butt of the blade down on his hand. The king grunted as the bone snapped. Still, he kept his hand in place.

Rainer took a step toward her, panic twisting his stomach in knots. "Cece?"

She ignored him.

"One down, many more to go," Cecilia said. "You could save us time and yourself pain if you just agree to help."

Davide said nothing. Cecilia brought the blade down again, breaking another bone. They went back and forth like that until most of the bones in Davide's left hand were broken.

Rainer was horrified. It was impossible to tell if he was more disturbed by Cecilia's coldness or the fact that her circumstances had forced her to confront a side of herself that even he'd never seen before.

He hadn't believed her when she said the goddess was really just a part of her—that she was sharper and colder now—that he was clinging to a memory of her. Rainer's thoughts careened in different directions. His heart beat faster, his breath shallow with panic. He had spent a lifetime protecting Cecilia from herself but he didn't know how to protect her from this.

Davide stared at Cecilia, air hissing through his teeth. Sweat dripped into his eyes and his body hunched around the pain. "*Princess*, even if I wanted to tell you everything, you must know I'm under Cato's influence as well." His face softened.

Without the mask of a sneer, his resemblance to Xander was uncanny. Cecilia must have seen it too. She took a startled step back. Rainer rested a hand against her back, but she shrunk away from him. The movement triggered a creeping panic that wound tight around Rainer's throat.

She circled Davide. "What can you not do?"

Davide winced as if fighting through the chaos in his mind. He gritted his teeth. "I can't help *you*."

Cecilia studied him. "But you could help Xander."

Davide nodded. "I could help my brother."

"Is he okay?"

"As okay as I am," Davide said, a flash of grief and pain in his eyes.

Cecilia's hand came to her heart and she flooded their bond with fear and grief.

"You really love him." Davide sounded surprised.

"Of course I really love him," she snapped. "Why else would Cato think he could use him to control me?"

"He's lucky to have you," Davide said, his voice holding a softer edge. "He never wanted that, you know. Love. Not good for spare princes who need to make political marriages. I don't think anyone was more surprised than Xander that he fell in love with you. He tried not to tell Cato anything about you. He really fought for you, but he failed. We all do. Cato breaks everyone eventually. Even Xany."

Cecilia and Evan both flinched at the nickname. Cecilia's anxiety surged through their bond. Rainer wanted to reach out to her, but he kept his hands at his sides.

"I could make you help," she said.

Davide nodded. "I can't just *tell you* what would be best."

It was as good as confirmation. They needed to read between his words. He couldn't help them, but he could say what wouldn't help.

"I could make you release your brother. It would be in your own self-interest. It would help *you*." Cecilia selected the words carefully.

Evan's eyes brightened. He nodded in approval at her wording. Rainer was never as good at strategy as Cecilia. Since he'd always had size, strength, and skill advantages, he never paid as much attention to it as he should have. Being so petite meant she had to be incredibly strategic in all of her fights. He had a new appreciation for her and Evan as they played a mental chess match with Davide.

"It would help me. It would ensure my survival. That's something I could do," Davide said.

"How long would it take?" Evan asked. "That's just information. It's neutral. Not helpful or unhelpful."

Davide considered the words and then nodded. "A day to get back, a day to find a good time to release him, and then a day or so for him to escape to Olney City. It would be best if this was my idea."

Cecilia's eyes lit up and she nodded. "None of you will remember anything other than the king taking a spill from his horse that shattered his hand. I'll heal a few bones to make it less obvious and you'll return to Cato, thinking it was your idea. If you have the rest healed when you get back, you should have no permanent damage."

She took Davide's hand in her own and held his gaze. He flinched as she settled into his mind. After a few quiet moments, Davide laid down and went to sleep just as all of his hunters had. Cecilia partially healed his hand before rising to her feet. Evan and Cal made it look as though the entourage just stopped for the night by lighting fires and stowing horses and gear.

"Are you sure this will work?" Evan asked.

"I removed his memory of the five of us and implanted a memory of the horse getting spooked and throwing Davide and shattering his hand," Cecilia said. "That made them stop for the night earlier than expected, which will explain their delay in returning. Then I pushed in thoughts of releasing Xander as the only way to ensure Davide's survival."

She rubbed her arms and shook out her hands.

"Are you cold?" Rainer asked.

She shook her head, not meeting his eye as she walked to her horse. "Just not used to the magic yet. It always leaves me feeling a bit strange."

He reached for her but she mounted her horse and took off at a gallop toward Olney.

Rainer rode behind her. He wanted to talk to her—to feel something from her—but she'd kept him locked out of their connection the whole ride home.

Several agonizing hours later, after arriving home and bathing, he was finally alone in the cottage with her and she couldn't avoid him anymore.

She sat on the couch combing out her hair, still wet from her bath. "You can just say it. I already saw it on your face. You're afraid of me."

Rainer sat down beside her. "I'm not afraid of you. I'm afraid *for* you—of what this war will turn you into. I'm afraid of what you will need to become to survive this and it's a thing I can't protect you from. That is what I hate."

Cecilia brushed her thumb over her inner wrist. "You judge what I did."

"I don't."

"Say it all you want. You wear your judgment like a second skin. I'm not the only expressive one among us."

Rainer sighed. "Don't put that on me. I just told you how I felt."

"Just admit it! You judged me for hurting him and not feeling bad about it!"

"You judge yourself!" Rainer shook his head.

"Only because of the look on your face."

"Fine! The Cece I know, my best friend, would never get joy out of hurting someone. But I saw you enjoy hurting Davide. Even if he deserved it. Even if you were just paying him back. I hate to see this war change you."

"Who can remain unchanged by war?" Cecilia crossed her arms.

They both knew the answer.

He could. Rainer hadn't changed.

Her sadness broke through the anger in their connection. "This is hard enough without your judgment," she rasped, teary-eyed.

Rainer wished he could take back the words. He didn't mean them. Everything he felt was grounded in disappointment in himself for not being able to save her from needing to be so cruel and his frustration that he couldn't allow her to be what she needed to be. He hated that he made her feel anything other than loved.

It was unfair to expect that she could go through so much and stay the same sweet woman she'd always been.

Cecilia's hand fluttered over her heart, and she looked like she might cave in. "I might have to become someone you don't like, and that breaks my heart. Of all the things I've been through, that judgment is the one thing that makes me uncertain that I can do what I have to. You don't know what this is like. You were always the person that understood me the best. Until Xander. He looks at me and he sees me. He doesn't judge me like you are right now. That's why I fell in love with him. I'm not just some idiotic schoolgirl with a crush on a handsome prince. He's the first person who ever looked at me and saw *me*—all of me—and didn't judge. He doesn't love me in spite of my flaws. He loves me for all that I am."

"Cece—"

"You fell in love with a girl who's gone. So just stop. Don't look at me like you love me. This *is* me, and I know from the look on your face that this version of me is someone you couldn't ever love."

The words were a punch in the gut. Rainer felt sick.

He took her hand in his. "Of course I want this version of you. I want all of you. All the time. The only reason I haven't seen that side of you is that you haven't *let* me until now. Please don't mistake surprise for judgment."

She yanked her hand back. "How do you know you even want me? Maybe you're holding on to this so tight because you don't know what else to want. If you let go of me you'll have to define yourself, apart from me."

The words burned. She always cut right to the core of him.

Is that what I'm doing? She told Rainer she was happy. She told him why she loved Xander so much. It made sense. Maybe she was right, and he was clinging to her to keep himself from floating free—from having to figure it out alone.

"It's just magic that binds us together. Magic and nostalgia," Cecilia said, but he could see on her face that she didn't completely believe it.

No one in his entire life made Rainer more impatient than Cecilia. He was desperate for her. His entire life was about self-control and discipline, but he had so little left.

She'd felt what he did when he kissed her. Consumed. Lost and found in the same moment. Rainer knew she had or she would have never told him not to do it again.

He got too close. Now Cecilia was trying to run away. He'd let her do it before, but he wouldn't let her do it again. He said he'd fight for her and he wasn't about to give up now.

16

CECILIA

Three agonizing days dripped by as Cecilia waited for Xander to return. She'd driven Aunt Clara mad with her pacing and she'd driven herself crazy poring over any book in the royal library that mentioned Cato.

She should have had fingertips riddled with paper cuts and dark circles under her eyes, but her unnatural healing meant she looked entirely unaffected by her crushing worry.

Now she had nothing to show for all her research except a not-so-subtle summons to a stupid ball to raise funds for the Olney war effort. King Hector Teripin had cornered her in the library, and despite Cecilia's best attempts at getting out of it, she ended up greeting guests beside the royal family.

Lively music kicked up again, making her jump. The frantic playing of the musicians was in direct contrast to how exhausted Cecilia felt.

She looked around the tent, remembering the day months ago when she'd walked into the same tent for the Godsball, where she'd first met her husband. Tonight she wore a spectacular scarlet silk gown on the off chance that Xander made his way back in time to see it. Though she'd grown more accustomed to elaborate gowns that showed more skin, she still felt a little like she was wearing armor that made her a more confident version of herself.

The fashions of the ladies of Olney Court were a strange mixture of look but don't touch. Show but don't share. Dresses showed a scandalous amount of skin but dances were always proper and distant, and all affection was a performance of lips pressed to hands and formal curtseys. What a precarious line women were expected to walk.

The more time that passed since her encounter with Davide and his men, the more she doubted her abilities and the memories she had planted. Creating false memory was challenging. It required a great eye for detail—capturing the right lighting, realistic facial expressions, detailed vocal dialects. Despite years of imagining bedtime stories, Cecilia was worried her imagination or her new magical skill had fallen short.

After an hour of greeting gawking guests, Cecilia was finally free to roam the party. She ignored King Hector's encouragement to talk up the war effort to the noblemen, instead wandering the periphery of the party, trying not to call any attention to herself.

Evan entered the tent. Cecilia caught his eye, but he shook his head. No news on Xander. She tried to ignore the ache in her chest.

"Nice tiara," Evan said, sidling up next to her. "Xander would get a kick out of seeing you in it. Then he'd probably say something really loudly in front of everyone about wanting to see you in that and nothing else."

Cecilia laughed even though she wanted to cry. A swell of love for her husband bloomed in her chest.

"Just be patient," Evan said. "He might have been farther away than we expected. It might take him longer to get back." He nodded to their friends on the other side of the tent. "I'm going to go update Cal and Sylvie. Are you staying here for a bit?"

"I'm not sure," she said.

"Where's Rainer?"

Cecilia shrugged. "After the whole thing with Davide, he's giving me some space, but he's here somewhere."

The corner of Evan's mouth kicked up. "I know. Just wanted to let you know that you did what you had to do. War is messy business and I know how badly you want to get Xander back."

Cecilia was desperate to know Xander was safe. She wanted to throw herself into his arms and tell him how much she loved him, yell at him for saving her instead of himself, kiss him until he felt how grateful she was for it all the same. Most of all, she was eager to look into his eyes and be loved and understood in the way that only someone so similar to her could.

"I'm probably going to sneak out and go to bed soon. I just need to be alone."

Evan looked like he wanted to say more but thought better of it. He nodded and disappeared into the crowd.

Cecilia wandered closer to the entrance of the tent, hoping for a clear exit strategy.

"Excuse me, Your Highness?" The small voice came from behind her.

She spun to find a dapper little boy with neatly combed hair.

"Well, hello!" she said.

"A man asked me to give this to you," the little boy said, smiling shyly as he handed her a rose from the queen's garden.

She stared at the flower in the boy's shaky, outstretched hand before taking it.

"He also said to give you this." He handed her a piece of paper folded like a bird.

"*Find me,*" it read.

"What did the man look like?" Cecilia asked.

Her mind was a whirlwind of thoughts: hope for her husband's safe return and fear this was another of Cato's cruel games.

"He was tall, and he had dark hair and a sword, and he said he was a real prince. I've never met a prince before, or a princess," the boy said, his eyes wide.

Cecilia ran from the party, trying to tamp down the hope swelling in her chest as she raced through the queen's garden. She expected to find Xander on the bench where they first spoke, but he wasn't there. She sat down to wait.

Cecilia couldn't stop fidgeting as she stared into the roses. The autumn evening held a chill that hinted winter was close. Cecilia shivered. The night was too cool for the dress she wore, but a vain part of her wanted to make a statement in case she found Xander. A strange sense of déjà vu settled into her bones.

She idly rubbed the inside of her left wrist with her thumb, wondering if she should have told the others she was running off. Thinking better of it, she decided it was best they keep their distance until she was sure that Xander was really himself and not Cato in disguise.

"Bad night?"

She whipped her head around, eyes wide.

Xander stood behind her. She hadn't even felt a shift in the air with his presence. She stared at him as the memory of the first night he spoke to her came back, her vision of it clear as the night it happened. A colorful bruise blossomed along the left side of his jaw, nearly blending into his stubble, and his hair was damp, as if he'd just bathed. She had to keep herself from running to him.

Xander took a step forward, and she flinched. There was a manic look in his eyes. He was himself, but also not.

He frowned. "Are you afraid of me?"

Cecilia shook her head. "I like to think of it as more of a healthy skepticism. I just want to be sure that you're really you."

With Samson's warning about how Cato could disguise himself fresh in her mind, she looked Xander over as if she'd be able to see the seams of Cato's magic.

"Read me, love. I promise it's really me." Xander took another step closer and his eyes softened.

She tuned into his energy and could feel anxiety, higher than he usually felt, as well as relief and the sharp edge of desire. He certainly *felt* like Xander.

"How did you get away?" she asked.

Xander sighed. "That's what you want to ask me?"

Cecilia shook her head. "No. I want to ask what you were thinking, making Rainer save me instead of you. I want to slap you for doing that. I want to ask if you've been hurt or tortured. I want to ask so many things—" Her voice broke. "But I *need* to ask how you got away."

"You wore your hair down," he said, finally smiling. "You rob me of breath in that dress."

It took every ounce of restraint not to take a step toward him when all she wanted to do was throw her arms around him and bury her face in his chest.

His gaze landed on her head. "I like the tiara. It suits you, although I think I'd prefer to see you in *only* the tiara."

She laughed. "That's exactly what Evan thought you would say."

He smiled and her cheeks heated under his gaze. He was so close she could smell his bergamot and cedar scent all around her.

"How did you get away?" she asked.

He reached out and played with one of her curls, running it between his callused fingers.

"Davide let me out. He must have figured out that Cato having me meant he wouldn't need Davide to run Argaria. Self-preservation has always been one of his most enduring qualities."

Cecilia cupped his face in her hands. "Are you all right? Did he hurt you?"

"Nothing I couldn't take."

Xander tried to sound casual, but the flicker of fear in his eyes broke Cecilia's heart. He took her hand in his before pulling back, leaving another paper bird in her palm. She turned the bird over in her hand. Scrawled in his perfect handwriting on the side were the words "*Beautiful Cece, you were worth it.*"

The words unraveled her.

"Can I kiss you now?"

Xander looked at her with an intensity that sent a flood of heat through her body. She nodded and he kissed her hard, pressing her tight against his body. Cecilia's legs went out from under her. He sat on the bench and pulled her onto his lap, continuing to kiss her with reckless abandon. She didn't realize she was crying until he pulled away to kiss her tears.

"All's well, love. I'm all right." He wrapped her up as if his arms could block out haunting thoughts for both of them.

"I was so worried," Cecilia whispered. "How can you be so calm?"

"Because I'm always calm."

"You didn't look so calm when Cato tried to take me," she said.

A shadow passed over his face. "That's true. I heard the fear in your voice and I saw you trying to fight your way out, and I admit, I lost my temper a bit."

"A bit?"

"More than a bit. I would have cut through half the Argarian army to get to you, but it still wasn't enough. I'm sorry I gave you a scare. It won't happen again," he said, pulling her back into a long, slow kiss. He drew up the hem of her dress, rough hands sliding up the soft skin of her thighs.

"Xander, I have to tell you something. And we're in public," she chided.

He kissed down the column of her neck, continuing to let his hands wander under her dress until one reached the apex of her thighs.

"That never bothered you before. No one is around. It's dark. I've dreamed about taking you right here since the first night out here in the garden. I need you. Gods, you don't know how much I need you." His voice broke, and he leaned his forehead against hers. He brushed his fingers over her. "Did you miss this, Cece?"

"Yes." She moaned as he increased the pressure and pace of his fingers against her.

"Did Rainer keep you warm while I was gone?"

Cecilia froze, a gasp stuck in her throat. "What?"

"Did you kiss him?" Xander asked, his face unreadable.

She hesitated. "That's what I was going to tell you. I only did it to get information out of my sisters."

Xander arched an eyebrow. "What does that have to do with kissing Rainer?"

"Gods, if I know. They asked me to do it, and I wanted to be like you and do whatever it took to get you back. We said we would both do whatever it took. Remember? The goddesses had information, so I did what I had to. It didn't mean anything."

"It always means something with you two," he said, rolling his eyes. "I'd prefer you kiss any other man or woman in the kingdom."

Cecilia took his face between her hands. "I only did it to get you back. I lost an archery contest to Sayla, and that was the price I had to pay, and then Samson made me do an exchange for the information of where to find Davide. It was worth it because he did exactly what we'd hoped he would do. You're here now. You had to have known it was me from the state of Davide's hand."

Xander smirked a bit. "It turns me on when you're that vicious."

"He's your brother."

Xander shrugged. "He deserved it. Did you like it?"

"Breaking Davide's hand? I know I shouldn't have, but yes."

Xander frowned. "No, did you like having an excuse to kiss Rainer?"

Cecilia squirmed in his lap. "I only wanted to get you back."

"That's not what I asked."

"Yes, I liked it. He's a good kisser."

"Better than me?"

She sighed heavily. "Is it a competition?"

"Everything is a competition."

"No, he's not better than you." *It's impossible to compare.* "I'm sorry. I shouldn't have, but I was desperate."

"You can make it up to me right now," he said.

Xander kissed her again, like he was trying to see how much of her he still had dominion over. The hand between her legs continued to rub against her as she whimpered. He brushed her panties aside, slid a finger inside her, and groaned in approval. "Always so eager for me. Want more?"

Cecilia nodded and he took her down to the ground, her tiara tumbling into the grass. She fumbled with the buttons of his pants, looking around wildly.

"Relax, love," he whispered. "I'll hear if anyone gets close enough to see their precious goddess on her back in the dirt."

Cecilia relaxed in his arms as he slid inside of her, right there in the queen's garden, where they'd first talked months before. He thrust into her, the soft, cool grass at her back in sharp contrast to the hard heat of his body flush against her front. He watched her intently, as if studying her reaction to every move he made. Cecilia bit her lip to keep from crying out, afraid to draw attention.

"Is my princess afraid that everyone will find out how badly she needs to be fucked?" Xander whispered in her ear.

She moaned louder as his teeth nipped at her neck.

"I can already feel your pussy fluttering around me. Do you want to let all those fancy courtiers know how perfect you sound when you come for me?"

"Xander," she groaned. The dirty words made her feel incandescent with lust. He knew she liked it, but he'd never been so vulgar.

"What would people who praise their sweet little goddess think if they knew how you prefer to be worshipped—hard and fast and dirty in the queen's garden?"

Cecilia clung to him as the tension built in her. Lightning simmered through her body, waiting to strike. He picked up the pace, and she struggled to keep quiet.

"Say that you're mine, Cece. Say that you belong to me and I will give you what you need." He slowed his thrusts to a gentle rocking as she whimpered. "Say it."

"I'm yours," she said, frantically reaching for his hips, trying to get him to move faster.

He continued to tease her. "You belong to me, love. Don't forget that."

With that, he moved hard and fast, his hips claiming along with his mouth. All the tension, fear, and confusion of the past few days came down on her at once. Her release crashed over her so fast, she couldn't help but scream as his hips churned against her, prolonging the climax.

He pulled out suddenly, and she whimpered as he shoved her dress higher, spreading her legs obscenely and burying his face between her thighs. Cecilia dug her fingernails into his forearms as he pinned her hips to the ground to stop her from squirming. Xander devoured her like she was his last meal, and right when she was on the brink, he pulled away.

Her pathetic whine split the silence.

"So needy." Xander prowled back up her body, nipping at her ear as he pushed inside her and whispered, "You taste like you belong to me."

Her head fell back as she groaned. Jealousy made Xander feral and Cecilia would have felt guilty if his way of managing that envy hadn't made her so mindless with desire.

"Maybe next time I'll fuck you in front of the entire court, so there's no mistaking who makes you feel so good," Xander said.

Tension coiled in Cecilia's body, her thighs shaking as another swell of pleasure crested.

Xander chuckled into her neck. "Seems you like that idea. Too bad I'm so set on being the only one who gets to see how perfect you look wrapped around my cock."

He swallowed her scream with a kiss as she fell apart. Xander finished with a grunt, the determined set of his brow softening as he brushed the hair out of her face.

Every muscle in her body went limp. Cecilia hadn't realized how tense she was until that moment. She was so spent that she wasn't even certain she'd be able to walk home.

Finally, he pulled back, buttoning his pants and pulling her dress into place as he helped her to her feet. He swiped her tiara from the dirt and placed it on her head.

She'd expected that his energy would feel more settled but he still seemed restless and angry. "Are you well, love?"

Xander frowned. "Did you not enjoy yourself?"

Cecilia's legs were still shaky as she slid her arm through his. "You know I did, but you were a bit more intense than usual."

He cupped her cheek. "Did I hurt you?"

She shook her head. "You just don't seem yourself. Did Cato do something—"

"I don't want to talk about that now," Xander snapped.

She winced and took a step away from him.

Xander rubbed a hand over his face and reached for her. "It wasn't pleasant but it's over now and all I want is to take you home so you can make me forget."

Guilt bloomed like weeds in Cecilia's heart. She'd taken too long to break him free from Cato and it was clear with the anger and fear swirling around him that the damage had been done. "Of course. Whatever you need."

The cold breeze ruffled her dress as they walked back to the cottage. Something was clearly off, but forcing both of them to relive whatever horrors Cato had inflicted on Xander wouldn't make either of them feel better.

All she wanted was to take away his pain the way he'd been doing for her the past few weeks.

Inside the cottage, she lit candles with her fire magic. Moonlight slashed across the bed, still crumpled from her restless sleep the night before.

Xander sat down on the edge of the mattress and blew out a heavy sigh.

Cecilia paced around the kitchen. "Can I get you tea? Or I have some leftover lemon cakes or—"

"Love, don't fuss over me. Come sit."

She crossed the room and Xander pulled her into his lap. The bruise on his face was dark and mottled in the firelight. She placed a hand over it and he cupped her palm as she healed him.

She was trembling by the time she finished, her mind full of questions she was terrified to ask. "Is there more to heal?"

He was trying so hard to be strong, but his eyes were glassy as she cradled his face. "Not yet. Let's not go there yet. Just let me hold you." He buried his face in her neck.

Cecilia stroked his hair. "I'm here. You're safe. I won't let him hurt you again."

Xander let out something between a sob and a laugh as she held him. "Gods, I need you." He kissed her neck and up her jaw before meeting her lips. "You don't know how much I need you." He pulled back and his gaze was full of anguish.

Grief and fear swirled around him in a torrent and she wanted to take it all away and make him feel anything else. Something was wrong. She could not put her finger on what it was but there was a roughness in his touch and an intensity in his gaze that seemed sharper, angrier than ever before. Although she wasn't afraid of him, she was afraid *for* him and any wounds she could not see. She wanted to ask what he had gone through, but she trusted him to open up when he felt comfortable, the way he always had with her.

"Will you show me your memory of our wedding?" Xander asked, his voice barely above a whisper.

She opened her mouth to ask why and then thought better of it. He'd obviously been through something awful and she was too relieved to have a way to help him. She held her palm against his neck and pulled up the memory.

They watched Cecilia getting ready, her tears over Xander's thoughtful gifts, walking down the aisle toward him, and the rush of joy and love she'd felt during their vows.

When it was over, he blinked up at her, looking puzzled.

"What?" she asked, reaching up to remove her tiara.

Xander stopped her. "Later. I just want to be close to you."

"Anything you need." She would do anything to take away his pain, to assure him there was no darkness in him she couldn't love and accept, the way he always had for her.

"I need you in that tiara," he said, lips skimming her ear. "In *just* that tiara."

She shivered as he unbuttoned her dress and set her on her feet. Silk slid over her hips, pooling on the floor. She pulled off his shirt and boots and he slid off his pants. The knot in her throat unwound when she found no more bruises or wounds on his body.

He only gave her a moment to look before yanking her into his lap. She felt completely ridiculous in the tiara but he clearly loved it.

Lust poured out of him as he reclined, his hands gripping her hips. "Gods, this is what fantasies are made of."

Despite the fact that they'd been using their intense physical connection to soothe each other for weeks, something rang false in it now. There was a hunger in Xander's eyes, a desperate clutching in his touch that filled her with as much dread as desire. Something was not right with him.

"Xander—"

"Please, Cece."

And that was all he needed to say. Loving him was a fever that never quite broke. She'd give him anything he wanted.

17

XANDER

Xander was wide awake when the faint sound of fishermen's bells began ringing on the Olney City docks. He'd already watched the sun rise, the light in the cottage turning from lilac to pink to bright gold. He used to wish he had paint so he could capture the view from the cottage windows in the mornings while Cece slept. Now he just wished he could remember that version of himself.

He brushed Cece's hair from her forehead. She slept peacefully with her cheek pressed over his heart, her body half on top of him like she was afraid he'd disappear if she didn't pin him down. Truthfully, part of him was already gone.

His mind churned, calling up old memories he knew Cato had somehow altered. He could not find their edges, or read what rang false in them. He only knew he'd been robbed of all his joy and instead an undercurrent of bitterness laced every moment with his wife.

He watched her version of their wedding, kept turning it over in his mind, watching it and then recalling his own memory. While he knew that hers must be the truth, he couldn't reconcile it with his own. Her memory showed her face full of joy and wonder, but in his he only saw fear in her eyes and longing when she looked at Rainer.

Xander was used to bruises and the ache that came with a fight. He'd been trained to withhold information even when tortured. But Cato's torture was beyond his wildest imaginings—the way he'd leeched Xander of his most precious memories, not by wiping them away but by warping them into nightmares. Everything that was precious to him was now a maddening tangle of truth and illusion that he could not pull apart.

He called up the night he'd found Cece bathing in the river. He could have sworn she'd been as caught up in their kiss as he had. But when he watched it now, he found hesitation in her touch and her eyes wide open while she kissed him back, like she was looking for someone else. Only the memories of his time spying on her in Olney remained untouched.

He'd wanted to ask Davide if he'd endured the same torturously slow poisoning of memories. Cato was careful to keep the Savero brothers apart, but his influence would explain why Xander's brother had grown so distant and cruel over the past few years. It was a dangerous thing for the trickster god to hold power over the king of Argaria. Nothing good would come from it.

Xander studied Cato the best he could with what little time he had. The one benefit of being the younger prince was that he'd been trained to lead Argaria's army and years of military tactics had taught him how to take on a more powerful and better-positioned enemy. The last eleven years honed his observation skills, so he studied his new adversary with the same single-minded focus he'd given Cece.

Watching her for a year made Xander wise. He knew exactly how to approach her and offer her what no one else had. He saw the way she banged her fists against the cage of propriety when she could, admired how she'd make herself less but with a fierce contempt in her eyes. At first he'd planned to use what he knew to manipulate her. At least that's what he told himself. But that first night when she spoke to him in the garden, all his well-laid plans burnt to ashes.

He'd listened to countless hunters brag about how they'd tame her, but Xander had only ever wanted to see her wilder. Weak men liked to break women to prove they could. But Xander didn't want a broken damsel. He wanted a feral goddess.

So he found the slightest rupture between Rainer and Cece and like a thumbnail in a hairline crack, he pried them apart.

But it wasn't enough anymore. The fear in his heart was too wild. The sorrow grew tight, like a breath trapped in his chest, threatening to rupture. There were too many ways to lose her—too many threats with more compelling magic.

Rainer McKay could be the selfless good guy, but Xander would lie, cheat, and kill to protect his wife. He didn't care if it made him a villain; he would suffer all of Cato's twisted games if it meant he could have even the smallest chance of insulating her from the god's wrath.

As if sensing his restlessness, Cece stirred. Her fingers slid up his side.

"What's wrong?" she mumbled, her voice still heavy with sleep.

He brushed his thumb over her jaw.

She blinked up at him, a crease forming between her brows. "You're worried."

"Make me feel good," he said, in the same way she'd said it to him for weeks. Xander finally understood what she meant. *Make me feel connected and alive. Make me feel like I'm not about to be crushed under impossible grief.* She'd meant *help me not feel so broken by loss.* Now he felt as confused and untethered as she had when she came into her powers.

And she did exactly what he asked without further question. She pressed her lips to his and all the tension in his body dissipated. He shifted her so she was straddling him and hiked her nightdress up around her hips. She shrugged out of the thin straps, the red silk sliding over her chest to pool around her waist.

"Gods, these are perfect," he murmured, cupping her breast and brushing a thumb over her nipple. She shivered at his touch, pulling him into another kiss.

He would never get enough. She was petite but so strong. She could easily have pinned him to the bed, but she let him have her however he wanted. He loved the danger, but mostly he loved how she was so vulnerable with him.

He flipped her beneath him, sliding inside her in one hard thrust, her back bowing as she gasped his name, her eyes hooded with desire.

This was what he needed. Her hands on his skin, clutching desperately like she never wanted to let him go, her breath ragged in his ear murmuring, "I love you. I love you. I love you."

She blinked at him, tears in her eyes. He saw so many questions in that look, but he didn't let her get them out. He picked up his pace until she was clenching around him, her muffled shout buried in the crook of his neck as she fell apart and he followed.

For a moment, they lay still, their heartbeats slowing as he kissed her. She rolled onto her stomach, a smile on her face as she leaned a cheek against her hands.

"Tell me about your trip. Tell me about your sisters," he said, running his fingers up her spine.

She smiled, her eyes brightening. "Sayla is insane and more of a predator than I anticipated. But Desiree was okay, I suppose. Once she was done playing with our friends like they were toys, she was somewhat helpful."

Xander's mind filled with visions of Cece and Rainer curled together on the forest floor, of Rainer kissing her, of the way he found any excuse to touch her. Xander's stomach turned over as he tried to pull away from the torrent in his mind, only to be flooded by every tender moment he'd witnessed between his wife and her guardian.

"And did you spend your night watch time with Rainer?" He'd thought the question would be a release valve on the pressure building in his chest, but his heart kicked even harder against his ribs.

Cece rolled her eyes as she sat up and slid her nightgown back into place. "No, I took watch with Evan so I could pepper him with questions about Sylvie." She paused, chewing her lower lip. "Before you were taken you were about to tell me something important. A secret. Evan said—" She hesitated again. "Evan said that there are rumors that you might be the son of your mother's consort and I wondered—"

Xander nearly choked on his surprise. Evan must have really come around on Cece to trust her enough to share that information.

"And what else did Evan say?"

His taunting tone was unnecessarily mean, but he hated that Evan had volunteered this information. He had no right to share something that further weakened Xander's position with Cece. His chest grew impossibly tight, his hands balling into fists at his sides.

She hesitated, her heartbeat quickening. She clasped her hands, her thumb brushing over her inner wrist. "Just that there was no evidence that it was true but that rumors existed and that having a consort wasn't unusual."

Of course. Now he could see what this was about. All the longing glances between Rainer and Cece were scorched into his brain. The way she'd screamed Rainer's name and kissed him when she thought he was dying. Cato hadn't even touched that memory. There was no need. It was savage enough on its own.

She shifted away from him, clearly sensing his anger.

"So this is just a starter conversation for you asking for a consort." Xander's laugh came out bitter and brittle. "Let me guess who you might pick."

Fury burned through his blood. Of course. It always came back to perfect fucking Rainer McKay, with his relentless pining, and his noble nature, and his direct connection to Cece's heart.

Xander's perilous grip on control slid away. He'd fallen through the trapdoor in his mind that led him back to the same revelation over and over. As long as Rainer McKay existed, Xander would never bear the full weight of his wife's affection. Their love was too old, ran too deep, was rooted into every memory, struggle, and triumph, and wrapped around her godsdamned heart. It was arrogant to think Xander could really compete, and he couldn't bear a lifetime of that.

For a year he'd watched Rainer and Cece attend crowded parties and court events, stray to opposite sides of the room and yet always be able to find each other at a glance. As if someone could blindfold either one of them, spin them around, and still they'd instantly be able to point at the other.

Xander loved Cece the way fire loved air. He was furious at her for making him love her when she couldn't love him back the same. No matter how much she burned for him, there would always be a part of her he could not reach. Rainer's pull on her felt cosmic, undeniable, like the moon tugging on the tides.

That awareness was a seed in his brain that took root and never stopped growing.

"I want you to have your bond severed."

The shift in Cece was immediate, the tremble in her limbs turning to granite, her eyes glowing a brighter blue.

"No." She crossed her arms, blowing out a disbelieving sigh. "We've been over this. You have asked and I have answered. You may bully Evan and King Hector and whomever else you like, but you will not bully me." She shook her head. "Why do you insist on pitting yourself against Rainer?"

"Because every time I think there's a chance you will choose him." The admission ripped out of him, leaving behind a messy wound. Ever since Rainer admitted to her how he felt, Xander couldn't shake the feeling she might not have married him if she had all of the information.

"When will this jealousy end?" she asked.

"Jealousy." Xander let out a scornful laugh. "Jealousy is a petty shadow of what I feel. My envy could raze kingdoms."

She poked him in the chest. "Your envy is the childish fit of a spoiled prince."

He gritted his teeth. "You kissed him twice in the past week." *And you liked it.*

She hadn't even bothered to deny that when he asked her. Perhaps he should appreciate the transparency, but his stomach twisted every time he thought of it.

She threw her hands up. "I had to. I said I would do whatever it took to get you back and I did. I don't regret it because you're here and you're whole. I am sorry for what I had to do and I'm sorry for enjoying it. What more can I do?" Raw desperation laced every word.

Xander waited to feel appeased by her words but the pounding heartbeat in his ears didn't relent. She couldn't give him reassurance because it didn't exist.

"Where is this coming from? It was never this bad before." She swallowed hard.

Xander rubbed the back of his neck. "I just can't get it out of my head. All the longing glances you give him. The way you spoke your wedding vows while looking at him—"

"Wait... What?" She stared at him. "But I showed you my memory of our wedding. Does it not match yours?"

He shook his head.

She thrust her hand into his. "Show me."

Xander pressed her palm over his heart, closed his eyes, and pulled up the memory of their wedding night. He showed her how she'd walked down the aisle toward him without ever looking at him, her eyes fixed on Rainer the whole time. He showed her how when she kissed him after their vows, she was still looking at Rainer.

She jerked away from him, blinking wildly to clear the magic from her mind. "That's not how it happened. I don't understand—"

"What's to understand? You are all I have left. I need—" He swallowed hard, his mouth suddenly dry. "I need your assurance."

She shook her head. "That's a lot to put on someone. I cannot love you enough for everyone you've lost just as you cannot do the same for me. I have two kingdoms on my back. I cannot carry your loneliness and my own. I cannot convince you of my love any more than you would believe me if I tried. If you cannot feel it. If it's not enough now, it will never be. I will always be connected to Rainer but I choose *you*."

"When you didn't know how he felt," Xander snapped. His voice was hoarse, strained by some untamed need, by the pure desperation of wanting proof of the truth beneath the web of broken memories in his mind.

"I cannot love you enough, Xander. Enough does not exist for you and me. There's nothing I can give you that you don't first need to give yourself. I cannot make you feel worthy—" Her eyes were wide and glassy. The sky darkened and rain began to drum against the windows. "Godsdammit. Stupid storm magic—"

Her lower lip trembled, and her hands fisted at her sides. Her heartbeat kicked up and the magic pulse of her anger hit him in the chest, the instinctive way she started to summon a storm with her frustration reverberating through him. Xander loved her haunted, sharp edges; didn't mind being bloodied by them as long as she let him close enough to do so. She was so infuriatingly uncontainable and while it drew him in, it also served as a painful reminder that he could never truly possess her whole heart.

He wished he could pin her love down—make her want him more than anything else. He was tired of being second, tired of being a spare. His whole life he'd kept the bottomless well of need tucked safely away. He'd put family and duty first. Just this once he wanted to be first, if only to Cece. He wanted some kind of tangible proof that he had the greatest sway over her. Still, he knew he could never own her. She was too fierce and wild to be contained, but it didn't stop him from wishing for certainty where life had given him none.

Xander reached out to the storm, a gentle caress to her wild, unbridled chaos. She instantly let him take over, and he lived for that trust and surrender. The way she understood magic and could pass it back and forth with him. He wrangled the tempest like a trainer breaking a horse from a wild thing into a steady stallion. The storm clouds dissipated, blowing out to sea and leaving spattered glass and a rainbow in their wake.

Cece watched the color arch against the sky, cheeks flushed, a trembling hand pressed to her heart. "Please do not be another person who wants more than I can give." Her voice was barely above a whisper but it slid between his ribs like an assassin's blade. "I cannot promise my people safety. I cannot promise the gods success in slaying this villain. And I cannot promise you that I would make a different choice because I do not know what I might have done differently, but I don't think this is really about Rainer."

She turned to face him, her shoulders slumped in defeat. "All I can tell you is that I choose you and the more you doubt me, the more certain I am that your doubt comes from some hole inside your heart that I could never fill because you will not let me in. Not really. I have given you all of me. I've shared my broken heart and my fears and my failures no matter how it hurt to let you see them." She placed her palm over his heart. "I have kept my vows and you have kept your secrets."

The truth was on the tip of his tongue but the moment he tried to speak it his whole body seized up in agony, a violent burning spreading through his veins. He shuddered and stumbled into Cece. She caught him, and he leaned his forehead against her shoulder.

The burning ebbed as he released the desire to defy the trickster god. He knew the feeling well, experiencing it every time he tried to defy Cato during captivity. Cato didn't just want to hurt her. He wanted Cece to be completely demoralized.

Xander worried that he had the hold on his wife—enough of her love and devotion—to do just that. He worried just as much that he didn't. For now, he was meant to pull Cece's strings and he hated the powerlessness of being a tool in his wife's torment.

"My love?" Her lips brushed his temple. "What happened?"

He bunched his hands in the back of her nightgown, fighting the urge to cry. "I cannot defy his orders."

"Cato's orders?"

Xander nodded.

She frowned. "But I thought he couldn't use his magic on a Savero."

"Clearly that isn't true."

This was it. He wanted to stop but he'd already pushed this off as long as he could. Every time he thought of not following Cato's orders, his blood started to burn again, the stinging sensation spreading from his heart.

A cold sweat rose on his skin. He gritted his teeth against it but it was no use. "You want to know a secret, love? You made a deal to save Rainer and now I am paying the price."

It was a lie—a vicious, wild swing that he couldn't take back. Cato's manipulation made him say it, but his jealousy made him enjoy the way she flinched—but only for a second, only until horror swept over her face. Then he felt awful.

"Rainer almost died and you made a deal to save him." He couldn't keep the bitterness out of his voice. "You were so desperate to save him, you didn't consider the cost. That's what Cato does. He doesn't hurt you directly. He hurts what you love."

"No—" Her eyes went wide in horror.

"He ruined all my memories of you."

18

CECILIA

The cottage floor creaked beneath her pacing, every groan a reminder that after hours of Cecilia's best efforts she'd made no progress at all in helping Xander determine reality from illusion. In fact, she'd only confused him more.

Cecilia was exhausted. She'd come to the end of her memory magic for the day, and although Xander encouraged her to use her goddess powers to fix him, she didn't feel comfortable trying to rebuild memories. It was one thing teaching him to call up what existed, but untangling the muddled mess that Cato had created was something else entirely.

Luckily, Evan backed her up on the decision. Rainer didn't, but she thought his faith in her was more out of guilt and habit than grounded in reality.

Finally, Evan insisted on taking Xander for a walk to give both of them a break and hopefully coax Cato's plans out of Xander.

"This is all my fault," Cecilia said.

She couldn't help feeling like they'd spent months preparing for the wrong type of war. They'd expected to be engaged in the field with weapons. Instead, they were fighting a different kind of combat that required a level of mental fortitude she wasn't sure she possessed.

Cato was not his father, Endros. He played mind games, not war games.

"Slow down, Cece. You'll pace a hole right through the floorboards," Rainer said softly.

"I can't. I did this. I made that stupid deal and now Xander's mind is scrambled and I don't know how to fix it."

Rainer stood, blocking her path, his hands braced on her shoulders. "Just breathe. It's going to be okay. I know it doesn't feel like it now, but it will. We have Xander back. You're going to get through to him and everything will work out."

"How can you say that? You're supposed to be the worrier," she said.

A smile broke over his face. "Because I have faith in you. If there is a way, I know you will figure it out. You're the antidote to my anxiety."

Cecilia loved and hated that Rainer's words soothed her. Xander was back, and he was as safe as they could make him now. She'd healed the bruise on his jaw, the only physical injury that remained from his time with Cato. It was just his mind that she needed to solve.

She sat at the kitchen table. Rainer poured her a cup of tea as Xander and Evan returned from their walk on the beach. She scooped in spoonful after spoonful of sugar and glanced at Evan over the steaming cup, hoping for a clue to what he discovered. The hunter shook his head. Clearly, Xander had shared nothing about Cato's plans, and that meant it wasn't obvious if he truly didn't know or if he simply didn't want to say.

So far, Cato's plan was perfect in its wretchedness. Once again, she was reminded that all good magic required an exchange. She bought Rainer's safety by sacrificing Xander's. It wasn't fair. She should have been the one to pay the price for that mistake. The guilt stretched wide beneath her skin, threatening to tear her open every time she saw the haunted, confused look on Xander's face.

"There has to be a way to undo this," Evan said. "Go through it again step by step."

Xander sighed. "He had me pull up a precious memory. He could see all my weak spots. The way you held Rainer's eyes a second too long. He has such a talent for misery. He hooked into my jealousy and amplified it. Then he tore it through the whole night. I watch what's in my mind now and feel sick with envy. Then, he pulled up the next precious memory of you and did the same. He found every hint of jealousy and anger, took all of it, and turned it into a nightmare."

Cecilia had restored his own memory of their wedding night, but Xander's anger and envy remained. The emotional strings cascaded into a tangled knot in his mind and Cecilia could not unwind them.

"The memories may be false, but the feelings are real," she said. "It doesn't seem to matter if I replace what was ruined with his own memories. Intense emotions will always overpower true memory—the feeling leaves an imprint that draws your attention more to the emotion than the memory itself."

Evan smacked his hand against the wall in frustration. "There must be a way."

"I can try my goddess powers, but I'm not sure that one godly power can undo another."

Xander tenderly kissed her sapphire wedding ring and sat down across from her. "How do you feel?"

"You shouldn't be asking me. I should ask you," she said.

He smiled weakly. "I should always ask you, love."

"Guilty. Horrible. Helpless. I just want to take away your pain."

Xander's eyes darkened, as if a storm was settling inside of him. "I have to tell you something else."

They all froze. Evan and Rainer stared at the two of them sitting across from each other at the kitchen table.

Xander licked his lips. "Remember right before the invasion in Olney? When I said I had something I needed to tell you."

Cecilia was certain her heart had stopped beating. She couldn't breathe. The entirety of her focus narrowed on her husband.

"Yes." Her voice was barely a whisper.

"I've been keeping a secret. A horrible one," Xander said.

Cecilia stared at him, frozen.

"I lied before. It's not your deal that traded me to Cato. It was my own. The morning we left for the Cave of Longings, before I woke you up, I made a deal with Cato." He turned to Evan. "And that's why he can influence me now. He can't manipulate a Savero unless they make a deal with him."

Cecilia's blood turned to ice in her veins and she shook her head. It couldn't be true.

"What was the deal?" Evan asked.

Cecilia was breathless with anticipation.

Xander swallowed hard, wincing like he was fighting an internal battle. He finally met Cecilia's eye. "I made a deal to keep Cece. Cato offered me a path to marry her without my brother's interference. He assured me it would happen even once she knew who I was. I made a deal to marry her and hold on to her love in exchange for a favor to be collected at a time of Cato's choosing. But I suppose he doesn't even need the favor now that he can manipulate me at will."

Cecilia stared at her husband, the shock rendering her breathless. Her vision went dark, narrowing to a pinprick until, finally, she sucked in a breath. Rage blistered her insides. Fury at Xander, at Cato, at everyone who'd left her alone in the wilderness, in enemy territory, without knowing who she was. Everything that she'd worked so hard to make peace with was ripped open all over again.

Xander had built their marriage on a lie. The foundation of their love crumbled with one simple admission. He'd had so much time to tell her but chose to leave her in the dark again. She'd been unmoored from the anchor that she'd attached herself to through all the chaos and betrayal, and she felt completely lost.

"How could you?" she gasped.

Xander hung his head. "I wanted to keep you. I had you for a moment and you were beautiful and open, and I couldn't stand to give you up so soon. I needed more time. Of all people *you* should understand the desire to want some semblance of control over who I married."

She shook her head. "Wanting it and forcing your will on someone else are different things."

"Yes, well, the joke's on me," Xander said. "I disappeared for a few days to be tortured—all to save you from whatever horrible fate Davide had in mind for you—and you can't even keep your hands and your lips to yourself. You weren't worth the deal I made for you."

Cecilia sank back in her chair.

Xander shuddered. He seemed like he was fighting an internal war with himself. He squeezed his eyes shut, hands pressing to his temples.

"You don't mean that," she said firmly.

"Does it matter if I do? You won't forgive me for that. I kept it from you for too long. I broke your one rule. I did the same thing again. I took advantage of your kind heart. You'll never forgive me."

"If I wasn't worth the deal, then why would you care?" Cecilia challenged.

"I don't," he said coldly. Suddenly, his face and posture changed, and she had the distinct feeling of looking into the loving eyes of her husband once again. "Cece." Tears streamed down his face. "I do care. I love you. I'm so, so sorry. Forgive me. Please say that you can forgive me. I should have told you. I tried a few times, and then I stopped trying and I shouldn't have. I hate that I didn't just tell you from the very beginning, but I was so afraid to lose you. Please." He grabbed her hand across the table.

Cecilia's instinct had always been compassion, but she'd grown tired of forgiveness being an expectation from the men in her life. What a luxury to be so catered to by the world that he felt owed compassion for such an enormous omission.

But Xander had broken something irreparable between them. Trust was a delicate thing. It took months to build, but only seconds to tear down. She looked at her hand in Xander's. Regret hung so heavily on him that she could barely stand to be so close to him. His regret did nothing to soothe the deep ache in her chest. She felt shattered, uncertain she'd be able to put herself back together, and furious with herself for allowing herself to be wounded in such a way by the same man twice.

"I'm sorry he made me say all of that stuff about your deal with him. He wanted to make you feel guilty and demoralized. But I'm sorry I kept this from you."

Xander closed the distance between them, knelt, and wrapped his arms around her waist, resting his head in her lap. She looked down at her broken husband, running her fingers through his dark hair. She was certain she'd never seen a more handsome liar in all her life.

Evan caught her eye, and she nodded toward the door. Rainer and Evan left, though she assumed they wouldn't go far.

"My love." Xander looked up at her with glassy eyes. He took her hands in his and kissed them both. "I couldn't bear to lose you. You were the first person who ever saw me. The only thing I ever really wanted for myself."

She shook her head. "But you took away my choice. How could you?"

How could he when he'd known from the start how important having agency over her future was? She'd believed he truly understood her, even after she found out who he was. She looked at him and was certain that he understood who she truly was at her core. That he loved that person—but now she felt like she was looking at a stranger.

She stared at her husband with grief and disbelief warring in her chest. For so long she thought she'd conjured love out of loneliness. In a world that wanted her small and contained, Xander seemed a small miracle. But his confession brought their whole history into question.

"I let you see everything about me. I let you—" It hurt too much to say. She let him see how broken she was. She let him see her weak and he'd held so much back.

Xander wrung his hands. "I know it's unforgivable."

"How am I ever supposed to know if what I feel now is *real*, Xander?"

He shook his head. "I don't know."

"I would have married you if you told me that day. I was ready to run away with you, Xander. You didn't have any faith in me, but worse, you didn't have faith in yourself."

He looked like she'd slapped him. "I thought you were my only chance at love, and it was the first time I ever felt truly afraid. I was desperate, and I made a really stupid, selfish decision for which I am now paying the price. I wish I could have saved you from paying it, because you don't deserve it and I love you so much."

Cecilia felt helpless with rage and grief. "You did exactly what everyone else in my life did. You let me believe a lie. You didn't feel like you owed me the truth."

"It was selfish and horrible. I'm begging you. Please forgive me. I will do *anything* to prove it to you. I'll spend the rest of our lives making it up to you. I will never lie to you again. I swear on my life."

She threw her teacup across the room, tea splattering the doormat as it landed with a clatter. "I don't want you to swear on your life, Xander. You started our relationship with a lie and I forgave you. But then you knew how much it would hurt me, and you started our marriage the same way."

"I didn't know when I made the deal."

"But you *did* when you married me." Her voice was shrill in the small room.

Recognition settled into his face, reflecting her shock and sorrow.

"You could have told me your mistake then, and we could have figured it out together. But you kept me in the dark, where I've been my whole life. I laid all my fears bare, while you hid."

Cecilia looked down at her hands. Her wrist was rubbed raw from how hard she'd been running her thumb over it. The silence grew taut between them.

The first time Xander lied to her, he'd been saved by the fact that Rainer's betrayal happened at the same time and hurt worse. This time she bore the full brutality of it—felt the way both leaving him and staying would hurt in equal measure. She was furious that he'd left her with no way to remain unscathed. He'd coaxed her out, made her open fully, only to wound the most tender parts of her heart, rendering love a weapon instead of a sanctuary. Worse, it tainted the filter through which she viewed each memory—everything that was once bright and shiny now muddled with grief.

He sat back on his heels. "You can't forgive me."

She tilted his chin up so he'd meet her eyes. "Every time my heart breaks, I think *it can't get worse than this. Nothing can break my heart worse than this.* And then you happened. I just hope nothing will ever break my heart worse than this, because I don't know if I could survive that."

Xander looked stricken. His face paled and his hands clenched in her dress. Cecilia was furious. She wanted to take a wild swing to spread the hurt around so it wouldn't crush her under its impossible weight.

"We're married now, so you *kept* me. I love you enough that I couldn't stop if I wanted to, but I will never trust you again. And that lack of trust will eat away at what love still lives here. I will be nothing to you but a ceremonial wife, and when this is over, I will take a consort and you should take one too, because whatever more is between us is over."

Xander's face was a picture of utter devastation, as if he'd expected her expedient forgiveness.

Cecilia wished she could harden her heart against loving him. She wished for the goddess to come and block her from having to look at the love on his face.

She pushed her chair back and pulled away from Xander's grip. She left the cottage and walked by Evan and Rainer, down the cliff trail, across the beach, all the way to the water's edge.

Cato had blown her life apart. Nothing was as she thought, and the deep, searing hurt in her chest—so sharp she could barely take a breath—was a constant reminder.

She stared into the crashing waves, trying to match her breathing with the rhythm of the sea.

"You were right, Adira! He was a fool! You were all right. But no one has anything to say now, do they? None of you want to pop in and say you told me so?" she shouted out into the sea.

Cecilia waited for tears that never came. Whatever was broken in her left no room for any feeling but emptiness. Maybe Cato had won already. It hadn't taken him long. He'd found the exact right knife to twist to bring her to her knees. He swept her beautiful future right out from under her. He robbed her of the one relationship that she was certain she could count on.

What choices might she have made differently? She imagined a thousand different lifetimes that were lost to her now. Lifetimes where Xander owned up to taking Cato's offer back in Argaria and they built something real. Ones where he owned up to it and she walked away, and let her heart want what it always had deep down. Those were the lifetimes where she ended up with Rainer. Whether or not he meant to, Xander had put her face to face with the very thing she'd felt nothing but guilt for wanting since they'd married: her love for Rainer.

It didn't matter, though, because all of those lifetimes were lost to her. All she had was the cruel one in which she lived. She'd need to see the way through on her own.

She was alone again. *Alone. Alone. Alone.*

For all her fighting, she was right back where she'd been all those months ago in the Cave of Longings—left in the dark with only her grief and rage to keep her company.

19

XANDER

Five Months Ago

Xander sat in the tub behind the mountain cottage, staring off, his breath rising in little white puffs in the icy dawn air. He'd been up most of the night trying to form a plan while Cece slept beside him.

The snow had finally stopped, or rather he'd finally stopped it. He'd been afraid she would notice him feeding his magic into the storm, but she'd been too restless and distracted. The storm had given way to gray skies and a crisp, blustery mountain morning that smelled like home.

The water in the tub cooled, but Xander refused to get out until he had a plan for how to keep Cece. He couldn't bear to lose her after the past two days. She'd let him into her body, but more importantly, into her heart. It was a thing he never knew to want and now could never live without. Although she hadn't said it, he could see it in her eyes. He'd never felt such an intense connection to someone, had never met someone so willing to be vulnerable, had never loved a woman so desperately.

Xander lived in certainties, and he'd known for some time that he was in love with Cece. In the darkest corner of his mind, he'd hoped for her to return those feelings, but he hadn't believed it possible until she agreed to run away with him. He could not let her go when he was so close to having the one woman who could be all things to him.

If he wanted to keep her, he needed a way to save Rainer, but he couldn't fathom how to pull it off alone. If he just had one more person with him.

Evan would have a well-thought-out plan. Teddy would encourage Xander's wild hope. He wished he had time to write to his friends, but he'd stalled as long as he could, and if he didn't intercept Davide today, Rainer was sure to be hurt. Then Cece would never forgive him.

"You've found yourself in quite a conundrum, Your Highness."

Xander whipped his head around. No one ever sneaked up on him, not with his hearing, but Cato stood in the snow just a few feet away.

"Cato."

He'd only met the trickster god in passing before. This was the first time they'd spoken. Xander was relieved for the bargain that his ancestors made with Cato that prevented him from manipulating anyone in the Savero bloodline.

"You've gone and fallen in love with the Lost Goddess."

Xander could have denied it, but there was no point. "I have."

Cato's lips quirked up in a half-smile. "The question is, what are you going to do about it? Even *you* aren't foolish enough to think you could really just run off with your own personal goddess. Not with everyone in two kingdoms looking for her."

Xander shrugged. "Maybe I could."

"She may be tiny, but she's quite memorable with those pretty blue eyes, perky tits, and that tight little ass. I expect she'd draw attention anywhere she went."

Cato's crude words turned Xander's blood to ice. It was bad enough catching Rainer staring at her backside all the time. He didn't need gods as competition as well.

"I know what you're going to say," Cato said. "She's more than just a pretty face. Spare me the lovesick poetry. I'm here to offer you a bargain."

"No."

Cato grinned as if delighted by the refusal. "You don't even know what I'm offering."

"I'm not interested."

"Not even if it could help you keep your goddess? Marry her. Keep her despite your considerable lack of disclosure about your identity as her sworn enemy." He paused for effect. "Do you really think she'll be so forgiving after you've taken something from her that she can't get back? She's going to despise you."

Cato gave voice to all of Xander's deepest fears. He hated himself for even considering it, but Cato's words had a stranglehold on him. Gods did not throw around bargains lightly. He'd learned that from his father.

"What's in it for you?" Xander asked before he could stop himself. Before he could let his better judgment catch up with him. Before he could let Evan's voice—constantly chiding him in his head—talk him out of it.

"Just a favor."

Xander's breath rushed out in a puff of white. "What favor?"

"I haven't decided yet."

Xander considered it. Cato would never make a deal that didn't benefit him directly. He didn't do favors. Xander's father repeated that nearly daily when he and Davide were young.

Xander studied Cato's body language. The god attempted to appear relaxed, but his white-knuckled grip on his arms negated his casual lean against the back of the cabin. He *really* wanted this bargain.

"I'm not foolish enough to believe you'd do this out of the kindness of your own heart."

Cato chuckled darkly. His slate eyes glowed with power. "Maybe you're wiser than I gave you credit for. You're right. I'll want something significant when the time comes. I'll want your help and you probably won't like it. But you're asking all the wrong questions."

Xander shivered in the bathwater, but he didn't want to stand there naked in the cold talking to a god, and his robe was too far to reach from the tub.

"I'll take the bait. What should I be asking?"

Cato grinned at him, and Xander knew he'd stepped right into some kind of trap.

"You should ask if you can bear to lose her. You know the moment she finds out who you are, what you had will be over. She'll never forgive you for knowing what she is and leading her into a trap. She'll never forgive you for putting the life of that guardian she's so in love with at risk. She'll hate you for taking her from one prison to another, and for stealing from her. Did you enjoy her enough to make that loss worth it? To give her over to your brother and let him bed her? Those are some questions."

Cato's words sliced through Xander with savage precision.

"She's a stubborn little thing," Cato mused. "I doubt she would be so forgiving once she knows who you are and how you've spent half of your life in an enemy court looking for her, and followed her for a year at her father's request. Do you think she'll appreciate the violation of her privacy?"

Xander still said nothing.

"Can you convince yourself of your ability to live without love now that you've had it?"

Cato had him, and Xander should have known he would before the god ever spoke. He had centuries of experience manipulating people to do exactly what he wanted, and his power went well beyond using his magic.

Xander cursed inside his head.

"I can manage your brother, so perhaps the last question you should ask yourself is what is she more likely to forgive: your betrayal, or you making a deal to keep her because you love her too much to lose her?"

Cece was so passionate, she would be much more likely to forgive

Xander's desperation to keep her. He wasn't certain of that, but from what he'd learned in all his time watching her for the huntmaster, he had to gamble on that being the better option.

It would be easier to beg forgiveness when they were married. Cato's deal guaranteed him that much. He'd have time to win her over and explain.

Evan's voice nagged at the back of his mind. He'd tell Xander that if he was charming enough to win her over against her better judgment once, he could do it again. But Evan had never been in love. Xander wasn't willing to risk love on his charm, even if he'd basically lived on charm his whole life.

Xander rose out of the water and made the only choice that he could live with. He stood there naked in the cold in front of the trickster god. He wasn't going to make a deal so important sitting in a bathtub.

He stepped out of the water, the icy snow setting an instant ache in his feet, and shook Cato's hand.

"You've got a bargain."

Xander knew from the look on Cato's face that he'd made a mistake, but it was too late to take it back. Cato walked around the edge of the cabin, and by the time Xander followed, he was gone.

Xander tried to comfort himself by repeating that Cece would keep loving him, but it somehow felt hollow after making a deal for her love to begin with.

She would forgive him. He'd have a lifetime to make up for it. Now it was up to him to make it a long one for both of them.

———

Now

Xander stayed where he'd been on the floor, begging for Cece's forgiveness.

There was nothing here for him. He saw her face fall. He heard her heartbeat waver. He'd only glimpsed her devastation at his confession, and he'd never hated himself more.

He'd broken something irreparable between them. Even if she eventually forgave him, she would never trust him again. She'd never bare every vulnerable part of herself to him.

He'd miscalculated, been too optimistic. It wasn't worth it. Xander wished that he'd thought more like a strategist when Cato offered him the deal. He was his impulsive, single-minded self, and it wrecked Cece.

Wishing was pointless. He couldn't take any of it back now. He also couldn't get clear of Cato's manipulation. He didn't have any more devastation to inflict, but his mind was still clouded by all of Cato's influence. His memories were jumbled, and he felt irrational anger toward Cece and Rainer. He had to keep reminding himself what was real.

Overwhelmed and confused, he tapped each of his fingers to his thumb, the way he'd been taught to calm down as a child.

"He's still in your head, isn't he? It didn't go away with telling her," Evan said.

Xander knew he was standing in the cottage doorway, but he didn't want to face his friend. "Yes."

He had to return soon. The burning beneath his skin set in now that his task was complete. That was what Cato had told him; it was the only way to figure out Cato's plan and truly protect Cece. As much as he wanted to stay and comfort her, he had no clue how to even begin to do that. He turned to face his friend.

"Xan, why didn't you just tell me?" Evan asked. "I would have helped you figure it out. I wouldn't have left your side. He never would have taken you."

Xander rose to sit at the table and met Evan's dark eyes. "I should have. I just couldn't give her up. Ev, when I made the deal with him, it broke that family bargain I didn't know about. Which must be why Davide changed, too, though I don't know what deal he made."

Evan's eyes widened. "How did your father never warn you?"

Xander shook his head. "I doubt he knew. He wasn't foolish enough to make a deal, though it's likely why he was always more wary of Cato than Endros. Now Cato can manipulate me at will and there's nothing I can do. It's hard to tell what's real. I know I love her but I'm also so irrationally angry with her. He ruined so many of my good memories with her. He can't wipe them out like she can, but he corrupted most of them."

"Why didn't you tell me what you'd done?" Evan asked.

Xander slammed a hand on the table. "I couldn't. Not until I told her what he wanted me to tell her. It's all true. I did these things. I hurt her. She will never forgive me."

Evan leaned against the wall, rubbing his chin. "I wouldn't underestimate her. Don't give up yet, Xander."

"I crossed the one line, to the one place I can't come back from. I was supposed to be the one person who always gave her choices, who always encouraged her to decide for herself. That's what I fought for, all the while taking away her options in secret."

Evan frowned. "Wouldn't Cato's influence have stopped working on her once she was a goddess?"

Xander froze. It hadn't occurred to him before. "I'm afraid to hope for that."

Evan sat across from him at the table. "I have to say that this all makes a lot more sense now. I knew you were hiding something, and I knew you were pretty extreme about Cece, even for you."

"He claims he made me more obsessive."

Evan scoffed. "You don't think he did?"

"I'm clearly not the best judge of these things, but I don't think so," Xander said. "I think Cato wants me to think that too badly. I think he's counting on me believing it, but I think I actually love her that much—my usual obsessive self, but on borrowed time. I knew she would find out, so I felt a need to push things forward as fast as possible, to get as much in as I could before she found out."

"If you love her, fight for her, Xander."

Xander rubbed the bridge of his nose, the urgent need to leave soon burning under his skin. The pain increased by the moment and it wouldn't let up until he returned to Cato. "I might never get out from under this manipulation and until I can, I'm a danger to her. I'm just another tool to hurt her."

"What are you going to do?"

"I'm going to fight for her from the inside. I have to go back."

Evan grew pensive. "If you go back, he'll kill one of you. He doesn't need two Savero heirs."

"I know. There's so little I can do now. If I go back, I can at least try to protect her from whatever is coming."

Evan threw his hands up. "Seeing you hurt would hurt her worse and you know it. For someone like Cece, it's much worse to see the people she loves suffer than to suffer herself. How do you not get that by now?"

Xander pounded a fist on the table in frustration. "I cannot do nothing. I am a prince, a hunter, and a spy. I can find a way out of this."

Evan balled his fists at his sides and sighed heavily. He tapped each finger to his thumb on each hand, summoning patience. "It's against everything in me to let you go back. I can't just let you walk back into this because you feel guilty. I've already lost Teddy."

Evan hadn't spoken their friend's name since he died and hearing it then was like being plunged into ice water.

It had been almost twelve years since Xander had last pulled rank on him, but he knew the look on Evan's face. "I am Alexander Maxwell Savero, Prince of Argaria, and you are my guard, and you'll do as I command."

Evan gritted his teeth. "Or I could tie you to that chair and beg the princess for forgiveness for disobeying you. She's mad right now. When she cools down, she'll be back to yelling at you and throwing things and you'll do what you always do and flirt your way out of it."

Xander shook his head. "Not this time and you owe me, Ev."

It was a low blow, but Xander was desperate. Their eyes locked, and Xander knew he had his friend.

"I'm going to write her a love letter and ask you to give it to her, and then I'll be gone."

"Xander, that is ridiculous. We can figure this out. The last thing she needs is you wandering back into Cato's hands."

"I have to. Our bargain is already tugging on me. Listen, Cato is afraid of Cece. I don't know why because her power can't affect him. I can't figure it out here. We're on our heels with him every time. The only way I can really have an impact is to figure out what he wants and try to stop him from the inside."

"This is a terrible idea." Evan ran a hand through his hair as he let out a frustrated sigh.

"Maybe. But we only have bad ideas to work with right now."

"It goes against everything in me to let you go, Xan."

"I know. If it would make you feel better, I can strike you with lightning real quick so you don't feel like you let me."

Evan didn't smile at his joke.

Xander wrote down everything that weighed on him and prayed it would bring Cece some comfort.

———

Beautiful Cece —

Here we are again...another love letter. I didn't even know what I started months ago with that little bird note.

Of all the things I've ever done, this is the worst. I worry that before this is over, I will somehow hurt you worse. If that happens, please know it's the last thing I want.

Love isn't supposed to hurt. I know that, and if I could save you from everything that hurts you with another bargain, I would. Maybe that makes you think I've learned nothing, but what I wish you would realize is that it means I love you too much to see you hurt at all.

Please look beneath whatever else I do and look for the love in it. I love you more than words can say, and I know what a fatal mistake I've made in our relationship. If I understood you then the way I do now, I promise I never would have made it. Even so, I should have told you sooner.

I'm leaving because staying won't ensure that I don't hurt you, and I believe it will actually make things worse. I may have lost a lot of my memories to Cato's corruption, but I will tell you the thing I remember and love most.

The night you told me you were afraid of the darkness inside of you, you wiped your tears away like you were angry that they had the nerve to appear. You tried to hide your emotions away. You tried to hide your hurt and fear, but I saw them. You let me see them even though you were afraid of what I would think. I felt so privileged and wholly unworthy that you let me see that.

In that moment, I hated the world that made you feel ashamed. I hated everyone who said you were too sweet, too kind, too emotional...too much. I hated them all, because seeing that part of you hidden away is a crime. You aren't too much. You are just the right amount. That memory lives in my mind, even still in this mess, and it both tortures and comforts me.

I am made of mistakes. I have made so many in my life, but believe that I don't regret any of them as much as I do taking away a choice from you. My heart may have been in the right place, but my head wasn't. I hope you'll find it in your incredibly big heart to forgive me and try to salvage what we have built, but I wouldn't blame you for giving up.

My love for you is bigger than magical bargains. Bigger than a crown. Bigger than all of my mistakes.

You are the dream I didn't know to want until you were standing right in front of me in that wet bathing gown under the full moon. You robbed me of breath that night and every day since.

Love, Xander

———

He folded the paper into the shape of a bird and handed it to Evan. He pulled his friend into a hug before tearing out of the cottage and riding off.

It killed Xander to leave, but he promised to protect the delicate parts of Cece. He'd done a terrible job of it so far. It was time for him to do better.

Xander rode back into Davide and Cato's camp hours later. The late afternoon sun blinded him. He stopped at the edge of camp, shielding his eyes with a hand as he overlooked the tents of the Argarian encampment below.

He had the impulse to reach into his jacket pocket. His fingers grazed a scrap of paper and he thought his heart might stop beating. A faint smile danced over his lips as he pulled out a slip of paper with his wife's loopy handwriting.

———

I slept much too well without you to wake me up every hour. I am so glad you're home. Whatever storms we must weather, let's meet them together. I love you.

———

Clearly she'd written it before he confessed. The note nearly shattered his resolve. Xander read it several more times and, through repetition, her words gave him the strength to ride to Cato's cabin and finish what he started.

20

CECILIA

Cecilia wanted to hate Xander so badly. Staring out over the Adiran Sea, she tried to summon hatred the way she did memory but only found love. Unfortunately for her heart, his betrayal did little to change the way she felt, and it certainly didn't release her from the commitment she'd made. She still needed her husband to be okay.

Waves crashed, their salty spray ghosting over her face. The gray sky swirled as if taking its cue from her mood, though for once it wasn't because of her summoning.

She'd thought she was making a choice when she married Xander, but it turned out she'd been missing two critical pieces of information that made that choice seem like an illusion.

What might she have done if she knew Rainer loved her before Xander proposed? What might she have done if Xander admitted his deal right away?

It was impossible to know, but she could not stop turning the questions over and over in her mind, like puzzle pieces that didn't fit together no matter how she flipped them.

"Cece?"

She'd expected Rainer to follow her down to the beach after

Xander's confession, but Sylvie stood behind her instead, her long blonde hair tangling in the breeze.

"Rain came to get me. Thought maybe you could use someone to talk to."

Cecilia turned back to look out at the sea. "I'm waiting to cry."

Sylvie stepped beside her. "Maybe you're out of tears."

"Maybe."

"Do you want me to get Rain?"

"No, it was smart of him to find you. I tell Rainer everything, but I think this is something even he can't understand."

"I'm not even sure I can," Sylvie said, dragging a toe through the sand.

"But you know what it's like. You know how vulnerable it feels to let someone into your heart like that. You know what it is to put yourself out there...to let someone into your body—" The pain stole her breath.

"I do. I'm sorry. I can't imagine what that betrayal feels like. Most men will never know what that's like."

Cecilia rubbed her inner wrist, grains of sand adding a harsh bite to the normally soothing movement. "I feel like such a fool. I was walking around flaunting this relationship, but it wasn't what I thought it was. The whole time I was with someone who agreed to manipulate me just so he could keep me. He had so much time to tell me, but he chose not to."

Sylvie interlaced her fingers with Cecilia's and squeezed her hand.

"I don't mean to throw a pity party, but, gods, could there just be one person who doesn't betray my trust?"

Sylvie squeezed her hand again. "I won't."

"I know. You're the last one left."

Silence stretched between them. There was nothing to distract Cecilia from the swirling in her mind but the crashing of the waves and calls of the gulls.

"I don't think I can fix it. I said some horrible things to Xander because I was hurt."

"I'm sure he knows you don't mean them. He knows your heart," Sylvie said.

"Maybe I do mean them. I don't know how we come back from this."

"You don't. You can't." Sylvie said it so matter-of-factly. "I don't see how you can with that kind of breach of trust. You can only start over from somewhere else. It's not fair that the world expects you to stay open in the face of so much experience that should inspire you to do the exact opposite, but if you want to make things work with Xander, you can. And before you argue with me, I am not suggesting that you just forgive him. I want to rip his throat out for hurting my friend like this. What I'm saying is that back in Argaria, something inspired you to give your trust to him in the first place, after he proved himself a liar once. Who's to say that if you can rebuild from that once, you can't do the same thing again?"

Cecilia sighed. "I don't even know where to start."

"You don't have to know right now."

"I'm furious with him."

Sylvie laughed. "Good! Be mad! Xander doesn't deserve to be let off the hook. The man deserves a good grovel. But you are a princess and a goddess. You have an opportunity to create a world for women better than the one we currently live in. Use the power that you have and the power that your relationship gives you to make sure that young girls in this kingdom and Argaria have options, and don't need to rely on the men in their lives to give them power. You can create a world where women can claim power for themselves so that no one has to rely on men to be the purveyors of truths they so selectively share. Use your anger and your frustration and your husband's love for you to create something bigger than just this. Fight for more than just you and your relationship. Fight for all of us."

Could Cecilia really do that? Was she thinking about her power too literally?

"I don't know how."

Sylvie shook her head. "Of course you do. You've always been doing this in your own way. And if there is one thing I know about my friend Cecilia, it's that she's much more comfortable fighting for other people than she is fighting for herself. Use that to sustain you. I know you love Xander. In this moment, when you feel let down by his love, find another motivation to carry you through until you can rebuild something new. You don't have to figure it all out now. And if you can't do that, you can always petition to dissolve the marriage. Marriage is a contract and just because you agree to it doesn't mean you have to stay in it, especially if you were misled. If I'm not mistaken, you have more information now."

Cecilia stared at Sylvie.

"What?" Sylvie asked.

"When did you get so wise?"

Sylvie laughed. "I've always been this wise, but it's more advantageous to let people believe I'm vapid. Easier to manipulate suitors if they don't think I'm smart enough to do it."

Cecilia threw her arms around Sylvie, relieved to have such a smart and brave woman as a friend. To be known and understood by someone was the highest form of love in Cecilia's book. It was a relief to have a friend like Sylvie who understood her worldview, even if she didn't fully understand the experience. Perhaps she hadn't been as alone as she thought all along.

They stayed there for a long time, holding each other as the sky darkened and the chill in the air chased them from the beach.

They reached the top of the cliff trail, and found Evan leaning against the cottage doorframe. Cecilia knew something was wrong immediately by the look on his face.

"Where is he?"

Evan held his hands up. "I tried to stop him."

She pushed by him, racing into the kitchen. "Where is he?"

"He went back to Cato, and before you yell, I tried to talk him out of it. He said he had to go as part of his bargain."

She gaped at Evan. "Then you tie him to a godsdamned chair, Evan. He is obviously not thinking clearly. Why would you let him do that?"

"I threatened to, but it physically hurt him to stay. He thinks he can get more insight working on the inside of Cato's army than out here with us, and after hurting you so much, he thought it was best to give you some space. He left you this."

Evan held out a letter.

"I don't want that," she said, swatting at the paper.

Evan sighed. "I think you will once you read it."

Cecilia cocked an eyebrow. "Did you read it?"

"Had to make sure it wasn't something else to torture you."

She snatched the letter, hands trembling as she unfolded it.

"Before you run off to read that, I have an idea. It might be a long shot, but at least it will give us some kind of action to take and maybe the start of a plan," Evan said.

"I'm all ears," Cecilia said, sitting down at the kitchen table.

"I think we should try to get some Godsbane. If it could subdue your powers, we could try to use it on Cato, and maybe that could be what helps us turn the tide on him. I doubt it's a move he would expect. He expects you to play fair, Cece."

Cecilia played with a loose thread on her dress sleeve. "But how do we find it?"

"That's the part I think you won't like."

"Oh gods," she sighed.

"Exactly."

Cecilia groaned. "You want to involve more gods?"

"I was thinking maybe your brother, Devlin—"

"What does the god of wisdom and reason have to do with finding Godsbane?" Cecilia asked.

Evan held up his hands as if to brace against her anger. "He might know where we could find such a thing. He is a scholar, and if anyone is going to know where to find a rare herb or how to find Cato's weaknesses, it's going to be the godly historian."

"I know I should argue with you and make a case for why I think it's a terrible idea, which I do, but I just don't have the energy. Any idea where we might find him?"

Evan nodded to a book of mythology that lay open on the table.

"Rainer suggested we start with the myths like we did with the rest of the gods. It's worked so far. According to the books we looked at, there's supposed to be an old abandoned library hidden in the hills just east of Olney City. It would be a quick ride, and even if we don't find him, we won't have wasted much time."

Cecilia sighed, looking out the window at the setting sun. "All right. We'll leave tomorrow morning."

Evan frowned. "I thought you'd fight that more."

"Well, you're in luck because I'm fresh out of fight today," she said.

"I hope a good night's sleep brings it back, because I find you disturbing without it," Evan said.

Cecilia could only sigh. She didn't know what would lift her spirits but she doubted another family reunion would do the trick.

———

For four years Cecilia had walked into dark caves alone, leaving a restless Rainer outside. Even now that she was bringing him along into an unmarked cave, that same uneasiness shot through their connection.

She frowned into the darkness. "This has to be it." The only other cave they'd found was too shallow and showed signs of recent animal activity without a hint of magic.

Pure hope propelled Cecilia forward as she led their group into the cave, the scent of damp moss hitting her as she crossed the threshold.

"I don't like this," Rainer whispered.

Cecilia promptly ignored him, snapping a flame to her fingers and walking into the dark.

They'd searched the hillside for Devlin's hidden library for hours until Cecilia and Sylvie felt a pulse of magic from the cave. As experienced memory witches, they had been eager to enter, but the men had hesitated.

They stumbled in the dark for a few long minutes. A light flickered ahead of them, growing brighter as they rounded a curve in the cave wall and the narrow space widened into an area that looked like a very large root cellar. Tall candelabras with wax dripped into puddles on the dirt floor, and bookshelves lined every wall.

"I think I preferred the Wailing Woods to this," Evan whispered as they made their way through leaning stacks of books and dusty, bowed shelves. The air was thick with the smell of parchment and ink. Old maps of Olney hung between gaps of shelves, and the few lit candles illuminated swirling dust motes. The stacks of old tomes stretched all the way to the dirt ceiling, where roots and ivy clung. Most looked like a stiff breeze or a ghostly hand might topple them.

Cecilia squinted into the dim space. The rows of bookshelves seemed to continue on forever into the darkness. "I suppose if this is the right place he'll just pop up like everyone else."

She'd braided her hair into a crown around her head, and she wore an intricately embroidered crimson tunic with the Savero family crest. As mad as she was at Xander, she didn't want any subtlety in her appearance. She was a princess and a goddess, and she meant business. In truth, she was trying to appear strong when she felt her weakest.

She was focused entirely on finding Godsbane and looking for any other weaknesses Cato might have. The sooner he was out of the way, the sooner they could start untangling the mess he'd made of the two kingdoms.

The candles guttered and a breeze fluttered loose pages. The library was the type of creepy, dilapidated place that felt haunted. A spirit peeked around a bookcase in the corner before ducking away.

Rainer cleared his throat. "Cece, are there—"

"Spirits? Yes." She grinned at him over her shoulder. "I never know if you want me to answer that question honestly. They're all standing right behind you."

She was certain he knew she was joking, but he looked anyway. Cal stifled a laugh.

"Honestly, I am so looking forward to never having another adventure again. I thought I'd seen my last musty old cave when you finished the Gauntlet," Sylvie whispered. "If the rest of my life is just me sitting on a settee somewhere eating candies, I think that will be as much adventure as I can take."

Cecilia rolled her eyes. "Liar. You'd be bored in a second. I take you on the most fun quests. Don't pretend not to love it."

"Maybe next time we could go somewhere less creepy," Cal suggested, his eyes narrowing as he peered down a dark row of shelves.

Cecilia drew up short and brought a finger to her lips.

"Are you all going to just creep around my library or are you going to come in and tell me what you want? I have things to do." The voice startled all of them.

A man walked out from a row of books in front of them.

"Devlin," Cecilia murmured.

"Greetings, Your Highness." Devlin dipped into a mocking bow.

Cecilia rolled her eyes. "Great, you're just as charming as the rest of the family."

"I'm not the god of charm. I'm the god of wisdom and reason. Now, what do you want?" He sat down at a table with a stack of books.

In the dim candlelight, Cecilia could see the similarities between her half-brother and herself. The god had slightly lighter hair, but the same blue eyes, and as he sat peering into his book, he tapped a finger to his lips the same way she did when she was concentrating.

"We need to know where to get Godsbane," Rainer said.

"Can't be done." Devlin didn't look up from his book. "If that's all, please see yourselves out."

Cecilia crossed her arms. "Why not?" She moved forward, shoving books carelessly off the chair. A cloud of dust rose as they thudded on the floor and she planted herself in the seat.

Devlin's eyes bored into her. "The only place Godsbane grows is in the Wilds, and there's a cost for harvesting it. An exchange. The magic there is powerful."

Cecilia shivered, remembering the creepiness of the Wilds, the barren area she and Rainer rode through on their last Gauntlet run.

Hardly anything grew there save for the hardiest of plants, and the air held an eerie chill no matter how warm the day.

"Can't one of us just go harvest some?" Evan asked.

Devlin huffed a weary sigh. "Only those with magic can harvest it and sometimes the Wilds take a tax."

"What kind of tax?" Cecilia asked.

Devlin continued paging through his book. "It varies. Could be a life tax, as in a few years of life—" He nodded at Sylvie. "Or a beauty tax, like wrinkles on your pretty face. The price correlates to whatever the harvester values."

"Sounds ominous," Evan said.

Devlin thumbed his book. "You want to use it on Cato."

"Yes. We were hoping to," Cecilia said firmly, trying to command the god's attention.

"It's not possible to catch him off guard. Best to assume the trickster knows you better than you think." He finally made eye contact with Cecilia. "He plans for all moves and countermoves. Trying to use Godsbane on him would be a mistake."

She leaned forward in her chair. "And it's my mistake to make."

Devlin frowned. "Indeed. I wish you were not so desperate to make it." He tilted his head back, as if the lot of them were a terrible inconvenience. He stood abruptly and dug through a stack of books, pulling out a volume on ancient herbs. The language in the book was not one that Cecilia recognized—it was more symbols than letters—but the picture Devlin pointed to was the most important part.

"I heard about your husband," Devlin said. "You know, there are three ancient rings that block godly influence. You might have considered those useful before you aligned yourself with an enemy prince."

Cecilia's heart raced at the prospect. "Where can we find them?"

Devlin balked at the question. "That's the question of the decade. We lost them after the War of the Gods and I've been searching for them since."

Cecilia threw her hands up. "A lot of help you are."

He shrugged. "I will not take that as a slight on my generosity. I'll continue my quest to find them and be happy to share my findings."

Cecilia sat back, deflated.

"You know that all of us gods can see different types of truth, but the trickster can read intentions as well as deepest desires. Be mindful of how to tip your hand. Best to keep your mind elsewhere when he's around." Devlin's eyes fixed on Cecilia and he grew quiet for a moment. "Do you know the antidote to war, little sister?"

"I wish I did," she said.

"It's hope. If you want to defeat an enemy, you either break their will or revive it. People fight when they're desperate, but they live when they're hopeful."

"Great, more riddles," Cecilia sighed. "Any other sage wisdom?"

"If you fear your powers, you'll never understand them, and if you're unwilling to try, then you've already lost. Is that direct enough?" Devlin's eyes narrowed on her.

She nodded. "How do you make an army hope?"

He blew out an exasperated sigh. "I have given you all the answers. What else do you want from me? I have much to do. Now, remember what I said and do not write it off if some of it is more helpful than other bits. I trust you can see yourselves out."

Evan looked like he wanted to ask more questions, but Cecilia waved him off and walked back the way they'd come with the group on her heels.

"He was sweet," Cal said dryly.

"As sweet as the rest of them. They say you can't choose your family and yet I'd still like to choose a different one," Cecilia said, her voice echoing in the cave. She squinted at her friends as they stepped back into the daylight.

Evan untied his horse. "We should go straight to the Wilds. It's a much closer ride from here than from Olney City. Princess, you'll head back to the city with Rainer. Cal, Sylvie, and I will go to harvest the Godsbane."

"I'm not letting one of you pay whatever magical price this is going to take. That's ridiculous. I will get the Godsbane," Cecilia huffed.

"I doubt it's a good idea for a goddess to be in a field of Godsbane," Evan said. "If there's an attack on Olney City while we're gone, you can defend the people much better than the three of us can combined. I know you hate to take help, but this is something we can actually do."

Cecilia sighed heavily. "I should argue with you, but I know you'll just do it, anyway."

"I will." Evan smiled.

Cecilia glanced at Cal and Sylvie. "Are you all sure?"

Sylvie waved a dismissive hand. "Harvesting a magical plant? I've got this. I'll cast a protection spell for the three of us and a mirror spell for whatever magic is in the Wilds. We'll practically be invisible."

Cecilia hugged Sylvie. "Please be careful. I need the three of you back in one piece."

Evan tugged Cecilia aside. "You know Rainer won't let you face Cato alone."

Cecilia nodded, her gaze straying to Rainer. "Just get the Godsbane and I'll take care of the rest—assuming you'll back me up."

Evan nodded, then turned to mount his horse.

They didn't give Cecilia time to second-guess, riding off a moment later and leaving Rainer and Cecilia to ride back to Olney City together.

21

RAINER

Rainer couldn't remember the last time he'd felt so completely drained. The adrenaline of meeting Devlin, whose histories he'd spent his youth reading, had long worn off, and he was left with only his own anxiety and Cecilia's restlessness buzzing through their bond.

Cecilia sat on the beach with her knees pulled into her chest, drawing spirals in the sand beside her. The stoicism she'd worn all day was gone, replaced by a whirlwind of emotions that played through their connection as she stared out at the sunset over the retreating sea.

Rainer sat next to her, tentatively bringing his hands to her hair. When she said nothing, he unpinned her braid, freeing her curls before gently rubbing her scalp. She sighed, relaxing into his touch, though grief bubbled through their connection.

Her loud sniffle cut through the soothing sound of waves. "What if none of it is real? I know I have to keep it together now but I can't seem to—"

"Cece, you listen to me." He tilted her chin so their eyes met. "You fall apart whenever you need to. If you hold it in, it will be a distraction. I will always be right here to listen."

She blinked away tears in the fading sunlight. "Promise me you won't make a deal with Cato. Tell me you haven't."

"I crescent promised I wouldn't before. I won't and I haven't. I swear."

"Would you tell me right now if you had?" she asked.

"Yes."

"Even if it would break my heart." Her voice broke at the words.

"Yes, even then. I swear I haven't." Rainer brought her hand to his heart.

"Rain, I still love him. I love him so much."

"I know." He ran his fingers through her hair. "We all know."

Her lower lip trembled. "I said horrible things. I said I would never forgive him. I told him to take a consort. I told him I was his wife in ceremony only. If something happens to him, I'll never forgive myself. Why do I do that? Why do I hurt other people when I feel hurt?"

Rainer sighed. "Because some stupid guardian taught you to meet an opponent blow for blow. Xander knows and loves your temper."

"How can I trust what I felt was even real?"

Rainer brushed a tear from her cheek. He could not believe he was about to defend Xander Savero, but he would have done anything to take away Cecilia's pain. "Didn't you fall in love with him before he made that deal?"

She nodded. "I don't know. Cato could have somehow manipulated me."

"Wouldn't his manipulation break once you became the goddess? And didn't Desiree tell you that gods can't manipulate love like that?"

Cecilia paused, considering his words. "I used to think that love was so simple. That you loved someone, or you didn't—that there was only one way to love. But now I know that nothing about love is simple. It's an exchange. A give and take, and to be vulnerable in the way I need to love someone—I don't think I can do that with Xander anymore."

Rainer kissed the crescent scar on her hand. "Okay, so then you can't."

"But I can't give up on him," Cecilia said. "I don't know how not to love him. He's suffering, and even if it's his own mistake that got him there, he would never let me suffer like that."

Rainer nodded. "I know he wouldn't. It is one of his few redeeming qualities."

"I wish he had less of them. He's so easy to love."

"Speak for yourself," Rainer huffed.

She blew out a surprised laugh. "Rain!"

"I'm kidding. If he wasn't trying to get under my skin all the time, and if I wasn't also in love with you, it would be easy to like him."

They stared at each other, his casual admission of love bringing everything to a halt.

His mind drifted to his father, as it often did when things slowed down enough for the nagging voice to rise above the chaos in his mind.

When Rainer was young, Raymond McKay made a game of punishing him for falling short of expectations. Not with public humiliation or disapproval, but by destroying the few sentimental items Rainer and Maura—his mother—cared about. The practice only grew worse when his mother passed and could no longer be a buffer between father and son. Then, Raymond had set about erasing bits of her. It was woefully motivating, and as angry as it made Rainer, he would be the first to admit that it worked.

He'd never told Cecilia about how his father's cruelty inspired him to be better, how the threat of destruction of Rainer's few sentimental items kept him focused and at the top of his guardian class. He was afraid Cecilia would burn Raymond alive with her anger. But underneath, Rainer knew he was just afraid of sharing his failures when there was so much at stake.

Cato's cruelty now made him feel similarly helpless. Rainer did not know how to counter this type of emotional warfare, but after a lifetime of being bullied, he was certain he should have been better prepared.

Cecilia's hands shook. She blew out a slow breath.

"What do you think, Cece?" Rainer asked.

"I think—" She swallowed hard. "I think I was a fool for love. I wanted to be loved so badly. I think I convinced myself I was buying time and safety—" Her voice cracked and she fell silent.

"There are much worse things to be a fool for than love," Rainer said. "You couldn't have known. When I said I didn't trust Xander, I never expected this. I know you don't want to hear it and frankly, I can't fucking believe I'm saying it, but I know Xander loved you. He made a mistake. A terrible one, but he did it for a reason I can understand."

"Don't defend him." She sat up straighter.

"I'm not. I'm trying to defend *you*, Cece. Right now you need to trust your judgment, and I'm telling you that it's sound." Rainer ran a hand through his hair. "I know what it's like to know I'm losing you and feel desperate to hold on. I know what it's like to make a mistake that breaks your heart, and to wish I could save you from it. Worst of all, I know what it is to feel your pain. I don't blame him for wanting to spare you."

Her gaze locked on his and she held her breath before squeezing her eyes shut and breaking the trance.

Rainer drew her out slowly, a practiced and delicate art it had taken him years to learn. "What do you think?" he repeated.

"I think—" Cecilia's whole body shook. "I think—"

Anger, fear, grief, love, frustration all swirled through their bond.

"Maybe I thought I was buying my freedom when I married Xander, when really I was buying a prettier cage with a little more room to grow. I love him, but I think I was so used to negotiating what I wanted that it felt normal to give in—like getting any one thing I wanted was a success. I think if I lived in a world that allowed it, I would have chosen me. I would have waited."

Bitterness seeped into the words. The dam was broken and everything rushed forth at once, but Rainer was used to weathering her onslaughts of emotion.

"I think that I should have seen myself in the place of power to negotiate," Cecilia said, her voice choked with emotion. "I was too busy staring down what I was losing. Too busy trying to figure out who I was without all the roles and responsibilities someone else assigned me. In a day, I lost trust in everyone I loved. I was so busy trying to hold on to that one last semblance of control, I forgot what I wanted the whole time: the power to make my own choices. I should have given myself a chance to figure out who I was on my own. There's not really anyone I can blame for that except myself. But this isn't really about blame. It's about facing reality. I fell in love with the first person who gave me the kind of love and attention I should have demanded all along. I owed it to myself to want more."

Cecilia went silent, tears streaming down her cheeks and dripping onto her scarlet tunic.

Rainer squeezed her hand and gave her an encouraging smile.

She took a deep breath that rattled through her body as if she was much older than twenty-three. "I think that women in this world are raised to believe love is sacrifice, to give and give of themselves until they have nothing left—until they are a hollowed-out vessel for a man's desires. I convinced myself I didn't believe that, but I still acted like I did. I sacrificed too much, and the only person I can really blame is me, because that was a choice I made. Love is about having faith. It's the ultimate surrender. And men like power too much to stomach such a surrender."

She raked her fingers through the sand and wiped her eyes on her sleeve. "I want to stop exchanging pieces of myself for power and love. I want to feel like I am worthy exactly as I am, and I think I am the only one who can make myself feel that way."

The words struck him like a well-aimed arrow. Rainer swallowed hard, the revelation settling like a stone in his stomach. *He* had made her feel that way—that he could only love her gentleness. Every word that came to mind felt too small to explain his regret.

She pressed a trembling hand to her heart. "I don't want to be someone who is ruined by hurt. I want to be brave in the face of it." The pain in her eyes left Rainer breathless. "But what if I can't come back from this?"

The admission shattered him. Rainer had seen her defeated when her father died, but even after the initial fright she gave them, she bounced back. Now she just looked lost.

"Cece—"

She held up a hand. "You don't understand what it's like to trust someone like that, Rain. To let them into your heart. To show someone everything about you. You only get to trust like that once. It only takes one time for it to be broken. You don't know what that's like because the world doesn't ask men to be vulnerable that way to begin with, but it expects it of women."

Rainer was speechless. He'd taken vulnerability for granted in all the women he'd been with, but he'd taken it for granted most with Cecilia. He'd been afraid of the risks she took, pretending to himself it was wise of him not to do the same. He hadn't considered what it took to open up to that kind of hurt because he'd been afraid of it his whole life.

He'd never let someone close enough to let him down—not even Cecilia. He'd always thought she was so reckless, but now he was struck by the foolishness of playing it safe.

Cecilia was so much wiser than he'd given her credit for. It was easy to be brave with a sword in your hands—much harder to be brave with your heart in them. That was her kind of brave.

Her hands shook, and she dug her nails into her palms to still them. "I feel like this might break me. I know I have to keep going, but I can't see the path forward."

Rainer tugged at their connection. Nothing made him feel more violent than seeing Cecilia upset. If he had his way, he would eviscerate everyone who hurt her—Xander included. It had taken years of trial and error, and every shred of his self-control to understand when to fight for her and when she needed to fight for herself. His impulse was always to show her gentleness when she was so wounded, but it didn't feel right for the situation. She needed tough love.

"Only you can decide what breaks you, Cece. You're not in a palace anymore, or enemy territory. You're free. There's nothing left to hold you back. You can't pretend to be powerless because you're not. So the choice is yours. Will you continue to fight for your freedom or will you build another cage?"

He held his breath, unsure whether to expect more tears, rage, or silence.

"Maybe I never was trapped in the first place," she rasped.

"Maybe you never were."

"Maybe this is more my fault than I want to admit and it's just been easier to blame the rest of you."

"Maybe you made the best bad choice, but it was still a bad choice," Rainer said. "You did your best. You fought for us, but now it's time to fight for yourself, Cece. You were scary strong before all of this, but now you're even stronger. I wish I could have spared you the heartache that made you that way, but I can only stand beside you as you try to rebuild."

"I still love him," Cecilia whispered.

"I know."

"I still need to fix him."

"I would expect no less. None of us are giving up on Xander. At the very least, he's our best shot at peace for both kingdoms, and at best, he's a friend."

Her eyebrows shot up. "Since when?"

"I didn't say we were close, and he hurt the woman I love, but before that there was a tenuous friendship forged in the fire of trying to keep a reckless goddess alive."

She grinned and laid back in the sand. Rainer lay down beside her.

"Do you think that Evan, Cal, and Sylvie will get the Godsbane?" she asked.

"Yes."

She laughed. "You answered so fast. What happened to Rainer the worrier?"

"I've got to pick something to believe in, right? I have to believe in this team that we've built because the alternative is not an option. I have to believe that the five of us—six if you count Xander—have what it takes to save Olney—to build something better."

She slid her hand into his and squeezed as they stared up into the darkening sky. The first stars appeared, twinkling bright against deep violet.

"I think what we need is a spell for courage to pick you up when you're feeling lost, and remind you of who you are," he said, turning his head toward her. "What do you call the words you say when you're weaving a spell?"

A hint of a smile played across her lips. "An incantation."

"So we need an item to exchange and an incantation." He held up her hand, brushing his thumb over the crescent scar on the outside of her palm. He reached into his pocket and pulled out the green satin ribbon.

Cecilia's eyes went wide. "Is that—"

"Your favor?" Rainer placed it in her hand. "Yes."

She looked at him with tears in her eyes. "You kept it."

Rainer suddenly felt embarrassed by his attachment to the ribbon, but the wave of nostalgia and joy that warmed their bond let him know that she was just as moved by it.

"You told me it was magic and that it would make me brave. I have carried it on me every day since, so I can attest that it works."

Cecilia gasped out a laugh, fresh tears streaming down her cheeks. "I can't believe you still have it."

"It has served me well for a very long time." He took the ribbon from her hand and tied it in a bow around her wrist. "It's my most prized possession, but maybe you can borrow it for a bit—to remind you that you're not alone when heading into battle."

She nodded, playing with the frayed ends of the bow. "So this favor is my exchange, but what about the incantation?"

"We want to cultivate courage both in action and emotion. How about something like—" He paused, trying to form the sentiment in his mind into something clever. He traced her scar with his finger. "Brave with my hand. Brave with my heart."

"Brave with my hand. Brave with my heart," she whispered as if trying on the invocation. "I like it."

"So you'll say it any time you feel lost. Any time you need the reminder."

She nodded, looking from the ribbon on her wrist to the stars blinking to life above them.

He turned to look at her in profile and was reminded of the night nearly six months before when he lay in a field watching the Summer Firestorm meteor shower with her.

"Tell me the one about the village where it rains stars and wishes," she said.

Rainer grinned. He knew Cecilia loved the story he'd made up that night because she'd asked for it more than once, and because it was where he found the bookmark in the book of stories he'd written for her. He wondered what the tale reminded her of.

Rainer saw it in her eyes that night. Hope. The story he made up with her in mind was about hope, because when he looked at her smile under the sparkling starlight, it inspired him to hope for all the impossible things he wanted. Cecilia had a way of making people feel foolish not to hope for life's long shots.

So there, in the dark, he told his story to the woman who inspired it.

———

"I cannot believe something so small can bring down a god," Rainer said.

The finely ground powder shimmered in the light pouring in through the Reznik Estate kitchen windows. Sylvie shook it into a vial.

"Let's just pray it works. I pulled up the memory of what Devlin said and followed every step, so it should be perfect," Sylvie said.

Rainer looked from her to Cal. "What did it cost?"

Sylvie shrugged. "I know Devlin said it would cost us something of value but if it took some price, it's not one we are aware of so far."

Rainer thought of his friends losing something unknown to a

magical exchange for this herb made him very uneasy, but what was done was done.

Sylvie turned her gaze on Cecilia. "Are you sure you're ready for this? Do you think it will work?"

Cecilia shrugged. "Only one way to find out."

Rainer wanted to shake her. How could she look so relaxed when their plan had so many points of failure?

After falling asleep on the beach the night before, she'd woken eager to move forward with their plan and face Cato. Rainer hated the plan. He didn't want to let her within striking distance of Cato, let alone across a table from him drinking tea that would neutralize her godly powers.

When Cal, Sylvie, and Evan returned, exhausted, from the Wilds that morning with the Godsbane, they'd suggested that if Cecilia invited Cato to tea, he wouldn't be able to resist. Evan and Rainer would lay in wait while Cecilia served him Godsbane tea and set about a fake negotiation for Xander's release. Once Cato's godly powers were negated, Evan and Rainer would come in and help Cecilia stab him with her Godkiller blade. Rainer hated the plan, and even Evan seemed concerned with all the points for failure, but they didn't want to wait and see what surprise Cato might bring straight to Olney if given the time.

Sylvie pulled Cecilia into a hug and whispered something in her ear, nodding to the pot of tea already steeping on the counter. Sylvie's secondary magical affinity was earth and she always made the best blends of tea. After seeing the state of Rainer's brutally bitten-down nails years earlier, she'd started making him a soothing mixture she appropriately named "Rainer's Anxie-tea." He still drank it every evening, though it didn't quite seem up to the task of staving off impending war and *your best friend is a goddess* restlessness.

Casting one last meaningful glance at Evan that looked half-threat, half-flirt, Sylvie ducked out the door, leaving Rainer, Evan, and Cecilia alone in the kitchen.

"Go to the sitting room and I'll bring the tea," Cecilia said.

Rainer led Evan into the sitting room. Evan took the huntmaster's usual leather armchair in the corner, allowing him to see both ways into the room, a clear sign of his training. Rainer sat across from him in a plush chair by the fireplace. He poked at the fire just to have something to do with his hands. He'd protected Cecilia from so many threats over the years, but never from a god.

The breathless terror of watching her fight Endros was still so visceral that Rainer froze up every time it came to mind.

Cecilia carried in a tray with tea and biscuits. She poured the steaming tea into three cups. She handed one to Evan, placed one aside for herself, and handed the last one to Rainer, with lemon and mint and a little bit of sugar, just the way he liked.

"Don't look so anxious, Rainer. We have a plan," Evan said.

Rainer took a sip of the tea, the bold taste spreading warmth through his chest. "Would you want Xander sitting powerless across from Cato?"

Evan cocked his head. "Isn't he already?"

Rainer rubbed the back of his neck, taking another gulp of tea. "Point taken."

Cecilia sat down beside him and brushed her thumb over his brow. "I found a worry, but I'll fix it in a hurry."

He smiled in spite of himself. "I wish that you weren't so eager to be a hero."

"And I wish you weren't such a fun-sucker," she countered.

He laughed. When he was young, the taunt got under his skin, but now that he took himself less seriously it only made him smile.

"What's done is done," Cecilia said. "Grimon delivered our invitation. We have a couple hours. Don't worry until you have to."

His mouth suddenly felt dry. He took another long pull of tea, but it didn't help. His head felt heavy and a sudden fatigue pressed in on him from all sides.

He glanced at the untouched teacup in Cecilia's hand. "Is yours too hot?"

She shook her head. "Just not thirsty at the moment."

Rainer blinked. His eyelids felt impossibly heavy. He rubbed his eyes, trying to focus on Evan across the room. Evan, whose tea sat untouched beside him.

His chest grew tight, adrenaline kicking his heart into gear to try to fight the sedative in the tea. He looked down at his nearly empty cup before blinking at Cecilia. "What did you do?"

Guilt bloomed through their bond. "I'm sorry. I knew you wouldn't be able to stay away and I won't be able to concentrate if he manipulates you."

The room grew dimmer and Rainer fought to keep his wits. He tried to press forward to wretch and throw up the sedative but he only slumped to the side.

"You fucking traitor," he growled at Evan.

"I'm sorry, but your reaction makes me certain we made the right decision."

Rainer turned his wild gaze back on Cecilia but the fatigue was dragging him down fast. The last thing he saw before the darkness took him was Cecilia's guilty frown as she guided his head to a pillow.

22

CECILIA

Cecilia tried to put Rainer's look of betrayal out of her head.

She forced herself to sit still. It was her choice to make all the others leave so she could handle Cato herself. They'd all done their part to make sure she was as prepared as she could be. Evan was on the beach trail listening for her shout so he could step in and help her fight Cato once the Godsbane took effect.

If this went right, their entire nightmare could be over today. She steeled herself against the fear of failure.

Brave with my hand. Brave with my heart, she thought. The words were comforting, even if Rainer wasn't there to say them, as was the faded green ribbon still tied around her wrist. She could not believe he'd held onto it all these years and never told her, but she was happy for the nostalgic comfort of it.

Her plan was not ideal since there were quite a few opportunities for failure—if Rainer had noticed her slipping the sleeping tonic into his tea; if Cato didn't want to join her for tea; if the Godsbane didn't work.

But Cecilia was no longer willing to sit still and wait for the battle to come to her. She wanted to take it to Cato. She was willing to go for a high-risk, high-reward plan since it was the only one they had.

She sat on the window seat, staring out at the sea in a red dress fit for the Princess of Argaria. Months ago, when they'd returned to Olney, Xander had insisted she order a bunch of clothing fit for a princess, but she hadn't worn much of it, except for the silk and lace undergarments that he loved.

The thought of him sent a pang of hurt through her, like a splinter lodged in her heart, the constant hurt made worse by attention.

Outside, the midday sun sparkled on the waves. She took a deep breath of the salty air that floated in through the open window. It had been nearly six months since she and Rainer set out on the Gauntlet run that started the mess they now found themselves in. The chaos in her life might have been someone else's creation, but it was up to her to solve it.

Rubbing her thumb across the inside of her left wrist, she took in the new topography of the skin forever scarred from her fight with Nessa Ducrane, the white slash on her wrist a constant reminder of her love for her husband.

Love he betrayed with his lie. Love that might not even be real.

"Little Dove, so kind of you to invite me to tea."

Cato's voice made her jump but she didn't turn to look at him. *Don't seem eager. Stay calm.*

"So glad you could make it," she said.

"The invitation surprised me after the state I left your husband in."

She slowly turned to face Cato.

"I like the princess costume—very lovely." His heavy gaze traveled over her.

"And you look like the god who ruined my life." *Act natural.*

Cato rolled his eyes. "Nonsense. You ruined it just fine on your own. I simply provided you with the options you so badly wanted." He looked around the cottage. "Will your friends be joining us?"

"I thought it best we meet one on one."

He smirked. "Shame. I'd hoped to chat with your love."

She rolled her eyes. "You already have."

"No, your *other* love." He picked invisible lint from his tunic. "It's so hard to keep them straight. You're such a busy woman."

Cecilia's eyes narrowed. "Stop the games. I'm not in the mood."

Cato arranged his lips into a pout. "But I'm always in the mood. I'll give you credit for being brave, Little Dove. Stupid, but brave. Where's your dagger?"

"Close enough, but I'd prefer not to give away its location to someone who can teleport."

His gray eyes flashed with glee. "Fair enough."

She looked him over. "Where's yours?"

"I left it at camp. I have no desire to hurt you, Cece."

She cocked her head to the side.

"Fine. I have no desire to *physically* hurt you, Cece."

"How do you do it?" she asked. "Travel like that?"

Cato shrugged. "I just bend where I am and fold it to where I'm going, like a piece of paper."

"But there's so much more to magic than—"

"I simply remind myself that my will is greater than the world's."

He said the words as if it were as easy as breathing, but there was terrifying truth in them. Magic required intention and force of will as much as an actual connection to power.

"Tea?" She gestured to the kitchen table.

Cato sat as she retrieved the kettle and poured the hot water into the teapot filled with tea and Godsbane.

Don't seem overeager. You're neutral. Nothing matters. Everything is fine. You're just heartbroken. The last thing she needed was for Cato to read her intentions. It was part of why she'd forced her friends to leave. She couldn't take the chance of one of them tipping him off to the plan.

Cato nodded, studying her carefully as she laid out a plate of biscuits and poured them both tea. As she expected, he waited for her to take a sip. She knew she'd have to drink it, too. She was counting on the element of surprise and her years of training and not her goddess power.

Cato smiled as he took a long sip of his Godsbane tea. He studied her face as he ate a biscuit. "So what can I do for you, *Your Highness*?"

"I want you to fix Xander or help me fix him."

His eyes went wide. "You want to make a bargain?"

She choked on her tea. "No bargains. I simply want my husband back and you've had enough fun playing games with him. I'm offering you my word, which is better than yours so far."

Cato sat back in his chair and crossed his arms as if considering. He took a long sip of tea and Cecilia forced herself not to look at how empty his cup was. She didn't know how much it would take, but so far, she felt no different. When she'd been hit by the Godsbane arrow, the effect had been immediate, but perhaps it was different when it didn't immediately enter the bloodstream. She took another sip.

Stall, Cece. Be heartbroken.

"While you consider it, can I ask you something?" she asked.

He shrugged. "Of course. Whether I will answer is the real question."

She rolled her eyes to hide her desperation to know for sure. "I suspect you can't actually influence someone to love someone else. I think it was fully my choice, and I love him this much on my own, with none of your influence. Most of our relationship has grown since I became a goddess, and that means your power wouldn't work on me."

Cecilia stared at Cato expectantly as she lifted her knee under the table and tapped the spot where Evan had secured her Godkiller blade. Relief flooded her when she felt the sheath there, waiting for her.

"That wasn't a question," Cato said.

She huffed out a breath. "Did you actually influence me, or did you just help him in some roundabout way for the sake of making a bargain?"

His lips quirked up. "Clever goddess. You figured it out. Even the gods can't make someone love. You must have learned a thing or two from that pesky sister of yours. Desiree really has a bone to pick with me." He sipped more tea, and Cecilia refilled both of their cups.

"How did you get around the bargain?" she asked.

"I convinced Davide not to meddle in the way he wished, which was technically enough to help Xander marry you."

Cecilia tried to hide her devastation but she could tell she'd slipped up by the way Cato leaned forward to watch her. Better he look at that. Better to perform her grief for him than allow him to see the truth in her heart. She took a scalding sip of tea and blinked back the tears in her eyes.

"Xander was the last person I could count on to see and understand me, and you ruined that. You must be so pleased with my pain."

"On the contrary, Goddess. Pain is a regrettable but necessary side effect of isolating you. It speaks to your kind heart that I had to work so hard to do it. I know it's easy to make me a villain, but I promise I'm on your side."

Cecilia laughed bitterly. She wiped a stray tear from her cheek as she drank more tea, trying to hide her rising panic. Her power still buzzed beneath her skin.

"You think I want to destroy you," Cato continued. "But that couldn't be further from the truth. I want to set you free. If you know history, you know your father is the only god I helped kill. The rest of the gods were killed by their so-called 'worshippers.' The same people who praise you for your strengths and talents now will be the very ones who come for you when you don't do what they want. It may be hard to see when you're new and shiny, but they will come for you eventually as they have for the rest. They will blame you for things outside of your control. It is the nature of mortals to seek power and to annihilate those who have more than they do. The only way to avoid the same fate is to bring them to heel."

She stared into his steely eyes. "You are going to claim you didn't have a hand in your father's death?"

Cato shrugged, taking a sip of his tea. "Are you going to claim the old man didn't have it coming? That if I hadn't set you two on a collision course you would have let Endros live?"

Cecilia looked away, trying to shove down her frustration. Power still pulsed beneath her skin. It almost felt like it was reaching out to Cato.

"When you're young, it's easy to tell the villains," Cato continued. "As you get older, you find there's much more gray area. It becomes harder to discern where the line is. When you live as long as I have, you might begin to see human rhythms. The centuries harden your heart. Someday you'll see enough of humanity to understand that villainy is in the eye of the beholder."

Cecilia shook her head, using it as an excuse to check his teacup. It was almost empty. "I hope I never live long enough that I lose my love for other people."

"Be careful what you wish for, Little Dove. Your wishes have agency to come true."

There was no menace to his tone but it still felt like a threat. Though he did have a point. "Why do you hate love?"

Cato picked at a thread on his cloth napkin. "Love is the only true weakness for those of us who are immortal. I'm trying to keep you alive, Cecilia. I haven't lived this long by offering up my weakness to mortals so that I can be manipulated."

Cecilia frowned, sensing regret and fear coming off of him in waves. She'd expected he would be better at hiding his emotions, but he'd let that much slip. "No, that's not all of it. It's only part."

He crossed his arms, narrowing his eyes. "You want my sob story, Cecilia? You want me to share my secret pain like your weepy mortal lovers?" He rolled his eyes.

"I want to hear the truth."

"You want to hear how my father killed anyone I got close to for a century until I learned my lesson. I can pull many tricks, but never once did I fool him. He always found them and I am lucky he did, because we watched your family get picked off one by one, all brought down by their love of mortals—some by the lovers them- selves. And there you sit, thinking I'm cruel when I'm just trying to save you the heartache and keep your soft heart beating."

Cecilia swallowed hard. "Why should you care if I live?"

The crease in Cato's brow softened. "Because forever is a long time not to have a friend."

She didn't fully believe him, but the loneliness swirling through the air around him suggested it was at least partially true.

His eyes passed over her, and she did her best to look heartbroken.

"This tea is delicious," he said, holding her gaze as he drained his cup. "I haven't had a Caprinos tea from the Wilds in some time."

Cecilia stared at him. "What did you say?"

"The tea. It's rare. From the Caprinos root in the Wilds. It's scarce since most people get creeped out by that place. It tastes fresh. Did you just harvest it?"

He was messing with her. He had to be. Evan and Sylvie had followed Devlin's instructions to the letter when harvesting the Godsbane. Sylvie was a memory witch with a perfect recollection of the location of the plant, what it looked like, and how to prepare it.

Cato's grin turned feral. "I see you trying to figure out where you went wrong. The answer is in what I've said before. There's no one who doesn't owe me a favor—even the god of wisdom and reason isn't above making the mistake of bargaining with me. Devlin had to pay his debts eventually."

Cecilia's palms grew sweaty and her heart pounded as she stared at Cato. For a moment she sat there frozen in shock and panic.

It was a point of failure in their plan she hadn't even considered. Devlin hadn't helped them. He'd sabotaged them. She wanted to scream when she called up the memory. Devlin had literally told her in no uncertain terms that it wouldn't work.

"It's not possible to catch him off guard. Best to assume the trickster god knows you better than you think," Devlin had said. *"Rest assured, Your Highness, he already knows what moves you will make. To try to use Godsbane on him would be a mistake."*

"Bold of you to drink the tea yourself," Cato said, leaning back in his chair. "I enjoy this game we're playing."

Cecilia couldn't speak, torn between grabbing her blade and

trying to stab him across the table and staying still in the sights of a predator.

"What was the rest of the plan once I drank what you thought was Godsbane?" he asked. "I know you must have that blade stashed. Or was the guardian going to burst through the door and take care of me?" He called over his shoulder toward the front door. "You failed, Guardian!"

He turned back to look at her as recognition tore over his face. "You don't have backup. What's keeping me from just grabbing you and taking you back to my camp?"

Cecilia shrugged. "I suppose I'm the only thing to keep you from doing so."

"You know I came here with the good intention of making a deal with you, no tricks. I thought we could solve this Olney problem amicably."

She scoffed. "So you felt it was an amicable move to try to kidnap me? To successfully kidnap my husband and ruin his mind? That felt *amicable*?"

"Compared to the destruction I could cause." Cato was quiet as his eyes passed over her again. "I'll have to retaliate. If I let an action against me go unpunished, people will think I've gone soft. People come for the gods who show weakness. I can't make exceptions."

"Have I not been punished enough?"

"Only I say when it's enough, Little Dove."

Cecilia narrowed her eyes at him. "Why do you call me that?"

He smiled as he leaned forward in his chair. "Because it suits you."

She sighed. "What do you want from me?"

"Whatever you will give me and also everything else."

Hearing Rainer's words in his mouth chilled her blood. Had he been spying that day after she told off King Hector? Her heartbeat hammered in her ears. She shifted her hand to her lap in case she needed to grab her dagger.

Cato studied her quietly. "You know you shouldn't let a little impulse control problem turn you off of your powers."

Cecilia laughed. "Only you would call murdering an entire battalion of hunters an impulse control problem."

"It takes time to learn how to wield such power. I'm not surprised that you couldn't handle it right away. But the more you practice, the more you learn. Tell me—what have you learned?"

Cato was too curious.

Cecilia leaned forward, matching his posture—an old trick she'd learned from training with her father. Mimic body language to show strength. "Nothing of consequence."

Cato scoffed. "Spending so much time being mortal has made you too ruled by emotion. The only currency worth having in this world is power, and you have it in spades, but you're afraid to use it. This is what love does. It makes you weak. It makes you vulnerable when you most need to be strong. Your precious kingdom is on the brink of war, and all you can do is worry about your husband and your broken heart."

Cecilia stood, slamming her hands on the table. "You think you've got me pegged? How about you? Centuries of living and the only thing you want is power. How *original*! You and every other man in the world. What a godsdamned bore you've turned out to be."

Cato's brows drew together as the insult landed. "You think I just want power? You think it's so simple. Cecilia, this monarchy—the men who ruled this kingdom for hundreds of years created a program that relied on child warriors. They bound you to another for a lifetime when you were just six years old. They've stripped away every ounce of autonomy and free will your whole life, and yet you want to save it. You want to beg for scraps within a broken system." He let out a harsh laugh. "I want to break the entire thing and start again."

Cecilia laughed. "No doubt with something that benefits you much more."

"Of course." He slammed his fist on the table, rattling the cups in their saucers. A flash of silver light lanced through his eyes and he winced like he was struggling to control himself. "Who says what's best for me isn't also best for the people of these two kingdoms, who have known nothing but war for their entire history? There was strife long before the War of the Gods. We could unite the two kingdoms, you and I. Gods from opposing kingdoms working together. You could have your precious Storm Prince. You could rule both kingdoms. You could create the kind of change you wanted to see in the world—help the women in both kingdoms become autonomous. Maybe even stop the guardian training programs and make joining the hunter army voluntary instead of compulsory for the lower class. We could establish a government run by common folk, with our guidance of course. You could change the patriarchal politics of this world. You haven't even considered that we might want the same things."

Cecilia rolled her eyes. "You don't make the best first impression."

Cato arched an eyebrow. "I saved you in the Reflection Forest."

"Fine, you don't make the best next few impressions. What's in it for you?"

"I'm done being under someone's thumb. My father and I spent centuries struggling to control the Saveros. Centuries with so little progress. I have nothing against the Storm Prince. Honestly, he has the kind of distaste for ruling that I could work with. You could be his queen, Cecilia. You could reconcile. I'm sure even you could forgive him. After all, you think of love as your superpower."

She eyed Cato skeptically. She didn't believe the rosy picture he was offering, but she was curious why he would offer it.

Cato's grin widened. "Want to know a secret I haven't even admitted to Xander?"

She nodded hesitantly.

"I didn't manipulate his emotions at all. He was that in love with you with none of my influence. He's a little obsessive, but Xander is as he's always been, a man of extremes."

Cecilia wasn't sure if she should be relieved. On one hand, she felt more confident in her marriage. On the other, she felt a little intimidated that he could feel so strongly and still not tell her the truth. But deep down she didn't know if she could take Cato at his word.

"So you see, I actually didn't manipulate either of you, until I kidnapped him, of course. I only kept Davide away so you could get married. I gave you your happily ever after." He waved his hand dismissively. "Honestly, the two of you owe me."

Cecilia frowned. "You only gave us something so we'd have something worth trying to save."

He cocked his head to the side and gave her a pitying look. "I saw my opportunity to use you against each other to set this entire plan in motion. Usually the most obvious solution is the best one. You both already loved each other, and you were spurred on by Xander's intensity. You don't have to pretend to me you didn't enjoy it. You were the beneficiary of some very focused attention, and you didn't mind it until someone wanted to use it against you."

Cecilia's anger flared. She wished she could use it to make Cato combust. The truth was that even if Cato hadn't manipulated her, Xander was comfortable with her being manipulated to begin with. What she felt might be real, but it did nothing to fix what was broken between her and Xander.

Cato tipped his chair back. "I want the freedom to use my power at will. I want freedom from fearing that people will rebel against me, try to control me, or take me out when I don't comply, like they have so many other gods. I want the world that existed when this all started with safety for men *and gods*. Unfortunately, the only language men speak is power. If I have to control those in power to ensure my safety, I will. You don't survive centuries without understanding the minds of men. You might find me cold, Cece, but when you live as long as I have—if you're lucky enough to do so—you'll understand."

"I don't believe you," Cecilia said.

"Then I suppose you've learned something. It wouldn't be wise of me to reveal my full plan until I'm ready to set it in motion, and it wouldn't be wise of you to believe everything I say. When the time comes, you'll know. The longer you hold out the more I'll spread the misery around, and you know it won't be you who suffers for it. It will be all the people you love. If you're not with me, you're against me, and I do so hate to fight, even with a worthy adversary." Cato stood with a start. "Send word when you're ready to give in, Little Dove. I'll be seeing you soon and I apologize in advance for the fallout of this attempt on my life, but like I said before, I can't let it go unpunished."

With that, Cato opened a slice in space and stepped through, disappearing from her cottage and leaving her with nothing but the fear of retaliation and the smell of pine and leather in his wake.

23

CECILIA

Cecilia had several hours to decompress from Cato's visit but felt no clarity about how to handle the trickster god. He wasn't a brute like his father, and with every bit of new information about him, she was less certain of what exactly he'd do. He was the kind of opponent she used to dread training against—strong, cocky, and unpredictable. She'd combed through his words and all of her siblings' advice and still she felt no more certain of how to beat him.

Though she'd felt Rainer's panic and a sharp yank on their bond a few moments before, it still startled her when he tore through the cottage door. His hair was wild from sleep. He folded forward, his hand over his heart as he struggled to catch his breath. His green eyes furiously searched her for injury.

She tried to force a casual smile as she held up her hands. "Before you yell at me, I had to. I knew you wouldn't stay away and you can't get mad at me for knowing you too well."

Rainer closed the distance between them. His hands gripped her shoulders, eyes burning into hers. "Ask me to kiss you."

She took a step back. "What?"

"Ask me to kiss you *right now*," Rainer growled. His hands squeezed her arms harder, his body practically vibrating with need.

She looked at his lips and then met his eyes as a shiver ran through her. "Rain."

"Please. I promised I wouldn't unless you asked me to, and I want to keep that promise, but I need to kiss you right now."

He pushed her back against the wall, pressing his trembling body against hers. Heat spread over her skin. One of his hands held a firm, proprietary grip on her hip and the other tilted her chin up. He lowered his head, his stubble brushing her cheek.

"I thought you would be gone," he said. "You have no idea how terrified I was. I thought I lost you."

He brushed his lips down her neck, and Cecilia shivered. Her entire body felt liquid. His breath danced over her collarbone. She leaned her head back against the wall, squeezing her eyes shut.

"I can explain," she rasped.

She brought her hands to his chest, but he grabbed them and pinned them against the wall above her head, which only sent another rush of heat through her body. He'd never been so assertive with her and this new side of him was intoxicating.

"No. You drugged me," Rainer whispered against her ear. "You're going to listen to what I have to say."

She swallowed hard as he brushed his lips over her cheek. He met her eyes again, and there was no mistaking the look in them. Desire snaked through their connection, hot and prickly. If she let him, he wouldn't hold anything back, and she could not let that happen. If she let him kiss her, she would want more, just like he so obviously did, but she was still married to someone else, even if that marriage was built on a lie.

He pressed his hips into hers and continued to murmur into her neck. "I was terrified I'd wake up and you'd be gone already. I was afraid I'd never see you again, or when I did, you would be someone else. Someone broken." He spoke every word against her skin. Goosebumps covered every inch of her skin, and her heart thundered in her chest. "Ask me to kiss you, Cece."

"I need—" She'd almost let the careless word slip when she didn't know what her body needed. It was making a very compelling case for needing everything Rainer could give her. Instead, she sent that need through their bond and she wasn't sure if he was responding because he truly felt it or because guardians were compelled to respond to their witch's needs.

"You are so unbelievably maddening. You do the most reckless things. You could have been hurt. You could have been killed and I never would have had a chance to hold you again." Rainer punctuated each sentence with a brush of his lips on her neck. "Ask me to kiss you."

His hips ground into hers and she felt him hard against her. She lost her will to argue with every word, with every breath dancing over her skin, with the tightening of his hand on her wrists above her head. She wanted everything he was offering at that moment. His lips said one thing, but his body said that he wanted to take her right there against the wall. That sounded very good to the pent-up, stressed-out part of her.

Yes. Her brain was loud, but kissing Rainer would solve none of her problems.

His lips hovered over hers.

"No," she panted.

Rainer dropped his head back and let out a sigh. He released her hands and stepped away, leaving her cold and aching.

"Gods, you are torture."

She laughed nervously. "I didn't do anything."

Rainer swallowed, his green eyes bright with desire. "You don't need to."

She rubbed her neck. "I thought you would just do it, anyway."

"You don't want it."

He was wrong. She absolutely wanted it, but what she felt was complicated.

Rainer's throat bobbed. "I would never take something you don't want to give me. This is about what you want."

Cecilia swallowed a lump in her throat. She didn't realize how badly she needed to hear those words until he'd said them. Guilt settled like a stone in her stomach.

"I'm sorry that I took your choice away today, but I knew you wouldn't be able to stay away when I was scared. Will you forgive me?" she asked.

His face grew stern. "Don't ever do that again."

Cecilia cocked an eyebrow at his words. They were the same ones she'd said to him after the last time he kissed her.

"I will only promise not to if you promise you will stay away when it comes to Cato. I know it goes against your every instinct, Rain, but if he gets to both of you, I am screwed. We all are."

Rainer studied her face carefully. "Okay. I promise."

"No. I want a crescent promise."

His eyebrows shot up. She held up her left hand.

He hesitantly clasped it. "I crescent promise I will stay away when you ask me to."

Rainer hugged her. They remained there, breathing together in the gathering dark as he sent peace through their bond.

His heart was the tether that brought her back every time she wandered too far, and now, more than ever, she needed to remember who she was.

But Cato's warning was clear. Every time she let herself closer to Rainer, she put him more at risk. Although she'd faced all previous villains with Rainer by her side, she was going to have to find a path forward on her own.

———

After tossing and turning all night, Cecilia finally gave up the notion of sleep when the sky was still dark. Rainer had reluctantly returned to his apartment the night before, and she was glad to have the cottage to herself.

In the half-light, she moved through the morning stretch routine that Xander liked to call "huntress foreplay." It was a combination of mobility and breathing exercises that kept her calm and grounded, and reduced soreness. But the suggestiveness of some of the poses meant that he interrupted her mid-routine most mornings.

As the room brightened with the rising sun, she took a sip of tea that had long grown cold. She crossed the room to the window seat, watching the sun peek out from the sea and light the striated clouds like pink and purple fingers scraping across the sky.

She replayed her conversation with Cato over and over, trying to untangle her emotions to see the complete picture clearly. Cato's game only became murkier as he revealed more of his cards. It was easier when he was clearly classified as a villain in her mind, but now she saw him in a new light.

He would not have been so forthcoming if there wasn't something he wanted, but she couldn't puzzle out what exactly it was. It seemed everyone wanted something from Cecilia, and she was tired of being used.

She expected to feel relieved Cato hadn't manipulated her into loving Xander, but she only felt robbed of the relationship she'd thought she had.

Being wanted was a quick stitch slipped in the pattern of her life —an escape hatch swinging open at the exact right moment. Xander had given her a way out that she was eager to take, and she had loved him for it. She *did* love him. But she'd been too restless, too rash, too reckless and desperate—happy to throw herself into marriage the way she did into any thrilling, dangerous thing.

Xander led her to believe he understood her. He was furious at everyone who treated her like a means to an end while using her in his own way. He had someone who loved and understood him—a huntress with a love of the forest, a witch who understood the thrill of magic, a goddess who would always keep him safe. Most of all, he had a lover who was vulnerable, who offered him the most secret parts of her heart, while he chose to only show what he wanted her to see.

Cecilia had believed there was nothing they couldn't overcome together, but suddenly a chasm yawned open between them, and she was unwilling to wait to see if it devoured her along with her love.

She could not see the way back to Xander, but worse, she felt like she'd given him too much, strayed too far and lost the path back to herself.

She'd made love a safe place for Xander. She loved him deeply, but she'd forgotten how to love herself.

She could spend a lifetime wondering what she might have done differently if she'd known about Xander's bargain or Rainer's love for her before her wedding, but it would do her no good.

Cecilia grieved the love she'd thought she had. Though she hated what Cato had done and said, she saw the truth in his words. Love was a tether for her when her world was turned upside down. The only way to know what she truly needed in her life was to slice the ties that still bound her so that she could see what she wanted without anyone else's influence.

For once, she resolved to choose herself.

Today, she would keep vigil and grieve. Tomorrow, she would go to King Hector and explain the godly bargain that had been struck in exchange for her marriage to Xander. She'd ask the king to dissolve their union—not to hurt Xander, but to give her the space to process what she wanted on her own.

Cecilia slid the sapphire and diamond ring from her finger, along with her plain gold wedding band. She tucked them into a pouch and hid them inside a hollowed-out book on the shelf where she kept precious things that hurt too much to look at.

She expected to feel lighter, having decided, but even knowing it was the right thing, all she could feel was her heart breaking.

PART III:
WHAT LOVE DOES

24

CECILIA

Cecilia's day started poorly. She'd woken to Evan knocking on her door just after dawn. His spies reported that the Argarian army was no longer split around the periphery of Olney; it was centralized in one spot. Cato seemed to use his power to transport his troops along with himself. Moving those numbers took significant time. Evan believed having them in one spot was a strategic move to make it easier to move them all at once. The problem was that no one knew where they would choose to attack.

Instead of going to see King Hector to get her marriage dissolved, Cecilia spent most of the day sitting around a map with her friends, trying to guess what Cato's retaliation would be for their attempt on his life. They'd spent the rest of the time poring over every magic and mythology book they could find, hoping to glean more detail on Cato's powers or spells that might help restore memory and undo his manipulation. For all their searching, they found nothing, and with movement from the Argarian army and daylight fading, they shifted their attention back to figuring out how to protect the people of Olney.

"I can't imagine that they'll use the same exact attack plan twice," Rainer said.

"But you also can't rule it out," Evan countered, rubbing his temples.

Cecilia sighed, shaking her head. "I need some air."

She plucked her cotton gloves off of the counter and stepped outside, hoping the cool air and late afternoon sun would help clear her head. She grabbed her shears and distracted herself from the dread brought about by Cato's promise of retaliation by tending to her garden.

The silk of her dress caught on thorns as she bent over the bushes Xander had given her as a wedding present.

While she might not have been able to detach herself from Xander officially, trimming back the bushes felt oddly therapeutic, as if with each snip she was pruning back a part of herself that would grow back stronger.

A shadow passed over her as she reached for a branch at the back of one bush.

"Enjoying your wedding gift, love?"

Cecilia spun toward the voice as she felt the familiar crackle through the air. "Xander!"

She was so shocked to see him she couldn't form any other words. He looked terrible. Dark circles shadowed his cloudy eyes, tarnishing their usual bright golden hue. For the briefest moment, a half-smile appeared, as if he was charmed by the absurdity of her gardening in a dress fit for a princess. But that glimpse of her husband was gone in an instant.

The cottage door creaked. She didn't have to turn to know Rainer was behind her.

"What have you been up to with all of your free time?" Xander asked, sneering at Rainer.

"Trying to figure out a way to help you. I know it's taking a while, but it's complicated," Cecilia said.

"You can stop." Xander's voice was devoid of all emotion. "I'm tired of this."

Cecilia closed the distance between them and brought a hand to

Xander's face. He flinched but didn't stop her, pressing his cheek into her palm. His composure wavered, and he closed his eyes.

"Come back to me," she whispered. "You dropped your news and ran away. We need to talk about our future."

"We have no future, Cecilia." Xander said her full name like it was a curse.

She opened her mouth to speak but Evan appeared beside her and beat her to it.

"Xan, I've known you my whole life and I've never seen you act so foolish, which is saying something. We have all been trying to help you, no one more than Cece."

She gave Evan a grim smile. She wasn't sure anyone but Rainer had noticed how she had stayed up most nights poring over books since Xander's confession.

Evan pressed on. "I've always known you as a man of your word, and I don't care what kind of magical spell you're under. I was there when you got married and I heard the words you said. You owe Cece better. You owe all of us better."

Cecilia never heard Evan speak to anyone that way, especially Xander.

"You're going to defend her. *Really*?" Xander shook his head. "After she kissed Rainer twice while we were married. Some loyal friend you are. I may have lied, but at least I've never cheated on my wife. At least I wasn't running around Olney kissing someone else like a common whore while my husband was being tortured."

The words struck her like a slap. Everyone held perfectly still, waiting for her to respond. She was humiliated her friends were there to hear Xander's cruel words.

Cecilia grabbed Xander's hand and recalled the fresh memory so he could feel how she felt.

"Are you happy now? You hurt me. Does it feel good?" she asked.

His eyes were wide and pained.

"Xander?" Evan asked as he stepped toward the two of them.

Just as quickly as the pain rose to the surface, Xander's face clouded over again. He grabbed the dagger from his waist and stabbed Evan in the stomach.

"Evan!" Sylvie shouted, running forward with Cal.

Cal drew his sword, but Cecilia held up a hand, warding him off. She fixed her furious gaze on Xander. "Can you fix it, Sylvie, or do you need me?"

"I can do it," Sylvie said, her voice tight with emotion but certain. Cal stepped forward, keeping himself between Sylvie and Xander.

Xander laughed. "I see you've got yourself your very own Olney witch, huh, Evan? Who would have thought it?"

Rainer stepped closer to Cecilia. Xander's gaze tracked his hand sliding to her lower back.

"Rainer McKay, always trying to play her savior. So gallant." Xander sneered. "Well, you can't save her from this one."

Cecilia swallowed the lump in her throat. "Haven't you done enough? Do you really want to do Cato's dirty work for him?"

Her resolve splintered. She grasped at anything from her training that would help. Her father's voice rose in her mind: *"When you're small, you have to run toward the blade if you want the advantage."*

She took a step forward. She was a goddess, and she needed to prove to herself more than anyone that she could face this alone.

"Always have to prove how brave you are, don't you?" Xander looked like he didn't know whether to be annoyed or impressed. "Let's see how brave you are when you read this." He held out a royal dissolution of marriage.

"I don't understand," Cecilia mumbled.

"Read the names, love," Xander said.

She froze when she saw her name and his.

"There's the face I was waiting for," he said.

She shook her head in disbelief. "It's a trick. This is just Cato messing with me."

"It's not. I petitioned King Hector myself. He was all too happy to have the goddess out of the clutches of an Argarian prince. I thought your infidelity would be enough to sell it, that and his desire to be rid of me, but it wasn't—not technically. Not when I couldn't prove it. So I had to use what I knew would work."

Xander watched her face like he was waiting for something to dawn on her.

Grief and fury warred in Cecilia's heart, and beneath that, a savage hurt yawned open. How dare he take away her choice again. How dare he call her a whore when he traded away his integrity, hoping to rob her of agency.

She bit her tongue to keep from voicing her thoughts.

"I was finally able to convince Hector when I explained your biggest flaw. One so big that no man could fault me for wanting out of this joke of a marriage." Xander laughed bitterly.

Cecilia heard Cal and Sylvie helping Evan to his feet behind her, but she couldn't turn away.

Xander gave her a brittle smile. "So he finally granted me what I wanted so much when I explained the exchange for your powers. He dissolved our marriage on account of the fact that you're *barren* and therefore *worthless* as a wife."

The words punched the air out of her lungs. She couldn't move. She couldn't think. She stared at him, unblinking, unbreathing, unthinking. Hurt bloomed like a bruise beneath her skin.

He beat her to it—robbed her of the opportunity to decide for herself once again.

"I have to admit, I thought you'd have more of a reaction," Xander taunted. "Do you know what's funny about all of this? Despite it all, I know that no matter what I do, you'll still belong to me. You'll go on loving me. I'll still have your heart."

Finally, air flooded Cecilia's lungs. With the breath came the pain. It hurt worse than anything. It hurt worse than almost dying. Worse than the betrayal of everyone she loved. Worse than her soul almost tearing from her body in the Cave of Longings. She couldn't process it. The flood of swirling emotions—rage, grief, betrayal, and bone-deep sadness—tore through her.

I can survive this. I can survive this. I will survive this.

It didn't feel like it but she knew she would. She was immortal and as far as she knew, no god had ever died of a broken heart.

Cato's retaliation was worse than she'd expected, but Xander had taken his most brutal shot and she was still standing.

Cecilia kept her face serene, her breath even, and her heartbeat steady. Then she stepped forward, handing the paper back to Xander.

"I'm sorry I couldn't give you what you wanted," she said, her voice devoid of emotion.

Those words cost her. Every moment of stoicism now would be paid in tears later. Xander had spoken to the fear that had dogged Cecilia since they'd married—the very thing she knew she could never give him that he wanted so badly.

Grief swelled around Xander, his anger swelling like a storm front.

Cato's manipulation might have been to blame for some of it, but Xander hit her where it hurt, and before that, he'd lied to her. He built the foundation of their marriage on a lie that he could have revealed and healed long before he did. The blow he'd just dealt simply ensured that the already crumbling castle fell.

Cracks formed in Xander's facade. The quickest flash of sadness lit his eyes. He'd always seen Cecilia exactly as she was, and he'd used the thing he knew would pack the biggest punch, just like she knew acting unfazed would have maximum impact on him.

Love was an exchange, and Xander and Cecilia had just exchanged killing blows. They both knew it. Love was handing someone the means to wreck you. That's what they were now, two human ruins a breath away from collapse.

"Run along to your keeper," Cecilia said. "Tell him that was a good shot, but I'm not impressed that he can't even do his own dirty work."

Xander stalked away, and Cecilia turned to face her friends.

Three sets of wide eyes stared at her. Rainer was the only one not looking at her. His gaze followed Xander's retreat. He placed a hand on her shoulder.

Her resolve cracked at the contact. She'd put on a brave face, but it was fading. The darkness inside her reared up, the grief she'd tried to pretend away by knotting it into an intricate ball in her chest coming unraveled.

"Cece—" Sylvie started, but Cecilia just held up a hand.

She fought desperately for control over her emotions.

"Not yet," Cecilia murmured. She looked at Rainer. "Is he gone? Is he far enough away that he won't hear?"

"Give it another minute."

The five of them stood there in silence. No one moved.

"Okay," Rainer said finally, signaling that it was safe and triggering a flood of grief and anger.

Cecilia crumpled to her knees and Sylvie slid down, meeting her there and wrapping her friend in her arms.

Sylvie held Cecilia as she sobbed. "Why didn't you say something? That was the exchange? You can't have children? I'm so, so sorry."

The old scar on Cecilia's heart was torn wide open. Everything she had packed neatly away—everything she'd come close to accepting—tumbled back out. Rainer knelt behind her and hugged both of them. Cal and Evan joined a moment later.

Cecilia was wrapped in all the love of the people she was closest to. She wanted it to make her feel better, but it did nothing to diminish the scalding hot pain in her heart. She felt broken. Her body shook with sobs and she didn't care who saw or heard; it felt like her heart had been torn from her body and trampled by wild horses.

They stayed there for a long time. Until the light faded and the air chilled with early evening. Finally, they peeled away, giving her space.

"Cece, he didn't mean that. He didn't mean that," Evan said.

She shook her head. "He did."

"I know he didn't."

"Please don't defend him right now," she rasped. "You know what he did doesn't change how much I love him. It doesn't change how hard this is, but I was going to do the same thing. Not out of spite, but because I needed to figure out what I wanted without the pressure of already being trapped. I just hadn't expected him to share all of that—"

Evan hesitated, guilt swelling around him. In all the time she'd known Evan, she'd rarely felt any emotion from him—only a hint of worry when Xander was first taken. "I knew. Xander told me the day you told him—back in Argaria. He felt so guilty for saying something about you two having kids. He kept beating himself up about it. I spent half that night talking him down. And that was how he felt after hurting you accidentally. There's no way he could hurt you that intentionally without feeling it too. I'm sure he didn't mean it."

Cecilia took a deep, shaky breath. "That might be true, but now he's done something I can't undo, and beyond that, he's put me under threat in my kingdom with the thing that would hurt me the worst. King Hector did not know what I exchanged. Only Xander, Rainer, and, apparently, you knew. The Teripins won't be happy to find out that there won't be baby gods and goddesses running around protecting Olney." She ran a hand through her hair. "There is only one piece of good news to come from this miserable day."

"What's that?" Evan asked.

Cecilia laughed bitterly. "Cato is eager to take away what little stability exists in my life, so at least that lets us know he's desperate."

"This is all *his* doing," Evan said.

"Cato can't create, Evan," she said. "He can only enhance. Somewhere in him, Xander had to feel that way. Children are important, especially to royals."

Evan opened his mouth to say something but quickly closed it.

Cal shifted beside her, placing a hand on her shoulder. "Rez, I'm really sorry."

"It's okay." Cecilia squeezed his hand. "Actually, it's really, really not for so many reasons, but it's certainly not your fault, Cal. You owe me no apology. I'm sorry to you and Sylvie and Rainer and Evan for dragging you halfway across the kingdom, thinking it would make a difference. I wasn't ready to give Xander up. Foolishly, I thought I could get through to him. I still do. I'm sorry that I put you all at risk.

It was selfish of me to even ask you all to come try to clean up my mess."

Sylvie took her hand. "You know that we all chose to go. None of us needed to. We wanted to. Cato is an asshole. If you thought I was going to stand back and let him pick on my best friend, you are not as smart as I've given you credit for."

Cecilia gave her a half-hearted smile, but she was weary. Bone tired. No part of her felt immortal in that moment.

"I can't say what it means to me that you've all been there for me this whole time," she said. "I've been really selfish and I'm sorry for that. I'm going to have to finish this. I don't want to give Cato any further way to hurt us, so I'm going to ask the rest of you to stand down for a bit. My heart is so broken—" Her voice cracked but she pushed through. "I couldn't bear someone else getting hurt."

"Cato picked a fight with all of us. I want to punch him in the face personally," Sylvie said.

Evan looked at Sylvie with admiration before turning back to Cecilia. "Obviously you know I'm not sitting out while my best friend turns into a lunatic, so you should count me in. It's personal for me, too." He patted the bloodstain on his shirt. "We'll give you some time to process this, but you know how to reach us when you're ready to make a plan."

He and Cal got to their feet and walked Sylvie home, leaving Cecilia and Rainer alone.

He silently helped her onto shaky legs and led her back to the cottage.

"What does it feel like to you?" she finally asked.

For a moment, Rainer looked confused, but then he pressed a hand over his sternum. "Like fury and despair. Like a dark and heavy grief I've never felt personally. It feels like what you felt back in Argaria after you found out about everyone lying to you, but it's sharper. It feels worse. Is it worse?"

"It is."

"I wish I could help."

Cecilia sighed. "You are. Just by being here."

"The moment he said it I felt how hard you had to fight for restraint. You're so strong."

She looked away. "I don't feel strong. I feel like I'm crumbling. I'm humiliated, and I'm too sad to even touch that. Xander did that. He chose to hurt me like that publicly. He was as vicious as he could be. It wasn't enough just to hurt me by leaving me. He also wanted to shame me, and that came from him. That's what's killing me. Some part of him wanted to do that."

Rainer shook his head. "You don't know that. The madness could have created that part of him."

"I never thought *you* would defend him."

"I'm not. I'm saying we don't fully understand how Cato's power works, and if it can build on itself. It's possible that thought never existed within Xander, but after all this madness, it was created and then Cato fed it. I've also given up on trying to understand Xander's moves. Every time I've thought he was doing something selfish, it turned out to be something to somehow keep from hurting you worse, and I can't help feeling like there's more to this."

Rainer's words called to mind the letter Xander had left her.

"You're trying to make me feel better, but I don't want to feel better right now," she said. "I need to feel how awful it is, or it will just be a distraction later."

"I will always try to make you feel better. I hate to see you hurt. What can I do?"

"What you always do. You can tuck me in and tell me a story."

She ducked into the washroom, taking off her dress and leaving it in a puddle on the floor, like blood from the invisible wound she'd been dealt. Staring into the mirror, she vowed never to wear a dress fit for a princess ever again. She might have thought that becoming the goddess had slain Princess Savero, but she was officially dead this time. That suited Cecilia Reznik just fine. She wasn't cut out to be a royal, even if she might have been the only woman in the two kingdoms cut out to love Xander Savero.

By the time she emerged from the washroom, she was so exhausted that she fell into her bed, which, thanks to her Aunt Clara, had been washed and no longer smelled like Xander's skin. She thanked the gods for that small mercy, because if his scent lingered after the day she had, she might have lost her mind.

Rainer laid down on the couch across from the bed, whispering a story about a thief who sneaked into a magical card game thinking she could win a favor from death, only to have him trick her into drinking poison and end up working for him instead.

As Rainer's smooth voice cut through the dark cottage, Cecilia's mind wandered to Grimon's words when they found him in the woods months before. *"Love is power. They're one and the same,"* he'd said. He wasn't wrong. Loving Xander gave him the power to crush her. Grimon told her that free will was the antidote to the whims of fate and she was done letting fickle fates decide things for her.

Though Xander had robbed her of the chance to pull away on her own, the result was the same and she needed to keep Rainer at a distance for the time being. Beyond just wanting to have the space to figure out what she wanted out of life, it was best for Rainer. The idea of him being used as a weapon against her was unbearable.

Cecilia would never give love the power to ruin her again. That was her sacred vow to herself.

She'd let Rainer stay for now to help her through the worst of it, but after that, she'd pull back. It was for their own good and she knew well from fairy tales you couldn't call yourself the hero unless your behavior reflected it. To keep Rainer close when it put him in danger was selfish, and she wasn't about to become the villain in her own story.

25

XANDER

Xander managed to temporarily avoid the burning magical pull back to Cato's lair. He'd ridden out of Olney City in late afternoon, thin sunlight slashing through the trees. Now the world was dark. He could have pressed on, but he pulled his horse to a stop in a dense stretch of trees a few miles from Cato's cottage.

He stretched out on his blanket, staring up at the night sky peeking through the treetops. Finally, the vicious ache of losing Cece caught him.

Xander had never felt so broken and untethered. He'd lost his parents, his brother was as mad as he was, and now he'd lost the one person who made him feel connected, happy, safe.

He forced himself to watch the memory on repeat, torturing himself with the look on Cece's face when he called her barren. What a ridiculous word to describe her. Cece was full of life, always moving and brimming with warmth.

Maybe Xander had learned nothing. Maybe he was still deciding for Cece, but what he wanted was to give her the freedom and time to decide for herself what she wanted with all the information.

It was foolish to hope that she'd still choose him, but he let himself dream about it for a moment as he tried to settle the sick feeling in his gut.

The memory ended, and he called it up again from the beginning.

He'd almost laughed upon finding her pruning the roses in a spectacular gown. The look on her face when she read their names on the dissolution of marriage that said: *Why won't you fight for me?*

But that was what he was doing, in the best way he knew how.

When Xander looked down the line, he couldn't imagine a lifetime of being Cato's tool to brutalize the woman he loved. No matter how the god had twisted his jealousy and anger, his love remained like a poison in his blood, as strong as it had ever been.

Xander had suggested the dissolution idea to Cato. It was a strategic move on Xander's part, even though it absolutely destroyed him. The trickster wanted the quick win. He was in a hurry to get to Cece. If Cato was thinking clearly, he would have thought about the long game, as he usually did, and told Xander not to end the marriage that gave him access and control. But whatever power Cato had stolen from his father, Endros, had left him impatient. It was a lucky break for Xander.

As much as it broke Xander's heart, he was relieved when King Hector dissolved the marriage so easily. Xander didn't actually say anything about infidelity or infertility to King Hector. All he'd said was that he wanted to dissolve his marriage to Cece, and Hector had been thrilled at the prospect. He didn't press Xander for an explanation, and that was a relief. The fewer people who knew what Cece had exchanged, the better. Cato had ears everywhere. The last thing Xander needed to do was give Cato any more opportunities to wound his wife—ex-wife. Xander could not blow this now, or he'd have hurt her for nothing.

He couldn't let Cece be alone and broken-hearted her whole life. She deserved whatever joy she could salvage when this war ended. If this war ended. It went against every instinct in Xander to give her the freedom to be with Rainer, but she deserved some kind of happiness.

It was a way to force her to choose for herself once and for all, and it gave her the freedom that she both needed and deserved.

Though he wished he could have found a delicate way to get her to give up on him, he could only see that one path forward. She fought fiercely for the people she loved, and Xander was lucky enough to be one of them.

The burning started in his feet and spread up his legs. He knew it was the bargain with Cato calling him back, deciding he'd had enough rest. Resistance was futile.

Xander mounted his horse and continued riding down the moonlit trail.

He hoped someday Cece would see that he'd done it to save her, that he could explain. He thought nothing could be worth seeing the hurt in her eyes. Her entire face might have stayed neutral, but he knew those eyes, had memorized their every expression, and there was no pain she could truly hide from him.

How foolish he'd been to feel relieved that she was immortal. With so much focus on her being physically strong, he'd forgotten there were much worse ways to hurt.

Still, he wanted to defend himself to his friends. He wanted to explain. He wanted to do so many things, but he'd tapped into the other side of him—into his fourteen years as a spy—to hold on to the kind of self-control it took to be cruel to his best friend and the love of his life. Choosing the two of them had been intentional, since they would fight the hardest for him. He stabbed Evan where he knew he could be easily healed, but he needed the hunter sworn to protect him to see that he was lost. He needed Evan and Cece to leave him to clean up his own mess.

He crested the hill, taking in the flickering lantern lights of the city of Rowdane and the Argarian army camped in tents on its borders. Seeing the near entirety of the army in one spot filled him with dread, not just as a military strategist, but as someone who loved both kingdoms.

Xander turned left at the camp and made his way to Cato's commandeered cottage as the burning in his body receded. Nausea flooded him as he approached the door. He composed himself before facing Cato. Now, more than ever, he could not afford to let anything slip.

Cato needed to believe that Xander had dissolved the marriage to hurt Cece, not to unbind her from the mistake he'd made. Xander hated her, but really he loved her. He did the kindest thing he could think of, in the cruelest way possible.

He scrubbed a hand over his face. Technically, the dissolution made it as if they'd never been married at all. As if Cece had never walked down the aisle like she'd stepped right out of his dreams. As if he hadn't blinked back tears as she spoke her vows with so much trust and love in her eyes. As if he hadn't felt like he might burst from joy and relief the first time he kissed her as his wife.

In a moment, the last few months of his life were wiped away. The same months that had brought some of the highest highs and lowest lows he'd ever experienced. Although it would have been easier to erase them, he wouldn't have given up the wreckage of those memories for anything. They were messy and beautiful, much like the woman he shared them with, and even in their gnarled, twisted states, there were glimmers in his mind left untouched. Small moments that still left him breathless, like the way she was so grumpy in the morning until he kissed her, or the way she ran her fingers through his hair idly while she read. They would haunt him forever, but it was better to be haunted by the loss than ignorant to the joy of experiencing that kind of love.

Forcing himself to take deep breaths, he tapped the fingers on his right hand to his thumb. He leaned against the side of Cato's cottage for a long time, settling his nerves.

Finally, he entered.

Cato looked up with a grin. "Your Highness, I assume your endeavor was a success."

Xander scowled. "Yes."

"And how did she take it?"

"She said—" Xander cleared his throat. "She said nice try, but why don't you try doing your own dirty work next time?"

Cato frowned, a hint of menace in his eyes. "Were there tears?"

Xander shook his head. "No. She just said she was sorry she couldn't give me what I wanted."

Cato's eyes went wide. "Tricky goddess. What is she playing at?" He leaned back in his chair, rubbing the scar over his right brow.

Xander shrugged. "I got the impression she's just exhausted. To Cece, the waiting is worse than the battle itself. She was raised to fight."

"Or perhaps she's secure in her backup plan. Was her guardian there?" Cato's gaze burned into him, waiting for a reaction.

"They were all there," Xander said plainly.

Cato crossed his arms. "Perhaps you're right. Our forces are merged here, but maybe we should wait them out, attack when their nerves are fried. Give them a chance to fight amongst themselves. Mortals are so predictable in that. Right when they're burned out and their hope is almost extinguished, that's when we'll attack."

"Why do you care if she has hope?" Xander asked before he could stop himself.

Cato's gaze snapped to his. "Because hope is the most dangerous thing in the world. No matter what side of a war you're on. You should know that, Savero. It's what inspired you to think you could go back there and convince Cece to forgive you in the first place. You were so angry until you thought you could win her over again."

"Hope seems a strange thing to fear," Davide said.

Xander jumped. He hadn't noticed his brother in the room.

Davide sat quietly in the corner, poring over a book on war games. His eyes met Xander's for a second, as if trying to emphasize something.

"You could live centuries and still find nothing more chaotic and unpredictable than hope. Some day you might understand," Cato said dismissively.

Something clicked into place in Xander's muddled mind. As soon as the thought sprang up, he forced it away. The trickster couldn't read minds, but it was clear he could read desires and intentions, so

Xander forced everything important from his mind the second it came up. It was exhausting.

Instead, he thought about how much he hated when Rainer touched Cece, how she leaned into his touch. He hated the way he could practically see her pulling strength from the guardian as Xander tried to hurt her badly enough that she'd stay away. He thought about anything else to keep his mind busy.

"Very well. We will hold off on the attack for now and let them stew in their misery," Cato said with a grin. He stood and slipped through a slit in the air to wherever he slept each night.

Davide stood, nodding at Xander. "I hope you've been paying attention."

Then, his brother turned and retreated down the hall without another word.

Xander breathed a sigh of relief and hoped that the delay in invading would give Cece time to rebound. She needed to figure out which of her powers scared Cato so much. Hopefully, this push toward rage and grief was enough to get her out of her comfort zone and inspire her to try.

He had never been one for blind faith, but he believed in Cece. If anyone could find a way to defeat a centuries-old god, it was her. She'd already done it once. If Cato thought hope was something to fear, then Xander knew for sure it was the only thing worth embracing.

No, when Cato talked about hope, the look in his eye was wary. Davide's words played through Xander's mind. It was as if he was trying to point Xander's attention to something in his own subtle way. For the life of him, Xander did not know how to weaponize hope and it seemed crazy to try.

What had he said to Cece when she was afraid of her goddess powers?

"Cece, you are hope embodied. You are a light in the dark. I am certain that whatever you become will only be a reflection of who you are as a person. And that is a goddess I would like to meet."

The idea hit Xander like a bolt of lightning.

All the gods had additional powers, and he might have been looking at the answer the whole time. If Cece could control mind and memory, perhaps she could also control inspiration and motivation. Perhaps something else in her powers was the key to why Cato was so concerned with her, so eager to control her. The god wouldn't have bothered with her if she wasn't valuable. He loved his games, but he refused to waste his precious time, even after living for so long. Everything Cato did was intentional and well-thought-out.

Xander stepped outside and made his way to the edge of the forest, far enough from the camp to avoid prying eyes. He wasn't sure if it would work but he said a prayer, hoping to summon Grimon.

"You are the last person I expected to summon me. I didn't think you were a fan of mine, and you know I'm not a fan of yours."

Xander rolled his eyes. He'd seen the way the god's gaze lingered on Cece. The way she'd fawned over Grimon when he showed up months before in the woods still brought forth a surge of jealousy in Xander.

"I need you to deliver something to Cece and I didn't know how else to go about guaranteeing that Cato doesn't see it," Xander said.

Grimon frowned. "I'm not sure that's the best idea right now."

Guilt twisted Xander's stomach. "I promise this isn't part of a game. I think I figured out something about her powers."

"Only two people know about her powers for sure, and one of them is Clastor himself."

"Who is the other?" Xander asked.

Grimon frowned at him. "Forgive me, but I'm not willing to give Cato the information that will help him answer all the questions even he can't manipulate the answers to."

Xander sighed. "You may know the gods, but I know my wife."

"Ex-wife," Grimon corrected through clenched teeth.

Xander held out the folded bird note. "I have about five minutes to get back before he notices I'm gone. Are you going to help or not?"

Grimon looked at the bird note and then back at Xander's eyes, as if trying to solve a complex puzzle.

"You don't have to understand. Just take it. The message is on the outside. You can read it. I'm not just fucking with her." Xander couldn't keep the impatience out of his voice. "Please?"

Grimon took the note and nodded. He read the message and pursed his lips.

"She will know what it means—I hope." There it was again. The word that Xander clung to like his life depended on it.

"It doesn't make us even," Grimon said.

Xander cocked his head to the side. "Never expected it to."

Grimon turned to leave.

"And Grim? If I call you again, will you come?"

Grimon turned to look at him again. "That depends on what you say."

Xander nodded. It was the best he could hope for.

The god of death evaporated into a cloud of smoke, leaving the smell of cinnamon and ash in the air.

26

CECILIA

Outside, hunters and servants scrambled through town, trying to fortify Olney City for an attack.

Inside her cottage, Cecilia tried to fortify herself against the pain in her heart. The days had trudged by at a glacial pace.

Torturing herself with perfectly preserved memory, she watched her and Xander's wedding over and over. Sifting through the memories, she tried to puzzle out what she'd missed. She picked at the cracks and seams of the memory until madness threatened. Maybe that was Cato's plan—to let her drive herself mad. The goddess of mind and memory losing her mind would be too perfect, even for Cato.

She refused to drag herself from bed until she knew what first step to take for herself, but she still felt flayed by her interaction with Xander. The angry hurt twisted like brambles inside her until she felt pinned under the blankets.

A loud knock at the door startled her from her brooding. It wasn't Rainer. He'd been giving her space, though she felt his constant reluctance through their bond. The knock sounded again, louder and too insistent to be Sylvie.

Cecilia sat up, grasping her dagger.

"Cecilia Juliette Reznik, you better let me into this cottage right now or I'll be shouting your business for all to hear," Aunt Clara called, rattling the front door with another loud knock.

Cecilia jumped out of bed, dropping the blade on her nightstand, and crossed the room. She threw open the door and squinted into the sunshine, her eyes narrowing on her aunt's disapproving face and the basket in her hands.

"I don't want company," Cecilia said, her voice scratchy from disuse.

Clara pursed her lips. "It was one thing to give you your time when your father died and you became a goddess, but now I have to hear that your husband dissolved your marriage from the Olney rumor mill? You may not want company, but it's what you're going to get."

Her aunt pushed her aside, barging into the cottage. She set the basket on the table before crossing the room and throwing open the curtains. Cecilia wanted to hiss like an angry cat, but she trudged after her aunt.

Clara opened the windows, letting in the cold sea air, and began stripping the linens from the bed. She bundled them up and threw them in a basket before pulling fresh ones from the cedar chest in the closet. Cecilia reluctantly helped before collapsing into the bed.

Clara crossed her arms and let out an exasperated sigh. "Oh no. Absolutely not. Up! Right now. Get in the washroom. There will be no more sulking alone today. We're going to eat and we're going to talk about all of this."

Cecilia grimaced. "I'm fine. I just really need some alone time."

Clara rolled her eyes. "I know. That's why Rainer McKay has been living in my kitchen, baking up all manner of things and asking me what I think you'd like."

"He is?"

Clara nodded. "He is. It was one thing when you left me alone with my grief for my brother, but I'll not let you push us all away at once."

The guilt sobered Cecilia. She trudged to the washroom and began pumping cold water from the well, using her fire magic to warm it to a comfortable temperature.

Clara stood in the doorway, waving a hand at Cecilia's clothes. "Off."

Cecilia frowned, but Clara just rolled her eyes. "This is no time to be modest, Cecilia. Just get in the bath."

Grumbling her discontent, Cecilia shuffled out of her leggings and sweater and climbed into the bath. She was surprised when Aunt Clara knelt beside the tub and poured water over her hair. No one had washed her hair for her since she was a child, and she'd forgotten how soothing it was to be cared for in such an intimate way.

"Now, do you want to tell me what happened with your husband?" Clara asked, her voice softer.

Cecilia swallowed hard, happy to have the excuse to hide her tears by rinsing her hair.

Clara wiped her eyes with a washcloth like she was a small child before working conditioning potion through her long hair.

Cecilia clasped her hands together, rubbing her thumb over her wrist. "It was all a lie. Maybe not his love, but our relationship. Xander was okay with a god manipulating me into loving him, and even though that didn't actually happen, that he could know how important agency is to me and still seek to take it away—" Her voice broke and her thoughts fragmented into a hundred little hurts. "He said I was worthless as a wife because I cannot have children."

Clara stroked Cecilia's shoulders. "Oh sweet girl, I'm so sorry."

A shuddering sob broke loose, followed by several more, until she was hugging her aunt and dripping water all over the washroom floor.

"My darling girl, you are priceless. Watching you grow into a brave, kind, smart young woman has been the joy of my life. Do not let yourself believe words a cruel god put in the mouth of your husband. Better yet, don't let your value be determined by any man. That's a surefire way to end up feeling inferior and unsure of yourself."

"But I love him." Cecilia felt more pathetic the moment the words left her lips.

"You can love and respect him without letting his love define you."

The words hung in the air like a spell, their magic digging at the roots of what Cecilia needed to do. She'd always done such a good job at loving everyone around her, seeing the unique and wonderful things about each of them. But she'd never taken the time to learn to love herself.

Clara folded her hands in her lap. "I may be old and James died just before you were born, but I remember the feeling of being swept up in someone. I know the way it feels all-consuming. But if I had let myself believe I was only what I was to James—if I'd let him define me completely—I would have never recovered from his death."

Cecilia studied her aunt carefully. She'd never heard her talk about her late husband. James had died in the War of the Gods and Clara had moved to the Reznik Estate to recover, only to end up helping take care of baby Cecilia.

"It's not just that he ended the marriage," Cecilia said. "It was that he stole the ability to choose that from me, too. I made the first decision for myself that I have since the last Gauntlet run—maybe ever, if I'm honest with myself. And Xander robbed me of it again."

Clara frowned as she rubbed vanilla-scented oil into Cecilia's skin. "Why were you going to end it?"

"Because I wanted to start over with a clear head and all the information."

Clara smiled softly. "Not so simple, is it?"

Cecilia shook her head. "No. It's not."

Clara's face grew serious. "You'll never be fully disconnected from either of them. They both have parts of you. But what you need to ask yourself is what would you want if you weren't concerned with anyone else's feelings?"

Cecilia rose from the lukewarm water. Clara wrapped her body in one towel before wrapping her hair in a second. As Cecilia got dressed, Clara laid food from her basket on the table and had a full feast ready by the time Cecilia emerged.

She sat down at the table and let her aunt pile a plate with food. She wasn't hungry, but as soon as she tasted the pasta, her stomach grumbled, demanding an end to her grief fast.

"Gods, that's good," she groaned as she popped a noodle into her mouth.

"Rainer made it. And the muffins. And the lemon cakes. Honestly, Cecilia, that boy has been living in my kitchen these past few months with no clue what to do with his grief."

Cecilia filled her mouth with food to shove down her guilt.

"You can be a friend to him without sacrificing yourself."

Cecilia scoffed. "Easy for you to say. He's not wrapped around your heart."

Clara sipped her wine. "I have watched you two love each other since you were teenagers. What's changed?"

Cecilia shifted uncomfortably. *He kissed me like he could bring me back to life with his love.* "We aren't children anymore."

"So you want to pull away from both of them so you can find yourself and what you want?"

Cecilia nodded.

"And it has nothing to do with Cato using someone you love to hurt you?"

The delicious pasta turned to ash in Cecilia's mouth. "I can't let him hurt anyone else to get to me. It's best if I keep my distance. It's selfish to put everyone else at risk."

Clara sat back, her arms crossed. "So, you are content to let another man control you?"

The words were a wake-up call. Cecilia thought she was being wise, but she was just handing Cato her power. Love had insulated her from so much hurt, and now she was playing right into Cato's hand by shoving it away. She was allowing the architect of all of her misery to define who she would be.

"You're right," Cecilia said breathlessly.

Shoving Rainer and Xander and everyone else away, hoping to

keep them safe, wasn't brave with her hand and it was definitely not brave with her heart. It was the action of a fearful, cowardly girl who wanted control of everything.

"You can redefine who you are and choose while still letting people support you. The point is to make an informed choice and I don't see how you can do that hiding in this cottage like a hermit," Clara said. "Now, let's go for some fresh air on the beach."

Cecilia grumbled about the cold, but Clara ignored her. Strapping her Godkiller dagger to her thigh just in case, Cecilia's mind floated to Clastor's words about the weapon.

"It can kill any of the living gods but also, if the moment comes and there's a loss you truly cannot survive, you can have that person stab you through the heart with that dagger. You will die, but they will live."

Cecilia remained baffled by the spell her mother had placed on the dagger. She wasn't sure she could survive *any* more losses. Her heart was already broken.

"Stalling?" Clara taunted, breaking Cecilia's trance.

She wove her arm through Cecilia's, leading her out the door and down the cliff trail. A stiff wind blew in off the sea, ruffling Cecilia's still-damp hair.

"I'll catch a cold," she complained.

Clara shook her head. "You're a goddess. You've never had a cold in your life."

Shrugging up the hood of her cloak, Cecilia pressed on after her aunt.

Clara paused, planting her butt in the sand, patting the space next to her as she laid back and gazed up at the dusky sky.

Cecilia studied her aunt in profile. "I'm sorry I did not spend more time with you after Dad died."

Clara squeezed her hand. "Oh no, sweet girl. Leo would not want that. He was never one to share his feelings much, but he was so proud of you. So in love from the first moment he brought you home. Don't get me wrong, he looked terrified and so awkward holding a baby, but absolutely enamored. He wouldn't blame you and I don't either. But you hid with your grief."

Cecilia blinked back tears. "I miss him so much. I didn't know how to face you or Rainer."

Clara's face softened, the smile lines around her eyes going slack. "No one knows what to do with grief. It is ravenous. Grief is communal. If you don't share the load, it will crush you."

Nodding, Cecilia turned her face up to the sky.

"They say the first stars of night are the luckiest," Clara said, a hint of teasing in her voice.

Cecilia sighed, fighting off a smile. "They do not."

"Well, just in case. Let's make a wish."

"My last wish didn't turn out like I expected," Cecilia said, her mind drawing up the night she'd watched the Summer Firestorm meteor shower with Rainer months before. She wondered if Rainer's wish had come true. She still desperately wanted to know what he'd asked for.

"Perhaps the practice will make you choose something wiser."

Cecilia stared at the sky, waiting for a star and inspiration for a wish.

———

Cecilia sat on the cottage window seat, staring out at the sea, trying to ignore Rainer's eyes on her, and dreading King Hector's plan to march her around in front of the people of Olney to instill confidence for the war efforts. Her friends all agreed it would help, but Cecilia had her doubts.

Two weeks passed with no movement from the Argarian army. King Hector itched to attack them where they were in Rowdane, but after the last invasion, the huntmaster worried the waiting was just a ploy to draw their forces away from Olney City. So the Olney army stayed put and a restless energy spread through the ranks.

Cecilia was uncomfortable in the role of hero and didn't know exactly what people expected of her. She felt more like a prop the king was using to inspire confidence than an actual help. The thought of all those expectant eyes on her twisted her stomach in knots.

Rainer's eyes burned into her. She didn't have to look to feel them.

Cecilia felt more like herself, or at least more like the new version of herself. Grief still tugged at her in strange moments, but she moved through it. She let Rainer walk on the beach with her in the morning and was happy for the way he filled the silence with mindless chatter or storytelling. He didn't ask her to share anything, even if he felt what she did through their connection. He let her have her space.

Anxiety swirled through her as she turned to face him. Even as she dreaded playing the role of goddess and savior, her mind kept dragging her back to the loss she had yet to make peace with.

"What's on your mind, Cece?" Rainer asked.

"I don't even know if I knew that I wanted to have kids until I knew I might lose it. I was so focused on everything else that I never thought about it. Is that strange?"

He frowned. "No, I don't think so. You had a lot going on. You were busy, but you also thought you had time."

"Do you want children?" she asked.

If the question surprised Rainer, he didn't show it. "I used to think so, but I look at my own father and wonder if I'm qualified."

Fury tore through her. "You are a hundred times the man Raymond McKay could ever be. You'd be a wonderful father, Rain."

Rainer ran a hand through his hair. "But do I really want to raise a bunch of little warriors to go fight someone else's war? What opportunities would really exist for them? I've thought about it but it doesn't feel as simple as yes or no."

Cecilia studied his face carefully. "Is that true, or are you trying to say what you think I want to hear?"

Rainer laughed and sat down beside her. "Cece, I've given up telling you what you want to hear. What would be the point? I think I always imagined myself as a father, but the larger implications of what those kids would have to grow up and be is more complicated."

With the Gauntlet torn apart, and the kingdom at war with

Argaria, it wasn't clear what would happen to future guardians, witches, and hunters.

Cecilia hated that Cato had made good points about the way they were raised. It was barbaric to raise children as warriors from such a young age. Though she didn't regret her own bond, removing agency was a sore spot for her. Bonded duos were matched when they were too young to comprehend fully what it meant to make any type of lifetime commitment.

Rainer narrowed his eyes at her. "Is that what you really wanted to ask me?"

"Yes," she lied.

She wanted to ask him if having kids was a deal-breaker for him. She wasn't really sure why she wanted to know that. It made little sense and, in the grand scheme of things, it hardly seemed important at that moment. Still, she couldn't let it go.

"I don't think it is," Rainer said. "I think you want to ask if I would be disappointed if I was with someone who couldn't have children."

Apparently, he knew what she was thinking. "Did you somehow gain the ability to read minds on our magical travels?"

Rainer laughed, the sound resonating pleasantly in her chest. "No, I just know you. I'll answer, but I need you to answer something first. Why do you want to know that?"

She squirmed under his gaze. "I'm trying to satisfy my curiosity—for research."

She knew he wasn't buying it, but he smiled as he looked from her lips to her eyes. She hoped he didn't kiss her, even though a big part of her wanted him to. She wanted to have every thought and fear and emotion wiped from her mind. She wanted to obliterate all the heaviness weighing her down, but she knew she wasn't ready for it.

"For *research* purposes only, I would say that if I was in love with someone, I wouldn't care," Rainer said. "I would tell my love that there are many ways to be parents. If that's what she wanted to do, we would figure it out. I would also tell her that I would be happy just to be with her, even if that meant no kids. I would try to love her enough to make up for it."

The words echoed what Xander had said to her, and a wave of grief crashed over her. Cecilia blinked back tears.

Rainer frowned. "Oh gods, I'm sorry. I didn't mean to make you cry."

She laughed as she brushed the tears away.

He tilted her chin up so she would meet his eyes. "Cece, you are so much more to me than what you can give me."

His words stole her breath. For weeks she felt like she'd been dropped into the middle of the sea, forced to tread water and pray for a rescue. Rainer's words were a lifeboat.

"I think maybe that's something the world has tried to convince you," he continued. "That you're only worth what you can do for people. I think I participated in that for a while and I'm sorry. You are everything to me, and I don't need anything from you. You owe me nothing."

Cecilia swallowed hard around a knot of relief. He made it very difficult to keep her distance.

"I know Xander acts like you belong to him. But you don't belong to anyone but yourself, Cece. All that I hope is that there's some part of you that thinks that maybe you belong *with* me." Rainer smiled and the light shining through the cottage windows gilded him.

It felt to Cecilia as if the entire world was conspiring against her desire for space. She fought the urge to reach for his hand. She belonged to herself and she needed to act like it. She needed to focus on the problem in front of her.

Her nerves were fried from waiting for an attack. She hated being held in Cato's suspension, with nothing to do but wait for bad news.

Rainer looked toward the door. "So I know you've been trying to pretend that the event this afternoon isn't happening, but there are people relying on you."

Cecilia sighed heavily. "I do not want to be paraded around like some divine savior to the people of Olney. This is the dumbest idea I've ever heard. How will that help anything? Who would make such an insane suggestion?"

"I suggested it," he said.

Wildfire fury tore through Cecilia as she hopped to her feet. "Are you out of your mind? You thought I was sad and that it would feel better to have people come to pay homage?"

He held his hands up. "No, I thought it would bring people hope to feel like they have a goddess on their side. I thought if people met you, they would love you as much as I—as we all do."

She was certain Rainer felt her fury, but instead of taking a step back, his gaze dropped to her lips, and the fire in her body moved south. For the first time in weeks, desire flared in her blood. It would have been so easy to press onto her toes and drag his lips to hers, but she could not afford to lose focus.

She stepped away. "Fine. Let's get this over with."

Rainer smirked. "You have to be nice to people. It will settle the restlessness in town."

Cecilia cupped her hands around her mouth. "Hey everyone, we know we lied to you for years and sent your children into danger in the wild to unlock a magic that we know really lived in just this one girl, but come get on board with our war efforts. Keep the faith!"

"You might not want to be the one with the power, but you also hated being powerless, and that's how these people feel. Where's your compassion, Cece?" Rainer asked.

Cecilia pursed her lips. She knew Rainer was right, and she hated him for it.

"Put on something goddessy." He gestured to her closet.

"Why don't you pick? I don't know what goddesses wear, unless we use my sisters as examples, in which case the suggestion would be basically nothing."

She expected Rainer to blush, but his gaze heated. "Maybe you should try that. I can imagine that's one effective way to drum up worshippers. I'd be first in line."

Her heart beat against her ribs like it was trying to break free, and she flushed. She tore her eyes away from Rainer's.

He'd never been so flirtatious with her. She couldn't tell if it was how he truly felt, or if he was just trying to inspire a defiant reaction.

"I'm serious, Rain. You pick. I don't know what people expect," she said, waving a hand at her closet.

He chuckled and made his way into her closet, emerging a moment later with an elaborate gown.

She groaned at the sight of it. "I forgot that was still in there. How did you find it so fast?"

Two years before, for her twenty-first birthday, Rainer wanted to throw her an elaborate party. She'd insisted she just wanted to have a nice dinner with friends. He had decided it would be a fairy-tale-themed dinner and had commissioned a dress fit for a fairy queen from a local seamstress. It was a beautiful shade of teal, with elaborate rainbow flowers thick around the hem that wound up the dress like a tornado of wilderness. It was a beautiful, whimsical dress and Cecilia secretly loved it, even though she pretended it was juvenile. Still, she hadn't worn it since because it felt like something too personal to share with the world.

She ran her fingers over the flowers. "The fairy queen dress?"

"I think it suits you."

"I think you're out of your mind."

"Yes, I have crazy good taste," he taunted.

She crossed her arms. "For a child."

"I know you love this dress." Rainer moved so close that she could feel the heat coming off of his body.

She drew in a breath and dug her fingernails into her palms to keep from leaning into him. "You know nothing."

His fingers skimmed her cheek, tilting her chin up. "Cece."

She met his eyes. "Rain."

Tense silence bloomed between them before he turned away. "I'll send Sylvie in to help you get ready."

She stared down at the fairy queen dress, wishing it had the magic to make her feel less nervous.

27

RAINER

"Go home to your families and be with them tonight. Tomorrow, be prepared to fight," King Hector said. The late afternoon sun glinted off of his golden crown as he held his hands up to the crowd in a benediction.

Half the crowd murmured solemn assent, as if they hadn't been on edge and ready for weeks. Others touched their lips and hearts in reverence as they looked at Cecilia. The gesture filled Rainer with pride. Cecilia had done exactly what he knew she could do. She'd given the people of Olney new resolve.

When she spoke to the crowd, her voice was calm and even, though Rainer stood close enough to see the way she trembled and felt her fear through their bond. Still, she'd persevered, her bravery inspiring his own as it always did.

Rainer had tried so hard to turn down the volume on his love so she could hear herself alone the past few weeks. It was difficult work, holding back the tide of it, but every time she brightened, seeming more herself, he was certain it was worth it.

King Hector guided Cecilia toward Prince Marcos, whose pink cheeks and slumped shoulders betrayed his embarrassment. Marcos had always been a bit uneasy around Cecilia. Rainer knew they had a history, but every time he asked Cecilia about it, she'd just smirk and say it was a secret for her and Marcos alone.

Cecilia smiled indulgently at the prince, but her gaze darted to Rainer almost immediately and he knew her well enough to recognize a cry for help. Why the king was insisting on pushing Marcos and Cecilia together when he knew she couldn't provide godly heirs was beyond Rainer, but he started toward her to interrupt anyway.

Before he made it three steps, he was intercepted by the last person he wanted to see.

Raymond McKay grabbed his arm. "I have been trying to set a meeting with you for two weeks. You haven't been avoiding me, have you, boy?"

Rainer stared at his father, trying to keep his face placid. He was twenty-six years old and had both height and weight advantages on his father, and yet the man still made him feel small with just a few words.

"I've been quite busy and since your many letters did not indicate the nature of our business, I assumed it wasn't more urgent than the defense of our kingdom," Rainer said tightly.

Raymond pursed his lips, raking his gaze over Rainer, shifting his eyes to Cecilia standing among a crowd of people gathering for blessings.

"That girl has risen high. I will admit I underestimated her value. That was short-sighted of me," Raymond said.

Rainer didn't like the way his father assessed Cecilia, always calling her "that girl" like he didn't know her name. Dread pooled in Rainer's stomach. Cecilia's growing apprehension buzzed in his chest, and he just wanted to get to her and get out of the crowd.

"What do you want?" he snapped.

Raymond's eyebrows shot up, but he recovered quickly. "I hear that Prince Savero has ended their marriage. I was always very discouraging of you having anything but a professional relationship with the girl, but I can admit when I'm wrong."

Rainer crossed his arms. "Is that what you're here to do?"

Raymond huffed out a sigh. "Yes. What do you want me to say?

She's valuable in ways I hadn't anticipated and she's clearly been in love with you since you were young. This is your chance, Rainer. The Gauntlet is no more."

His father said it like completing it had been a minor accomplishment.

"You've become an advisor to the king. She is the last hill to climb, the highest you could hope to rise, and she is within reach."

How quickly Rainer had forgotten that Raymond McKay was yet another reason he'd never allowed himself to show the world how much he loved Cecilia. His father had a dark gift for wounding people with words, for twisting simple sentences into vicious barbs, and Cecilia was so sensitive. Rainer couldn't bear for her to become a target and so he'd stuffed his feelings down deep and kept her secrets.

Rainer clenched his fists at his sides. "Cecilia is not a conquest. She is a *person*."

"She is an immortal goddess with untapped social power," Raymond countered.

Rainer let out a brittle laugh. "Of course you want me to chase after her now."

His father's face pinched in disgust. "How are you so weak and sentimental you won't capitalize on this?"

Maybe it was the way Raymond dismissed the Gauntlet as if it was nothing, instead of a pursuit that had nearly ended his son's life. Maybe it was the fact that he hadn't even come to visit Rainer when he was laid up in the healer's clinic after nearly dying on their last Gauntlet run. Maybe it was the way the words finally made it clear that there would never be a height Rainer could reach that would be good enough.

After years of waiting, Rainer and his father had finally reached a true line in the sand between them: Cecilia Reznik.

Rainer shook his head. "I don't know what you're suggesting, and I don't want to know—"

"I'm your father, and it's my job to take care of you."

Rainer's laugh sounded broken in his ears as he met his father's dark gaze. "I'll not make her a toy you can break to control me. Her well-being is my focus, and it has nothing to do with who she is to these people and everything to do with who she is to me—who she always has been."

Rainer looked up at the dais, but Cecilia was no longer beside Marcos. He looked over the crowd but didn't see her anywhere. He sent a surge of panic through his connection, and peace floated back a moment later. She was farther away; he could tell by the faintness of the feeling.

"I have to go—"

Raymond grabbed his arm. "Consider what I'm saying. Your birth father had a famous bond and love story too, you know."

Rainer turned away, but not fast enough to ignore the way the words sank beneath his skin and crawled deep into his bones. The man had a gift for knowing exactly how to reach Rainer, even when his own approval was no longer compelling.

Pushing through the crowd, Rainer tugged on his bond with Cecilia, surprised to find her much farther away than expected. He ran to the stables and saddled Zeke before riding down the trail beyond her cottage and into the woods. Finally, he reached the grove where he and Cecilia used to train. She sat facing away from him in the shade of the wisteria trees, her dress pooled around her.

For weeks Rainer had watched Cecilia struggle with the end of her marriage and the realization that it wasn't the relationship she thought it was. There was nothing he could do to comfort her or take away her pain. Rainer felt her grief wrapped around his own. He'd never seen Cecilia so broken.

While Xander's love was obvious, Rainer understood why Cecilia wanted to discount it. It was hard to look at something that hurt so much and call it love. It was the same reason he could never use that word to refer to the constant conniving Raymond McKay did to boost Rainer's status.

Something about Xander's abrupt choice to end their marriage nagged at Rainer. It was so out of line for the depth of Xander's feelings, but it also made little sense that Cato would approve a move that made Cecilia harder to control. What was the endgame?

Rainer dismounted and allowed himself a rare moment to stare. Cecilia's dark hair was woven with wildflowers and piled neatly on top of her head, exposing the three-freckle constellation that stretched from her shoulder to her neck. He'd thought of kissing each one at least a hundred times over the past few weeks.

"You found me," Cecilia said without looking at him.

"Why did you run off?"

"It was a little lonely out there, Rain."

"Everyone wanted to see you."

She sighed. "No, everyone wanted their goddess. No one wanted to see *me*."

Rainer sat in the grass next to her. "I wanted to see you."

"Well, you were the only one."

"What's really on your mind? Is it Xander?"

She frowned. "He's always on my mind, but that's not what is bothering me so much right now. When I was in the Cave of Longings, the spirits in the cave said that I would always be alone. Always isolated."

"But you had me. You always belonged with me, Cece," Rainer said.

"I didn't, though. You were confident and talented and charming. Everyone loved you. They only hung out with me because I was with you. No one actually liked *me*."

Rainer shook his head. "That isn't true."

"It is. Even with you, I was alone. I couldn't be fully open to you because of how I felt. I was a lady, but they didn't accept me because I didn't want the same things and I always had dirt under my nails. I was a hunter, but hunters didn't accept me because they didn't like being beaten by a woman. I was a witch, but I could only control half my powers, and most of the other witches were afraid of me. There was always some part of me that was isolated."

It wrecked Rainer that she'd felt that way, and he could do nothing to undo it.

"You know you can tell me anything, right? Truly," Rainer whispered.

"I know I can. I feel like I've grown up and I'm this goddess now and I'm still so isolated. No one treats me normally and no one ever will, and it's just one more thing that separates me. And if all I can do is erase memories, that's a pretty shitty power. They're all looking at me like I'm a hero and I don't know how that will help anyone."

Rainer took her hand in his. "I doubt that is your only power and I think in order to figure it out, you actually would have to try. You've been so afraid of hurting someone that you won't try. What happens if you reach past the darkness? Is something else there?"

She frowned. "I don't know."

"Will you try it with me?"

Cecilia drew her hand back. "No! Absolutely not."

He took her hand and placed it on his chest. "Cece, I know you are here to do amazing things. I know your gifts go beyond what you've seen, like when you had the invading Argarian army surrender. Everyone else has been treating you so cautiously, but I won't let you run scared now. You're going to try, and even if you don't trust yourself, you're going to trust me."

She looked surprised by his conviction. He tried to close off their connection so she wouldn't feel how scared he was to let her try.

She leaned her forehead against his, her breath ghosting over his lips. "I won't risk hurting you."

"I think that's precisely why it needs to be me."

"I can feel how scared you are," she rasped.

"That's because I'm afraid I won't be able to stop myself from kissing you when I'm this close to you."

She jerked back in surprise. He smiled and brushed a loose hair back from her face. It wasn't a complete lie. He felt it whenever she was close.

"It would break my heart if I wiped your memory," she said. "You'd lose everything—how to fight, all your years of training, our entire history. It could all be gone in the blink of an eye."

He shrugged. "Then I will just get to fall in love with you all over again."

She sighed, exasperated. "Okay, but if you feel like you're losing yourself, say something."

He watched her face intently. Her brow scrunched in concentration. He felt a faint tingling where her hand rested in his.

"I feel something."

She tensed. "Is it bad?"

"No, it feels—good. Keep going."

Rainer's whole body was warm and tingled like it did when she kissed him. The sensation grew, stretching beneath his skin. Finally, she pulled it back and released the power, blinking her eyes open to look at him. He stared at her.

He couldn't stop the impulse. He kissed her, half expecting her to push him away—but she leaned into him. She ran her fingers through his hair and pulled him closer.

He wrapped his arms around her, guiding her back to the grass. One arm stayed wrapped around her and the other hand found hers. She wove her fingers through his, and the sweetness of the gesture unraveled him. His whole body felt like it was awash with sunlight. Like he was being warmed from the inside out. Like he was about to leap off a tall peak but knew he wouldn't fall, that he would instead float up into the air. The world spun, and he felt dizzy with boundless joy. There was such a lightness in his body. He grinned as she finally pulled away.

She didn't seem upset, just surprised. "Rain, why did you do that?"

"I was overcome by this feeling that I could win you over. I don't —" He was breathless. "I'm sorry. I know I promised I wouldn't kiss you again unless you asked me to. I don't understand."

Rainer wasn't prone to impulse control issues, but the sensation she pressed into him was overwhelming.

Cecilia's fingers brushed over her lips.

"Can I do it again?" Rainer asked.

Cecilia's cheeks pinked. "I don't think that's a good idea. If you do it again, I won't want to stop you, and then we will just be out here kissing forever, letting the world fall apart."

"Honestly, that doesn't sound so bad." His fingers brushed along her jawline.

She shook her head like she was trying to clear it. "Rainer, I'm still—"

"I hate that you're still hurting. It makes me hate him."

"I know. If someone did to you what he did to me, I would feel the same way."

"Yes, but I know that's not him. Xander—your Xander—wouldn't do that."

"My Xander is gone." Her grief sank through their bond.

Rainer closed his eyes and tipped his head back. "Maybe not. Cato can add influence and manipulation through new memories, but he can't get rid of the old. Shouldn't you be able to remind Xander what's true? Either way, if you do to him what you just did to me, it might be—" He struggled for an appropriate word. "Clarifying."

She grinned. "Weren't you just kissing me a minute ago? Why help him?"

"Because I will always do whatever I can to take away your pain, and because I know you're not really ready to let him go yet. You don't believe he's really gone."

Cecilia swallowed hard. "What did the power feel like to you?"

He ran a hand through his hair. "It felt like nostalgia. It made me think of all the moments before when I desperately wanted to kiss you and didn't. I think that's why I did that. Even thinking about it now, I have such an overwhelming urge to do it again."

Cecilia's blush brightened and she avoided his eyes. "Is that all?"

Rainer paused, considering how he felt. "No, it also made me think of this memory I forgot. One time when my mother tucked us both in—I would guess you were probably nine, and I was eleven and I thought I was too cool for our fairy tales. My mom knew otherwise, so she pulled me aside and said that I set the example for you and if I started acting too cool for fairy tales that I would ruin your imagination. She said that was one of your greatest gifts and that you didn't have a mom to tell you stories and that it was my responsibility to make sure you didn't lose touch with dreaming. I can still hear her saying it. *Someday you will be old enough to need those fairy tales again.*"

Rainer shook his head, warmed by the memory of the woman who raised him. "I completely forgot about that night but I think that's part of the reason that I kept up the storytelling all these years. I never wanted you to stop dreaming. I wanted to be part of the dreams you were making for yourself."

Cecilia frowned. "I never knew that you wanted to stop story time."

"I didn't. I already got so much crap from the other kids in training for having you as a best friend. I think I was afraid of being soft. But I always loved story time. You tried so hard to stay awake, but you always fell asleep early and I used to make my mom keep going, even after you were asleep. She knew I liked it too. Gods, I miss her."

"Me too," Cecilia whispered. "I miss her all the time. She was always so kind to me."

Rainer frowned, an idea forming in his mind.

Brushing her thumb over the space between his brow, Cecilia grinned. "I found a worry, but I'll fix it in a hurry."

Rainer shot to his feet, a growing suspicion winding through him. "I have an idea." He yanked Cecilia to her feet. "I think I know what your other power is."

He helped her onto Zeke and jumped up behind her. They rode in silence until they reached Sylvie's house.

Sylvie finished coaxing several buds on a rosebush to bloom with earth magic. She smiled when she turned and saw Rainer and Cecilia. "What are you two doing here?"

"How's your grandfather?" Rainer asked.

Sylvie's brows shot up. "Not very well. The sickness has his mind most of the time. We remind him of things, but he can't retain them. He's gone much more than he's here."

"I think Cece can fix it."

Sylvie and Cecilia gawked at Rainer. "What?" they said in unison.

"You told me before that memory is more than just the brain making a copy...it's also the emotion. That power you used on me brought such nostalgia. What if you can use it to fix those lost in their own minds?"

Cecilia frowned, looking from him to Sylvie. Doubt and fear slid through their connection.

"You can do this. I know you can."

Rainer didn't want to pressure her, but she needed the push, and not because it would prove she was powerful and valuable to the kingdom. He wanted her to prove she was powerful to herself.

She is the last hill to climb, the highest you could hope to rise, and she is within reach.

Raymond's words wormed their way back into his mind and Rainer vowed never to make Cecilia feel like a currency he could exchange for honor and recognition.

His father had tried to train all the softness out of him, but time and again Cecilia reminded him that soft was just a different, more subtle type of strong. Steel could bind, but so could love.

28

CECILIA

Cecilia hesitated, staring at the door to the Brett Estate as if it led to her doom. She was so afraid to fail and make things worse.

"Think about it," Rainer said. "You gave me back a memory I thought I'd lost. It was like you lifted this wall between old and new. I didn't even know I lost it. It wasn't like when you share memory because it wasn't a memory you had. It was one of my own and you recovered it."

"We've learned about keeping inventory and archiving old memories and venting things we don't need," Sylvie said. "Perhaps your power can put up and take down walls between memories or help someone rebuild bridges to old memories."

Cecilia shook her head. "I don't know that I can fix it. I don't want to be cruel. What if I can't—"

Sylvie squeezed both of Cecilia's hands. "This disease is cruel. He doesn't even know who we are most of the time. Please, if you think there is even a chance that you could help, try."

Cecilia let Sylvie lead her into the back of their house, where her grandfather sat looking out the window. His gaze was vacant.

"You can do this. I know you can," Rainer whispered, placing a hand on her shoulder.

Cecilia knelt next to the old man's chair and took one of his hands between hers. She closed her eyes. Grandpa Brett's body tensed momentarily, then relaxed. His mind was a maze of detours and dead ends.

"What was his wife's name?" Cecilia asked.

"Harriet," Sylvie said.

"Think of Harriet," Cecilia whispered.

Immediately, a delicate face popped into his mind. Blonde hair and dark eyes and high, round cheekbones. The feeling was bright, colorful, and pulsing with love, but Cecilia could only see a few thin connections to vague memories. She tugged on that feeling of love and little spots lit up all over his mind like thousands of candles. The feeling of loving his wife was the key to reconnecting the lost memories.

Slowly, Cecilia wove them one to the other, the dormant memories growing brighter and more detailed as she went until they latched on to memories of children and a whole new feeling that she connected. On and on she went, trying to weave the tapestry of Grandpa Brett's mind back into one cohesive picture.

They stayed like that for a long time. When Cecilia finally blinked her eyes open, the old man was staring beyond her.

"Sylvie?" he asked. Sylvie ran toward him. "Sylvie, where was I? I was lost." He turned and looked at Cecilia. "You found me. I was lost, but you brought me back."

Sylvie screamed for her parents. Her grandfather recognized everyone right away. He'd lost most of the past few years, but he knew who everyone was. He remembered his earlier life. He was lucid and coherent.

Sylvie guided them to the front of the house and hugged Cecilia again. "Cece, there are so many more. So many more people with this horrible illness. You can fix them. I'm going to go celebrate with my family, but thank you."

Cecilia was shocked that her magic had worked.

Rainer swept her up into his arms in a hug. "I told you. I knew that there would be something good."

She laughed through her tears. "I'm sorry I can't stop crying."

"You've always been so strong. It's okay to let yourself feel what you feel."

"I don't want you to think less of me."

Rainer brushed the tears from her cheeks. "I would never think less of you. I don't know how you're still standing. Here, with me, you don't have to pretend, okay? Feeling nothing isn't brave. It's easy to just shut off big emotions. Trust me, I know. But what you do—feeling everything. Letting all of it in. That's brave. It's why you understand people. It's why you can hold memory and fix it. If you couldn't feel it all, you wouldn't be so good at what you do. I wish I could do more to help you, but if the only thing I can do is hold you when you cry and encourage you when you're doubting yourself... that's what I'm going to do."

She tucked her head into his chest and squeezed him. "Thank you for believing in me."

For the first time since she'd realized who her true enemy was, Cecilia felt the barest hint of hope.

———

Cecilia strolled alone down the beach beneath her cottage, still trying to shake off the nerves from her speech the day before. For once she wasn't interrupted by Grimon and she was happy for the solitude.

Rainer offered to go with her, but she enjoyed taking her morning walks alone, and after their kiss the day before, she needed the space to clear her head. She sent him off to check in with Cal and Evan.

She'd felt so triumphant healing Sylvie's grandfather that she'd come dangerously close to giving in to her feelings for Rainer. The timing would have been all wrong.

All of her thoughts and feelings were twisted together in an impossible knot—grief wrapped around longing, love wrapped around rage. And at the center, a steady ball of loneliness. She stood at the edge of the water, allowing a steady pulse of tide magic to flow through her body. It was her weakest form of summoning, which meant the delicate work of making tiny waves required the entirety of her focus. The work was menial—first-year magic—and yet she still struggled with such fine skill from lack of practice. She laughed as her tiny wave rushed up, splashing the hem of her dress.

She released her power and listened to the steady waves crashing on the sand. It served as soothing music as she let her mind sort through the complex emotions swirling inside her. She closed her eyes, inhaled a cleansing breath.

"You've been busy."

Cecilia jumped. She turned and found Xander standing behind her. All at once, it felt like the ground had fallen out from beneath her feet.

"Xander?"

The corner of his lips quirked up in a half-smile. "Goddess."

She frowned at the term of endearment. "Don't call me that."

"Why not?"

"Because I prefer when you call me Cece."

He rolled his eyes. "I don't care what you prefer."

"Yes, you do. You're usually such a good liar, Xander. You're getting rusty. Why are you here? You're a single prince now. Shouldn't you be out chasing ladies of the court or something?"

Cecilia didn't want him to see how much he'd hurt her, but it didn't sound nearly as casual as she'd wanted it to.

He gave her a dazzling smile. "You're certainly spunky today. What has you in such a good mood?"

"If you must know, I've just figured out how my powers work."

"Really? And here I thought it was just because you have the freedom to be with Rainer. I broke off our marriage, so you moved on. I must admit, I didn't realize it would happen so quickly. It feels like you were just trying to prove me wrong."

"About what?"

Xander's eyes glimmered with malicious intent. "You were trying to prove that you don't belong to me."

Cecilia frowned. "I don't."

He stalked toward her and she tensed. He brought a hand to her cheek in such a tender touch that she leaned into it.

"Look at the way you respond to my touch. I did always enjoy that." He smirked.

"It doesn't mean I belong to you."

His eyes softened for a moment. He leaned down and kissed her gently. Cecilia let him, just for a breath, before pushing him away.

"Don't play with me, Xander. I'm tired of games," she said in a half-growl, half-sob, her heart still undecided on which emotion dominated.

Xander's brow furrowed. "Why let me kiss you when you're free to have Rainer?"

Cecilia sighed. "Because I love you. It has nothing to do with ownership."

He kissed her like he was trying to claim her and she tried to claim him right back. The kiss was a fight over who cared more, who had more to lose, who hurt who worse.

"You are the sweetest torture, love. Say that you belong to me," he whispered against her lips.

Her heart thundered, her body eager for the relief his touch brought. "I don't."

Rainer was right. She only belonged to herself, and she always had. She framed Xander's face with her hands and pressed her newfound power into him. He fought against the sparkling lightness of the power but she felt it spreading through him.

"Come back to me, love."

Finally, Xander broke her hold, stumbling away from her. She studied his face for any sign of recognition. His eyes were wild and confused.

"I know you don't know what's real, but I can fix it, Xander."

Xander studied her. She felt his anger even before she saw it reflected on his face.

"You're hurt," she breathed.

"I'm angry."

"Then why do you care if I belong to you?"

"Because Cato tore you away from me, but he didn't take the wanting," he screamed. "I barely have a memory of loving you before it turned to poison, but when I see you, it's like my whole body is a storm. I can still taste you, still smell your skin. I can hear the sounds you make when I touch you, and I can't stop wanting you. I can't put words to it."

Cecilia blinked back tears.

"Can I, Cece? Can I have you?"

Xander's face was so desperate that a sob broke out of her.

"No, you can't."

His face fell, and for a split second, she saw the grief before the anger took over. He took a step toward her. "I want you to show me."

"Show you what?"

Xander's eyes were glassy. "You and me. Show me. I hardly remember anything. I remember you bathing in the river. I remember being snowed into the cabin. I remember you walking down the aisle toward me and I remember almost nothing else. There's no feeling around it. It's like I'm watching someone else's life. Please, Cece, put me out of my misery."

Cecilia cupped his face in her hands and brought to mind all of their memories. In the garden during the solstice festival, fighting in the wild, kissing her in the Godswoods, teasing her while they rode together. On and on, she poured in everything she could remember of him. Then, she showed him her memories after he was taken, how he broke her heart when Cato had him taunt her. She bared her whole soul, allowing him to see just how much it hurt her when he ended their marriage, how much she'd cried for him, how much she wanted to save him.

Xander's hand pressed against the back of her neck, his lips moving with a barely audible rhythm.

Cecilia's eyelids grew heavy. Panic kicked up a storm in her chest as she realized he was using his soothing spell to put her to sleep.

"Xander, no—" she said, her voice barely a whisper.

"I'm sorry. I put it off as long as I could."

He swept her into his arms as the darkness dragged her under.

29

CECILIA

"Time to wake up, Goddess."

Cecilia blinked blearily, looking up at Cato's smug face. She swung with all her might and her fist connected with his jaw before he could react. He stumbled back, laughing.

"What do you want and why on earth did you send Xander to do your bidding again?" Cecilia snapped.

She sat up with a start, the table creaking beneath her as she glanced around a small, unfamiliar cottage kitchen. Power still buzzed beneath her skin. She wasn't sure if she should be relieved or worried that she hadn't been dosed with Godsbane.

Thin orange sunlight slashed through the windows. It was late. She'd slept most of the day. Xander could have brought her anywhere and with Cato's help, she could have been transported all the way back to Argaria. With any luck, she was in Rowdane where Davide had assembled the army.

"You ruined my toy," Cato said with mock sulkiness.

Xander paced the short hallway that led away from the room.

Cato grinned. "You know you only confused him more. Once again, you've done more harm than good."

Cecilia ignored the jab. "Why am I here?"

"I thought perhaps I've taken the wrong approach with you," he said. "I've tried to convince you through force twice with little success. Consider this one last peaceful chance to work with me. Perhaps that will show you that while I can't love the way mortals do, I have a softer side."

Cecilia burst out laughing.

"That wasn't meant to be humorous, Little Dove."

She looked at him skeptically. "The sudden change of heart is a little hard to believe after you've spent so much time hurting me."

"My methods are regrettable, but you need to understand that I don't feel the way you do. Those of us who have lived for centuries, those of us who have seen the rise and fall of empires, we don't bother with trivial things like love. I can't feel love like you do, but I can want things."

"That much is clear." Cecilia's eyes flickered over Xander.

His hands were clenched in his freshly shorn hair. He looked incredibly handsome—his skin glowing and his face cleanly shaven—though his eyes bore the same haunted look they had the last time she'd seen him. Cato must have had him healed, or at least made him look every part a prince without a crown. Xander stood frozen in her gaze, but his fingers tapped his thumbs over and over like he was counting out heartbeats.

Cato followed her gaze. "Tell me what you did to make him so out of sorts."

"I gave him his memories back. Mostly from my perspective, but I have a lot of his own too."

Cato shook his head. "Little Dove, you should know better. You're a trained memory witch, but Xander is just a beginner. You might have dabbled with teaching him a thing or two, but did you teach him how to archive and vent?"

Cecilia's blood turned to ice, dread pooling in her gut. How could she have forgotten? It was the first thing that she learned in memory magic class. If a witch took on too much outside memory without learning how to archive older memories and other people's shared memories, and vent unnecessary ones, the witch could literally lose their mind. Their sense of self would be shattered and crowded out by other people's memories.

"Oh my gods," she breathed, staring at Xander. "*I did this.*"

Cato shrugged. "You can't take all the blame. I made him obsessed."

"You can only enhance what exists. You can't create."

"Fair enough. I made him *more* obsessed," Cato said. "Even so, he's not gone yet, but you're definitely approaching the limit of giving him too much. Pull out what you've given him and teach him how to inventory and archive first."

A swell of hope bloomed in her chest. Maybe she could fix her mistake. She studied Cato. He might be lying. It was impossible to ascertain the limits of Xander's mind. Everyone had different boundaries and Cato loved to wield guilt like a weapon.

"Xander has always been so jealous of your guardian. You know, you might be even more like Clastor than I gave you credit for. He was always known for his many love affairs."

"A couple kisses is hardly a love affair, and the stalking is creepy," she huffed.

"I have to keep an eye on you. I like to know my enemies better than they know me."

"I'm not your enemy."

Surprise flashed in Cato's eyes. "Aren't you?"

"I don't think we want different things. You suggested that yourself."

"I don't think you have any idea what I want." The heated interest in his gaze filled her with apprehension.

"Well then, enlighten me, because it feels like you just want to drive me beyond the bounds of my sanity," Cecilia said. "You may be hundreds of years old, but you're playing childish games."

Cato licked his lips. "I want *you*, Goddess. I want what all these foolish men want. You are my only equal in this entire world. You and I, we are meant for each other. We are inevitable."

A hysterical giggle burst from her lips. "You *must* be joking."

"I'm not." His gray eyes studied her.

Cecilia swallowed hard, chilled by Cato's confession. She'd seen how powerful men acted when they didn't get what they wanted. They made a mess or they took it anyway.

She shook her head. "I'm not available or interested. Plus, our temperaments are not at all suited to each other. Why would I want someone who could never love me?"

"Do you need to feel special?" Cato asked. "I've lived centuries and I can tell you with confidence there is nothing I've wanted more than you, Cecilia."

"There's a difference between *want* and love. Want is about possession. Want is selfish. You can want someone badly and not love them. Love is about giving. It's about selflessness. If you'd ever had love in your long life, maybe you'd understand that wanting someone, even if it's more than you've ever wanted anything else, won't ever replace what it is to be seen and cherished. An imitation of love would never do if you'd ever had the real thing."

Cato stared at her. She held her breath, wondering if he'd be angry and vicious or calm and calculating. The closer Cato stood to her, the more she sensed the way the power he'd stolen from Endros didn't serve his temperament.

Where Cato's games required patience and moderation, his father's powers of chaos and wrath propelled him toward impulsivity. Cecilia hadn't considered how taking on extra power had affected the god. Cato was trying to cut magical corners—but magic required an exchange, and he was exchanging control for strength without realizing it. It was something she could use to her advantage.

"You want what I can give you. You don't want me," she pressed.

She walked a delicate line, trying to pull information out of Cato, testing the boundaries of Endros's rage that lived just beneath his skin.

Cato cut through the space between them so quickly it was hard to track. His hands gripped the table on either side of her legs, his face so close she felt his breath on her skin. The scent of leather and pine surrounded her like a cloud, and she knew if she had still been mortal, she would have been under his influence instantly. She looked into his angry gray eyes.

Although they'd fought before, she hadn't considered his size as intimidating then. He stood even taller than Rainer, and he had a physique that hinted at years of training and a very active lifestyle. He was handsome in the glowing, unnatural way all the gods were. His hair was so dark it cast a bluish hue. His gray eyes glowed silver as his anger grew. An old scar through his right eyebrow made her shudder as she wondered what it would take to scar a god like that. But it was less his good looks and formidable size that made him domineering; it was his presence, which seemed to swallow up the humble cottage. He seemed woefully out of place in such a quaint space, exuding the kind of power that belonged in a throne room.

"I assure you, Goddess." His gaze dropped to her lips. "I want you. You don't live as long as I do without knowing your own mind. Any man—immortal or otherwise—would be foolish not to recognize that you are a rare woman."

His eyes flickered brightly with power. Cecilia tried to read his emotions, but they were a swirl of sharp, prickling desire, fiery rage, and quiet, tingling intrigue.

"If you want me, then you'll let Xander go."

Cato looked down at her lips. "I cannot. He made a deal. The laws of magic require I follow through. Bargains with gods are binding."

The silence grew heavy between them. Cato leaned close, his cheek nearly brushing hers. Cecilia couldn't deny that she felt an invisible cord between them, as if his very proximity tugged at her. Perhaps it was the magic in her recognizing his, or simply the curiosity of being so close to the only other living god. The longer he remained so close to her, the harder she found it to remember why she shouldn't just give in to him.

"Wanting is a waste. I promise I would give it up if I could," Cato whispered. "Do you feel it too, Little Dove? It feels like you're reeling me in and I don't want to struggle against the line."

She read his emotions again. The hot anger had cooled to a warm frustration, and the desire was so prickly that goosebumps erupted along her skin—the feeling unnatural, but still compelling.

Xander cleared his throat and Cato backed away slowly.

"What was that? Were you messing with me?" Cecilia swallowed hard.

Cato's nostrils flared and his pupils dilated as his eyes met hers. "No more than you were messing with me." He shook his head, looking away.

"Tell me about Xander. What breaks his deal with you?" she asked.

Cato laughed. "Bold of you to ask. I won't hand you the way out."

"It was worth a try," she said. Cato ran his fingers up her neck, drawing a line of shivers. "Don't start."

He sighed. "I wish I could see inside your head. Instead, I'm reduced to common stalking. You are the only person in the world I cannot influence, and yet you somehow manage to be the only person I really want to."

Cecilia frowned. "You don't actually want to. You must realize that by now."

"I don't?" he asked.

"No, you want me to come to you. You want to win me over and you'd be disappointed if you could make me do it. You'd be bored with me the same way you are with everyone else, eventually. The only reason you want me is because you can't influence me. I would be the only person you could tell for certain wanted you. You're lonely—lonely like only you and I are. You want me to choose you. That's why you keep toying with me."

Cato arched a brow. "And why I keep toying with your men."

"My men?" Dread formed a new fissure in her heart.

"Yes. Xander and Rainer."

Cecilia froze. "No."

"Yes. Both of them."

Rainer had *promised* more than once. She was sure he wouldn't, but she suddenly felt less certain. "That's a lie."

"Is it?" Cato's grin turned wolfish. "What did your guardian want most, Cecilia?"

She shrugged, attempting to appear casual. "I don't know."

"Of course you do."

"I don't."

"Then you're the blindest woman in the two kingdoms, because everyone else can see that there's nothing in the world that Rainer McKay wants more than a way to be with Cecilia Reznik. A way where you could choose him and no one could say anything. Why do you think he didn't say you were the goddess? Why did he leave you with Xander? I told him it was the way. I convinced him it was how he could get what he wanted."

Bile rose in Cecilia's throat. Her mind clouded over with doubt. Rainer wouldn't do that. He couldn't have.

"Cece, your heart is racing," Xander said quietly, cutting through the silence. He'd stopped pacing to watch them.

Cato's grin turned feral. "I had them both this whole time. Surely you must have suspected. It's always been about me trying to win you over, Cecilia."

"And you had to clear the board to do it," she sighed.

Tears burned in her eyes. She thought that the hurt inside her couldn't get more brutal. When Xander admitted his secret and then dissolved their marriage, she thought she couldn't feel more wounded. But the revelation that Rainer could lie to her so easily hurt more than anything else.

"You're hurt," Cato said plainly. For once, he didn't look like he was happy about it. There was doubt in the scrunch of his brow. "I can teach you to harden yourself against the hurt, Little Dove."

"If there comes a time when I don't feel hurt, I hope they burn me on a pyre." Bitterness wove through the words.

A nagging voice tugged at the back of her mind. She knew Cato was preying on her deepest fear. *Remember,* the voice in her mind whispered.

She thought back to when Rainer was in the cell in Argaria and remembered how she could keep the goddess powers away, and then of all the times he tried to distract her from the pull of them. *Remember.* She thought of when he willingly pushed her into Xander's arms, when he officiated her wedding. She thought of when he almost died and the seriousness in his voice afterward when he promised to never make a deal with Cato. *Remember.*

"You're lying," she said, finally meeting Cato's surprised eyes. "You never got to Rainer."

For a moment Cato just looked at her like she was a fool, but then he started clapping. "I really thought I had you there. You should have seen your face. You are way more fun than I ever expected you to be."

The tension left Cecilia's body at once. "I've had enough games for one day. I've no interest in working with you peacefully. I want to go home and I want to take Xander with me."

"Do you want to make a deal? I'll trade Xander for you. We can seal the deal with a kiss," Cato taunted.

She crossed her arms. "I'm not falling for that one again."

His grin made her blood boil. "I know you feel like you have to say that to save face, but I could tell you liked it when I kissed you before. I know you feel the pull between us today." He leaned casually against the wall as he spoke.

"Whatever you need to tell yourself. If I trade myself, what happens to Xander?"

"Honestly, that deal doesn't really work. He would stay here with you to ease his obsession."

"*Fix him.*" Impatience crept into her voice.

Cato shrugged. "I don't know how."

"That's a lie."

"It's not," he said. "I don't know how to undo what I did. He's paranoid and jealous and possessive. He hates you and also all he can think about is you. Then you overloaded him with memories. It's a fine line between love and hate. I don't know how to undo it. Truly. We made a mess I don't know if I can fix. Xander, what are you thinking about right now?"

315

"Fuck you," Xander said. His body went rigid, and the room filled with the leather and pine scent of Cato's magic.

"Stop!" Cecilia yelled.

Cato grinned as he released Xander from his power. "I will let you stay with us and try to fix him with me."

"I don't want to stay with you."

"That's the only deal I'm willing to make right now."

"I'm not making any deals with you," she said.

"Fine, no deals, but if you stay and hear me out, I will help you fix him."

Cecilia tried to see any other angle, but he was clearly desperate for more time to convince her to work with him.

"Fine, I'll stay," she said. "Very temporarily, but I need a message delivered to Rainer, so he doesn't worry, and you cannot mess with it. And we fix Xander before I listen to any of your nonsense."

Cato's eyes lit up with excitement. She wrote Rainer a note, assuring him with a crescent promise that she was okay.

Cato disappeared and returned a moment later, having delivered the note.

Cecilia walked over to Xander and put a gentle hand on his shoulder. He jumped and flipped her onto her back on the floor. Straddling her, he brought a dagger to her neck. Cecilia tried to breathe, but he moved so fast that it knocked the wind out of her.

"Xander!" Cato's tone was casual yet scolding. "You're not supposed to hurt her. Drop the knife."

Xander's hands shook. "I need it to stop. I need her out of my head. I can't tell what's real."

He looked at Cecilia with tears in his clouded eyes, but he dropped the knife. His hands came to her throat and she tensed. She didn't know which version of him to expect, but he leaned down and kissed her softly on the lips. It surprised her, and even though she was still afraid he might try to choke the life out of her, she kissed him back. She pushed her sparkling power into him once again.

"Okay, enough of that," Cato said, pulling Xander off of her. She sat up, looking at Xander's stunned face. He looked so tortured and confused.

"Cece, I'm sorry. Did I hurt you?" His voice was so small, and he looked horrified.

She pulled him into her arms and hugged him. He tensed and then buried his face in her neck, taking deep breaths.

"Olney summers," he whispered. He placed a soft kiss on her neck and she sighed. "You really smell like lemons and lavender. That's real." His voice was quiet and heartbreaking.

"Yes, that's real," she whispered.

"Must you constantly be touching?" Cato asked. His voice was laced with so much contempt that Cecilia almost laughed.

"It's how I work, Cato," she said.

"You have to be touching?" he asked.

"It works best to be touching the person if I'm trying to share memory."

Cato frowned. "Well, must he enjoy it so much?"

"I didn't realize gods were so jealous."

He scoffed. "I only envy power, but we gods can be a bit possessive."

She shook her head. "I don't think he knows how he feels about it. He's conflicted."

Xander pulled back from her. "Don't talk about me like I'm not here. I still have half my mind."

"Fine. How do you feel?" she asked him.

"I don't know. It's all tied together. I'm jealous and angry with you. I feel ashamed and furious, and also I want you so badly it hurts. I don't know what's real. It all feels the same to me," Xander said.

"I'm going to show you how to inventory and archive, okay? It will help you make sense of what's in your head."

Xander nodded. Cecilia pressed gently against his mind and tugged at an emotional thread.

"See this," she whispered. "This is my emotional signature. Now find all the memories that have this and gather them together."

She waited as Xander slowly retrieved each one. It was tedious at first, but as he got used to the process, he became quicker at recognizing and tugging the memories loose until they were wrapped together.

"That's perfect. You're learning so quickly," she said. "Now you want to tuck it away in the back of your mind so it's there if you need it but it's not front and center with everything else."

It took Xander several attempts to tuck the memories into a far corner and keep them there.

"What's something you put in his head, Cato?" Cecilia asked.

"I told him you imagined it was Rainer when he made love to you," Cato said.

"Gods, why are you such a prick?"

Cecilia tucked Xander's face into her neck, keeping her voice so soft that only he would hear. "Xander, show me a memory that Cato gave you."

He obeyed, Cato's false influence wrapped around the memory.

"Okay, find all the ones that look like this and do the same thing you did with the memories I gave you."

The process took much longer because some memories had a tangled quality that connected them to others, but eventually he'd collected them all and tucked them carefully away.

Cecilia opened her eyes and looked at Xander.

Cato looked back and forth between them. "Did it work?"

Xander shoved her onto her back, her shoulder blades hitting the wood floor with a thud as he kissed her feverishly, one hand woven through her hair as he hiked up her dress.

"Okay, enough of that," Cato said, yanking him back.

Cecilia stayed on the floor, panting.

"Is this just a ploy to make me jealous?" Cato asked. "Because if it is, it's working."

"How should I know if he's going to kiss me or try to kill me? You made him this way. I'm just trying to get through to him," Cecilia said, her cheeks warming.

"I need you," Xander rasped, his voice desperate.

Her archiving was clearly a temporary solution and not a true fix.

"Okay, let's take a break. Walk it off, Xander. Things are getting a little too intense for my liking," Cato said.

Xander stood with a huff and walked out of the room.

Cato narrowed his eyes at Cecilia. "You think you can win him back by confirming the true things, but you can't rip out all the bad things I put in. His mind is poisoned by his love for you. You can strengthen the memories you shared, but you can't erase what I've done. I preyed on what already existed. He has an intense jealousy of you and your guardian. Why is that, do you think?"

Cecilia climbed to her feet, refusing to let Cato see the intensity of her love for Rainer. Better to be casual, to make herself look selfish than admit what Rainer really was to her.

"It's because I have a long history with Rainer and he's connected to my heart. What man wouldn't be jealous of that? I could show you, but it feels too cruel to show you a thing you'll never have. You'll never be able to manipulate someone into being a true friend."

Cato's eyes blazed with fury as Endros's power overtook him. He pressed her back into the wall and the wood shuddered from the impact.

"I will have everything I want. Even if I have to burn down your whole world to get it."

Cecilia sighed. "That's the problem. If you burn my world down, I will never feel anything for you but contempt. Friendship and acceptance are not things that you can steal. You can only earn them through gentleness."

He scoffed. "You're an incredibly strong immortal goddess and you like Rainer because he treats you like you're fragile."

"No, I like him because he knows I'm strong, but he's gentle with me anyway. He sees me as I am and he asks for nothing. You have neither the desire nor the capability to do that."

Cato sighed, scrubbing a hand over his face. "You don't know what I'm capable of yet, Goddess. I've lived quite a long time, and I believe I can always learn new things."

"And you want to learn to be vulnerable? To be gentle? To be kind?" she asked.

"No, I don't want to, but if it's what you require, I will teach myself."

Her eyes went wide in surprise.

"That shocks you, Cecilia?"

"Yes."

"It shouldn't," Cato said. "I told you before, I've waited a long time for you. A human lifetime is the blink of an eye. You and I, we can live for hundreds of years—thousands if we're careful. We're frozen in time. We were truly made for each other. God of manipulation and goddess of memory. Fate could not have set us on a more obvious course."

"Is that what you think?" She laughed in disbelief. "You think your meddling makes fate?"

"Cecilia, you are the only other living god. You are the only person who could understand me. I want you and I will not stop coming after you until I have you," he insisted.

"If you like games, then you should enjoy that."

Cato shook his head as he crossed the kitchen and leaned against the hearth. "This is the one time I don't want to play one. I'm shooting straight, Little Dove. I'm telling you my true intentions. I want you and only you."

"You want the power I can give you."

The trickster god waved a dismissive hand.

"And you hardly know me."

"I know you hate getting up early," he said. "You would do anything for the people you love. You are fiercely protective. Your loyalty is admirable, if not ill-advised."

She wasn't foolish enough to believe that all he wanted was her. Cato was always a few moves ahead, and that was way too simple a motivation.

"Those aren't things you know," she said. "Those are things you've stolen. You haven't earned them. You don't know what it is to get to know someone, to learn what they like and don't like, to learn what the sounds they make in their sleep mean. You've never taken the time to know someone so well that you can read every look on their face, even without a magical connection. You don't know what it is to do anything unselfish for someone else because you love them and want to protect them."

"And yet I still know them," Cato said. "Personally, I find the way you swing from feeling to feeling so violently compelling. I know how much you enjoyed your husband's company in the bedroom, in particular his talent with—"

"Do not finish that sentence."

"—his tongue," Cato finished, a delighted twinkle in his eye. "I have centuries of experience, in case you were wondering."

"Gods!" Cecilia covered her face with her hands, trying to hide her flaming cheeks.

She was suddenly aware of Cato's proximity. He was much too close to her once again. His breath danced over her cheek, and she felt the same supernatural pull to him as she looked into his gray eyes.

"I thought you'd be impressed by my persistence, Little Dove," he said, tucking a curl behind her ear.

"Perhaps you could try impressing me with your restraint," she said.

"As I recall, you enjoy a lack of restraint. I seem to remember an incident in the queen's garden with Xander." His voice was rough, sending a shiver through her.

She wasn't actually interested, but there was a strange magical pull toward him—his magic reaching out to brush against hers.

She turned away and saw Xander standing in the doorway. "I should go."

"Oh, don't run off, Cecilia. I was just having some fun with you," Cato huffed.

She pinned him with a look. "I think we have very different definitions of fun. Why doesn't Xander try to leave?"

"The deal. He has to stay, like a good little pet."

She walked toward Xander but he held perfectly still, like she was a bear about to attack him. She placed a hand on his cheek. He closed his eyes and leaned into the touch.

She turned back to Cato. "Can we have some time alone?" she asked.

Cato's eyebrows shot up, and he smirked. "That sounds dangerous. Now why would I allow that?"

She gave him her winningest smile. "It would endear you to me."

"Letting you fuck your ex would do that? How?" He laughed. "I can't wait to hear this one."

Cecilia rolled her eyes. "I just want to see how he acts when you aren't hovering."

A flicker of pleasure lit his eyes. *This* was what Cato wanted—for her to think there was nothing worth saving. He would allow it because he wanted her to believe Xander was a lost cause.

He wrung his hands and frowned. "I think we both know how he will act if I leave you alone, but if you say it will win me your favor, I will give you one night. You can go back to his room."

Cato ushered them down the hallway into a small bedroom, then winked as he closed the bedroom door and left them alone.

30

XANDER

Xander was wary the moment the small bedroom door creaked shut behind them. He knew Cato wouldn't wander far, but the thought of being alone with Cece called forth both excitement and dread.

The moment she'd looked at him on the beach, Xander saw a goodbye in her eyes. He wondered if she knew she'd made a decision, or if she was too surprised by the sight of him to realize. She'd let him kiss her, but for the first time ever, she held something back.

That hesitance stoked his desperation into an inferno. He felt the way his lies had made her cautious where she'd once been wild. His dishonesty had slammed closed the door of her heart, barring him on the wrong side.

Cece clasped her hands, rubbing her thumb over her inner wrist as she took in the rumpled bed and the sparse decor. Faded sunlight cast the room in gold, illuminating dust motes swirling around her like glittering stars.

"How do you feel?" she asked.

Xander sighed, trying not to pick at the memories he'd carefully tucked away. He still felt confused, agitated, and always like he was missing the full context of their relationship.

"Angry. Afraid," he said.

"Hmm." She closed the space between them, her eyes focused on his mouth as if daring him to kiss her.

Xander hated wanting her so badly, hated the way his desperation made him weak to anything she offered, hated the extraordinarily high cost of loving her.

Her hand came to his cheek, and he was comforted by the contrast of her soft skin and the calluses on her palm from using her bow.

"I know it's hard, but stay with me," she whispered.

He met her eyes and stilled, finally seeing her for what she was—the woman he loved with all his heart, the one person in the world he would do anything for.

"Cece."

Nothing had ever felt as good as seeing her and letting her see him. Their eyes locked and all the war and pain and love of the past few months passed between them.

"You are so reckless to be alone with me." He backed away from her a few steps.

She shrugged. "I know you won't hurt me. You didn't want to do that. You were confused and scared."

"I thought it was a dream. One of Cato's nightmares." Even in sleep, Xander couldn't escape the trickster god twisting his love for Cece into something poisonous that ran through every fond recollection of their time together.

"I forgive you." She touched his face so tenderly. "I promised to hold on even when it was hard—to fight with you and for you. I may not be your wife anymore, but I won't forget those vows. I won't let you push me away and stay in this mess alone."

Xander hung his head. "But I hurt you."

"I'm fine. Nothing even hurts," Cece said, gesturing to her body.

"I'm not talking about that. I'm talking about when I made the deal with Cato."

She tried to slide her mask of calm back into place, but he saw the truth.

"Don't pretend—not with me. I know that of everything I've done, that's the thing that hurt you the most, and I know it's the one thing I can't come back from. It's the thing he's used to spur on my rage. I know I'm just mad at myself. You have to let me go."

She shook her head, chin jutted in defiance. "You're still you, Xander."

He leaned his forehead against hers, breathing hard. Relief coursed through him before jealousy flared again.

"Have you been with Rainer?"

Cece stepped away, her calves bumping the bed. "That's not your business."

"That's a yes," Xander snapped.

"It's not your business. *You* left *me*, Xander. You have no right to the way that I've dealt with it. You have no right to more of my heart." Her pulse kicked up. "I'm leaving." She pushed out the bedroom door and ready to storm down the hallway, but Xander caught her wrist and pulled her back against him.

"Don't leave while you're angry. I'm sorry. I don't want to be this way. Please don't leave yet." He wrapped his arms around her from behind, tucking his face into her neck, and she relaxed.

"You hurt me. Worse than anyone ever has," she rasped.

He spun her in his arms, cupping her face in his hands. "I know there's no excuse. The worst thing I did was before I was ever influenced. I know I can't fix it. I'm so sorry. I hate myself for hurting you, but please stay with me, just for tonight. Please let me have you for just one more night. It doesn't have to be anything else. Just let me hold you for a while. Please, Cece." The floorboards creaked as he lowered himself to his knees, hugging her waist. "I'm not above begging."

She looked down at him with tears in her eyes and nodded. Xander couldn't decide if he felt relieved or panicked by her decision. He rose and sat down on the edge of the bed, pulling her into his lap.

"Every day I wonder what would have happened if I made a different choice and told you who I was when we were in the cabin instead of making a deal with Cato. I have so many regrets, but the biggest one is hurting you. You are the one thing in this life that made me hopeful."

Xander wasn't the man she'd fallen in love with, and he didn't know if that man was even in him anymore. He wrapped his arms around her and she relaxed into him.

"How is it now?" she asked.

His chest grew impossibly tight. This was it. The room was on fire—their love burning down around them. All of their moves and countermoves formed a pattern—like dancing a Reldan in reverse, the passion bleeding out with each step. "I'm afraid you'll never let me have you again, and that's making it worse."

She pulled away and met his eye, and he saw it again; that glimmer of goodbye.

"If you knew it was the last time, what would you do?" she asked.

His thoughts were too overwhelming for him to form words.

She placed a hand on his cheek. "Don't think about it. It hurts too much to name it. Just show me."

His fingers made quick work of the buttons on her dress, the seams groaning as he yanked it down. She kissed him fiercely, wrapping her legs around his waist as he lifted her. He was starved for the sight of her, for the way she touched him with so much tenderness, for the taste of her—sugar and tea and lemon.

But this kiss tasted like goodbye, like she was trying to have the last word and that word was "Sorry."

His hands trembled. "Tell me you love me."

"You know I do," she murmured. Her eyes were shining with unshed tears. "I always will."

He kissed her again and they were lost in the pull of each other, in the grasping, desperate need to get as close as possible. His hands were in her hair, but his heart was in her teeth.

His stomach tumbled. He wasn't ready. It was too soon. The frenzy overtook him.

Xander's lips rarely left her skin and when they did, it was only to murmur apologies into the crook of her neck, the space between her breasts, and the curve of her hip. He'd charted this territory so many times it was imprinted on his brain.

The most precious magic he'd ever cultivated was how to shrink the world down to just the two of them—how to love someone so much that time and reason burned to ash and left only the raw, heart-rending knowing between them. A five-word love story written with touch that would linger a lifetime on their skin. *I will always love you.*

Cece stayed with him. She let him try to make up for breaking her heart, and it seemed like she might have fallen a little more in love with him for trying so hard.

Xander tried to memorize the sound, taste, and rhythm of fierce, wild, beautiful Cece. There was no end to his desire. Nothing even took the edge off of it. Nothing ever had.

Finally, they collapsed in an exhausted, breathless heap, skin raw from the passion. Cece brushed his hair from his forehead. They were quiet for a long time before Xander summoned the strength to speak.

"Sometimes I wonder what would have happened if I had just had more time to win you over at court. I wonder if I would have just run away with you. Do you think you would have gone for that?" Xander asked.

"I don't know."

"You wouldn't have left him." Jealousy beckoned, but he fought to stay.

She frowned. "Maybe we shouldn't talk about Rainer."

"What will he think about this?" Xander asked.

"About what?"

"About you staying with me tonight."

She sighed. "Xander—"

He couldn't imagine watching Rainer with Cece the way Rainer had with him over the past few months. Xander had made a real show of trying to bait him, but Rainer clearly had access to restraint the prince lacked.

"He doesn't know yet," she whispered.

Xander arched a brow. "How you feel? You haven't told him?"

"I didn't know, or else I've always known."

He couldn't have put Cece and Rainer's story into better words himself. "It's just as well. I could never share you."

She propped herself up on her elbow to look at him. "You'd rather have none of me?"

"No, but I couldn't control the jealousy before this either. You're the only thing I ever wanted to myself. I never wanted to be a king. Honestly, I never even cared about getting married, but when I fell in love with you, it broke me open. I cannot love in half measures. The thought of having none of you—of someone else having all of you— breaks me. But I know what it would do to me and to you if I could only have part. I've hurt you so much already." He brushed a tear from her cheek, but she refused to look at him. "You wanted me to fight for you like you fight for me."

"I don't know what I wanted, but I wanted to feel worthy of a fight."

Xander sighed heavily. If only she knew. If only she understood. He *was* fighting for her, just not in the way she expected.

"You are. I'm sorry I can't do it how you want. I made the selfish choice before and I'm trying to make the unselfish one now. I thought that letting you go would be the kinder thing. Rainer said once that you never let him take care of you, but you let me. Let me take care of you one last time by staying away from you, no matter how much I don't want to."

"But what if you can break the obsession?" she asked.

"I'm still not sure I could share you, especially with him. Rainer has always been better at loving you, Cece. You and I both know that."

Cece looked at him with tears in her eyes.

"Love, don't look at me like that. You don't understand the strength it takes to say no to you."

There was nothing else to say, so he kissed her. He pulled her onto his lap and moved with her, with all the sweetness between them. Kissing her tenderly, touching her with a gentleness he never knew he possessed until they met. He felt the torrent of grief, shame, passion, and ecstasy. He gave Cece every last piece of him, and she stayed connected to him.

When she finally faded off to sleep, he idly ran his fingers through her hair. He stared at the pout of her lips as warring emotions tore through his head. He had little chance of getting out from beneath Cato's influence, but he was happy to have had the chance to be with her again.

Xander hoped he'd given her the closure she needed.

He'd lost Cece long ago, but he saw it on her face as she slept. Grief and love mixed with acceptance. She wasn't giving up on him, but she was letting go of their love story. She was letting herself be free.

Xander clung to her, wishing for the same peace but finding none.

31

CECILIA

Cecilia woke to early morning light slashing through the cottage window, casting the dingy, graying wood walls in golden light.

Xander's lips brushed her shoulder.

"Please?" he whispered.

"This is the last time." She sounded more certain than she felt.

Saying goodbye to him felt like weeding the remnants of love from her heart, leaving her full of holes where she'd ripped out leftover affection.

Everything was different, as if some of Xander's aggression from the previous night had burned off. All sense of urgency was gone. He moved slowly, kissed her softly, as if he was trying to savor each moment. There was such a reverence to his movements. He caressed her face, her neck, her shoulders, like he was trying to make sure to touch every last inch of her skin, following each touch with a flurry of kisses.

Cecilia felt such a swell of longing for the man she thought might be gone forever. He moved with her until she was breathless and every inch of her skin tingled. He was so tender with her, she wondered if he was holding back, or if the obsession had waned. When she sat there tucked against him afterward, he finally spoke.

"It's still there," he said, as if reading her mind. "I just know how much you like when I'm gentle."

He drew long lines from her neck to her collarbone and then down over her shoulder, and despite the gentleness, his gaze was intense.

"I thought about what you said last night. If it was the last time, I would tell you I never wanted to cause you any pain. Even when you smile, I can see it in your eyes. They always sparkle, but they seem to have lost some of their joy, and I know I'm responsible. I always loved you and no matter what happens, I will love you. You taught me how to forgive myself before. Part of me hopes you will teach me again if I can ever get free of this—" His voice broke.

"Xander—"

"If this was the last time, I would tell you that Cato could never manipulate me into being this obsessed with you if I wasn't already halfway there myself. I remember that. I remember not being able to keep my hands off of you. I remember the way it felt impossible to stop kissing you. I know that was real even before this." He swallowed hard. "And if this was the last time, I would thank you for holding me together while my world fell apart. You deserve to be happy without guilt."

Xander had given her so much when she'd stopped wanting things for herself. He'd inspired her to figure out what she wanted in the first place. He reminded her of her courage when she forgot it, and he saw her when no one else had. There were so many reasons why she would always love him, but she knew this was his way of letting go and it hurt all the same.

The windows rattled with the breeze, startling her into action. "I have to go."

The crazed, unfocused look returned to Xander's eyes. "I know."

"I wish I could break you out. I wish you could come with me."

"Cece." His eyes pleaded with her. "Don't give up on me getting

331

my mind back, okay? I know I'm not all right, but please don't write me off yet."

She brought a hand to his cheek. "I never would. I will figure it out."

She washed up and was mildly disturbed to find that Cato had left her a set of her own clothes—a tunic and leggings that he must have retrieved from her cottage.

She kissed Xander one last time, then returned to the kitchen where she found Cato waiting.

"Long night? You look like you were ridden hard and put to bed wet," Cato laughed.

"At least I don't look like an asshole," she said.

"Little Dove, you know I'm joking. You look lovely and radiant as always. All that *exertion* makes you glow."

She crossed her arms. "Why do you call me 'Little Dove'?"

Cato smirked. "Because it suits you."

"That's not an answer."

He shrugged. "Are you sufficiently convinced of the futility of your mission? Are you ready to end this chaos? Truly, it does not need to be this way. Join me and cease this ridiculous warring." He shook his head. "Honestly, it's just so much work."

Cecilia sighed. "You're right. It would be easier to just surrender. You should try it because you'll never win me over."

Cato's eyebrows shot up, and his eyes glowed dangerously. "Never say never. Never is a challenge. Never is a promise you can't keep."

She brushed her hand over the dagger strapped to her thigh. Even within striking distance, she wasn't sure she'd be successful in killing Cato.

He tracked the movement. "Feeling brave?" He stepped close enough that the toes of his boots brushed hers. "Are you nervous about being so close?"

Cecilia could practically taste the words. "No."

"I love how sweetly you lie."

She felt hooked by him—or maybe it was just the effects of his power. He couldn't influence her, but his essence seemed to draw her in. Perhaps hers did the same to him. She leaned closer and Cato did the same until they were just inches apart.

Xander cleared his throat, and Cecilia stumbled away from the trickster god.

"What was that? What did you do to me?" she panted.

"I didn't do anything. What did you do to me?" Cato asked. He looked just as confused as she felt and she couldn't decipher if he was playing some kind of game.

"Nothing. I don't know," she stammered.

His grin grew wide. "What did you feel? I think I felt a hint of your power. It was like my whole body was full of sunlight and I felt something I haven't felt in a long time—"

"Disgust?" she suggested.

"Hope." He laughed in disbelief. "What did you feel?"

She rolled her shoulders as if she could shake off the sensation. "I have to go."

Cato stepped into her path. "When you walk out that door, you take with you the last chance for peace."

"That chance is a farce as long as you're breathing," she said. She shoved past him, ready for a fight, but he let her walk out of the cottage.

Just as she suspected, the valley below was full of scarlet tents of the Argarian army. She mounted the horse tied up beside the cottage and took a moment to orient herself. This was the town of Rowdane. For once she was glad of the way Rainer had drilled Olney geography into her when they were training for the Gauntlet. She turned her horse and kicked him into stride toward Olney.

As she rode, her mind wandered to all she'd lost. Her eyes stung with hot tears, which turned to sobs, forcing her to slow her riding.

Thanks to Rainer's relentless repetition, she knew exactly where she was. A red dirt trail blurred in front of her as she wove into a series of winding rock caverns. This had to be the Halls of Truth, the alleged home of Goddess Aelish.

Cecilia led the horse to a stream of water that cut through the dusty rocks and sat down on a boulder, trying to shove down the flood of emotions. She'd intentionally chosen this route back to Olney City in hopes of finding her last sibling. Now that she was sitting in the caverns, though, she wasn't sure she was ready to hear the truth.

"Hedging, little sister?"

Cecilia turned to see a pale, statuesque goddess with long, strawberry-blonde hair and blue eyes. A faint smile danced over her lips as Cecilia stared at her, wondering if thought alone was enough to summon her siblings.

"Aelish?"

"Very good!" the goddess of truth said, sitting next to her.

"I thought of you, and now here you are."

Aelish grinned. "What's weighing on your heart?"

"I think you probably already know," Cecilia said, wiping away her tears.

"I do, but I'd still like to hear you say it."

"Where do I even start?" Cecilia let out a shaky laugh.

"The gods, right? We aren't exactly known for our smooth love lives," Aelish said, placing a gentle hand on Cecilia's shoulder.

"I suppose not."

"Life is a great teacher. We get the lessons we need, not the ones we want. That's not what's really bothering you, though, is it? It's a lot, but that's not the acute thing." Aelish stared right through her.

Cecilia sighed heavily. "I thought it would hurt less to know for sure, but it doesn't."

Aelish looked at her skeptically. "That's part of it."

The goddess let the silence stretch, honing it into a weapon that forced Cecilia to speak.

"Gods! Are you always like this? So pushy?"

"I am simply the goddess of truth and you're denying yours."

A deep grief tightened every muscle in Cecilia's chest. "You don't always know when it's the last time you'll kiss someone. You rarely get to know that, but I knew. I knew it was the end even before Xander kidnapped me."

Aelish's eyes softened to something resembling sympathy. "You're getting closer."

"It's always been Rainer. I fell in love with him and it never faded. Maybe I always knew, but I couldn't ignore it that day in the forest when he almost died. I feel guilty, or stupid, like I should have known, like it shouldn't have taken falling in love with someone else to realize what I wanted because I knew way back in Olney before we left on that last trip."

"You did know, but Rainer didn't give you the option," Aelish said. "You can't beat yourself up. Cecilia, you are so young. The path was winding to teach you to trust yourself. There is an eternity ahead of you. You're just learning how to love and how to know what you want. You are bound to make mistakes."

Cecilia sighed. "I don't want to hurt anyone."

"Not hurting anyone else just means hurting yourself, little sister. The truth always comes out. You get to choose whether you run toward it even when you're scared or run away. You're afraid now because there's nothing holding you back. It hurts now because you loved Xander, and you lost the relationship you thought you had. You can mourn that. It's possible to honor what it was, to still love him, flaws and all, as he's always loved you. But even if he had never made those mistakes, you know the truth in your heart."

Cecilia felt exposed, raw, and so weary. "I never would have stopped loving Rainer."

Aelish's smile was gentle, but the revelation filled Cecilia with guilt. "Sometimes it's not about who you can live with as much as who you can't live without."

Cecilia could never give Rainer up. He was hers as much as she was his.

Aelish touched her shoulder gently. "I'm not saying this to hurt you, even though I know it will, but you need to understand. Not all love stories are meant to be forever. Some are just a shock to the system. Part of that will always be there. There's a fire between you that is forever and that won't change. It will hurt. It's not the kind of thing that disappears."

Cecilia sighed and looked down at the stream, trying to imagine the hurt she felt lasting forever.

"But you and Rainer are a soul-bonded match," Aelish continued. "That connection with him is only how it is because you want it to be. If you truly felt nothing, you could easily turn away. That connection would stay, but you would be able to easily love another. If you didn't feel for each other, the bond never would have formed the way it has. Soul bonds are real, but so is free will. You chose each other every day. If either of you had let go, the bond would have fizzled. You'd still feel things, but not as you do now. You're worried that it somehow took away your choice, but all it ever did was reinforce it and connect you deeper. It's a tremendous trust that stretches between you. It may feel ordinary, but some of the most potent magic feels mundane to those who are accustomed to it."

Aelish spoke to the deepest fear that plagued Cecilia's relationship with Rainer. Her life had already been more influenced by magic than she ever wanted it to be. It had poisoned so many of the good things. She'd worried that even the purity of her love for Rainer was tainted by ancient magic, but Aelish's words released her from the worry that what they had wasn't real. Still, that felt too tidy and convenient. She had the feeling she was being moved around a chessboard by yet another sibling.

"It's okay to be scared. But don't play it safe. Some risks are worth taking. Some things are worth saving, even at the end of the world." Aelish gave her a knowing smile.

"But what about what Cato said?"

Aelish rolled her eyes. "Cato believes that you are fated."

"But how do I keep that away? How can I be fated to three different people?" Cecilia balled her hands in frustration.

"Fate is a tangle, a half-formed tapestry that shows the most likely design, but we all have free will. Even we gods don't know exactly what will happen. We simply see the most likely possibilities. You are a goddess and you can decide."

They fell into a comfortable silence.

"How do I beat Cato? Any sage wisdom?"

Aelish grinned. "Tell me, do you play chess?"

Cecilia sighed. She was so exhausted of godly double-talk. "I do."

"Facing Cato is like playing a game of chess. He will try to bait you into making rash moves. He will prey on your emotions whenever he can. In chess, when is your opponent most vulnerable?"

Cecilia searched through her catalogue of memories, trying to remember all the lessons from her father over the board. "When they think they've won."

"Does he think he's won yet?" Aelish asked.

The thought unnerved Cecilia. "No, but I'm afraid to let him get to that point."

"The greatest players know when to sacrifice something valuable. Have faith in yourself and the people you've surrounded yourself with," Aelish said. "Have faith that you have more control over your future than you think. Have faith in the love that's pulled you through everything. It's okay to hope, even when things feel hopeless. Remember, where faith goes, power flows."

Cecilia continued to sob, her tears puddling in the red dirt at her feet.

"I wish I could stay and chat more, but I'm afraid I've already been in this realm too long," Aelish said.

Cecilia turned to watch her go, noticing that Aelish's body appeared more diaphanous.

"I'll be watching, Cecilia. We're all rooting for you. Don't forget what I've said." Aelish's eyes shifted to the ground beyond Cecilia. "Look at that, Stellaspo Tenebiso. I haven't seen those flowers in quite some time."

Cecilia whipped her head around. Sure enough, the exact flowers Xander sent her on their wedding day burst from the barren dirt, blooming where her tears landed moments before.

She looked back to Aelish, but the goddess was gone. She turned to the white, star-shaped flowers and pulled up the memory of reading the letter Xander sent with the flowers on their wedding day. She focused on the words.

"It's an Old Argarian word, but it translates roughly to a 'hope in the

dark.' They always make me think of you and the night we met. The fairy tales say they only grow on the old battlefields where a cause felt especially impossible or hopeless, and many fell believing in their cause anyway..."

What did it mean that flowers bloomed out of her tears? It wasn't exactly like she could flower Cato to death. Cecilia sighed. She needed to ride home, but her body felt like lead and her head was too full.

She'd been dancing around the truth since she left for her last Gauntlet run. It felt like a lifetime ago. So much had happened, but she knew the whole time that she could never love anyone the way she loved Rainer. She wanted to run toward the terrifying longing.

She was making yet another exchange, and even though it was right, it hurt.

She squeezed her eyes closed and took three deep breaths, inhaling a smoky cinnamon scent. When she blinked them open, she was looking into the icy blue gaze of the god of death.

"Grim, what are you doing here?"

Grimon shrugged sheepishly. "Aelish mentioned it was a tough day. I didn't want to add to it, but I've been looking for the right time to give you this note. I probably should have given it to you when Xander asked me to weeks ago, but you were so distraught."

It figured that Xander was suddenly everywhere at the exact moment she was trying to let him go.

She frowned. "So you thought you should decide what I can handle?"

"I'm sorry." Grimon sounded genuine, but she was still annoyed as she snatched the bird-shaped note from his hand.

———

Beautiful Cece – You are hope embodied. You are a light in the dark and I'm certain what you become will only be a reflection of who you are as a person, and that is a goddess I would like to meet.

———

Cecilia frowned. *Why repeat those words now?*

"What does it mean?" Grimon asked.

"It's what he said to me when he first returned home to Olney, when I was so scared of becoming a goddess. I just don't understand why he'd send this now."

"He wrote it the day he dissolved your marriage."

Cecilia frowned. "I have no idea what to make of it, but I need to get home. So thanks, I guess, for delivering this very late message."

Grimon's face softened. "I was just trying to look out for you."

"I've had more than enough of other people deciding what I can and can't handle for one lifetime," she sighed. "I'll see you later, Grim."

The god of death hesitated to accept her dismissal before fading into a puff of smoke.

Cecilia mounted her horse and continued toward home. As she rode, Xander's words blended with the flowers growing from her tears, which blended with Cato's nickname for her. *Little Dove.*

An idea sparked, burning through her mind, and she rode harder, eager to share with Evan and Rainer the first piece of good news in weeks.

32

RAINER

Waiting helplessly for Cecilia to return had scraped Rainer's nerves raw. Even though he felt Cecilia getting closer, he jumped when she burst through the cottage door. Evan leaned against the kitchen table with a forced casualty.

"How is he?" Evan asked before Cecilia had even caught her breath.

Cecilia's eyes were red-rimmed and puffy, but she seemed unharmed.

"I was worried," Rainer said.

"You got my note?" she asked.

"Yes, but still. I felt your grief. I wanted to come find you, but Evan made me stay here."

Cecilia gave Evan a grateful mock-salute. "Evan, I need to try something on you," she said. "I need you to tell me what it feels like to you when I use this part of my power."

Rainer's eyebrows shot up. Hopefully Evan wouldn't have the same reaction Rainer had the other day.

Cecilia took Evan's hand and the room filled with the lemon-lavender smell of her magic. He blinked his eyes open and looked at her.

"Well?" she asked expectantly.

Evan sighed. "It felt like sunlight filling my whole body, but there's something else. It reminded me why I started out to begin with. Why I always protected Xander. Why I led you all back here and risked getting killed. It's like it reconnected me with the possibility of avoiding war. Of building peace. However small it might be. It felt almost like hope."

Cecilia clapped her hands and bounced on her toes. "I think I finally get it."

"Care to fill us in?" Rainer asked.

She paced across the kitchen. "So I can melt minds. Horrible and also true. I can also return memories and rebuild memory structures and soothe ailments of the mind like with Sylvie's grandpa. But the piece we've been missing is that I can restore hope. I should have listened to what people were saying all along. Rain, you said something similar back when Teddy asked us about our bond. Xander said it and then when Cato touched me—"

"He touched you?" Rainer's hand fisted as he looked her over for injury again.

She waved him off. "I could feel his power and he could feel mine —not like it affected me, really, but just like I had a sense of it. Cato said mine felt like hope. I think he knew that hope was the key to this whole thing. We wrote off everything that my brother Devlin said because he betrayed us, but technically he told us that our plan wouldn't work and also he said that hope is an antidote to war and chaos. It's also got to be the antidote to Cato's brand of manipulation. I just haven't figured out how yet."

Evan blew out a breath. "It was right in front of our faces."

Cecilia nodded.

"I assume it didn't go well with Xander?" Evan asked.

Cecilia's face fell and a wave of her grief hit Rainer in the chest. He placed a hand on her shoulder and was relieved when she leaned into him.

"Cato has done a number on him. He claims he doesn't know how to fix Xander either, now that we've both messed with him. I assume killing Cato will fix him." She slumped into a kitchen chair. A wild pulse of grief and fear and anger punched through their bond, but Rainer did not know how to help her sort through it.

She swallowed hard, her eyes watery. "He's in terrible shape. Before, he was mean and vindictive, but now he's haunted. He doesn't know what's real and I don't know if what I showed him helped or just made it worse for him." She leaned more heavily into Rainer. "I tried to bring him back with me, but Cato wouldn't make a deal with me I could live with."

"What does Cato even want?" Evan asked.

"Me. He wants me," she sighed.

Rainer's stomach plummeted like he'd crested a hill on horseback too fast. "What?"

Panic twisted in his chest. He could not lose Cecilia, not when he finally felt he was winning her back. If Cato wanted Cecilia, there was almost nothing stopping him. Rainer was well-trained and had years of experience protecting Cecilia, but Cato was a god.

Without looking, Cecilia slipped her hand into his and squeezed.

"He thinks we are fated for each other," she said. "There's a certain pull toward each other that I didn't realize before because I was so busy planning out ways to murder him. I understand why he thinks that, but it's obviously never going to happen."

Evan shook his head and let out a disbelieving laugh. "I hope you'll forgive me because you're a goddess and all, but our lives would be much easier if everyone realized how impatient you are."

Cecilia shrugged and sat at the kitchen table. "And to think, not that long ago I couldn't even get a man to look at me."

"Bullshit. You had plenty of guys looking at you. You just weren't looking back, Cece," Rainer said, plopping down in the chair across from her.

She grinned at him. "Yep, I was too busy looking at you, and you were too busy looking at anyone else."

Rainer knew she was teasing, but he still felt guilty.

"Do you think you got through to Xander at all?" Evan asked.

"Maybe a little." She tried to make it sound light, but her face was lined with sadness. "I miss him, too. I promise I'm going to figure out a way to get him back. It just might not be an easy fix. I won't give up on him."

"I know you won't. I know I give you a hard time, Cece. I know that you care, and I know you won't stop trying. My frustration isn't with you. It's with the whole situation," Evan said.

"So what do we do next?" Rainer asked.

"I guess I can just walk around Olney trying to spread hope over the next few days," Cecilia suggested.

Rainer frowned. Hope would help soothe fears but he couldn't imagine how it would benefit them in active combat.

Evan rubbed his chin. "There was something Devlin said. Can you bring back that memory so that we can watch it again?"

Cecilia nodded, taking each of their hands as she pulled up the memory. The tension in Rainer's chest released as the familiar surge of her magic flowed through him. He loved watching her memories. Her height meant her angle on the world was so much lower than his, and her memories were always punctuated with sharp emotions.

They watched again as Devlin said, *"It's hope. If you want to defeat an enemy, you either break their will or you revive it. People fight when they're desperate, but they live when they're hopeful. Hope can command even the strongest army."*

Evan clapped his hands together when the memory was finished. "I don't think it's about inspiring the Olney Hunter Army. I think it's about reminding the Argarian Hunter Army what they have to lose. When you used your power on me, I wasn't thinking about fighting. I wasn't inspired to fight. I remembered the things that were important to me and none of them were fighting."

"So you think I need to use the power on their army and remind them what they have to live for?" Cecilia asked.

"Exactly! Fighting for something is easy. Living for something is hard. They just need the right inspiration," Evan said.

She looked wary. "I've never used that power on huge groups of people."

Evan arched a brow. "What happened that day on the beach?"

Cecilia cringed. Rainer knew she hated talking about it.

"I wasn't running the show then, but it was honestly like a reflex," she said. "Still, I was tired afterward, and that was only one battalion. I assume Cato has quite a few."

Evan frowned, sipping his tea and setting the cup back on the table. "I am not sure that anyone has the expectation that you can stop an entire army, but maybe you can do enough to minimize our losses."

The three of them sat quietly, considering it.

"And what if it doesn't work?" Cecilia asked.

"Then we're no worse off than we were to start with. We'll plan for the worst and hope for the best," Evan said.

While Rainer appreciated Evan's faith in Cecilia, he worried it was too much pressure on her and the power they still knew so little about.

"Think about it, Cece. I'm going to go take Sylvie for a walk, but I'll stop back to check in with you both in the morning," Evan said. He turned and left them alone in the cottage.

Late afternoon light streamed through the windows. Cecilia sprawled on the bed.

Rainer ran a hand through her curls. "Do you want to talk about it?"

She raised an eyebrow. "Do you want to hear about it?"

"I want to hear everything." As soon as he said it, he knew it was true, but he was worried from her hesitation that he'd change his mind halfway through.

"Are you sure?" she asked.

"I meant what I said before. I trust you will do what you have to do, and what you want to do. I might not love it, but I accept it."

She told him exactly what had happened. He didn't flinch, but he shut down their connection so she wouldn't feel the jealousy surging through him. He wasn't angry. Feeling envious of Xander Savero was nothing new. Mostly, Rainer just worried for Cecilia.

"Rain, I'm fine. Just in serious need of a bath." She bit her lip. "Cato almost tricked me."

"How?"

"He made it seem like he made a deal with you too, and for a minute, I believed him. Then I realized it couldn't be true, but it scared me. Rain, Cato cares about nothing. He has nothing to lose and everything to gain. He's never going to stop coming for me. He could get to you or he could just hurt you until I do what he wants."

Rainer placed his hands on her shoulders. "He cannot have you. Not ever. I won't let him. I will always come for you."

She nodded, but her eyes were full of doubt. Her dread flowed through their bond, bleeding into his. No matter how desperate he was to believe it, even Rainer didn't have the strength to hold back a god.

———

Rainer washed the dinner plates as Cecilia paced the cottage. She'd been home for a full day and hadn't stopped moving the whole time.

She leaned against the kitchen table. "So you and I, and Sylvie and Cal and Evan will help guard Hector and Marcos and Queen Elena. We report in two days to Olney Castle and then we—what? Just wait for Cato to show up?"

Rainer laughed at the exasperated look on her face. "What else can we do? He can literally appear out of nowhere at any time with an army behind him."

She poured herself a glass of wine and took a long gulp. Worry bloomed through their connection.

"What's bothering you other than the obvious?"

"I can't help feeling like this is a short-term solution. We solve for now, but Cato is immortal. I'm immortal. I won't age. Even you won't live forever, Rain. I hadn't thought about it until he brought it up. He could just wait you all out and get me isolated."

Rainer almost laughed at her concern. "If I know anything about you, it's that you could live a millennium and still not give him the satisfaction of giving in. I've seen you run on spite for a long time."

She smiled faintly. "Be serious."

"I *am* serious. Cato has met his match in terms of stubbornness, and I plan to be here for a long time."

Rainer had no intention of letting her go anytime soon. She might have forever, and he only one lifetime, but he would make it count. He would never take her for granted again, and he had the rest of his life to make up for all the times he had.

Cecilia seemed curled in on herself, lost in thought. He tried not to stare, but her blue dress made her eyes look even brighter than usual.

He dried the dinner plates, stoked the fire so it wouldn't die out overnight, and walked to the door to go to his apartment and give her some space.

Cecilia caught his hand, looking up at him, her eyes full of apprehension. "Will you stay tonight?"

"I'll stay as long as you will have me. I won't ever leave you. I know I'm pretty late getting here, but I will be here for whatever you need. I was an idiot our whole lives. I'm here for you. Mortal, immortal. I don't care. I've made a lot of mistakes, but I will not let you down now." He looked down at her. "Oh no, are you going to cry?"

"Maybe," she laughed, brushing tears from her eyes.

Rainer cupped her face in his hands. "I'm hoping one of these days that you will trust yourself the way I do."

"If you want me to stop crying, then you need to stop being so sweet," she sobbed.

He laughed. "I've got a lot to make up for."

"You don't. It's all forgiven."

Rainer hadn't realized how badly he needed that absolution.

Cecilia's gaze focused on his mouth and he had to fight the urge to throw her on the bed and kiss her until she was too exhausted to keep her eyes open.

"I would say it anyway because it's true—gods, don't look at me like that," he said, leaning away from her.

"Like what?"

"Like you want me to kiss you again. It's almost impossible not to. I'm trying to give you space, but when you look at me that way, I can't stop thinking about the way you taste, and now I know that you'll be even sweeter from the wine. Your kisses make every bad thing in my life fade away."

"That's just goddess magic," she sighed.

"It's not. Sometimes, just being close to you was enough to make me feel that way. It has nothing to do with magic."

She nodded, but he saw the doubt in her eyes.

Rainer swallowed hard, his heart thundering in his chest. *Now or never, McKay.*

"I couldn't love you before the way you needed me to. I wasted so much time worrying about the stupidest things. You were a goddess and I was just an orphan and I thought I couldn't possibly be worthy of you. But now I don't really care if I'm worthy or not because you are all I want. I'd walk across the two kingdoms just to hold your hand. I'm done wandering around trying not to be in love with you. You gave me a lot of chances and I wasn't ready, but I am now. I'll love you now like I couldn't before. I'm here, and I'm yours."

She was so close now. Her hands resting over his heart, her teary eyes fixed on his.

"There is no part of you too dark and scary for me to look at. No part of you is less lovely than the whole. No part of you that isn't worth being frustrated and challenged by you daily. I'm not running away anymore. I was made to love you and I'll never stop."

Before Rainer could even comprehend what was happening, Cecilia pressed onto her toes and kissed him.

33

CECILIA

C ecilia kissed Rainer like she could make up for all the history between them. A lifetime of wanting crashed down on her at once.

She was tired of holding back, tired of being good, tired of pretending not to want Rainer. She vacillated between guilt, grief, and relentless longing. The pendulum swung back and forth so violently it made her dizzy.

There was nothing in the world like the way Rainer kissed her—his hand at the nape of her neck, drawing her deeper into it. He was unhurried, as if there wasn't a war on the horizon, a god out for blood, and a kingdom counting on her.

She slid her hands beneath his shirt, relishing in the warmth of his skin and the way his heart beat so fast beneath her palms.

Cecilia wanted to give in. So much of her life had been about fighting. She'd been holding back so long; surrender was a living temptation.

Rainer backed toward the bed. He sat on the edge and pulled her into his lap, bunching up her dress. His hands on her bare thighs sent such a riot of sensations through her that she stopped breathing for a second.

Desire burned through her blood like a fever, like she'd embraced a sort of madness. She pulled off his shirt, and he fumbled with the buttons on the back of her dress until the sleeves sagged further off her shoulders and his hands wandered over the skin. He kissed her neck as she hiked the dress higher before pulling it over her head and tossing it on the floor.

So much of his skin was pressed against hers. There was nothing between them but his pants and her thin lace undergarments. He kissed her neck, leaving a trail of fire on her skin. Cecilia wanted his lips and hands everywhere. She was drowning in Rainer willingly, so utterly out of control that her entire body seemed poised to forget who she was and what doing more would mean.

"Stop," Cecilia said, jerking herself back.

She was really talking to herself, but Rainer pulled his hands away. Both of them sat there, wide-eyed, panting, hands trembling.

"I'm sorry," he whispered. His green eyes sparkled in the firelight, daylight dimming over the sea.

"Don't apologize, Rain. I kissed you. I was telling myself to stop. I just...I'm very overwhelmed and I felt like I was losing control."

"I felt like I wanted you to," he said, bringing a hand to her cheek.

She closed her eyes and leaned into his palm. "Gods, I want to. I've wanted you for so long, but I just don't want it to be like this. When there's someone else still in my heart. When I'm still grieving. I want it to be all about you. I want my mind to be clear."

Rainer sighed, shaking his head. "How is it I've accepted that Xander will always be in your heart, but you haven't?"

The words stunned her.

He grinned. "Rare to see you speechless."

"It's just not what I ever expected you to say."

He shrugged a shoulder. "It's true. There is no perfect moment. There's only the little time we have."

She ran her fingers through Rainer's hair. It was just long enough that it was starting to get the wave to it that she loved.

"But don't you feel jealous?" she asked.

"Of course. I've been jealous of Xander since the first time he had you all flustered at the Godsball. I just didn't know it was him I was jealous of. But I've accepted that he's a part of your heart. I would never ask you not to feel what you do. You've given up so much already. I don't mind sharing your heart if it means I get some small piece of it."

Cecilia was afraid of the way those words freed her of any excuse she had to keep Rainer at a distance. They removed the last barrier to being with him. He brought her hand up to his mouth, gently kissing her fingertips.

"I see you overthinking. As an overthinker myself, I recognize the signs." His hand on her cheek forced her to meet his radiant green eyes. "What do you want, Cece?"

She shook her head. It was too much.

He brought his other hand up, cupping her face, forcing her to hold his gaze. His dark hair fell over his forehead as he studied her face.

"Tell me what you want, Cece. There's nowhere left to run from this. Stay with me. Tell me what you want and I'll give it to you."

She leaned back and shook her head. He lifted her from his lap, setting her on the bed beside him. Sighing heavily, he rose to his feet and began to pace.

"Rain, it's so soon. I don't want you to get hurt."

It was weak. She didn't want herself to get hurt, either.

There were sacrifices she would have to make to survive the war to come, but Rainer was her hard line. He always had been. She'd tried to ignore it, but she knew the day the poison arrows nearly killed him. She'd known when she made the deal with Cato that it was a huge risk, but she didn't hesitate, because she'd always known that she never wanted to live in a world without Rainer McKay. Cecilia would never sacrifice him for this war. If it came to it, she would do whatever she had to to keep him safe.

Out of all of her friends, he was the one good thing—unchanged by war, unchanged by the harshness of the fight they were in. She would do whatever she had to in order to protect the man who'd spent his whole life protecting her, even if it meant protecting him from herself.

She was sure he already knew what she wanted. "Rain, I'm scared."

"I know what you're going to say, so please just shut your beautiful mouth and listen," Rainer said. "I've listened to you talk for weeks. I've listened to every excuse you've made up as to why we shouldn't be together. I let you talk and process everything, but it's my turn to talk now—hard as it might be for me to get this out. So please be quiet and let me try."

Cecilia stared at him, jaw slack, eyes wide, but she nodded.

"Yes, what I feel for you is influenced by our bond. How could it not be? I'm pressed right up against your heart. How could I feel the depths of your love and joy and frustration and anger and not fall completely in love with you? How could I know you for more than half my life and spend every day with you, and not want you? You are funny and kind and passionate and you fight for the people you love."

"But that could just be the bond—"

He pressed a finger to her lips. "I'm not done. What I feel for you is about much more than that bond. I tried not to love you—fought it as much as I could. You tried too, and yet here we are. Over and over, back in the same place. When I kissed you in the Wailing Woods, I thought the joy of it was going to knock me over. I've kissed you before, but that time you gave yourself over to it and I couldn't stop thinking about it. It felt like everything was right in the world. Then again, in Heartwood Valley. I knew then, when you said 'Don't ever do that again.' I knew what you felt because I felt the same—like I could spend the rest of my life kissing you and it wouldn't feel like enough."

She opened her mouth to argue, but he cut her off.

"Cece! Please, it's hard to get this out and I'm really trying. You thought I saw something dark in you with Davide, and that meant you didn't deserve me—that I couldn't handle it. But who could blame you for hurting those who hurt the people you love? I wouldn't hesitate to hurt someone who hurt you. I would never judge you for the fierce way you protect the people you love."

He caressed her cheek so gently.

"There is no part of you I don't want to see. There's nothing you need to hide from me, because I've always seen every side of you. I've always wanted to see them—even the dark ones. I've loved them before you even knew they were there."

Rainer brushed tears from her cheeks.

"I've had a lot of chances and I've messed up every one. I can't promise not to mess this one up, but I promise that I'm not going to let you push me away. I promise to keep fighting for you. I spent too long asking you to stand behind me when I should have asked you to stand beside me. I should have let you fight for yourself, but I was afraid you'd stop needing me. It was weak and small of me, but I always saw it and I'm trying to change."

He took a deep breath.

"I want to get into exactly your kind of trouble, no matter how anxious it makes me. I want you exactly as you are, because you are and you always have been the most beautiful person I've ever laid eyes on. I never want to fall asleep without looking into those big blue eyes. I never want to wake up without hearing you complain about how early it is.

"I've loved you so long that I don't even remember my life before loving you. I'm still figuring out who I'm going to be, but who I want to be is someone who fights for you. I want to be the kind of man who won't let you give up on yourself—the person who loves you best and knows you best in the world. I want to be someone who isn't afraid of the consequences of loving you, because I know whatever they are, they're worth it. Love gives you courage when you need it most. So if you need to borrow mine right now, you can. I've been borrowing yours for years."

The earnest words left Cecilia breathless, but Rainer pressed on.

"What I'm wondering now is if you'll let me love you. If you'll let me pick up the pieces with you. If you'll let me heal beside you. If you'll let me love you the way I should have all along."

"What if I don't know how?" she sobbed. "What if that part of me is broken? I'm afraid I'll never be able to love the same way again."

"Then love a different way. Love however you still can. The only thing I want from you is whatever love you can give me."

"But you deserve—"

"Let's let me decide what I deserve, okay? Let's make a deal that we'll stop deciding things for each other."

Cecilia nodded.

"I can't promise not to break your heart. I know I've done it too many times before, but I promise to do my best to never hurt you again. Now, can you stop running away and just let me catch you?"

She couldn't breathe. If she'd written everything she wished he would say to her, she couldn't have done a better job. One by one he'd pulled apart every argument she had for keeping her distance.

He sat next to her on the bed. "Brave with my hand," he whispered, his eyes meeting hers. It was a question that demanded a response.

"Brave with my heart," she replied.

He gently traced his fingers up her arm, over her shoulder, and up her neck. His eyes never left her face, watching her every reaction. Cecilia tipped her head back and closed her eyes, just concentrating on his touch.

Rainer was wanting personified. She'd loved him quietly for so long that bringing that love out into the light was terrifying. Considering the many dangerous and horrifying things she'd been through, it should have seemed far less terrifying, but for her, love was the most dangerous thing there was.

But love was also her salvation. Love was the last hard thing worth having.

"What do you want, Cecilia? Anything you want, I will make it so." Rainer breathed the words into her collarbone.

She couldn't control her trembling as his lips made their way slowly up her neck to her jaw. When she thought she couldn't stand it anymore, he finally kissed her lips. She climbed into his lap, her thighs bracketing his.

There was such a sense of certainty in it. It felt like something she'd been doing her whole life, like she couldn't remember a time before she kissed Rainer. She couldn't believe she'd gone so long between kisses. He eclipsed everything, blocking out time and thought and memory, and the only thing she could think of was him. The ocean-lilac-fresh-linen scent, the way his kisses tasted like black tea and whiskey, the scrape of his rough hands on her skin. He pulled back, looking into her eyes, waiting for her to say it.

"I want you. I want you so much. I've never wanted anything more in my life," she said, blinking back tears. "But I'm afraid."

"No." He pressed a finger to her lips. "There's nothing left to fear, Cece. I trust you completely and you trust me. All that's left is for you to trust yourself."

"What if I don't?" she whispered.

He kissed her with heartbreaking tenderness. "Then I will just kiss you until you're not afraid anymore."

He drew her into a deep kiss that dulled all the fear in her mind until all she could feel was a deep, driving desire for him. She was reminded of the time when her father gave her free rein of a bakery in town for her seventh birthday, and she'd eaten enough sweets to make herself sick.

Cecilia wanted to gorge herself on Rainer. She was so ravenous, she was shaking, unable to touch enough of him fast enough. He kissed her neck, her shoulders, her arms, any skin he could find until she was panting, driven mad by desire. Finally, he pulled off her lace chemise, and instead of continuing, he hugged her. The tenderness surprised her. She hadn't realized how much she was shaking until he made her slow down. She rested her cheek on his shoulder, tucking her face into his neck.

Being held that way, skin to skin, as his hand gently trailed up and down her back, might have been the best feeling in the world. Her heart slowed and her breathing evened, calming her as she sat there wrapped around him.

She was so incredibly relieved, because no matter how the world saw her—an impossibly strong goddess, a powerful witch, a huntress with uncanny aim—Rainer saw someone delicate he wanted to take care of.

For so long, Cecilia resented Rainer's gentleness because she thought he saw her as weak. Now she knew he simply wanted to take care of her like no one else would. Now she realized the immense courage it took for her to allow herself to receive that tenderness.

"Okay so far?" Rainer asked, kissing her temple.

"Yes."

"Do you want me to keep going?"

"Yes." She smiled, leaning back to look at him.

She shifted her hips and felt him hard beneath her. The sensation sent sparks all the way down to her toes.

She knew Rainer's body almost as well as her own from years of training together, but now it was a revelation. She ran her hands over his skin, feeling her way across the muscles and ridges. Her hand passed over the scar on his chest and the one on his neck, reminders of how close she'd come to losing him. She traced the outline of each one with her mouth, the words "I love you" on her lips as she kissed them.

It broke something loose in him. He flipped her over so she was underneath him and worked her underwear down, tossing it onto the floor. He kissed down her chest, teasing her nipples, then her stomach and hips, as she squirmed and moaned beneath him.

He lowered himself between her legs, his eyes full of heat and adoration.

"Rain," she said, reaching for him. She couldn't tell if she was shaking from nerves or so much pent-up desire.

"This is about you." His voice was rough, and his breath on her thighs sent a shiver through her body. "I told you I would kiss you until you weren't afraid anymore."

Her back arched and her head kicked back as his tongue slid over her. She writhed on the bed, fingernails digging into the sheets. He paid homage to her body as only someone who'd wanted the opportunity for years could.

Cecilia's whole body buzzed with pleasure as his palm spread out on her lower belly, holding her in place as he went to work. She marveled at the way he intuitively knew exactly what she wanted, even before she did, using his fingers to work her along with his tongue. He drew sounds from her she'd never heard before, and the pleasure built so quickly it startled her.

His lust rushed through their bond, mixing with her own. She hadn't considered how extraordinary it would be to feel what he felt in such an intimate moment.

The tingling in her body intensified until the tension snapped and she screamed his name, pleasure rolling over her in waves.

Rainer's face was painted in a triumphant grin. He kissed her trembling inner thighs as she relaxed into the bed.

All her fear had been replaced by desire.

He kissed his way up her body, finally meeting her lips in a long kiss.

"Do you want me to keep going?"

"Yes. Please don't stop," she said, breathlessly unbuttoning his pants.

He pulled them off and knelt between her legs, gloriously naked. Cecilia leaned back and stared at him. His skin was tanned from his morning swims, a sharp line of paler skin marking where his pants normally sat. The muscles on his torso seemed to form an arrow, drawing her gaze lower.

She was so eager for him and he'd taken care to get her ready, but his size made her nervous.

He smiled as he kissed her sternum. "I'll go slow. Don't be nervous."

He stayed there, poised above her, holding her gaze. He tugged on their connection, a sort of wordless request for permission, and she opened it wide.

"Yes," she whispered.

There was no more waiting. He pushed inside her with agonizing slowness. The fullness was almost too much, but he was so careful. He kept his eyes locked on hers, watching her reaction, waiting for her to adjust, kissing her softly over and over until she relaxed.

It felt so unbelievably good. She was torn between holding him exactly where he was and urging him to move.

"Gods, you feel perfect." Rainer's voice was a low growl in her ear, sending a shiver through her body.

Finally, he started to move. He kept their bond wide open. Cecilia felt the deep longing, the fierceness of his love for her, and overwhelming joy. A soaring ecstasy filled her chest.

She felt herself on the verge of tears, her heart cracked wide open.

Without breaking his perfect rhythm, he looked down into her eyes and said, "Cece, I love you so much."

Just like he always had, Rainer anticipated her needs, ready to give her whatever she required before she even knew she wanted it. He pressed on, quickening his pace, pulling her closer. He wrapped an arm around her, holding her in place so that he could drive deeper. She clung to him, unable to get close enough, unable to touch enough of him. He only brought his lips away from her skin to whisper how much he loved her.

Rainer was right. She didn't belong to anyone, but she did belong *with* him, and he belonged with her. The driving momentum of their bodies yanked hard on the tether between their two hearts until they were right up against one another.

She relished the feeling of his skin, the fullness of him inside her, the way her heart overflowed with joy, even after all the times it had been broken. Her body felt like the night sky, full of sparkling stars.

The unrelenting, building pressure and the sweetness of his kisses and his words drove her toward an impossibly intense release. They had both crawled back from death's doorstep and yet this still felt more powerful. The entire world stilled until the only motion was the two of them. She wrapped her arms around him, holding on as tight as she could, meeting his pace, feverish with need, until finally everything broke wide open, sending a riot of pleasure through her.

Cecilia wasn't sure if she screamed nonsense or his name as she catapulted over the edge. She felt him shudder and follow her. Her whole body was on fire with sparkling starlight. Tingles shot from her heart through each of her limbs. She'd felt nothing like it, and she never wanted the feeling to fade.

They lay there panting, allowing their heartbeats to slow in matching time, not wanting to move and shatter the perfect moment.

Finally, Rainer shifted, kissing her collarbone, her neck, her eyelids, her cheeks, each kiss like a snowflake dusting along her skin as he whispered "I love you" over and over.

She didn't realize she was crying again until he wiped a tear away. It was so much more than the physical. It felt like they were completely connected to each other. At that moment, she didn't feel isolated and strange. She didn't feel alone anymore. She felt connected and powerful, and so incredibly loved.

"Are you okay?" Rainer asked.

"Yes, I've never felt anything so amazing in my whole life. I wish I could hold on to that feeling forever."

He smiled, and for a moment she thought maybe her heart had stopped. It astonished her that his smile could still do that. After so much time, so much history, it still felt like being shocked back to life every time she saw it.

Rainer blew out a sigh. "You don't understand how long I've dreamed about doing that."

"Probably not as long as I did," she said.

"I was so afraid of this for so long because I think somewhere deep down I knew it would feel like this." He sighed. "Like being connected heart to heart and soul to soul. Like I couldn't tell where you ended and I began. I have never felt anything like it. I could feel what you needed. What you wanted. I felt this sensation like tingling starlight under my skin. It felt so good. I love you so much."

"I felt it too. Starlight. I love you, Rain."

He gently tucked her hair behind her ear, tracing her cheek with his fingertips. Cecilia wished she could go back and do it again, relive it a thousand times, but she also knew that what made mortal moments so precious was that they were fleeting.

Memory was a valuable and fragile thing. It tied them up in quiet strings, binding them together forever. It would have been impossible to explain the feeling to someone else.

"Will you share it with me?" she asked.

Rainer's smile was dazzling. "Of course." He slid his hand into hers and shared his side of the memory so that she could hold on to it forever.

"Do you think anything will ever feel so wonderful again? Will it feel like that every time?" she asked.

"Only one way to find out," he whispered, rolling back between her legs.

Twice more that night, she found out that it felt just as amazing as it had the first time. She fell asleep wrapped in Rainer's arms as she had for years. So many things were the same, and yet something massive had changed.

In the middle of the night, she woke from a pleasant dream and knew something had shifted. When she felt into the space around her heart, around their bond, she no longer felt the loneliness. The place in her that had been hollowed out for so long had filled in, as if it never even existed.

34

RAINER

The world outside the cottage was probably falling apart without them, but Rainer couldn't bring himself to think of anything but Cecilia sleeping in his arms. The distant ringing of bells at the dock and the bright light shining in the windows let him know it was well past dawn, but he had no intention of moving.

There weren't words for how amazing it felt to have her love; to be himself fully; to touch her when and how he wanted; to have permission to kiss her at will. Everything he'd locked inside for years burst free at once and he couldn't hold her close enough, couldn't kiss her long enough, couldn't quench the insatiable fire that roared in his chest.

The night before, when she stood in front of him, still at war with herself, he knew she was close to the tipping point. He almost had her, but he knew better than to ever be certain of what she would do. Despite their years of friendship and his direct connection to her heart, Cecilia Reznik still managed to surprise him.

Rainer had faced enemy hunters and slayers. He'd fought opponents much bigger than himself and been kept prisoner in Argaria.

He'd nearly died, but the scariest thing he'd ever done was stand in front of Cecilia and lay his heart on the line.

There was nothing sweeter than knowing how terrified she was but that she still risked it for him, that she surrendered finally to what they'd both felt for so long. In hindsight, it felt inevitable, but in that moment, it felt far less certain.

Rainer would have been happy just to hold Cecilia and kiss her, but he knew she wanted more. He worried it was too soon, though for him, it was a long time coming. It felt like they'd always been heading there and finally their timing matched up.

It was well beyond his wildest imaginings. Cecilia was vulnerable and sexy and so connected to him. He had never felt anything so amazing in his whole life.

Rainer tried to go back to sleep. He was exhausted, but his mind and body still buzzed.

Love. How could he describe what he felt for her in such a small word? She was the "happily ever after" to his "once upon a time," the home to which he'd always wanted to return but could never quite find the path. And now she was asleep against him.

Gods above, he still couldn't think straight with her leg thrown over his hip and her breasts pressing into his side. She was so soft, every part of her delicate and shivery. He loved how he'd murmured into her neck and she'd shuddered against him, loved the satisfied little hum she let out when he brushed his lips to her pulse, loved how she smelled the most like herself at that pulse point or just above her sternum. He stayed there, kissing that smooth skin like he could press his lips to their bond itself and thank the gods for it.

He was absolutely done for. Rainer was already so gone for her, but in that moment, he knew he would never love another woman the way he loved her. Their connection was so electrified, and it was hard not to wake her.

He could see their whole lives laid out before them. He wanted adventures and laughter and marriage. He wanted to raise children with her and watch her grow and change in front of him. Cecilia wouldn't actually age, and while he found it comforting that she would stay safe and healthy, it also filled him with fear.

What if she grew tired of him? What would people think when he was old and gray and she was still young and vibrant? He hated the idea of dooming her to be attached to him.

But logic and love could not live in the same place. What Rainer felt for Cecilia was well beyond anything rational. Love turned him inside out. He'd gladly let it over and over if it meant sleeping next to her for the rest of his life.

He pulled his attention back to the present moment, the way Cecilia always reminded him when she felt him worrying. He was the worrier, and she the reckless adventurer. Those were the roles they'd always held, and it worked. He loved her particular brand of chaos, and she loved his steady sense of order.

Truth be told, he'd never minded because she forced him out of his comfort zone, and he knew she was soothed by the way he always over-prepared.

Even as Cecilia slept, Rainer couldn't stop staring at her. He fought the urge to wake her, to cover every inch of her skin with kisses, to taste her and listen to the strangled sounds that broke free when he touched her. He'd seen sweet Cece, kind Cece, funny Cece, and glimpses of how effortlessly sexy she could be, but being with her was the first time he understood how much she could still surprise and astonish him.

She loved like a wildfire with little thought for the ruin it could make of her. She'd happily burn herself to ash for just one moment of the love she deserved.

Rainer had no intention of giving her any less than all of him. He had a ring. He had to fight himself not to wake her up and ask her then. It was way too soon. She was still healing. Everything around them was chaotic. He knew he should court her properly, announce his intentions, follow protocol, but a lifetime of following the rules made him strain against the chains of decorum.

His urgency wouldn't help anything, but he still felt so incredibly impatient for her. It was as if this was the ending he'd always been waiting for, and now that it was so close, he couldn't allow it to unfold on its own. He'd had enough adventure, enough heartache, enough waiting, and he wanted his happily ever after.

He'd watched her spend her whole life desperate for approval, desperate to fit in. He always wanted to shake her, to tell her it was ridiculous for someone so wild and courageous to try to fit in with people who were so scared and ordinary. She wasn't meant to fit in. She was meant to shine. Even when she tried her best, she'd failed because she was too bright for the rest of the world.

"I love you," he whispered.

Cecilia sighed softly, curling closer to him like the words reached her even in sleep. Rainer bent down and kissed the three freckles dotting the left side of her neck and she startled awake. Instead of pulling away, she pressed herself closer to him, and everything that was already awake in his body came to attention.

"I like when you wake me up like that. You should have done that years ago," she whispered against his lips.

"I know. I'll do it every night and every morning for the rest of our lives."

Her eyes widened slightly at the promise. If she was disturbed by the permanence of his offer, it didn't show, and warmth flowed through their connection.

"Did you just wake me for a kiss, or did you have something else in mind?"

He laughed as he kissed her again.

"Rain," she groaned against his lips.

Every nerve in his body came to attention as the bare skin of her inner thigh slid over his hip. He forced himself to pull back and look at her. She blinked at him with a bright smile.

"What?" she asked.

"I just wanted to make sure you were okay. That you didn't regret anything," he said, tracing the lines of her face with his fingers.

She frowned. "I told you before I would never make you something I regret, and I meant that. If I wasn't really ready, I would have told you."

"I was worried it was too soon, and you got carried away. I didn't want to rush you. I probably should have waited, but I wasted so much time before. I didn't want to miss my shot."

"I'm done doing things the 'right' way," Cecilia said. "It's never worked for me. I've made peace with the fact that I'm never going to be a traditional kind of woman."

"Funny, I made peace with that about seventeen years ago when we were bonded together."

She laughed.

"What? It's true. You were a little maniac. You gave me a heart attack once a week," Rainer said.

"I know. It was fun. I thought I'd be able to break you of the habit of worrying so much."

"I think you introduced me to that habit."

She giggled again. "I'm sorry."

He knew she meant about being such an unholy terror of a charge, but he could see an apology for the larger things. "I don't regret anything that brought us to this moment."

Apprehension clouded Cecilia's eyes. "It's so soon. I don't want you to feel like you're a rebound."

"I don't. I knew what I was doing when I kissed you. We don't have to have it all figured out now. You'll do what you have to for the kingdom and to get Xander back."

"But what if—"

"No more what-ifs. I'm the overthinker. Let's not change roles. I trust you. I'm crazy about you. I just want us to be honest with each other."

She nodded. She bit her lip, her gaze dropping to his lips. "Is that the only reason you woke me up?"

"I just needed to be kissing you, but now that you're awake, I'm open to ideas—" He hissed as she gave him a firm stroke with her hand.

"Did I do something distracting?" she teased.

Rainer relented to the pull of her, glad to be caught in the undertow for once instead of fighting hopelessly against it. He was done trying to swim against the current of love that ran between them. Their kind of love was an exercise in surrender and, for once, the lack of control didn't scare him.

35

CECILIA

Thanks to years of their storytelling ritual, Cecilia knew that the key to a good fairy tale was in making things seem most impossible before the hero's triumphant victory.

It should have been easy to form the words to tell Rainer how she felt, but it was nearly impossible to distill the vast expanse of emotions she felt for him into simple words. They just felt hollow when she put them to the page.

The idea to profess her love—and end the Xander and Rainer tug-of-war that she'd been at the center of for months—in the form that he loved most had come to her so suddenly she couldn't believe she hadn't thought of it sooner.

How did she capture the depth of her longing over the years, the disappointment of his rejection, the desperation of begging him to love her, losing him, the grief of it and the rebirth on the other side of unimaginable pain? How did she explain that he was the bright spot in the past year that had broken her down and hollowed her out? How did she explain that he was the bright spot in her whole life?

Cecilia wrote and rewrote as Rainer slept heavily beside her after spending the day in bed with her. He shifted and the sheet dipped, revealing a tantalizing view of his smooth, muscular back. She considered waking him again, but forced herself to focus. She had one more day before they were forced back into the utter chaos of court life, and she had to make it count.

It took all night, but by the time the sun rose and she dozed beside him, she finally felt like she had something that might be worthy of his eyes.

She was worried it was too soon. Other people would likely think so. Cecilia was still trying to heal her wounded heart. It would have been easier to wait until they weren't staring down the demise of Olney, but love was the last hard thing worth having, and it was something she was willing to fight for.

———

Cecilia laid out a blanket and a picnic in the grove where they'd trained together for years. The branches created abstract slashes of sunlight on the arrangement. Although the season had turned and most of the petals had fallen off the wisteria, coating the cool ground in purple dots, the spot was still beautiful and lush—the perfect place to tell someone you wanted to be with only them.

Tomorrow, they'd report to Olney Castle to begin their watch protecting the royal family from Cato. She had no idea what the future held or if their plan would work. She had one chance to get this right and she wanted to make sure Rainer knew exactly where she stood. Surely he felt her anxiety through their connection, but he was good enough not to say anything.

He propped himself on an elbow next to her, his shirt straining against his broad chest. She wasn't sure how she'd missed the changes in his body over the past few months. Clearly, he'd spent his hours of tortured longing working out, and it showed.

Cecilia picked at the fraying end of the green ribbon still tied around her wrist. She was unsure how to start after he'd shared so much of his heart the night before. Rainer watched her, sensing her anxiety, but leaving her space to talk.

"There's one more thing I didn't tell you yet. I didn't want it getting tied up with everything else." She fidgeted, trying to figure out the right words.

"What's wrong? You just told me everything, and now you're the most nervous I've ever seen you. You're scaring me." Rainer sat up, taking her hands in his.

"I ran into one of my sisters on the way back from my visit with Xander and Cato. Aelish."

"Goddess of Truth."

Cecilia nodded. "That's her. A bit cagey, but definitely wise. She made me face something that I've known for a long time but was afraid to face. I think because I never thought I could have it, and then when I finally realized I could, it felt like it was too late."

She wasn't sure if either of them was breathing as she thrust the book into his hands. "Can you just read this thing that I wrote? It's probably terrible, but I wrote it all down because I knew I would be a wreck."

Rainer looked down at the familiar book of fairy tales. She'd added her own entry behind all the ones he'd catalogued.

His eyes lit up, and he smiled as he opened to the page marked with her loopy handwriting. "Will you read it to me, Cece?"

She took the book, her hands shaky, and read him their story—an imperfect fairy tale about two flawed people who kept missing each other. A story without an end. A story that was theirs to add to every day for the rest of their lives. A story with a happily ever after that was, as yet, undefined. She read him the words that had spent years tucked away in her heart. *I love you. I've always loved you. I will always love you.*

When she finished, she could barely hold his gaze because the look in his eyes was pure love. She still felt unworthy of it, but it didn't stop her from wanting it.

"Rain, it's always been you. I fell in love with Xander, but I knew when you were standing with me in the back of the temple that day, if you had said there was a chance for us, I wouldn't have married him. I never stopped loving you, even when I fell in love with him. You and I were meant to be. I spent a lot of time pretending not to know it, but

I'm done. I will always love Xander, and I won't give up on him because I owe him that much, and because I wouldn't be me if I gave up on someone I loved. I would do it for any of you. You, Sylvie, Cal, Evan. I wouldn't give up on any of you. I can't give up on him. But, at the end of the day, I want to be with you. It scares me. I don't know what will happen. I know my life is long, and yours is going to go too fast, but I want whatever time I can get. I am done running from it. If you'll have me."

For a minute, Rainer just stared at her. Then he pulled her into a tight hug. One arm wrapped around her, and the other tucking her face into his neck.

He took a deep, shaky breath. "You don't know how long I have wanted to hear you say that. Gods, I love you so much. I wish I hadn't been such a moron for so long. I could have saved us both a lot of trouble."

"I don't regret any of it. If we hadn't gone through it, you would probably still be busy trying to follow the rules."

He sighed. "You're right. I can't regret anything that brought us together. So, what happens now?"

"I was thinking that maybe we could make a little magic like before." She winked at him.

"Cecilia Juliette Reznik! Are you suggesting that I make love to you right here in broad daylight in the middle of the wilderness? That's scandalous," he teased, but his eyes sparkled, and delight shot through their bond.

She flushed. "It's just a beautiful day and there's a beautiful view and I'm happy."

"I will not be looking at any beautiful weather or landscapes if you're naked. I'll only be looking at you." He bent and gave her a long, lingering kiss, guiding her down to the blanket.

Then, he did what he promised. He paid attention to nothing but her for the rest of the morning, until she was flushed, exhausted, and couldn't stop smiling, her heart practically bursting from joy.

It felt to her like she was making a choice, but there was no other choice to make. She'd known even while she was happy with Xander that in the most secret part of her heart, she never stopped loving Rainer. That love had grown and changed as much as she had. It burned to ashes and was reborn a phoenix a dozen times, but it was still the most familiar thing in her life.

The last words she'd written echoed in her head as Rainer grinned at her.

The world might have been crumbling around them. Alliances were shifting. The two kingdoms were poised to destroy each other. It was the end of the world as they knew it, and she still had so much to lose. It frightened her and also gave her courage, because love, especially his love, was something worth saving at the end of the world.

PART IV:
THINGS WORTH
SAVING AT THE
END OF THE WORLD

36

XANDER

Xander Savero had a secret tucked away in the vortex of madness in his mind. Every day, he balanced on a knife's edge—careful not to share it, but holding it close enough that he didn't lose it completely.

After his parents and Teddy died, it felt as if Cece was the string that tethered him to the world. Her mercurial shifts from goddess to wife were a melody to which he lived his life. Now his own excruciating shifts from villain to ally helped anchor him to reality.

He'd come full circle. He'd been sent to Olney at fourteen to find the Lost God. While he was loyal to his family and country, he'd spent eleven years in Olney and it felt more home to him than Argaria ever had. War benefitted no one. It was bad for both kingdoms. In fact, he was certain that it didn't even benefit Cato. It was simply a tactic he used to manipulate Cece.

So when the trickster god rushed him out of the cottage that morning, Xander worried he'd been found out. Instead, Cato used his power to transport the two of them to a grove. At first, Xander didn't recognize it, though the climate was distinctly Olney. The clear blue sky and sea breeze told him that much. Then, he saw Cece and Rainer and recognized it as the grove where they liked to train.

Though Cece had made it clear days earlier that she was saying goodbye, it was still jarring to see her kiss someone else. The impulse to sprint across the forest and throw Rainer off of the love of his life was overwhelming. Instead, Xander kept his breath even and calm beside Cato.

Rainer spent an excruciatingly long time kissing Cece. Both of them seemed so unhurried and content, as if they'd be satisfied to ignore the war coming to their kingdom and stay there kissing all day.

Cato would probably be annoyed if that were the case since he'd gone to the trouble of dragging Xander out there, but things intensified, Rainer hiking up her dress. Cece, always a bit of an exhibitionist, climbed into his lap.

Xander just wanted to leave. He couldn't stand to watch her be so happy with someone else, but he couldn't say he wanted to leave either.

Instead, he watched Cato out of the corner of his eye.

"You said she was a woman of many talents," Cato mused. He tried to sound unaffected, but Xander could see that the god was interested.

Xander wasn't foolish enough to believe Cato actually wanted a partner in Cece, but that didn't mean the god was above lust. Whatever his plan for her, there was no mistaking the look in the god's eyes.

"She's also exceptional with her mouth." Xander tried for indifference, but desire crept into his tone.

Cato smirked. "I know what you're doing. Watching me so diligently, looking for a weakness." He turned to look at Xander. "You think that there's something here worth saving, but there's not. Your Cece has moved on. There's nothing here for you, but there's a whole world waiting for you in Argaria, and once we conquer Olney, you can go anywhere you want in either kingdom. You can have any woman you want in the two kingdoms. You don't need to bother with her anymore."

Xander sighed, using annoyance to hide his panic. "And what if I still want her?"

"Still? *Really*? I thought I'd done a better job with you." Cato shook his head, his grin turning feral. "Fair enough. If you still want her, we will find a way to give you exactly what you want. I suppose we could always give her the option of me or you, and that makes you an easy choice."

Xander relished the dream of having Cece back, but it was just a dream. He'd lost his one chance with her and only had himself to blame, not that he believed Cato would actually do what he said.

Cato's eyes brightened with mischief. "I'll give you whatever you want. I just need something from you first."

Dread sank in Xander's stomach as Cato took his arm and yanked him through a split in space. He stumbled, trying to right himself back at the cottage in Rowdane that served as their headquarters.

Davide leaned against the wall outside in full battle regalia. It was startling to see him in armor, looking so much like King Damian. Even when he'd invaded Olney, he'd not been so well protected for battle.

"You summoned me," Davide said, a hint of annoyance in his voice as he bowed mockingly.

Cato grinned. "Of course. I was just trying to inspire your brother to think logically and make choices that are in his best interest, instead of Cece's."

Davide met Xander's eyes. It was like looking in a mirror as an awareness dawned on both of them.

"And here I was hoping for an explanation about why I just had to take a battalion to fight off Vincent's forces along Argaria's eastern borders," Davide said.

Xander froze. How could his cousin, Vincent Savero, have his own army after so many years of quiet? Why didn't Xander know they were a threat until now? He looked from Cato to Davide.

"I thought that he and Uncle William had given up on that idea. They were so actively trying to usurp the throne those first few years and then nothing," Xander said.

Davide shrugged. "Apparently, they were just laying low."

"How did he look?" Xander asked.

Davide shook his head, sunlight glinting off of his armor, high-lighting smudges of blood and soot. "I didn't get a good look at him, but it was only him and a couple hundred men. No sign of Uncle William, but it's been eighteen years since they were banished. It's a hard lifestyle out east. He could have passed. Either way, Vincent is clearly under the impression that we're unstable and this is the time to strike."

Davide was trying to bait Cato into responding—to get him to reveal more of his plan—or to distract him.

"Don't presume to know where this is going, Davide. Perhaps I just thought a reunion was in order. After all, you've lost so much family so recently," Cato taunted.

Davide blanched, his expression grim.

"What's one more?" Cato shrugged. He waved at Davide and Xander. "I'd like you to fight. Winner gets to be king of Argaria and, eventually, Olney."

Davide looked carefully from his brother to Cato. "Why?"

Cato huffed a bored sigh. "The last thing we need is competition once this is settled. I only need one of you. It's just much neater. Davide, you've been difficult and unpredictable, but you're also smart. You must have seen this coming."

Xander hated Cato with a fiery burning passion that could melt iron. It flared to the surface momentarily, and Cato smirked at him.

"I will not kill my brother for you," Xander barked.

He'd known it was a possibility, perhaps an inevitability. But now, confronted with it, he could not fathom it.

"You will," Cato said. "You don't have to like it, but you'll do it. As you know, I don't like to get my hands dirty."

The only time Xander had seen Cato even attempt to battle was the day he'd fought Cece, the day he'd taken Xander. He still wasn't sure how skilled the trickster god was. He'd largely toyed with Cece as a distraction, keeping his true skill veiled. He'd also never once laid a hand on Davide or Xander. Xander had long suspected that Cato hurting him physically would somehow undo their bargain.

Xander met Davide's eyes again.

His older brother gave him the slightest nod. "Scared, little brother? You love to brag about being the better swordsman. I thought you'd be eager to prove it." His words were dissonant with the pleading look in his eyes.

"When you're the best, you don't feel a need to prove it in every fight," Xander quipped.

Cato sighed. "Xander, your resistance bores me. I could make you do it, but I'm offering you the opportunity to cooperate on your own for once. Take it."

Davide stepped toward Xander menacingly and drew his sword. Xander unsheathed his sword. Although Davide was an excellent marksman, he lacked the regular practice in recent years to be a great swordsman. He didn't know when to commit or how to be patient for the right moment to strike.

They paused, momentarily distracted by a scout from the Argarian army who appeared at the bottom of the hill. Cato walked to meet him and Xander's gaze darted from the god and the scout to his brother. He strained to listen to the scout's message while giving the illusion of fighting.

Davide took a light swing with his sword. Xander broke the blow. He went to draw away but Davide grabbed his wrist.

"I'm sorry about Mother and Father—especially Mother."

Xander swallowed thickly, his grief a great, yawning maw waiting to devour him. "How did he get to you? Why did you do it?"

"He got to me when you left for Olney. I made a deal with him to keep you safe. I didn't know what would happen. I didn't know it was happening at all until recently. He was so subtle about it."

The world seemed to be closing in on Xander. The last mystery was finally solved and all the grief he'd postponed hit him at once.

Davide had made a deal to protect *him*, and in turn he'd lost his mind. Cato's cruelty was profound.

Davide's gaze darted to Cato. "He made me kill father so I would be king, but mother killed herself."

Xander stood frozen in shock. "What?"

"Keep your voice down," Davide snapped, nodding to where Cato still stood whispering to the scout.

"Mother woke up and realized it was me," he continued. "She seemed to know what was happening. I don't know how long, but she said that she wouldn't be a weapon against her own children, and if Cato didn't order her killed that there was a reason. Xan, she grabbed my hand and shoved the blade in so fast I couldn't react. She didn't know you had a deal with him and that he could control you. She thought she was saving us from being manipulated. I'm sorry." His apology winced out like a sob.

Grief burrowed under Xander's skin—the feeling too familiar. He reached for any other emotion, settling on the boiling rage he felt toward Cato and relief that Davide, the older brother who had always protected him, was still in there, underneath years of manipulation. He knew that Cato was responsible in some way but the guilt of being the very reason that he'd lost his brother was too much.

"I've been trying to protect you, Xany. For years. I know it doesn't seem like it. If you'd run before the wedding back in Argaria, Endros would have killed Cece. Breaking Cecilia's hand was regrettable, but I needed you to understand the danger. I would never choose to hurt her. I just needed you to believe I would."

Xander stumbled back before going at his brother again. Their fight was like running a combat drill and he hoped Cato was too distracted to notice that it was choreographed.

Xander couldn't think straight. "How are you able to tell me this? How can you fight what he does to your mind?"

"I hold on to the feelings." Davide swiped over his head. "He can manipulate the memories. He can enhance my jealousy and anger, but when I look at you, I still see my little brother. I still love you. Even magic can't break that. I still have the impulse to save you. I just remind myself that what I feel is real, even if what's in my head is confusing. It took a long time to get here and now you'll just be putting me out of my profound misery."

Xander was so startled he accidentally sliced the top of Davide's wrist. His older brother stumbled away, looking so weary that Xander fought the impulse to hug him. He looked from Davide to Cato, who was wandering back to them, a grimace on his face.

"How do I know I can trust you?" Xander asked.

Blood coated Davide's hand as he deflected another blow. "I don't know how to convince you other than to say I swear on Rip."

Xander stumbled a step. Rip was their beloved childhood dog. When they were young, Davide loved to tell Xander scary stories and play tricks on him, in the harmless way older brothers often did. So whenever Xander was scared of a story Davide made up, he made Davide swear on Rip that none of it was true.

"Are you afraid, Xan? I've always found that when you name the fear, it loses its power," Davide said. He held Xander's gaze over their crossed blades. "I'm afraid I'm going to have to kill my little brother like I did the rest of my family."

Xander swallowed hard. How could he name this fear? *I'm afraid of killing my brother, afraid of being alone, afraid of what will become of me with no love or family.* His stomach plunged. "Even named it feels no less compelling."

Davide nodded. "Well then, don't be afraid, Xan. I promise to make it a quick death for you. As you can see, I've improved since we last fought."

His eyes pleaded with Xander to fight. He lashed out with a crushing blow that Xander broke.

"Fight or be killed!" Davide commanded as Cato returned to his post by the cottage door.

Davide's desperation showed in the way he lunged for Xander. Xander deflected his blow and spun away. He wanted to fall to his knees and beg for the nightmare to stop.

Davide was better than he'd been in the past, but while Xander had spent most of his time fighting, his brother had been busy ruling, learning politics, and studying battle strategy. That lack of close combat experience showed.

Xander's anxiety spiked as they traded blows. He fought the lump forming in his throat. He'd lost everyone he cared about. He couldn't lose Davide, too. Whatever he'd become, Davide was still his brother. A king, a killer, but also kin.

Xander had no desire to be king. King was a role much better suited to Davide, who, when he wasn't manipulated, had the temperament to run a kingdom. He had none of Xander's impulsivity. He made dispassionate decisions, and he'd been raised for the role. Xander was woefully unprepared for such responsibility. He was still in the grips of the madness Cato had constructed in his mind.

He fought half-heartedly.

"Xander, finish him or I'll finish you," Cato said, sounding bored.

Davide came at Xander fast. In his rush, he left himself wide open.

Too late, Xander realized he'd done it on purpose. Years of hunter training made defending himself second nature. He blocked with one blade while slicing up with the other, cutting Davide through the gap in his armor.

No. No. No. Blood rushed in Xander's ears and the air whooshed from his lungs. He didn't mean to. It was an accident—a reflex from years of training.

"Thank you," Davide whispered, low enough that only Xander could hear. He drew back suddenly and the wound opened wide, blood rushing down his armor.

"No—" The word was a gasping sob, a desperate prayer to gods who did not care to listen.

Xander sunk to the ground with his brother. The cloud that surrounded Davide for the past few years lifted. Cato's bargain was undone by Xander's killing blow, dooming him with the knowledge that the only escape from his fate was death.

There was a lifetime of unspoken words in the look on Davide's face. Xander choked down a sob, his eyes blurring.

"Don't even think about giving him the satisfaction of your tears," Davide rasped. "I knew this would happen eventually, and you are the last thing I had worth saving. I'd do it all again knowing the outcome. You're my little brother and I love you and although I haven't done a good job of it lately, it's my job to protect you. You will beat him, Xan. I know you will. You're an optimist. You always expected the best of the world, and I thought that was stupid, but now I know it means you think in ways that other people don't."

He coughed up blood. "It's up to you now. You're the legacy of our family. Make it count. Fix this. Help our people. You were only supposed to find the Lost God, but you united all of these powerful people. Take their help." His breath sputtered. "Make it better, Xany. Promise."

Xander forced calm into his voice, but he didn't feel calm. "I will keep the peace. I'll make it better. I promise."

Davide smiled at him as he took one more breath, and then his chest ceased to rise again.

With one reflexive strike of a blade, Xander had slashed every string attaching him to anyone who loved him. He was entirely alone. His hands shook violently, his chest hollowed out by loss. It was pure stubbornness that allowed him to stagger to his feet.

He slowly turned his gaze back to Cato, forcing his face into an indifferent frown.

"Clean yourself up," Cato said. "We invade in two days, and we need to go over the entire battle plan."

Xander took one last look at his brother's body. It may as well have been his own because he didn't know who he was anymore. His life no longer resembled anything familiar. He thought he'd been alone before, but he never felt it more acutely than he did at that moment.

Xander had a secret. He would keep it as long as he could. Long enough for Cece to beat Cato. Long enough for her to figure out a way to get out from under the mess Cato made for all of them. He had faith in Cece because he had no other choice, but also because he'd been amazed by her fortitude over and over.

Xander counted on Cece's strength to inspire his own. He counted on Davide's faith in him. His own faith was failing, so he counted on the people he'd surrounded himself with.

37

CECILIA

Cecilia jolted awake, momentarily disoriented by the gray stone walls around her. She'd fallen asleep in her chair outside of Prince Marcos's suite in Olney Castle. It felt a bit like falling asleep in a tomb. She shuddered, wiping sleep from her eyes.

Rainer grinned at her from where he leaned against the wall across from her.

"Hey, sleepyhead," he whispered.

"Any news?" she asked.

Rainer shook his head. "All quiet out there this morning."

Cecilia rose and stretched. She, Rainer, Cal, Evan, and Sylvie had camped out with the royals as they awaited Cato's impending invasion. For two days, the castle courtyard had been filled with most of the Olney Hunter Army, preparing for siege, but now they were growing restless.

Davide and Cato needed to come for the Olney royalty to usurp the Olney throne. So it stood to reason that protecting the Teripins protected the interests of the whole kingdom.

Along with their regular contingent of guards, Cecilia and Rainer were temporarily assigned to protect Prince Marcos. Sylvie and Cal were guarding King Hector, and because the king didn't fully trust Evan, Anders Everett was assigned to protect Queen Elena. Cecilia needed to stay close to them to ensure Cato didn't take the minds of Olney's highest-value targets. If the Teripins fell, the rest of Olney would, too.

Cecilia began to pace. The guardians along the hallway paid her no mind.

For Cecilia, the waiting was much worse than fighting. She was on edge from the moment she woke until the moment sleep dragged her under.

She felt Rainer's eyes on her, but she was trying not to give much away about their relationship. Although the guardian and witch program had changed, they weren't about to flaunt what they had in front of the royal family. The last thing she needed was to rile up King Hector, who, for no reason that she understood, still seemed eager to push her toward Prince Marcos. Maybe he'd be satisfied without god and goddess heirs as long as she was there to ensure Olney's dominance.

Rainer stopped her pacing by stepping into her path. "Lady Reznik, I need you to help me check the south hallway."

She stifled a laugh at how official he sounded. She followed him around the corner. Before she could say anything, he tugged her against his chest and kissed her. Instantly, all the tension in her body eased.

"What was that for?" she asked when he finally pulled away.

"You seemed like you needed some help relaxing."

She played with the button on his tunic. "I know what would make me feel even more relaxed."

Rainer laughed. "I don't think we can get away with that right now, although it's a very tempting offer." He kissed the top of her head before leading her back to their post.

Marcos exited his room, looking more exhausted than regal and dressed entirely in his battle regalia.

"Your Grace," Cecilia said.

He smiled warily and started down the hall toward the throne room, Cecilia and Rainer following behind.

Hector and Elena sat atop their marble thrones, the queen in her more ceremonial armored breastplate and the king in full armor. Cecilia curtseyed and Rainer bowed as they took their post next to Prince Marcos.

Evan entered the throne room. "Your Majesties, still no sign of Cato or the Argarian forces."

"This is ridiculous. How long will it take them to strike?" King Hector grumbled. "Are they trying to bore us to sleep and attack while we're out?"

"It's not a bad strategy to wait until your opponent's nerves are fried. Especially if you have the luxury of moving an army all at once," Evan said.

The king glowered at him but Evan looked wholly unbothered.

Cecilia heard something faint in the distance. "Wait," she said. She closed her eyes and listened closely. "I hear death whispers. They're faint, but we should get ready."

She waved the group closer. Cal, Sylvie, Evan, Rainer, and the royals huddled around her. "Cato might know what I'm doing, and it's possible that what I do won't work at all. We need to be prepared for all outcomes. Remember our fallback plans. King Hector and Prince Marcos will stay close to us so they know when to give the order to let the Argarian army flee."

The group nodded, and Cecilia marveled at the absurdity of giving commands to the king and prince of Olney. Marcos was afraid enough of her, but she half expected King Hector to rebel just to refuse a woman's commands. She led her rapt contingent into the morning sun, where the half-asleep Olney Hunter Army was huddled in the courtyard.

"Everyone remember the safe word. If you fall under Cato's influence, just say 'Blackberries' and I'll try to cut the connection as quick as I can," Cecilia said. "Remember, I'll have to use my powers on you, so I apologize ahead of time for the intrusion."

The group nodded as the huntmaster ran through the ranks, rousing the sleepy soldiers.

Suddenly, a gash opened in the air and a battalion of Argarian hunters charged through. Even though they'd prepped the Olney Hunter Army on what to expect, hearing about something magical and seeing it were two very different things. The first few minutes were a bloodbath.

Cecilia pushed her powers toward the opening in space that Cato had created, but she was too far away.

"I have to get closer," she shouted to Rainer. He shook his head, but Evan was at her side in a blink.

"I've got it, McKay. Stay with the prince. Call if you need us," Evan said.

Rainer hesitated for a moment but nodded, and Cecilia flashed a quick, reassuring smile. She sent a surge of love through their connection as she walked toward the front lines, and his love reverberated back as she reached the opening.

Evan stood next to her along with a line of witches and guardians who were using their magic to push back the advancing Argarian army. Cato's gap in the air closed temporarily, staunching the flow of Argarian soldiers. Most of two battalions had made it through, pushing their Olney counterparts to the brink. She pressed her sparkling hope power out again, aiming for the first line of Argarian hunters.

At first, nothing changed, but one by one they began to look a bit stunned. They stumbled away from their fights in a daze. Cecilia pushed harder, drawing on as much power as she could. She was no longer afraid of the darkness inside her because it was where she found her strength. She dug deep and pushed her power wider, trying to encompass the entirety of the Argarian battalions.

Sweat dripped down her brow and her whole body shook as she tried to channel her power into the hunters in front of her. Slowly, they all stopped fighting, looking confused.

Evan shouted for Hector and Marcos.

"Any Argarian hunter who flees Olney now will be free to go

peacefully. We have no war with you. Go in peace and live long lives with those you love," Hector shouted.

The hunters hesitated, but once the Olney guards opened the gates, they poured out of the castle grounds in droves, leaving only a few Argarian hunters fighting.

"It's working!" Sylvie said excitedly.

Cecilia smiled half-heartedly. She didn't want to tell them that she already felt tired. The battle was only starting, but using that much power had taken a lot out of her.

"But where's Cato?" Evan asked, searching the field.

As if on cue, a slice opened in the air behind Hector, and Endros and Cato stepped through. Cecilia's eyes widened in surprise. She should have expected that Endros would be there. If her ascended siblings could visit the mortal realm, it made sense that he could too. He wouldn't be as powerful as when she fought him before, but he was the god of war, and his chaotic influence could counteract her own.

Cato clicked his tongue at her. "Little Dove, what did you do to my hunters?"

"I see you brought your father. Too scared to fight me alone?" Cecilia said.

"Cecilia, you know I don't wish to fight you at all—unless, of course, you consider it some sort of foreplay, in which case, I'd be thrilled to engage with you."

A surge of anger flooded her bond. She wanted to reassure Rainer, but giving him any attention at all would just make Cato focus on him, so she forced herself to keep her eyes on the two gods in front of her. She stepped between Cato and Marcos.

"Always protecting princes, it seems," Cato teased.

"Blackberries," Marcos mumbled.

Cecilia summoned earth and rooted Cato's feet to the ground as she spun to look at Marcos, who drew his sword and stalked toward King Hector. She seized Marcos's mind from Cato's grip, only for Endros to reappear in front of Hector and take a swing at him with his sword.

Rainer broke the blow.

Cecilia's heart leapt into her throat seeing him go up against the god of war. Endros might have been less powerful, but he was still formidable, if only for the short time he could stay in this realm.

She turned back to check on Cato, but he was already gone. A tear appeared on their left flank and another battalion of Argarian hunters charged through. Cecilia knew she had to use her power to stop them, but she couldn't leave Rainer alone with Endros.

"Cece, I've got it. Just go," Rainer yelled.

Endros turned his attention to her. "Little Goddess, I owe you a debt."

She shrugged. "You do, indeed."

"Did my boy deliver as I said he would?"

She grinned at Endros. "I'm still standing."

He frowned. "And so is he. He's not out of moves yet, Goddess. Don't be foolish enough to think you've seen his best work."

"Your power has made him sloppy. It works against his own."

Endros's eyes widened slightly. Either he was surprised she knew, or he hadn't noticed. His gaze shot past her to where Cato stood on his front lines, letting hunters through the rift in space.

"You didn't know," she mumbled as Rainer took another swing at Endros.

"Cece!"

She spun at the sound of Evan's voice.

Evan pointed to where Marcos had again turned on King Hector, the prince swiping his sword wildly at his father.

"Go!" Rainer shouted.

Cecilia took off toward Marcos, jumping between him and his father with her sword raised to block the blow intended for Hector. She grabbed ahold of Marcos's mind, but experienced the same spinning feeling as when she pressed into Xander's mind.

"Evan, I can't," she shouted as she continued to fight Marcos. She struggled to keep her moves defensive. Her strength matched his, but Marcos was fighting with an aggression she'd never seen in him. "Marc, snap out of it!"

"Can you put him out?" Evan asked.

She nodded. "Someone needs to get him out of the fray."

"I can do it," Cal said, shouldering through the crush of bodies.

Before she could grab Marcos, he elbowed her in the side of the head, knocking her aside and creating an opening to get to Hector. He drove his sword into the king's side through a gap in his armor.

Cecilia cursed as she grabbed Marcos's mind and put him to sleep. Cal caught the prince and heaved him over his shoulder. Evan defended them as they made their way back into the castle.

Sylvie sprung into action, using her healing magic on the king. Cecilia stood in front of them, guarding Sylvie as she worked.

"Do you need help?" Cecilia asked.

"No, I've got it, just don't let me get killed," Sylvie said. Panic oozed out of her, no doubt a result of the responsibility of saving the king.

The air split in front of them and Cato appeared. Xander stepped out behind the trickster, a mix of heat and hate swirling in his gaze.

"My love," Xander said quietly.

Cecilia was momentarily distracted by Sylvie calling for Rainer to help her get the king into the castle. Rainer bent low to assist but as soon as he stood with his arm around Hector's shoulders, Endros charged at them.

Everything happened too fast. Endros swung his blade and Rainer ducked. Sylvie jumped out of the way and threw out earth magic, growing roots up and over Endros's legs. But it was too late. Endros's blade struck true, slicing straight through Hector's neck, beheading him.

A scream lodged in Cecilia's throat and she fought the urge to vomit as the king's head rolled away. Rainer dropped the king's body and stumbled back, raising his sword, but the killing move took all that Endros had left. Flames rose from his legs, consuming his body, and when they receded, the god of war was gone.

Strong arms wrapped around Cecilia's middle, yanking her back against a firm chest. The familiar scent of bergamot and cedar cut through the metallic smell of the battle.

"Let me go, Xander."

"My beautiful Cece, what have you been up to since you left me with such fond memories?" The words weren't warm. They were an accusation.

She stilled as Xander pressed a blade to her throat. His lips grazed her ear as he spoke quietly amid the surrounding battle. She tried to elbow him, but he pressed the blade harder against her throat.

"Just listen. Cato knows what you can do. You need to work faster. There are another eight battalions along with the two that are over there fighting. Stay away from Cato or he will grab you and disappear and this will be a fucking bloodbath."

Cecilia kept her face neutral, but she wanted to start sobbing. Xander still had enough of his mind to help. She gave Rainer the briefest shake of her head and sent a spark of calm through their bond.

"I'm going to let you go now. Make it look good. Run to the front lines. I will try to keep Cato away."

Cecilia slammed her elbow back into Xander as she spun away. She kneed him in the groin and then punched him before turning and running past Rainer and Sylvie.

"Stay with me," she said, soft enough that only they could hear. "Don't let Cato get close to me."

She ran to the front line and stretched her powers wide, trying not to be daunted by the volume of soldiers still to come. She knew their plan was a long shot. They'd only hoped she could take on the whole army. The actual goal was for her to send as many Argarian hunters peacefully on their way as she could and trust that the Olney Hunter Army could handle the rest.

They hadn't been counting on Endros, and he did much more damage than she expected. It would have been nice to have her own godly family there, but they were noticeably absent. She didn't have time to think about it further as Cato opened another seam and two more battalions charged through the courtyard gates.

Rainer cursed and Sylvie sent up a huge tower of dirt to slow them. Cecilia pushed her powers out wide again, trying to encompass the two battalions on the left flank. She sent her sparkling power into each and every hunter and, just like before, they slowed their fighting before stopping.

Without Marcos or Hector to give the freedom to retreat to the battalions, they gave the signal to the Olney huntmaster, who sent the two battalions on their way. Once again, most of the hunters fled peacefully. Only a few stood and fought.

Rainer, Sylvie, and Cecilia turned their attention back to the hunters entering the gates.

Cecilia's legs felt like lead. She was exhausted, and every muscle in her immortal body ached. She forced herself to keep going, on and on, pressing her power into every hunter as they flowed through Cato's rift and sending away four more battalions of Argarian hunters.

She started to feel shaky on her feet. Rainer reached out to steady her. She didn't think she could keep going. It was an effort just to keep her eyes open. Cato still held the split in space open as hunters charged through, but she couldn't keep working.

Arrows arced through the air, one striking Cato in the center of the chest. Cecilia whipped around and spotted Sayla standing on a nearby tower.

Cato cursed and stumbled forward, losing control of his power, and the rift slammed closed. Cecilia didn't think. She charged toward him as the goddess of the hunt hit him with three more arrows.

Cecilia pulled her dagger from the sheath on her thigh, ready to pounce. A pair of strong arms caught her around the waist. Xander pulled her back against his chest yet again.

"Put me down, Xander!" Cecilia said, fighting his grip.

"I'm sorry, love, I cannot do that since you insist on ignoring my advice. I told you not to go near Cato."

"But I can finish this," she huffed as she swung her head back. Xander anticipated the move. An arrow shot past their heads. "That was a warning shot. Sayla is going to kill you."

Xander released his grip and Cecilia turned to look at him. She swung with her fist and he caught it like she knew he would. She grabbed his wrist and tugged hard, flipping him and slamming him into the ground. Cato was already rising to his feet, all arrows removed, all wounds healed. His murderous gaze swung from her to Rainer.

Cecilia saw her error immediately. She grabbed hold of Rainer's mind to keep Cato from doing the same and planted the memory of him promising to go check on Prince Marcos. She prayed he would forgive her for using her powers on him. Guilt sliced through her.

Cato faked a pout. "You stole my toy."

"You already have one," Cecilia said, jerking her thumb toward Xander.

Cato was much too close. She needed a distraction, and a good one, or he was going to grab her and disappear. She was desperate to escape. She somehow needed to take out another six battalions. She held out her sword as another arrow connected with Cato's shoulder.

Cato opened the rift behind him. More hunters charged through as he commanded his archers to take aim at Sayla. Cecilia spun to see Sayla salute and disappear into mist. Cecilia turned back to Cato, sword in one hand, dagger in the other.

"I told you before, I don't want to fight you, Little Dove. We could have done this the easy way with far less bloodshed. I told you this wasn't what I wanted. I need you to come with me now. We've danced around this and played this game long enough."

"I'm not going anywhere."

Cecilia felt a sudden burst of panic through their connection. Rainer must have realized that they were separated, or he felt her fear. At any moment, he would charge in to help, and she couldn't let that happen. Her eyes darted wildly over the field. Across the courtyard, Sylvie and several other witches and guardians fought off an attack on the Olney army's right flank. Overhead, the sky grew dark as Olney's witches summoned a storm.

A bolt of lightning tore from the sky as Cato grabbed Cecilia's arm, launching him several feet. Cecilia landed on the ground with a groan. It hurt her, but not nearly as much as it hurt Cato. The god groaned, rolling onto his side. Cecilia looked up and saw Xander pulling bolts of lightning and hitting the Argarian army.

"Fucking Storm Prince!" Cato grunted as he sat up.

Xander went rigid as Cato sunk his power into him. For the first time, Cecilia noticed sweat on Cato's brow. He had to have been getting tired, too. Although their power was seemingly endless, the human bodies they inhabited limited how much of that power they could channel in one day. The massive draw they were using was draining them both quickly. This was her best shot to kill him. Even if she was tired and slow, she wasn't sure she'd get another chance. She had to try.

She jumped to her feet and charged toward Cato as fast as her tired legs could carry her.

"Cece!" Rainer's voice cut through the rumble of the battle at the exact wrong moment. Her eyes met his over the melee. His face was a mix of horror and betrayal. She thought that her guilt might kill her. Rainer started toward her when his eyes went wide. Cato's hand clamped down on her arm.

"Enough, Little Dove. Wave goodbye to your guardian. You won't be seeing him again for quite some time."

Cecilia tried to jerk her arm away, but she was so incredibly exhausted she could barely stay on her feet.

Cato's hand was wrenched violently away from her arm and when she looked up, she met blue eyes the exact shade of her own. Clastor looked from her to Cato with menace in his eyes.

"Go!" Clastor yelled at her.

Cecilia took off toward Rainer and they ran across the field where four more battalions of Argarian hunters were engaged with Olney's army.

"Rain, I know you're mad," she said, afraid to look at him. "I don't know how much more I can do. Can you just make sure I'm okay?"

"I'll always be here to catch you, Cece." His voice was soft and full of relief. He wrapped one arm around Cecilia's waist, brandishing his sword with the other, ready to defend against anyone who came at them.

Once more, she reached out to the sparkling power of hope and pressed it wider than she ever had. Her legs shook violently. She leaned into Rainer and he held her firmly. Sweat soaked her hair and her clothes and her mind grew foggy, but she pressed on.

Her heart beat wildly in her chest as the fighting slowed. She pulled every last ounce of her power, tearing every drop of energy from her muscles, focusing her attention on the rest of the field. She gave it everything she had until her powers sputtered out; until her heart kicked hard against her chest and the world went dark.

38

RAINER

Cecilia shuddered and collapsed against Rainer. His heart clenched as he eased her down to the ground and checked her pulse. Her face was pale and bloodless but, to his immense relief, her heartbeat was strong, and her breathing was deep and even.

Scooping her into his arms, he looked out over the field.

The fighting had ceased. Bodies littered the front lines, blood soaking the courtyard. Smoke and ash from barely smothered fires filled the air, along with the sounds of swords being sheathed and groans from the wounded. Witches were healing and corralling injured hunters and guardians into tents.

Cecilia had saved both sides from immense casualties. It was more than they'd hoped for when they developed their plan, and more than Rainer felt certain they'd get given the twists and turns of the battle.

He turned back toward the castle. Clastor stood in the center of the courtyard, surrounded by rows of hunters kneeling in reverence. Despite his graying hair, he looked every bit a warrior in his shining silver armor.

Though seeing the gods walking among them had become a regular occurrence, it was still jarring to behold Clastor.

"Rainer McKay." The god's voice boomed, and Rainer wasn't sure whether to be humbled or genuinely afraid.

He tried not to look stunned that the god of all matter, Cecilia's birth father, knew his name. Rainer approached him with Cecilia cradled against his chest. Clastor dwarfed him in size, his assessing gaze burning into Rainer, but he refused to look away.

"Is she well?" Clastor asked, brow pinched in worry.

"I think she just fainted."

Clastor nodded, a hint of pride in his eyes. "She did a great thing. I can't stay here for more than another moment. Please get her to safety. Tell her we're proud of her. The rest would have been here if they were good in a fight, but we had every confidence in her. We still do."

"I will," Rainer said.

Clastor's face grew stern. "Be good to my daughter."

"I will, sir," Rainer said.

"She's a strong woman—so much like her mother. Don't let her convince you she doesn't need to be taken care of."

"Yes, sir." Rainer nodded.

"I told her you were better suited for her. Now don't break her heart."

Rainer swallowed hard. "I won't. I will give her anything she wants."

A sudden sadness passed over Clastor's face. "I certainly hope you will. Remember those words. They're easy to say but hard to follow through on."

Rainer wanted to hear more, but the god of all matter blurred at the edges and gently faded to nothing.

As his essence cleared, Xander came into view, looking disheveled and bloody. He staggered through the mess of bodies being shrouded for burial, past several of Grimon's priestesses blessing the dying. He glared at Rainer from the other side of the courtyard, his eyes filled with pure hatred. He looked like he wanted to cut out Rainer's still-beating heart. He started toward them, but as soon as he'd taken a step, Cato appeared and grabbed him, yanking him through a fold in space.

Rainer sighed heavily, knowing how much it would break Cecilia's heart to know that Xander had been taken again. Rainer had seen him stop Cato from getting away with Cecilia during the battle. He shuddered at the thought of what might have happened if Cato had succeeded, but there was nothing he could do about it now. He needed to get her to the healers and check in on Prince Marcos and Queen Elena.

———

Hours passed and Cecilia still hadn't stirred from her sleep. Rainer began to worry. She hadn't even moved when he'd carried her from the healer's suite back to the cottage. She'd stayed peacefully asleep as he washed her hair, taking his time to comb out the tangles. He used a washcloth to remove the dirt and blood from the battle and rubbed her skin with an oil that smelled like vanilla.

Cecilia slept through the rest of the day. Sylvie, Evan, and Cal took turns coming in to sit with Rainer while he waited for her to wake. The longer she slept, the more restless he became. He reorganized the bookshelves in the cottage, then pulled everything out of Cecilia's closet and rearranged it by color. He cleaned the cottage from top to bottom, but restlessness still dogged him.

He felt nothing through their bond, which wasn't unusual in sleep but still unsettled him.

The healers had found nothing else to fix, saying that she likely just needed rest, but she was a goddess and they weren't trained to treat an immortal. He pored over old mythology books, looking for any clue as to how to help. Once Evan left for the night, promising to be back first thing in the morning, Rainer climbed into bed beside her and fell into a dreamless sleep.

———

The first thing Rainer was aware of were fingers moving against his side in a slow, soothing pattern, the same way Cecilia used to do when she was starting to wake up.

He jerked awake, rubbing sleep from his eyes as he took in her smiling face.

"Cece!"

"I was wondering when you were going to wake up. You rarely sleep in like this," she teased.

Rainer was so relieved, he leaned down and kissed her. He crushed her body against his as he poured all of his fear and desperation into the kiss.

Someone cleared their throat. Rainer jumped back and saw Evan smirking at him from the chair next to the bed.

Rainer sat up straight, untangling himself from Cecilia and moving to the edge of the mattress.

"Don't stop on my account. It just looked like you were getting into it and I didn't want you to take any clothes off," Evan said.

Cecilia blushed. "No one likes an eavesdropper, Evan."

Evan just laughed.

"What happened? I figured it must be good if I'm here, and not in Cato's cottage," Cecilia said, her voice still heavy with sleep.

She sat up, rolling up the sleeves of the sweater that he'd put her to bed in. Gods, he loved seeing her in his clothes.

Rainer ran his fingers through her hair. "You passed out, but not before you stopped all the fighting. You were amazing. Cato might still have a few battalions, but the rest of his army is in the wind. It would take months for him to track them down and try to get them brainwashed enough to fight again. Especially after you used your power on so many of them. I doubt anyone wants to go up against that."

Relief broke over her face. "My father—"

"Clastor was there. He wanted you to know how proud they were of you and they have every confidence you'll finish this," Rainer said.

Evan laughed. "Then he put the fear of the gods into Rainer."

"What did he say?" Cecilia asked, delighted.

Rainer rubbed the back of his neck. "He said that he told you you were better suited to me. He told me not to break your heart, and I told him I'll give you anything you want."

"I like the sound of that," she said, winding her fingers through his. He kissed her knuckles.

"How do you feel?" Evan asked.

"Exhausted. Sore. Like I fought my own personal war." She looked around the room. "Wait, what happened to Cato? Where's Xander?"

Evan locked eyes with Rainer. "Clastor didn't kill Cato. I don't think he could have. He just wanted to get him away from you. Cato left with Xander."

"But Xander saved me," Cecilia said. "He saved us twice. He told me how many battalions Cato had when he held a knife to my throat. Then he hit Cato with lightning when he almost got away with me."

"I know, Cece. I'm sorry. I almost got to him, but it was too late," Rainer sighed.

Pain lit her eyes, but she pressed her lips into a firm line and nodded.

"It's not over. We'll get him back and you'll beat Cato. But let's try to look at that battle for what it was: a huge victory for us and the people of Olney and Argaria. You saved a lot of lives. The casualties were minimal—except for the king." Just saying it out loud filled Rainer with guilt. He'd failed in his protection duty.

Cecilia's eyes went wide at the memory. "Gods! Marcos is the king now." She giggled. "I'm sorry. I know this is an inappropriate reaction. I'm just shocked."

"What happened with you and Marcos?" Rainer asked.

She gave him a mischievous smile. "I will never tell. That's the King of Olney you're talking about, and sharing embarrassing stories about him might be treason now."

Evan's eyes went wide.

"So what do we do now?" she asked.

"I think we let you rest up," Rainer started.

"And then we find a way to get Xander back," she said, looking from him to Evan.

Even Evan looked skeptical of the idea. "I'll leave you two to it." He let himself out of the cottage.

Cecilia met Rainer's eyes. "Rain, I'm sorry I used my powers on you."

Rainer shuddered thinking about the moment he'd made his way into the castle to find Cal with Marcos and realized what Cecilia had done. He'd never been as scared as he was running back out into the battle. When he saw Cato grab her and felt her fear, sharp and fast through their bond, his heart sank. He shook his head, trying to get rid of the memory.

Cecilia pursed her lips. "I saw Cato reaching for your mind and I only had a split second to think. The only way I could guarantee that he wouldn't get in is if I did first. I'm sorry. I hate that I did it. I just wanted to keep you safe."

Rainer frowned. "You can't do that again."

"I promise I won't."

He knew she meant it from the look on her face and the heavy guilt that flowed through their connection.

"And?" Rainer asked.

"And I love you."

"And?"

Cecilia's grin grew wide. "And do you want to be mad, or do you want to kiss me?"

It was the easiest question he'd answered in months. Rainer kissed her and let all the worries of the past few days and what the future held drift away.

39

CECILIA

Three days after the battle at Olney Castle, Cecilia stood alone in her kitchen for the first time in weeks. Things in Olney City were quieting down. Life appeared to be returning to normal.

Evan's spies confirmed that Cato's army was all but dissolved. Two battalions still sat organized back in Argaria, presumably to protect Davide, whom they hadn't spotted during the battle or in days since, but the rest of the army had started the journey back to Argaria in peace.

A persistent restlessness grew in her heart. She couldn't shake the feeling that her job was only half finished. Until she defeated Cato, she'd only given him time to regroup.

Her stomach grumbled. Rainer was late returning from their favorite bakery with lemon cakes.

She stood by the kitchen table arranging roses from her wedding bushes into a vase. A shadow passed over the cottage door.

"Finally. I'm starving—"

When she looked up, Xander stood in the doorway, silhouetted by the sun, his expression unreadable.

"Xander." Cecilia froze.

"Cece."

Just from the way he said her name and his posture, she could feel the change in him. He was no longer the man who warned her of Cato's plan and saved her from being taken. He'd paid a price for betraying Cato. She reached for her dagger out of habit as he stepped into the cottage.

"What's the matter, love? Not happy to see me? Even after I saved you?" Xander's face was more bitter than hurt.

"You just don't seem like yourself."

"How could I be? I had to pay for what I did to Cato."

"Xan—"

He held up a dismissive hand and, for a moment, the pain in his eyes was real and unclouded. "Don't. I don't want to hear it." His frown shifted into a wolfish smile. "It's so good to see you again. You really gave me a workout last time we were alone."

She sighed heavily, continuing to fuss with the flowers with one hand, still holding the dagger in the other. "What do you want?"

"You know that I'll just catch the dagger if you throw it at me, although that reminds me of that night I found you bathing in the river. Could be fun to relive it." He winked, but there was no light left in his eyes. It felt more threat than flirtation. She wondered if Rainer could feel the genuine fear she felt now; if he would come running.

"Lots of memories here," Xander said fondly as he ran his fingers over the kitchen table. "Where's Rainer?"

"Closer than you think." The words echoed the night they met by the river. "What do you want?"

"Cato needs to see you."

A laugh burst from her, surprising both of them. "Then he should come and get me himself and not send his pet prince to retrieve me."

Xander's jaw clenched. She reached her senses out and felt him shift from boiling rage to icy jealousy.

"You know how impatient he gets."

"I don't care. Leave or I will make you leave." She felt her power flaring under the surface of her skin.

"Your eyes are glowing," Xander whispered. Longing crept into his gaze, but it was quickly snuffed out by rage. "You think you're so powerful, but you're really just a slut."

She clenched her fist. He was trying to bait her into something.

"Don't forget you're playing chess," Aelish had said.

This was just another move. Something to trick her into doing some permanent damage to Xander.

"I suppose it takes one to know one, huh?" Cecilia let her power recede.

"You were just waiting for absolution. Just waiting me out for your chance to be with Rainer," Xander said, shaking his head. "You used me to wake him up. He was always a fool—so in love with you and so unable to give you what you wanted. I could have had you in that garden the final night of the Godsball. I fed you a bunch of pretty lies and you were ready to let me do whatever I wanted. You were so eager. You would have gone along with it, just like you would have in the Godswoods. I may hate you, but I loved to make you beg for it."

She dropped her head back and ran a hand through her hair. "And I loved when you made me beg. Stop trying to bait me. If Cato wants me, tell him to show up himself."

"You may be immortal, Goddess. But your friends aren't. You'd be wise to remember that."

In the blink of an eye, she pinned Xander against the wall with the dagger at his throat.

"If you touch any of them, I will split Cato open and rip his immortal heart out before I stab it."

Xander's eyes were wide.

"Cece—" Rainer called from the doorway.

Xander barked out a laugh. "Of course. Cece is in trouble and Rainer comes running. You're so predictable."

"Everything looks like it's under control." Rainer sat down casually at the table.

Cecilia hadn't moved the knife at his throat, but Xander's mouth twisted into a wicked smile.

"This is a nice role reversal, Cece," Xander taunted. "Normally, it was me holding you up against the wall. I enjoyed that more than this. I think you did, too. Didn't you hear the way she screamed my name when I was deep inside her, Rainer? I knew you were right outside this door. I wanted to remind you what you couldn't have."

Cecilia always suspected that, but she hadn't been certain. Rage threatened again, but she locked it away.

"For a puppet, you sure talk a lot," Rainer said. His tone was calm, but anger snaked down their bond.

"I have lots to say when it comes to my Cece. I may hate her, but I can always appreciate what a great lay she was. Tell me, is she as much fun with you?"

"I am going to break your nose if you don't shut up," Cecilia hissed through gritted teeth.

"She's so wild. You should have seen her on our wedding night. I thought I loved that smart mouth before that night, but I liked it even better after. The way she was so eager to be on her knees for me—"

Cecilia slapped him. "Shut up."

Fear clouded Xander's eyes as he grabbed his cheek. "I told you. I have to bring you with me."

"If Cato wants me, he needs to come here himself."

"He won't, and he will just make a mess if you don't do what he wants," Xander said. "Plus, I'm going to stay here and keep talking about this with Rainer. I saw you two out in the wild the other day. You kissed her for so long I thought you were afraid to do anything else."

"I love the way he kisses me," Cecilia said.

Xander smirked at Rainer. "You were much too gentle with her. She doesn't like to think. She likes to surrender. She needs a firmer hand."

She knew Xander didn't understand how much strength it took her to allow herself to be touched so gently—how undeserving she felt of any kind of tenderness. It was hard to sum it up, how it felt simultaneously terrifying and joyful and liberating.

"Did you tell him about what happened the last time we met? How I spent the entire night inside you? How I had you every single way I wanted, and you loved it? I was surprised you could ride home," Xander laughed.

"Yes. He knows."

Xander looked genuinely surprised.

"She came home and told me everything. Then she told me she wanted to be with me and only me," Rainer said.

"You really told him?" Xander's face softened.

Cecilia nodded.

"Fair enough, but I'm betting she didn't tell you about the night we were alone in the cabin—when she spread her legs and let me take her virginity."

Cecilia summoned all of her patience as Xander grinned at her.

"I could have stopped that storm, you know. You had to have suspected that by now, Cece. I needed more time alone with you. Especially after the first time. I couldn't get enough of you. Did she tell you that, Rainer? Did she tell you how she begged me to teach her? I could have spent a week with her and it wouldn't have been enough. There isn't a surface in that cabin that I didn't take her on."

Rainer's calm was gone as he appraised Xander with obvious murderous intent. His hand held a white-knuckled grip on the table.

"You may be there now, Rainer, but I'll always be her first. I taught her everything she knows. Just remember that every time she pleases you."

Rainer's jaw ticked. "And I'll be her last."

He crossed the room and kissed Cecilia until her heart kicked against her ribs like it was trying to escape.

Xander was watching them when she finally pulled away, a new desperation in his eyes. "Cece, will you please come with me? Cato is just right down on the beach. He will hurt people if you don't come. You know he will."

"Fine," she huffed.

Rainer pulled her into a hug. "I'm coming with you."

"You're not. Cato made it clear that if I don't meet him, he would hurt one of you. Will you crescent promise to go check on the others?"

Rainer frowned. "Please don't ask me to do that."

"Please don't ask not to. Send Cal and Sylvie to protect Marcos. If Cato wants to talk, we can bet it will not be friendly. I want to make sure we protect our shot at peace. I know you want to be with me, but I can handle this, okay? What I can't handle is him hurting you," she whispered.

Rainer frowned and sighed. "I crescent promise."

His hands cupped her face, and he pulled her into a long, slow kiss that sent a flood of heat through her whole body. When she pulled away, she was flushed and smiling.

"I love you. Be careful."

Xander followed her out of the cottage. Her pale pink dress blew in the cold sea breeze, tangling around her legs. She squinted against the bright afternoon sun. As they walked, she felt a strangled desperation in the air around Xander, as if he was holding back a storm of emotion.

"Davide is dead," he whispered.

She froze. "How?"

"I killed him—"

"What?"

"Cato made us fight," Xander said, his hand trembling. "Davide wanted too much control. Apparently, it was harder for Cato to keep the reins on him, so I guess now I'm king. Easier to control. A weaker mind."

"That's not true. I know you're still in there, Xan. I still love you."

He looked shocked by how freely she said the words. "You shouldn't."

"Still haven't learned not to tell me what to do, huh?"

He swallowed hard. He seemed at war with himself.

"Xander, I'm so sorry. I know Davide was kind of an ass, but he was your brother. I know you loved him."

"I did."

"Can I hug you?" she asked.

He opened his arms, and she curled into him. It was so familiar, it took her breath away. He tucked his head into her neck and took a deep breath, surprising her with how quickly he surrendered to her. Finally he pulled away.

"I'm sorry." He squeezed her hand.

"Don't apologize. You don't need to apologize for him," she said.

"Xander, you know I don't like it when you touch my things," Cato said, his voice carried on the sea breeze.

Cecilia locked eyes with the trickster god and saw what she'd been waiting for since she realized he was the villain in her story: desperation. Nothing was scarier than a powerful god with nothing to lose.

40

CECILIA

"I'm not yours, Cato. I never will be," Cecilia snapped.

Waves crashed hard on the sand behind him as if to emphasize her words.

Cato clicked his tongue. "Like I said before, never say never. Never is a challenge." He winked, and she imagined stabbing him in that eye. "I've enjoyed this little cat-and-mouse game we've been playing, but I've had enough."

"You're welcome to resign anytime and I'll happily dispatch you," Cecilia said, patting the Godkiller dagger strapped to her thigh.

Cato shook his head. "Little Dove, you may be immortal but your friends are all so very breakable. I could do the same thing to them I've done to Xander."

"Threats won't win you my favor."

"I don't need your favor. I just need you to obey. You've tested my patience, but I'm tired of chasing you. You have all of my interest and whatever is left of my very cold mortal heart. What more do you want?" Cato asked.

"I want my life. I won't heel. I won't make myself small and obedient for you and you wouldn't like me if I did. This isn't a game you're willing to give up." Cecilia stood firm, her hands on her hips.

Cato frowned, a hint of doubt lighting his eyes. "It's not?"

"No, we've discussed it before. You want to win me over so I can be another one of your little toys. But I don't enjoy your company and I don't share your idea of fun. We aren't compatible, and I'm not interested in trying to bend to your every whim."

"I think you misunderstand my endgame."

Cecilia crossed her arms. "It seems like it's just to bring me misery."

"I wish you wouldn't say that. I would do anything for you. I know how much that matters to you. I would slaughter this entire continent to be with you."

"That's excessive."

Cato arched an eyebrow. "You like excessive."

"I am not impressed by murder," she said. "I told you before. Impress me with your restraint."

"You don't like restraint. You like power. Remember, Goddess, I've seen inside Xander's head. I know *exactly* what you like. I want you to be my partner in all things. My equal in every way. We can rule over this entire continent. We can have anything we want together. We can have your precious peace that you keep begging me for. I find war to be such a waste. I have no desire to see it go on. No one else will have to die."

Cecilia held up her hands to ward off his words. "I don't want to be caught or kept. I want to be free."

"You're a woman in this world. You'll never be free," Cato snapped. "Don't you see the ways you aren't now? There will always be people trying to use you. People afraid of you. If you give them a chance, they will revolt and resent you the moment you can't or won't give them what they want. This is what love does. It makes you weak. If you show mortals your weakness, they will find a way to exploit it. They are fickle."

Cato reached out for her, but Cecilia shrunk back.

"I know you fear it and you're right to. They might love you now —praise you as Cecilia, the healer of minds, bringer of hope—but the second you do anything they don't like, they will turn on you."

Cecilia shook her head. "You are a liar and a manipulator. I would be an idiot to believe any of the poison you spew."

"What would be the point now of lying to you? I'm showing you all the cards in my hand, Cecilia. We are the last two living gods. I had other plans for you, but things have changed. I think you are clever, bloodthirsty, and beautiful. You are my only equal. Forever is a long time to be alone, but you and I, we could have a long and happy life together. We could keep the peace. I will let you do anything you want."

"I don't want to rule people. I just want to be a normal, happy person," she sighed.

Cato scoffed. "Don't be naive. You know that's not in the cards for you. It wasn't in the cards before you came into your full goddess powers. You resented your isolation, but you were magnificent. Fierce and vicious. You were meant to be extraordinary. You weren't meant to be so *human*." Cato spat the last word with utter disgust.

She laughed. "Cato, you take with both hands and give nothing back. You're more human than you think."

His face twisted in a sour frown. "I'll make you a deal."

"I'm listening," she sighed.

"Be my partner, my equal in all ways, for the next ten years. If you are truly unhappy, I will let you go and leave you in peace with whoever you wish. I will fix Xander's mind and I won't cause any problems in Olney for the rest of my immortal life. I will leave all of your friends unharmed, both physically and mentally."

"That's it?" Cecilia asked. That couldn't possibly be his endgame.

Cato's eyes lit with triumph. "What's ten years when you have an eternity? You might end up actually liking me."

"That's all I have to agree to?"

He looked encouraged by her question. "That and you have to have a few children. I'll need heirs eventually, and ours would be the most powerful living gods that have ever existed. They would solidify our power. No kingdom could challenge us."

Cecilia looked at Xander, her heart clenching in her chest. Cato had torn through his mind. How could he not know?

"Xander." Emotion clogged her throat.

She didn't know it was possible that a revelation could both heal and break her heart at the same time.

"I never told him," Xander rasped. "I knew he might hurt you if he knew. I tried my best even after everything to protect the thing that would hurt you the most. I'm sorry for what I said to you. I needed you to believe it so you wouldn't say anything to him about it." He took her face in his hands. His voice was strained and desperate. "It killed me to hurt you like that. Cece, I know I can never be forgiven for what I've done, but I never told him. I knew it would put you at risk. I love you, so I kept that information as well as the thing that would hurt you most."

Cecilia threw her arms around him and sobbed. The dam broke open and all the hurt rushed out. She struggled to stay standing, but he held her. He hushed her and rubbed her back, kissing away her tears. She'd never felt so relieved.

Xander smiled sadly. "You looked at Rainer that day in the woods and said, 'Don't go where I can't go,' and you were in agony. I felt it in your words—the way the loss of him would shatter you—and I thought: *Cece is the only person who has ever made me feel that way.* I didn't know until that moment that you didn't feel the same for me, or maybe I did but I hadn't been so confronted with it. When you thought I was going to die back in Argaria, you were distraught and heartbroken, but when I watched you frantically rack your brain for a way to save Rainer as he lay dying, you were just inconsolable, like your soul was being rendered from your body. Love, I knew what would hurt you most, and I knew what a huge mistake I'd made."

Months had passed, and he'd said nothing about it. Desiree's words rushed back to her. *"Do you have no faith in your husband? Was he not behind enemy lines his entire life? Trust that he is the man you fell in love with. Someone nearly as tricky as the god himself. He's not out of moves yet, sister. Have some faith."*

Even in his worst moments, Xander had protected the thing that would be most catastrophic. The thing that would have obliterated her. At the bottom of the well of chaos and confusion, he was still the man she'd fallen in love with.

"I let him get to a lot. I needed him to believe that he saw it all. I'm so, so sorry, Cece. But I promise that's the one thing I would never give up. I wouldn't let him hurt you like that." Xander kissed her forehead.

"What in Grimon's Underworld is going on?" Cato asked. His gaze was murderous.

The absurdity of the entire situation hit Cecilia, and she burst into a fit of giggles. Cato just looked more confused.

Her exchange *finally* made sense. Fate was brutal all around, and for once, it was funny.

"Oh, it is just a little too much sometimes." She laughed hysterically, and Cato and Xander stared at her like she'd lost her mind.

"Cecilia, what is going on?" Cato sounded exasperated. "I just shared my plans for our future and you hugged your ex-husband and started crying and now you're hysterical. What is going on?"

She grinned at him. "Do you know what my father said? I know you were eavesdropping on us in the woods that night, Cato, but did you hear what he told me about you?"

"He told you not to make a deal with me." Cato looked confused and impatient.

"He said to not try to outmaneuver you, that I should let you outmaneuver yourself," Cecilia said.

"And why is that so funny?"

"Because he was right. You beat yourself and you don't even realize yet. It's ironic, really. After all the misery you've caused me, it is deeply funny."

"What is?" Cato demanded.

"You convinced Clastor to create the Gauntlet," she continued. "You helped him do it and you created the story around it and used your influence to spread it. You got witches to bind Clastor's magic to the caves and especially the Cave of Longings as the last step. Do you know what that magic was?"

He waved an impatient hand. "Yes, exchange magic. You had to

411

give up what you desired most to come into your full goddess power. You were lonely. You had to give up companionship."

"Do you know the problem with messing with that kind of magic when you're an amateur? Exchange magic is unpredictable. Magic belongs to those who study and understand it. Not greedy people who try to wield it like a weapon. You can't use it to manipulate," Cecilia said. "Companionship was my deepest longing—an end to loneliness. I see how you could think that it would isolate me from Rainer and Xander and leave me open for you, but it didn't. I don't blame you. I expected the same. Did you not notice that didn't happen? They were both with me still. Xander and I got married. Rainer was still my best friend." She looked at him with a challenge in her eyes.

Cato shook his head. "But I already owned Xander and your guardian wouldn't give you what you wanted."

Cecilia shook her head. "But I still had them. They both still loved me and I loved them."

Cato paled. The gears turned in his mind.

A wide smile spread across her face. "I thought what you thought —that I would never have romantic companionship—but it was a different type of companionship and connection that I lost."

She couldn't stop smiling. The thing that had been bitter medicine for her to swallow for so long actually turned into the killing blow for Cato. There was a poetry to it. When Xander hid the one thing that could threaten her safety, he'd unknowingly foiled the god's plans.

"No." The word was a breathless whisper on Cato's lips.

"I can't have children. That was my exchange. You were outsmarted by witches. They had to know that kind of power would throw off the balance in the world. Two gods creating a bunch of baby gods with no one to keep them in check. Imagine the chaos. The Gauntlet was about maintaining a balance in power. It may have hurt me, but it ruined all your big plans. They tricked you. You manipulated and influenced and you failed because you were outsmarted by a few witches."

Disbelief descended on his face.

"You and I are the last two living gods, Cato. There will be no more."

Cato shook his head. "I could still have children with someone else. Your mother was just a mortal witch."

She clapped her hands like a child delighted by a puppet show. "See, that's the best part. I suspect you can't. What did you have to give up to help the witches create the magic? It would need to be something equally important to create an exchange spell like that in the Cave of Longings. What was your deepest longing? They tricked you first by binding my magic in the Gauntlet, and you unknowingly helped the witches of Olney bind it so *you* would have been the one to make a sacrifice."

"A legacy of power." Fury tore over Cato's face and he let out a guttural scream. "Fucking witches!"

Cecilia took a step back. Her hand went to her dagger.

Cato paced. It was clear the power he'd stolen from Endros was affecting his impulse control. "How did you hide it?" His eyes flashed to Xander, his fury so potent that Cecilia could practically taste it.

Xander crossed his arms as he faced Cato. "You knew my father. King Damian believed in performing weakness rather than waiting for an opponent to hit you where it hurts. He taught Davide and I using chess and then later in court politics. You must have seen it—probably respected it. He thought if he showed his enemies a fake weak spot, they wouldn't be able to resist striking there, and they would never look for a less obvious vulnerability. *Only show a weakness that you can control, never where it actually exists.* There is a reason the Saveros have ruled for generations. You should have noticed. I offered something too tempting for you to look beyond. I offered my love for my wife."

"But that is your weakness," Cato argued.

Xander shook his head. "No, my weakness is seeing Cece hurt."

"But I did hurt her." Cato still looked baffled.

"Just not in the weak spot," Xander said quietly.

He knew he wasn't her true weak spot. Cecilia wasn't even sure she knew it herself until that moment.

Xander was a mirror, reflecting to her all of her blind spots. He was a prince, a hunter, a witch, and a man who loved her more than anything. For the first time, she could see the truth of his sacrifice, the reality of what he'd endured. He'd been tortured by Cato and his manipulation. He'd also been tortured their whole marriage, knowing and seeing it proven over and over that there was someone else Cecilia loved more than him.

"Why didn't you say something?" she rasped.

"Because I wanted to take care of you in the only way I could, Cece. You are the love of my life, but Rainer is the love of yours."

Xander let her down in unimaginable ways. He'd broken her heart and nearly broken her will when he ended things. He hurt her as deeply as he could, but in his own way, he'd protected her. And it had cost him everything.

She turned to face Cato. "So, are you ready to let me go now that you know?"

Cato stopped and turned toward her. "It wasn't just about children, Cecilia. I still want you."

"You ruined my life. You've been torturing me for months," she yelled.

"I will take everything you love," Cato threatened.

"You can't." She pulled out her dagger.

"I can try."

She sighed. "We've already talked about this. If you take everything I love, you will be immortal and alone forever."

He rolled his eyes. "You'll get over it."

"Try me! You're going to do this because you're angry now? No, that's not your thing. You're a strategist. Or maybe you're not. Maybe your daddy's power is weakening your own. This is about the big moves. You can see the long game."

She had him.

Cato bit his lip, and she could practically feel the heat of his fury.

There was a surge in her chest. Rainer shouted her name from somewhere behind her and she turned to see him running toward her. She could have killed him for showing up. That's what guardians did. They protected their witches. She'd tried to keep her emotions in check, but she'd failed. Now he was here at the exact wrong moment.

As mad as she was, it was also a relief to know she was never alone, no matter how perilous her task might be.

A terrible squelching sound cleaved through the air.

She turned back to find Cato's dagger buried in Xander's chest. Cato yanked it out.

Cecilia screamed, rushing to Xander's side. She caught him before he could fall, guiding him down to the ground.

"Cece," he whispered. "Cece, that did it. Hurting me broke the deal. I remember everything clearly now. I'm...I'm so sorry. I love you."

"Shhh, love, I know. I know. I always knew. Try not to move."

Cecilia put her hands over the wound, trying to stop the blood flow, calling every ounce of her power to heal him. It was a brutal wound, and she wasn't sure she could heal it fast enough. Blood poured out of his chest, hot and sticky between her fingers, soaking her dress as she worked frantically.

"Cece, it's okay if you can't. You can let me go," Xander rasped, but she just shook her head.

"Don't you dare, Xander. I will not lose anyone else."

She gritted her teeth as her healing power flowed out of her, rebuilding everything inside his chest. It was hard work, weaving her magic into delicate blood vessels, hard bones, and soft skin. Sweat dripped down her arms. Tears drenched her face. She could not lose Xander. She couldn't bear to bury someone she loved so much. Her magic tore out of her, burning through her reserves at a rate that would have been alarming if she wasn't so terrified that it wouldn't be enough.

After a few tense moments, it was nothing more than a vicious pink scar.

"You saved me." Xander hugged her.

She was so relieved and almost in disbelief that it had worked. He pulled back, leaning his forehead against hers. "I'm so, so sorry."

Xander was weak from the blood loss, and likely would be for days. She hoped he'd be strong enough to run if things went wrong with Cato, but he looked like he could barely sit up. He definitely wouldn't be able to summon to protect himself. He drew back suddenly, eyes wide, fixed on something behind her.

Time slowed as Cecilia turned to see Rainer frozen in place, a terrified look on his face. Fear sliced through her like an arrow.

"Blackberries," Rainer mumbled.

41

CECILIA

Cecilia could barely think around her panic. "Let him go, Cato."

She tried to call on her healing power just in case, but she'd used every ounce of her magic healing Xander. Just trying to summon made her dizzy, her vision growing narrow and dark. She'd have nothing left if Rainer was hurt.

Cato grinned menacingly. "I'm not above improvising. I thought about what you said, Little Dove. I thought about what you really wanted. Fortunately, your true weak spot came right to me. I suppose it would have been wise of me to ask Xander what it was from the beginning. But now, Rainer here has given me the opportunity to make up for it. I know a chest wound like Xander's would really drain you of your resources. No need for manipulation when a sharp blade will do."

Her blood turned to ice in her veins.

"Cato, stop it! Don't do this! You did this to yourself," she said. "I just pointed it out. Do not do this. *Please*."

She frantically tried to think of a way out. Cato was angled in a way that would make it hard to strike his heart with her Godkiller dagger. Instead, she grabbed Xander's dagger, holding it behind her

417

back as she rose to her feet. It wouldn't kill him, but it could at least distract him.

"Cato, please. I'll make a deal with you," she begged.

As fast as she could, she whipped Xander's blade toward Cato's shoulder, but he had already started moving.

Time bent, slowed, came to a screaming halt. Cato plunged his dagger into Rainer's chest and she felt it as if it was her own. It wasn't his life that she saw flash before her eyes. It was *their* life.

Rainer's fear and anguish rushed through their bond. He crumpled to his knees, and Cecilia caught him, easing his fall. She tried to summon her healing, but it sputtered.

Rainer's green eyes were wide with shock and fear.

"It's okay," he mumbled.

Even when he was mortally wounded, he wanted to comfort her. Tears burned her eyes as she lowered him to the ground.

"It's not okay. You promised not to leave me. In the forest, you promised," she sobbed.

"Just be with me. Just kiss me one last time. Please," he begged.

His voice was weak, and she hated the sounds coming out of his chest. Cato had hit something—if not everything—important. Despite the immensity of her overwhelming grief, she leaned down and kissed Rainer.

"Please," she begged. She didn't even know what she was asking for. "I love you so much. I just got you. You can't leave yet. Don't go where I can't go, Rainy."

Rainer's smile was pained. "It was worth it. It was worth this little time. It was worth my whole life beside you. I would do it again a hundred more times. I was made to love you." He coughed, blood bubbling on his lips, and she sobbed harder.

Cecilia prayed, silently calling out to her sisters, her father, anyone who would listen. She begged for help but nothing happened. She tried to call on her healing again, but it didn't work.

Xander knelt next to her. He tried his magic, but he was too weak from his wound. There was nothing left for either of them. He backed away to give them space, turning his attention to Cato.

She leaned her forehead against Rainer's. His pain burned through their connection, but even more than that, she felt love—so much love it was overwhelming. Like he was trying to give her enough to last the rest of her life. She brought her hand to her chest as the feeling swelled.

"Do you feel that?" Rainer whispered. "That's what you would have felt all along if I'd let you. That's how much I love you. I don't know how I held it back all the time."

She nodded, kissing him frantically. He was fading.

She shifted, her hand brushing her dagger. Suddenly, she remembered what Clastor said to her in the forest about her dagger—that if she ever found a loss she couldn't live with, she could use her dagger to trade with the person.

"Wait." She pulled it out and leaned in close so only he could hear. "I know you won't want to do this, but Clastor told me a secret about my dagger. It has a spell on it from my mother, Selene. I need you to stab me in the heart. It's the only way I know to save you."

Rainer shook his head. "You'll die."

"I won't. It will hurt, and I'll no longer be immortal, but we'll live. I don't mind giving it up. I never wanted to be a goddess. I only ever wanted you. Please do this one last thing for me. Don't make me live without you. Please, Rain. You said you would do anything I wanted." Her voice was high-pitched and hysterical. She was desperate for him to believe the lie.

He sighed and closed his eyes for a moment. She was afraid he was already gone, but then he opened them. "It's impossible to say no to you. I don't want to hurt you, but if you say so, I'll do it."

"I say so, and we both know I always get what I want," she said.

He would be furious at her for lying, but she didn't care. Rainer was her hard line. Cecilia would stand between him and a violent end one last time. She would straddle the veil between life and death and make sure he ended up on the right side.

Her desperate tears fell into the sand, sprouting little white star flowers all around them.

Cecilia leaned down and kissed him one last time. She tried to press all the sweetness of their whole lives together into that one kiss. She could have kissed him all day and it wouldn't have felt like enough, but they were out of time.

Her whole life had been about exchanges. It was fitting that her death would be one, too. She would exchange her life for Rainer's and it would be the easiest exchange she'd ever made. There was no hesitation in her heart—no doubt of what she'd do. There was only solemn resignation and a hint of fear at the unknown. A hint of grief that Rainer would be alone. And a hint of worry that he'd never forgive himself for what she made him do.

She put the dagger in his hand. "Do it, Rain. You promised you wouldn't leave me. I need you. It will only hurt for a moment. I can take it." She met his eyes, nodding to the green ribbon still tied around her wrist. "Brave with my hand."

"Brave with my heart," he whispered, tears in his eyes.

His normally steady hand shook, but he did it. He pushed the dagger into her chest. It was agony because he was weak, and he had to do it slowly, but mercifully, her mother's spell made it easy work of flesh and bone.

Xander and Cato screamed her name, but it was too late.

Cecilia slowly slumped down next to Rainer, pulling the dagger out. For a moment she stared at the blood pouring from her chest like it wasn't real. Then, she lay on her side looking at him, unsure of what would happen. She slid her hand into his, the same way they had slept next to each other for years.

They were so close together. She tried to memorize every fleck of color in his verdant eyes. The way his dark hair fell across his fore-head, the small scar on his jaw from when he'd first started shaving, the freckle under his left eye.

Suddenly, his body jolted, and a bright golden light surrounded him. It grew blinding, and she had to squint.

When it finally drew back, he sat up tentatively.

"Cece, you did it!" Rainer patted his chest, pulling his shredded shirt to the side to show a golden scar where the blade had entered.

She was so relieved she started to cry all over again as he crawled over to her and kissed her.

Rainer looked down at her chest. "It's not healing. How long will it take to heal?" He looked back at her face and then he knew. "Oh my gods, Cece!" Horror descended on his face at the revelation.

"I'm sorry!" she rasped. "I'm sorry I lied, but if I told you the truth, you never would have done it. I couldn't live in a world without you."

He blinked back tears. "So you'll condemn me to one without you. You'll have me live with the fact that I caused it."

"I'll have you *live*. I'll have you live a long and happy life. I'll rest knowing that I took care of you, and I would do it again. The same way. One hundred more times. I love you so much. Now, do you want to be mad at me, or do you want to kiss me?"

He sighed as he wiped the tears from his eyes and kissed her.

"You are my best friend, my partner, and the love of my life, and you made me kill you before you gave me a chance to ask you to marry me." Rainer looked down at her with equal parts frustration, grief, and love.

"You want to marry me?"

She smiled, but smiling hurt. Everything hurt. Her legs were cold. Her dress was too damp. There was blood everywhere. She was dying.

"I had a ring and everything. Took me long enough, right? I was going to ask tomorrow." His voice cracked, and it broke something open in her.

"Ask now. I think I'd like to spend the rest of my life with you." She smiled through her tears.

He let out a strangled laugh. "Only you would joke right now. I was hoping the rest of your life would be a little longer than a few minutes."

"Ask now," she pleaded.

"Cece, you are the bravest person I've ever met and also the most reckless. Being your best friend has made my life better in so many ways. I know without a doubt that I want to spend the rest of my life making up fairy tales, stealing lemon cakes, and going on adventures with you. I love you so much. Will you marry me?"

"Yes, I'll marry you." She meant it with her whole heart. She smiled, and he kissed her again.

"This is not the proposal I had in mind," he sighed as she winced. "What can I do?"

She grinned at him to hide her pain. "You can finally tell me what you wished for the night we watched the Summer Firestorm meteor shower on our last Gauntlet run."

Rainer looked devastated by the request, fresh tears rising in his eyes. "I can't tell you until it comes true."

"Then hold me one last time and tell me a story. Tell me the story of what our lives together would have been like."

She could feel the way the request broke his heart, but he did it.

He laid down beside her and carefully pulled her into his arms, telling her how they would renovate the cottage and what they would do with their days. He told her how they'd spend time by the sea and while riding and at target practice, and how they'd fall asleep in each other's arms every night, and how he would never wake her up before ten. He told her how they would travel beyond the two kingdoms and explore new lands, watch the summer auroras and the moon rise in the city of Estrellas in Novum, across the sea. How he would cook so she didn't have to. How he would never let her fall asleep without telling her how much he loved her.

It was her favorite story he ever told. She never wanted it to end.

As her soul tried to pull away from her body, she held on. She didn't want to miss any of the story. Rainer watched her face the whole time, as if trying to memorize her every expression.

There was another tug on her soul, and she knew she wouldn't be able to hold on. She wished that she could stay with Rainer. She wished she had a forever to give him, but all she had left was one last breath.

"Rain, if love was enough, I'd stay with you forever." It was barely a whisper, but she knew he heard it by the devastated look on his face.

He whispered that he loved her, but he didn't need to, because she felt it. Then she breathed out, and the world faded away.

42

RAINER

The moment the light went out of Cecilia's eyes, Rainer was instantly less. He felt their connection sever as if he'd been stabbed in the heart all over again.

Some piece of him fled with Cecilia's soul. Part of him had and would always belong to her—the same part he didn't want back, and yet couldn't bear to live without. Had he tithed that to her? Had she given nothing back? Why could he not keep some part of her?

Rainer was gutted—irreparably shattered. He curled around her body, trying to stave off the hollow feeling in his chest.

For the first time since they'd been bonded seventeen years before, he was aware of how much of their connection had been Cecilia. How her chaotic emotions would roll through him in rough waves. How he could always feel her warmth wrapped around his heart. But what really broke him was how much he'd relied on it, taking for granted that she would always be there.

Rainer held Cecilia's body in his arms, painfully aware of the stillness in both of them. They had always been in rhythm with each other, but now his heart beat on alone, a flat melody robbed of its harmony.

There was life before Cecilia, but once they'd met, there was nothing in his world she left untouched.

Rainer remembered his youth so well—how his thoughts slammed together, bouncing around like coins in a jar, his heartbeat a constant drum in his ears, the whole world too loud and chaotic. But the first time her bright blue eyes met his, the frenzied noise eased to a hum, lilting into a song that spun through both their hearts and settled in his blood. It wasn't until she'd snared him in her gaze that he realized the torrent in his mind could be tamed to something so gentle. When she looked at him, he knew for the first time that all would be well.

Just like how he knew now that nothing would.

The whole world tilted—tipped by the imbalance of her sacrifice. If lives had weight then surely hers weighed more than his. He waited for nature to right the wrong, to bring her back. He willed it desperately, and yet the world did not bend to his whims.

The green ribbon, still fastened around her wrist, flapped in the ocean breeze. Rainer wanted to tear it off and toss it into the sea. Its magic was just a spell between the two of them, but it worked too well, gave her too much courage, and he never wanted to see that stupid ribbon again.

He'd been punched, kicked, poisoned, and stabbed in the heart. He'd crawled back from death's doorstep twice, but the agony of this loss was far worse than any of it.

Once Cecilia had become immortal, he'd finally let his guard down. Despite everything, he'd felt relief. He could almost laugh at how foolish he'd been to think that she would be fine.

The smell of lavender and lemons hung around her, the last trace of her essence floating through the air like a cruel taunt.

A void opened up where her love had been wrapped around his heart. It threatened to suck him in. If Grimon was merciful, he would take Rainer too.

He waited for it, begged, but the god of death didn't come for him. He wouldn't. Grimon was as much at the whims of fate as the rest of them.

Cecilia had spoken, and she was used to having the last word.

Rainer felt furious—cheated by the world. How dare the fates steal her away when he finally had her!

How long had he loved her?

It was nearly impossible to remember the exact moment. Between one breath and the next, a spark ignited—his heart burning like a fevered star. His love for her felt ancient, as if born of the last gasping wish of a dying god—a wanting older than earth and story and memory—older than the stardust that made the world. She was a spell cast in his blood—his fairy tale ending. Without her, there was no magic.

When he was eight years old, he met a girl who became a friend, who became a crush, who grew up into the love of his life, and now she was gone.

It was impossible that she wouldn't be there, trying to ease away his worries with a brush of her thumb and a rhyme, whispering secrets to him in her sleep, saying, *"Do you want to be mad, or do you want to kiss me?"*

Gods, he wanted to tell her one more time how much he wanted to kiss her every day, all day. The relentless desire to do so was a constant distraction.

Rainer wanted her beside him, breaking down every reservation he ever felt about being with her until there was no option but to love her openly in the same immensely overpowering way he'd done in private for years.

Suddenly, Xander placed a hand on his shoulder, startling him out of the trance. Rainer sucked in a breath and it was agony to keep breathing when Cecilia wasn't.

"I know," Xander said.

He was the only one who could possibly understand.

It was as if all the light had gone out of the world. The sun could have ceased to shine, and Rainer wouldn't have noticed.

He couldn't see a way forward in the dark. His chest felt caved in. It was a pain he'd never felt before and wouldn't wish on his worst enemy. He wanted to lie down and die beside Cecilia.

He stared at the blood-soaked sand. The white star flowers that sprouted all around her seemed a testament to how hopeless and impossible life without her would be. How could she be so lovely and magical, even in death?

Cato knelt across from him and Xander, looking as stunned as they were.

"Why did she do that?" Cato asked.

"Because she had hope. Because she wanted the one person who wasn't ruined by all of this to survive," Xander answered.

Ruin fell short. There wasn't a word for how the loss broke Rainer.

"She did it because she loved him," Xander said. "It's the one thing you didn't account for in all your planning. You're ancient and wise, but you're also cold. Love is the last wildcard that exists. It is the thing you can't account for, because you don't know what it means to love. You only ever saw it as a weakness because to you, to sacrifice is weak. But it takes courage to love like that, and no one loves harder than Cece." There was a reverence in Xander's voice. He saw her clearly from the beginning, and it wasn't until that moment that Rainer really gave him the credit.

Rainer couldn't have said it better himself. No one loved harder than she did, and now her love was gone.

He wanted to strangle Cato. He reached for Cecilia's Godkiller dagger, but Xander grabbed his wrist before he could grasp it. He gave a gentle shake of his head.

Rainer knew it was the right move. He was too emotional to get a good shot at Cato, but he was so overwhelmed he didn't know what else to do.

He tipped his face up to the sky and let out an agonized scream. Gray clouds blotted out the sun, the whole world gone dark with the final breath of the last living goddess.

43

CECILIA

Death was darkness that pressed in on all sides.

Cecilia could not see Rainer but she felt him still. He was more distant than he'd ever been.

The darkness was suffocating and even though she no longer needed to breathe, it filled her with panic. She stepped forward and it was the strangest sensation of being there and also not. She snapped her fingers, hoping to summon flames in death the way she could in life, but nothing happened.

Bringing her hand out to the side until her fingers met a rough stone wall, she took a tentative step forward. Her footsteps echoed in the space even though she barely felt the ground beneath her. With every step forward her panic grew, but she forced herself to keep moving, one hand scraping along the wall, the other stretched out in front of her as she followed the feeling in her chest.

Cecilia kept moving, not allowing herself to give in to the panic that wanted her to lie down and cry. There was no sound but the percussive beat of her footsteps growing progressively more rapid.

She stumbled as she reached the end of the wall, her fingers flailing through the air. She shuffled to one side and then the other, but passages led both ways. It wasn't a tunnel. It was a maze.

She brought her hand to her chest, trying to tug on the bond that no longer felt solid.

"Please. Please. Please let me find you," she whispered.

The thinnest thread of a connection branched out to her left, as if the severed ends of her heart were reaching to Rainer's.

Cecilia imagined what people would think of her decision. For all her preaching, people would say she was just another woman sacrificing herself for the greater good. But she was done making decisions based on what everyone else expected. Her choice was selfishly motivated because she could not face a world without Rainer.

By either a small miracle or the sheer force of will, the maze grew slightly brighter and a slip of green ribbon appeared on the floor. She bent and picked it up, running the satin through ghostly fingers.

She was immediately reminded of a fairy tale she and Rainer read when they were young. Two children get lost in the woods and leave a trail of breadcrumbs back home. But now, perhaps as a taunt, her connection to Rainer had laid this ribbon out for her.

She followed the ribbon into the dark for what felt like forever and the maze grew progressively brighter. A flickering candle appeared ahead and she drew up short as she took in the shadow behind it.

"Cecilia?"

She came to an abrupt halt as the shadow lifted the candle, illuminating the face of Davide Savero.

Even in the dark he looked ethereal, radiant, and happy. Without the menace in his eyes, he looked so much more like Xander. "Lady Reznik, I'm sorry I was not myself at all our past meetings. I was hoping you could tell my brother that I am here and well. I expect he'll struggle going forward so please remind him: name the fear and you take away its power."

Cecilia nodded solemnly.

"Keep following this path. They're waiting for you."

"Who?" she asked, but Davide had already faded into the shadows.

She took off at a run, gathering the ribbon in swift handfuls until she came to the frayed ends and fatigue hit her hard.

The pull to Rainer was still there, like a path illuminated through a dark forest. She wanted to follow it but she was so very tired.

The smell of smoke and cinnamon filled the air and Grimon stepped out of the darkness beside her, a frown on his face. His pale blue eyes glowed. "I wasn't supposed to see you here for several more centuries, Lady Cece."

"I have to go back. I can't let go," she rasped. "Where are we?"

"You're in between. Not in the Otherworld yet."

Rainer's grief rushed through her chest. She squeezed her eyes closed and curled in on herself.

When she blinked her eyes open, a golden glow filled the air and Clastor appeared.

"Daughter. We had hoped that we wouldn't be seeing you for some time," Clastor sighed.

"I did my best."

She wouldn't take back her trade for anything, but now she doubted herself. "I'm supposed to be with Rainer. Don't take me. Please, if you love me at all. I've never asked for anything. This is the only thing I want. There has to be some way for me to go back."

"You gave it up for him," Clastor said, his face expressionless.

"I did. I would do it again. Rainer is everything. Please let me stay. I never wanted to be a goddess. I didn't mean to be. I only ever wanted to spend my time with him."

Clastor and Grimon were silent.

"Did you know I was going to die?" She looked between them.

"We couldn't be sure," Clastor said solemnly. "The fates only allow us to see possibilities. You were a moving target. Your emotional nature makes you a hard read. The only consistency in your life, the only steadiness—"

"Was Rainer," she finished. "That's why you all pushed me toward Rainer."

"We wanted you to live," Grimon said.

She locked eyes with Clastor. "You must have known when you told me about the spell on that dagger."

"I knew it was a possibility," Clastor confirmed.

"But you told me, anyway."

"I did," he said. "You have free will, Cecilia. We hoped you would choose to live. But I knew what it was like to live without your mother. I wanted to save you the suffering I felt when Selene passed."

Cecilia felt like she was drifting apart, growing fuzzy at the edges, the path back to Rainer growing fainter.

"I'm terrified I'll never see him again. I don't want to leave him. I love him. I wish I could stay. I don't want to go where he can't go. I want to go back."

Clastor frowned, then sighed in resignation. "Rainer is a good choice. Your soul bond can send you back to him."

"How?" Cecilia gasped.

"The spell your mother put on that dagger. It only works because of what you two have. I can only do this because you gave up your life for him—because your sacrifice was unselfish. You did it without knowing there would be a way back. You are the compassionate daughter your mother and I hoped you would be," Clastor said. "Your humanity is your strength."

Cecilia nodded.

"There are two things that you should understand before you go back," Grimon said. "The first is that it will be painful both physically, mentally, and emotionally. No one returns without a bit of darkness. Something must die off for you to be reborn, so understand that you will not be the same."

Clastor shifted, swallowing thickly. "The second is that you'll never ascend. You'll never join your true family in the Otherworld. You'll live a mortal life. You'll still be a witch and you may have some residual goddess power, but you will essentially be mortal. You'll go to the same afterlife as mortals and that spell on your dagger was a one-time thing," Clastor said. "You'll have a second chance, but not a third."

It wasn't even a choice. There was only one place she belonged, but she felt her connection fading the longer she stayed. A persistent magnetism drew her deeper into the dark.

"Please," she begged. "I have never asked you for anything. Considering you've been absent most of my life, this is the least you can do. I want to be with him. I hope you're not disappointed."

Clastor smiled. "I'm actually very proud, and I understand your choice. If I could have gone with your mother, I would have. I think she'd be very proud. I have watched you suffer and sacrifice a great deal to keep those you love safe. I've watched you go way out of your comfort zone to embrace power you never wanted and then use it to help people. I could never be disappointed. It's an honor to be your father. I'll be watching over you. Live well. Remember what we told you. You still have work to do. Grim will shepherd you back."

"Wait!" Cecilia said. "Will this undo my exchange?"

Clastor shook his head. "It wasn't my magic that created the Gauntlet. It was the witches of Olney that bound your power in those caves. They would be the only ones to know if or how such an exchange could be undone."

Cecilia tried not to look ungrateful, even if she wanted to argue that she'd had no real choice in making the exchange. Instead she threw her arms around her father. She'd never seen any of the gods hug, but he held her for a moment before nudging her toward Grimon.

The path before her grew brighter.

"Good luck, Lady Cece. Use this second chance wisely," Grimon whispered.

Suddenly, she felt herself falling, a dizzy stomach-sailing drop. She couldn't see Grimon, but she smelled cinnamon and ash.

Pain was the first thing she was aware of. Then it was the only thing she was aware of. Everything hurt in a bright, blistering fever of pain that burned through her.

The closer she got to her body, the more she could feel the injury, but she pressed on. She wondered if she'd made a mistake; she wasn't sure she'd ever felt such agony. For a few endless minutes there was nothing but the savage ache in her chest.

Cecilia pushed through the pain because the closer she got, the more she could feel the connection to Rainer.

There was an abrupt jolt as she slammed into her body.

A golden glow swelled behind her heavy eyelids. Muffled voices spoke, but she couldn't make out words. The glow grew brighter and brighter. She felt like her whole body was full of sunlight and warmth. The emptiness in her ribs filled up, the pain subsided to a dull ache, and after a few long moments, the glow faded.

"Cece? Can you hear me?"

She smiled at the sound of Rainer's worried voice. Slowly she blinked her eyes open and looked up to see three pairs of concerned eyes—one set green, one set hazel, and one set gray.

"Hey," she said.

"Hey?" Rainer choked out a laugh, rubbing the salty crust of tears on his cheeks like he couldn't believe his eyes.

She reached up and ran her thumb over the crease in his brow. "I found a worry, but I'll fix it in a hurry."

Rainer's grin grew wide.

"Say you're not mad now," she said.

"I'm a little mad, but mostly I just am so happy you're here," Rainer rasped.

She turned her gaze to Xander, who looked glassy-eyed and stunned.

"This is impossible," Cato said. He knelt on the other side of her body. "That was a Godkiller dagger with a soul-exchange spell. You exchanged your life for his. You shouldn't be here. It's impossible."

Cecilia's fingers grazed her dagger on the ground next to her as she grinned at the trickster god.

She once told Cato that she preferred love over power. For months she thought she'd been a fool to choose love as she watched everyone around her suffer. As Cato slowly ripped her world apart. As he introduced her to unimaginable horrors. But through every trial and every grief, love had been the blinding light that guided her through. It was the thing that tore her open and destroyed her, but it had also been the thing that stitched her back together.

She realized that love was a power of its own. The power to heal, or the power to destroy. The power to free or to chain. The power to crawl back from death because of a tether that connects to an earth-bound soul.

It all came back to love. The love of a father who wouldn't let his wild little huntress be tamed. The love of a guardian who protected his memory witch and reminded her of her courage to walk into the dark alone. The love of a prince who inspired her to define her own path instead of letting others decide for her. The love of a family of eccentric gods who gave her the support of a millennium of wisdom and the confidence to know that she would figure it out for herself.

She knew then she'd never underestimate love again. Love made her weak, but it took courage to face it. Love made her foolish, but it took wisdom to risk it. Love made her do reckless things she hadn't thought herself capable of, but it also brought her back to life.

And the greatest surprise of all was that the entire time Cato thought he was doing everything for power, when really he was also doing it for love, even if to him love was a hollow god's impersonation of real human love. Perhaps it was the best he could do. Perhaps some wounded part of him had made him bitter in his very long life.

"This is *impossible*," Cato repeated.

Remember. Her magic had always been about remembering. Now she remembered with new clarity what she'd learned from her sisters.

Cecilia's fingers gripped the dagger as their words flooded her mind.

"Remember that when Cato looks at you and sees a weakness, he'll exploit it. There is wisdom in hiding your strength until you need it. Pick your moment," Desiree had said.

"Which side of you do you think Cato is most likely to underestimate?" Sayla had asked.

"The human side," Cecilia had replied.

"In chess, when is your opponent most vulnerable?" Aelish had asked.

When they think they've won.

"A goddess can make her own fate," Adira had said.

Yes, she could. Yes, she would.

"A goddess with a soul bond, Cato," Cecilia said. "You always forget to account for love because you don't know what it means. Love means shifting fate, pushing its boundaries. Going beyond what seems possible because you would do anything if it means another moment with the person you love. I came back because I had something to hold on to. *This* is what love does."

Recognition washed over Cato's face.

Cecilia shot up and swung her right hand around. She plunged her Godkiller dagger into Cato's heart.

His eyes went wide in shock.

"I wish I could kill you over and over for all the pain you have caused me and the people I love. Enjoy your afterlife, Cato." She meant every word.

Now she knew for sure. It wasn't the mind-bending goddess, the lovesick princess, the powerful memory witch, or the talented huntress who killed the last living god. No, Cato forgot who she was first. Before she was any of those things, she was a girl who loved. She'd been raised by mortals, with love and compassion and warmth. The very things that Cato had seen as weaknesses were what made her strong enough to defeat him.

The trickster god collapsed and let out a strangled laugh. He narrowed his glowing gray eyes at her. "Do you think he could ever really love the girl you are now, Cecilia? A girl who's broken and crawled back from death. No one comes back the same, and one victory won't erase what you've lost."

Cecilia tried to ignore the way the words lanced her heart. Cato had such a dark gift for understanding exactly how to hit someone in their weak spots.

Cato's eyes locked with Xander's. "This is only the beginning. You all think killing me will be enough to bring peace, but I've already started moving pieces around the board. You have no idea the storm that's coming for you. Vincent Savero is just the beginning. Two brand new monarchs, both young and inexperienced. You have no idea the chaos that waits for you without me to hold it at bay." A laugh sputtered out of him.

Xander bristled at Vincent's name.

Cato's breath grew labored. "I always have contingency plans," he wheezed. "I've had hundreds of years to think this through. You won't be able to stop what I've set in motion."

He sucked in one last ragged breath and then the light in his eyes went out.

The last living god was dead, slain by a woman in love. Not a goddess, or a witch, or a huntress, or a princess. A mortal woman.

She turned back to Xander and Rainer. Xander looked like he wanted to hug her, but he sat back and Rainer practically tackled her.

He hugged her close and covered her face with kisses. "How are you here, Cece? How did you come back? You were gone. I felt the moment you were gone."

She pulled back and looked at him. She brought her hand to his heart and his hand to hers. "Because of this. Because you were the tether to bring me back. Because I sacrificed for you. I couldn't have come back for anyone else. That's what Clastor meant. Just you. I couldn't let you go. Not even death could take me away from you. That's how much I love you."

"I'm never going to be able to outdo that." Rainer laughed through the tears in his eyes.

"No, but at least now you have a lifetime to try."

He didn't wait for her to say anything else. He kissed her like he thought he might never get to do it again. Like she sacrificed herself for him.

Finally, she pulled away and turned to Xander.

"Are you well, Your Majesty?" she asked.

He grinned. "How can you make something so stuffy sound so sexy?"

Cecilia laughed and hugged him. "Never change."

"I'm glad you're okay," he murmured. "I'm so sorry. I should have stopped you from healing me. I should have known what he was going to do. I've spent enough time with him." He looked at her with glassy eyes.

She wrapped her arms around the king of Argaria. "None of us could have seen that coming. Don't blame yourself, Xan. You know that no matter what, I couldn't have let you die like that. I am so glad you are okay. I'm so happy to have you back."

He held her close and tucked his face into her neck as he'd done so many times before.

She brought a hand to his cheek. "I saw Davide when I was gone."

Xander pulled back to meet her gaze, his eyes full of grief.

"He said to tell you he was well and that you should name the fear to take away its power," Cecilia rasped.

Xander swallowed hard. "Thank you for that."

"It's good advice."

"I suppose it is," he croaked.

Pounding footsteps startled them both. They turned as Evan drew up beside them and took in the blood-soaked ground and the dead trickster god.

She turned back and ran her fingers through Xander's hair. "We will talk, my love, I promise, but right now I need to go home and get out of this bloody dress and rest, because I am exhausted. It turns out dying really takes a lot out of you."

Xander nodded as Evan helped him to his feet.

Cecilia tried to stand, but Rainer swept her up into his arms.

"Rain, I can walk."

"I am not letting you go, and that is not up for negotiation."

So she let him. Not because she couldn't do it herself, but because she didn't mind letting him take care of her.

44

CECILIA

Back in the cottage, Rainer pumped water into the bath as Cecilia sat on the edge of the tub.

Fatigue made her eyelids impossibly heavy as Rainer helped her up. He peeled the blood-soaked clothes from her skin and gasped.

"I know they're nice but you've seen them before," she teased, gesturing to her breasts.

He brushed his finger over her sternum and she shivered. A golden scar marked her chest where the blade had entered, a mirror of Rainer's, as if whatever spell had been cast on her dagger left a mark in healing to remind of what they'd survived. A constant reminder of what wasn't strong enough to break either of them. A constant reminder of her fearless sacrifice and his immense love for her. He climbed into the tub with her and helped her bathe and wash her hair.

Cecilia forgot what it was like to be in a fully mortal body. Everything hurt, and she felt so weak. The hum of power under her skin was gone, but she didn't miss it. Its absence meant she could feel the rhythmic beat of her heart, the heart that by some miracle beat on.

Finally, Rainer helped her dry off and led her to bed. He couldn't stop touching her or kissing her, and every time he pulled away, she pulled him back. He was tentative at first, afraid he would hurt her, but finally she pulled him close and kissed him like she had crawled back from death to do just that. His body jolted as if she'd shocked him, and he finally trusted that she could handle the power of his affection.

Rainer spent an eternity kissing and caressing her golden scar until she begged him for more. He kissed down her body, trying to cover every inch of her skin, peeking up at her to make sure she was still with him as he teased gasps and moans from her.

It wasn't their first time, but it was their first time with her being mortal, and he was so gentle. When she was a goddess, she'd felt so powerful in everything she did, thanks to her heightened senses. Now everything felt new again.

As Rainer kissed her inner thighs, she was aware of how powerful she felt being with him, even fully human. Not like a goddess, but like a woman in love. That was all she'd really wanted to begin with.

His lips and his hands were everywhere. When he brought his mouth down on her, her back arched and her pulse thundered. Every nerve in her body fired at once and she could barely breathe. He took his time with her, moving torturously slowly and making her feel each kiss, each swipe of his tongue, all the way down to her toes. The way he knew exactly what she needed was equal parts unnerving and wonderful. A delicious tension built inside her and she fell over the edge, her whole body vibrating with satisfaction.

Rainer took his time kissing his way back up her body, whispering "I love you" against the golden scar on her chest. She pulled him close, and he kissed her, a soft, slow kiss, like he was trying to bring her back to life.

Just like always, when he moved inside her, they both felt like they were full of starlight. Their connection was wide open and stronger than ever before, and it made everything much more potent. It astonished her how much they could feel from the other. What was once just a hint of emotion was now completely laid bare, and it was raw and powerful.

It was sweet and desperate and full of relief. And just like always, it felt like magic. He couldn't stop touching her, and she kissed him like she wanted to make sure she wasn't dreaming. She rained kisses all over his face and didn't let him go until their skin cooled and heartbeats slowed.

They fell asleep tucked chest to chest. Their scars lined up, perfectly in sync, just like the beating of their hearts and the rhythm of their breath. She got the best sleep of her life, knowing that they'd come home to each other, and that even though they took the long way, it was worth it.

———

Cecilia woke up with a sense of peace she had never known in her life. Fire burned bright in the hearth, but Rainer's spot beside her was cool.

The restless, searching part of her that had always felt unsettled was gone. There was nothing that needed doing. No war that needed fighting. No magic that needed tending. The only thing that she needed to do was lay in bed and rest, and that was the best feeling in the world.

Eventually, the weight of the grief and loss and darkness Grimon had warned her about would catch up with her. Eventually, they would need to venture out and explain what happened. Eventually, they would have to see to the tenuous peace between the two kingdoms. Teach and work and live—but for now, it was just the two of them.

They deserved to be happy and enjoy a hard-fought victory. The darkness that still lived in her beckoned, but she shoved it down. She needed a reprieve, however temporary.

She watched Rainer make her breakfast and felt like she might burst. He turned to look at her.

He grinned. "You aren't supposed to be awake yet. It's too early."

His hair was still mussed from bed and his pants hung low on his hips. He'd never looked so handsome and relaxed.

"Stop thinking whatever you're thinking or I'm going to come back to bed and your breakfast is going to burn."

She giggled, sitting up as he brought her a cup of tea.

They ate eggs and toast in silence and Cecilia caught Rainer studying her like he couldn't believe she was really there.

"I won't disappear if you stop looking at me, Rain. I'm really here, and I'm not going anywhere."

"I know you don't understand. I watched you die in my arms. I felt your last breath. You were *gone*. For a few minutes. It was the worst few minutes of my life. I felt the connection sever, and I felt like I died, too. I know you're here now, but that happened, and it was horrible. You're going to have to forgive me for feeling overwhelmed. You literally came back to life. I see you in front of me, but it's hard to believe with the worst thing that's ever happened to me so fresh in my mind."

"Oh Rain. I'm sorry. I didn't think about it," she said. She pulled him into a tight hug and ran her hand through his hair.

He relaxed into her. "I think you're stuck with me. It's going to be a while before I finally let you out of my sight. Do you feel okay?"

His fingers moved lazily along the skin of her waist, and it distracted her from the question. She closed her eyes, enjoying the sensation. When she opened them, he was smiling at her.

"What?"

"How are you feeling?"

"Fine. I'm just a little tired. That could be from the crawling back from death thing, or it could be from the fact that you kept waking me up to make sure I was breathing," she teased, kissing the tip of his nose.

He stood and disappeared into the closet. He emerged a moment later and knelt in front of her.

A lump formed in her throat and she blinked away tears.

"I really wanted to surprise you, but you had to ruin it yesterday by dying, so I figure I will just ask now. I know it's soon, but I figure I've already wasted enough of both of our time pretending I didn't want this. Say yes. Say you'll spend the rest of your life spinning stories with me—"

She dropped to her knees and kissed him.

"Yes," she rasped when she finally pulled away. "Of course I'll marry you."

Shocked recognition shot through her as he slid the ring onto her finger.

"Rain, this is my mother's ring. How did you get this?"

Rainer sat back on his heels. "After we got back from our trip, the huntmaster dragged me from my sickbed in the healer's clinic and gave me a talking-to—said I really screwed this one up and he didn't pull for me my whole life so that I could let you get away. He told me he knew it didn't look good for me but that if I—" His voice broke, his eyes going glassy and far away.

Cecilia knew he loved her father as much as she did. Leo's absence was a void in both their lives.

Rainer took a shaky breath. "He said that if I fought for you my whole life and stopped now that I wasn't the man he thought I was and that I should be used to how stubborn you are, and I would just have to find a way to be more stubborn. He said many people had let you down, me and him included, and that I needed to make sure not to keep doing it. He said you were a force of nature and if I wasn't ready to fight for you, that I didn't deserve you. And then he said that you always made your own decisions and who you wanted to be with was no exception, but that nothing would make him happier than us being together. He gave me that ring because I think he knew I would finally get around to asking you. I think he knew he might not make it out of this unscathed and he wanted me to know that I had his blessing. I think he'd want you to know, too."

Cecilia lost it. She threw herself into Rainer's arms and cried for the only father she'd really, truly known—the one who had raised her like his own. He'd let her make her own choices in a world that was constantly trying to take them from her. He didn't care that she was a goddess. When he'd looked at her, he saw his little girl.

She held onto Rainer—the only person who could understand or share her grief because he felt it too. He rocked her against his chest and smoothed her hair. The words burned her. She wished her father was there to see how far they'd come.

"He was always so proud of you, Cece. I wish he was here to see us now."

"You know, he knew you slept here every night."

Rainer paled. "Seriously?"

"He was the huntmaster. It was silly of us to think that we could pull one over on him. He trusted me and he loved you, Rain. You were like the son he never had. When we first got back and I spoke to him alone, he told me he thought it would be you and me. He was really thrown off by Xander. I think he was less offended by the fact that he was a prince of Argaria than he was that he wasn't you. He offered to get me out of it—to petition the king to say that I got married under duress. I just couldn't do it. I loved Xander, and I didn't want to break a promise I made. He raised me to be a woman of my word. I think at that moment he was a little mad at himself for doing that," she laughed.

"I wish I knew he knew the whole time. I could have slept in a bit," Rainer said.

She looked down at the ring on her finger, grief threatening to pull her under. Before that darkness could run away with her, Rainer pulled her into a kiss and the whole chaotic world narrowed to just the two of them.

45

CECILIA

Loud pounding on the cottage door roused Cecilia from heavy sleep. She groaned, snuggling into Rainer's chest.

"Cecilia Reznik, you better open this door right now or I will break it down." Sylvie's voice cut through the cottage and she resumed rattling the door.

Rainer kissed the top of Cecilia's head before rolling over and pulling on some clothes. "Get dressed so I can let her in."

Cecilia groaned, stretching her arms. Her body was pleasantly sore from a full day in bed and, though some of the fatigue of her ordeal remained, she found the ache a pleasant reminder of what it felt like to be human.

She pulled on a simple green cotton dress and wrangled her bed-ruffled hair into a braid.

Rainer threw open the door and Sylvie stormed into the room, practically tackling Cecilia into the bed.

"Take it easy, Sylvie. I'm not a goddess anymore and I've already died once this week," Cecilia said.

Sylvie's pale blue eyes were swollen and rimmed in red and her usually immaculate hair was coming loose from her updo. "I cannot believe you did something so reckless. I am so mad at you." She hugged Cecilia tight. "And also I'm so glad you're okay. When Xander told us, Evan and Cal had to hold me back from breaking down the cottage door to see you."

Cecilia brushed away Sylvie's tears, casting a glance over her friend's shoulder. Cal gave her a sheepish smile. "Sorry, Rez, we tried to give you both some time to rest."

Sylvie pulled back, searching Cecilia's face like she was looking for any change in her. Cecilia worried what she would see—that Cecilia had died and come back, bringing some new grief with her, or perhaps she'd left some part of herself behind in the dark.

Sylvie took her hands. Her fingers brushed over the engagement ring and she screamed. "Holy Clastor! You're engaged? To Rainer?"

Rainer nodded, and Cecilia grinned.

"Finally! Cal, you owe me a week's worth of raspberry tarts," Sylvie said, casting a smug smile over her shoulder.

Cal rolled his eyes. "Great, I'll never hear the end of it. I said it would take another month or two, but suddenly Rainer was in a rush."

"Gods, it only took you two your whole damn lives!" Sylvie said. "I told you, Cece! I told you at the Godsball that you didn't know your own heart and I was right."

"No, she always knew it. I was the idiot," Rainer laughed.

Sylvie jumped up and down, gleefully clapping her hands. "Rainer McKay, what did I say to you when you and I danced at the Godsball?"

Rainer shrugged sheepishly. "You said I was a fool."

"Other than that," Sylvie laughed.

"You said 'Rainer, you may be handsome but you're also a fool. You need to get it together and marry that girl before you lose her. She may not know how you feel, but I'm not blind. Now go kiss her and stop messing around.' That's what you said, Sylvie."

"And did you do that?" Sylvie asked sternly.

"No, I continued to be very dumb. But I can do it now." Rainer smirked. He leaned down and kissed Cecilia, long and slow, like they were alone and not standing in front of two gawking friends. When he stopped, she was flushed and breathless.

"I guess this will be a regular thing now," Sylvie said. "Too bad we won't be around to tease you."

Cecilia frowned. "Not around? What do you mean?" She looked to the door. "Where's Evan? I thought he'd be with you."

Sylvie and Cal locked eyes for a moment, some silent message passing between them.

"Why don't we go for a walk on the beach?" Sylvie suggested.

Cecilia took her arm, letting Sylvie lead her out into the cool autumn sunlight.

"What's going on?" Cecilia asked as they descended the trail.

Tiny pebbles mixed into the sand crunched under her feet as she navigated the steepest part of the trail, the sand growing warmer as they stepped onto the unshaded beach.

She watched Sylvie out of the corner of her eye. Her friend, normally so put together, looked completely shaken.

"Evan and Xander left this morning," she said.

Cecilia drew up short. "What?"

"Apparently, there are some disturbances along Argaria's borders, and with the army in ruins from Cato, they needed to get back as soon as possible. So they sent me and Cal to—" She dragged a slippered toe through the sand.

"To what?" Cecilia asked, crossing her arms.

"To collect what remains of Xander's things at your cottage and bring them to Argaria," Sylvie said.

Cecilia stared at her slack-jawed as realization dawned. "You're leaving."

Sylvie wrung her hands in her lilac dress. "Princes—*Kings* Marcos and Xander have asked me and Cal to act as Olney ambassadors to Argaria while we try to grow this new alliance. Evan thought he could use some help wrangling the Argarian court and Xander."

Cecilia arched a brow. "Oh? Did Evan think that?"

Sylvie's cheeks pinked. "Yes."

"And that's the only reason you're going? Strictly business?"

Sylvie waved a hand. "Strictly the business of keeping the upper hand and reminding him what he's missing."

Cecilia laughed and squeezed Sylvie's arm. "Who better to keep the peace than the woman who's had half of Olney court wrapped around her finger for years?"

Sylvie laughed. "I know. It's good to have my talents recognized." Her face grew serious. "This is the start, Cece. This is exactly what we talked about—giving women in this kingdom more options. I have an opportunity now because you put yourself out there. We can continue to grow this together."

Cecilia hugged her friend. Maybe Sylvie was right, and this was just the beginning. She liked the thought of the two of them working to make things better from opposite ends of the two kingdoms.

Cecilia shivered, looking out at the sea as the salty spray from the waves ghosted over her skin. "I'm happy for you, but a bit sad for me. I'm going to miss you." She choked back a sob.

"You'll miss me that much or you're hurt because he left without saying goodbye?"

Cecilia looked away, wiping the tears from her cheeks. Sylvie was so good at cutting to the heart of the matter. "He doesn't owe me anything, but I do worry about him after everything." She shook her head. "I will pack up his things, and I have something for you to deliver to him if you don't mind."

A quick shock of love passed through the bond in her heart. Clearly she was passing off too much of her grief to Rainer. He tugged on the bond, but she sent back a feeling of calm.

Sylvie nodded. "Of course."

"Before you and Cal leave, we should all have dinner at the house with Aunt Clara."

"I'd love that."

They turned and started back toward the cottage. Rainer and Cal were waiting for them outside.

The moment Rainer saw Cecilia, the tension in his shoulders relaxed. He swept her into his arms and planted a scorching kiss on her lips that she felt all the way down to her toes. When he finally put her down, Cal and Sylvie were laughing.

"Okay, if I knew you two were going to be this over the top, I would have never suggested you get together." Sylvie's tone was sarcastic, but her smile was sincere. "We'll see you tomorrow for dinner."

Cecilia nodded, and Cal and Sylvie turned and headed back toward town.

"Are you okay?" Rainer asked. "I felt your grief."

"I was surprised that Sylvie is leaving, that's all. I just feel a little raw."

Cecilia shut the connection between them and forced a smile. She didn't want to seem ungrateful. She thought when she came back mortal that she'd be free of the heaviness that inhabited her since the Cave of Longings, but it seemed to have grown and taken up permanent residence in her chest. She was afraid Rainer would feel that darkness pressed up against the light that he brought to her connection.

She'd read so many fairy tales, and when she read about happily ever afters, she'd never imagined them as an exchange, but that was what they were. She'd exchanged loss and grief, loved ones, parts of herself, parts of her friends, all for this happy ending.

She was grateful to be alive. All she'd wanted the moment she was gone was to be back with Rainer. She didn't understand why it felt so difficult to be the same happy woman she'd been before.

Rainer wrapped an arm around her waist and she leaned into his warmth, allowing it to block out the cold creeping into her bones.

Freedom had cost her her father, her sense of self, her marriage, and her life, but she finally had it. If she wanted to get free of everything that haunted her, she would have to fight for it.

Olney and Argaria had been at war for years, and now with two new kings, they had their first opportunity for peace. If Cecilia had learned anything from their adventures, it was that people hated change almost as much as they hated war.

The fight to establish and keep peace between the two kingdoms and fend off attacks from outside kingdoms would be a new challenge for all of them. Even after Cato's death, his threat loomed over all of them. They didn't know yet what sort of trouble they were facing, but she knew that if Cato had helped design it, it would be brutal.

One war was ending, but a whole new one stretched out in front of them. One they were far less qualified to resolve. Hope had seen them through everything they'd encountered so far. They would need it to see them through whatever was to come. They'd all made so many mistakes. She prayed they'd have a chance to make many more.

AFTER

Rainer

Rainer ducked out the bakery door, clutching a paper bag full of fresh lemon cakes as he squinted into the morning sun. A horse-drawn cart bustled by, kicking up a cloud of dust. When it cleared, he finally laid eyes on Cecilia. She stood in the shade of the building next door, a tight smile on her face as two little girls approached her with flower crowns.

"Thank you, Goddess," they said, touching their fingers to their foreheads and lips and hearts in a sign of reverence.

Cecilia blushed fiercely, darting a nervous look at Rainer as she stacked the flowers on her head. She hated the attention, and he understood. People meant well, but she didn't want to be reminded of what she'd done for Olney, or what it had cost her.

Two weeks had passed, but the restlessness in her had not settled and Rainer couldn't blame her. They were thanking her for dying. The memory shuddered through him. He was as desperate to rid himself of it as he was to never forget for one moment that Cecilia loved him enough to die for him.

But now he worried that she didn't love him enough to live for him and that thought terrified him. Each day, the city bloomed back to life, but she seemed to wither. Her smiles were more forced and she didn't want to go to town and be thanked for her service. She wanted to rest. Her melancholy broke through their bond and flashed in her eyes.

The little girls looked up at him with wide eyes. He bowed to them. "Ladies, I hope you'll let me steal her."

They nodded, giggling as they scampered away.

He curled an arm around Cecilia's waist, ushering her away from the crush of town.

"Sorry," he said, handing her the bag of lemon cakes. "It took longer than I expected. I know you don't like coming to town on market day."

She took a bite of cake, then another, and another, until her mouth was too full to speak. As they wandered away from town, the tension bled out of her shoulders and she finally leaned into him.

She only admitted that anything was wrong when she was asleep, murmuring feverish, tear-stained whispers into his chest in the darkest hour of the night. Each night he had to keep himself from shaking her awake and asking questions. He didn't want to push her. He'd learned that lesson the hard way already.

He would be there to listen when she needed, and would love her in the meantime.

Everywhere they went, people bowed their heads and whispered. "Soul bond" and "star-crossed" were often the only words that Rainer could make out, but it was always the same.

Only people who weren't on the beach that day could look at the two of them and see the dream without knowing what it was like to survive the nightmare.

The people of Olney spoke about their love story with stars in their eyes. Rainer and Cecilia had been just as starry-eyed before their last Gauntlet run. The truth of living through it was that it felt unresolved, as if it was still going on.

Happily ever after wasn't a fixed target. It was really just a new once upon a time, and it was his job to try to make their next story a much happier one.

————

Xander

For twenty-seven years Xander had prided himself on being a great fighter. He'd earned the right to brag. He was one of the most lethal hunters in the Olney army and that was a right worth bragging about.

It was especially bitter medicine to take that he'd lost the only battle that ever really mattered to him: the fight for the woman he loved.

The Argarian throne room was as silent as a temple. He hated the place with its tall, whitewashed walls and stained-glass windows. He hated the throne with its white marble sculpting—cold and hard like the rest of the mountaintop capital of Ardenis. Most of all, he hated the painting, still wrapped in brown paper and sitting on the throne beside him. He knew what was hidden inside.

Cece could not just let him go and tend to his broken heart. She had to send her favorite and most precious painting with him.

He pressed his fingers to the new scar over his heart. He could not seem to stop the impulse to check that it was still there. The scar reminded him that it wasn't all a dream—that he was really still here, even if he felt half gone. It felt as if he'd stolen his life back from death's clutches but he could no longer find the path forward to live.

Cato had taken the fight right out of him. How was Xander supposed to save a kingdom when he couldn't even save himself? He should have been worried about saving Argaria but he was focused on all he'd lost.

The whispers had already begun to spread through the court like wildfire.

"Xander Savero is a bastard."

"He's more Olney than Argarian."

"He's unfit to rule."

Xander was inclined to agree with them. He hadn't the slightest idea how to be a king, but if Cato's threats were true, he couldn't leave his kingdom in the hands of his vicious cousin Vincent.

He couldn't opt out. Just like Cece hadn't been able to opt out of saving them all from Cato.

Evan reminded him of that daily, very effective at ruling him with guilt. It was almost as good as having his family. Almost.

Xander was a king. That responsibility should have scared him to death, but he'd lived through a worse nightmare than he could have ever imagined—watching the love of his life die to save someone else who she loved more.

The only comfort he could take, if there was any to be had, was that she'd saved Xander and then Rainer. If it had happened in the opposite order, she wouldn't have been able to come back from the other side.

The truth was that he only had himself to blame. He knew what a mistake he'd made outside the Cave of Longings when Cece didn't kill him. He knew when she let him sit up and kiss her that he'd made the wrong choice. He knew she would love him anyway but he hadn't had the faith in her or himself to believe it.

Cato had blown Xander's life apart and turned it into a barren wasteland devoid of love and family.

The ghosts that haunted his life now weren't of those he'd loved and lost; they were the ghosts of all the lives he could have lived if he'd made one specific, different choice. He didn't know if it made him shallow to have lost his whole family and still be focused on the one person left living, but he didn't care. Cece was the only thing he ever truly wanted for himself.

Xander never wanted to be king. He never wanted to be wealthy. He never wanted people looking to him like he had all the answers. Now he had all three.

The throne room door groaned open and Evan stepped inside. "This is the last place I expected to find you."

Xander shrugged. "It's a quiet place to think."

"There's been an attack on our eastern border. They were flying your cousin Vincent's banner. It's possible some of the hunters who fled the battle in Olney defected to Alandane, where Vincent's army sits."

Xander sighed heavily. He leaned his head back against the cool stone throne and squeezed his eyes shut.

"I can send out a battalion," Evan said.

"No, I won't have someone else lead my army. The people need to see that their king is willing to fight for them. They've been through enough. I'm not going to ask my army to do anything I'm not also willing to do myself."

"You sure it's not just that you're a self-sacrificing bastard?"

Bastard. The word hit him like a blow. Evan had been so careful to never say it to him even in jest. Clearly he'd saved the first occasion for a moment when he wanted Xander riled up.

He gritted his teeth. "I'm sure."

Evan nodded in approval. "Good, I'll have them prepare your horse. Anything else you need? Perhaps you'd like to write to Cece, just in case."

Xander gave him a warning look. Evan had watched him wallow their whole way back to Argaria, and all but begged him to reach out to Cece for comfort. He thought she was a calming influence on Xander. Xander couldn't argue with that but he had no idea how to be just friends with the woman who'd thoroughly wrecked him. He would have loved to talk to her, but the thought of disturbing the peace she deserved stopped him from reaching out every time. He thought he would have a lifetime to make things up to Cece but he had no time at all. The least he could do was let her be happy.

He'd hurt her enough, and she'd still saved him, and she didn't owe him anything. He would take care of this on his own. He'd been alone most of his life. It was familiar territory.

Xander had only been back in the kingdom for a week and it was already starting. He'd always been an amazing fighter but he had seen enough battle for a lifetime. It figured that at the moment he most wanted to set down his blade and be done, the fight was at his doorstep.

The Adventure Continues in...

THE ST⚡RM KING

On a cold winter day, high in the mountains, a baby was born in the heart of a storm...

Xander Savero is reeling from the loss of his family and the love of his life. But there's no time for his broken heart when his kingdom is in peril. His cruel cousin is chipping away at Argaria's borders, leaving a trail of violence in his wake, and that's just the beginning.

The fiercest opposition comes from within Xander's own court, where nobles speculate about his parentage, commoners think he's an outsider, and assassins wait poised for the moment he drops his guard. Xander strives to put an end to the upheaval by marrying a princess from a stronger, more established kingdom. His decision plunges the Argarian court into a chaotic three-week festival, at the end of which he will choose a bride.

But more new faces at court mean more threats to Xander's life, compelling him to call in reinforcements from old friends. Cecilia's arrival is more hindrance than help, putting him face to face with the woman who shattered his heart, while he's still picking up the pieces. Together, Xander, Cecilia, and their friends must fight against a series of ancient spells, a spy in their midst, and their own haunted pasts to take down their faceless enemy before Xander and the kingdom both fall.

This exciting next installment features the same three POVs and a new one.

Buy it now:
https://www.amazon.com/gp/product/B0CS7G5XLN

Thank you for reading

THE MEMORY CURSE

Did you like it? Love it?
Read it under duress because you lost a bet
with a friend?

✦ ✦ ✦ ✦ ✦ ✦ ✦ ✦ ✦ ✦ ✦ ✦ ✦

However you feel about it, I would be so grateful if you would **REVIEW** it on Amazon.

Reviews help indie authors like myself reach new readers and they help readers determine if this book is for them.

Please take a moment to write a short review.

THANK YOU!

Scan the code to review

✦ ✦ ✦ ✦ ✦ ✦ ✦ ✦ ✦ ✦ ✦ ✦ ✦

You can also get a BONUS CHAPTER featuring Evan and Sylvie's meet cute by following this link:

https://starsagespirit.ck.page/tmcbonus

or scanning this code

ACKNOWLEDGMENTS

Here I am, yet again, writing an acknowledgments section and getting super emotional. When THE LOST GOD came out I had no idea what to expect. The love and support I've received since release have blown me away.

When I set out to write THE LOST GOD series, I wanted to write two equally compelling love stories. The great joy and grief of writing a love triangle is that, as the writer, you know from the start that one of those love stories is temporary. I broke my own heart writing this series a few times, the first of which was in this book. I really wanted to honor the short and sweet romances that stay with us, as much as the deeply-rooted long-standing ones. I did my best to do both justice and, if you bear with me, I swear I have every intention of helping as many characters as possible find their happily ever afters.

Once again, the first thanks go to Tanya. You were the earliest cheerleader for this series and pushed me to go for it during a very tumultuous time. You have continued to be a champion of this world and these characters and our biweekly calls are balm to the creative soul. It's safe to say that these books would have no blurbs without you.

Thank you, Liz. You once again dragged me kicking and screaming through a late revision, and were, once again, right about it. You've listened to me complain my way through edits and grumble over fears. You sat beside me (metaphorically - why did you move so far away?) as I worked through plot holes and character arcs, and you held the space for me to bring the pain.

Huge thanks to, Mike. You were both an early and late reader.

Thank you for all the time and effort you put into helping me be a more efficient writer, and for red-lining five hundred pages in five days and then doing it again a month later. Thank you for not letting me quit when I was frustrated and never letting me sulk over criticism. You have been my biggest cheerleader, not just with writing, but with everything else in life, and I am very grateful for that.

A heartfelt thank you to Andrea for taking the utter nonsense I spewed in my cover questionnaire and turning it into a masterpiece. The details are absolute perfection, and I am in awe of your ability to bring a vision that was murky in my mind to life. I'm thrilled with what you've created and can't wait to see what you continue to create for the series.

Thank you, Erin, for whipping my words into their loveliest form. Not only did you help guide this story into its final draft, but you affirmed the choices I made and relieved my worries in a critical moment. I'm grateful for your wisdom and gentleness.

Thank you to Stella and Hillary for bringing me to tears with your stunning character art, and to Nichole (Coco) for making such cool stickers and such a gorgeous pin. For three years, these scenes and these characters have lived in my mind, and you have all given them form.

An enormous wealth of gratitude to my beta readers: Christa, Michelle, Fil, Flynn, Lauren, Melissa, and Ashley. All of you helped make this book hurt in the best possible way. Also, a very big thank you to my anonymous sensitivity readers who kept me on the right side of that hurt.

Thanks to my biz witch coven: Amanda, Ash, Christa, Davis, Nora, Patty, Scout, and Winifred for your tremendous support through publishing and all other aspects of life. Your unique brand of magic keeps me inspired, and on track through all of the background work it takes to write a book (which is most of it).

To Megan, for not just being the lovely voice sending me memos on my phone, but also the lovely voice in my head that reminds me to be kind to myself when I'm struggling. I have listened to this voice memo you left me about fifty times, and these words always pump me up. I hope you don't mind me sharing with everyone else: "Creating is not a safe profession. Creativity, unfortunately, is not a place where we are going to be safe. You have to step outside of your comfort zone allow yourself to be seen, and know that not everyone will like you. That's really hard to do. And also, you are not a person who I have ever seen play small. You don't want to live a life where you hide parts of yourself away or don't let your creativity flow. Your stories need to be told. Your story is out there for someone who needs it more than you realize. To let the people who are sending negativity your way prevent you from sharing what needs to be out there in the world would be such a shame... ...This is just the first of many books that you have written and are going to write, and I guarantee you don't know how you're touching people's lives. The people you're touching the most may not be the ones who are going to be vocal—so do it for them."

Thank you to my friends and family both immediate and extended. You made it your mission to tell everyone you met about THE LOST GOD. I appreciate your unwavering support.

An immense thank you to my original ARC team. I will forever be grateful to all of you who responded to a stranger on the internet offering you free books. You championed THE LOST GOD and brought so much enthusiasm and joy to my first book release. I still get choked up when I think about it. Thank you for following me through THE MEMORY CURSE, and I hope you'll all remain with this story through the end. And many, many thanks to those of you new to the team. I am so grateful for your kind words, and I very much write these books for you.

Bookstagrammers, Booktokers, Bookish Swifties, The Kindred Book Club, my personal book club, and all other voracious readers who embraced this series wholeheartedly—I am so immensely grateful for your support. It might seem a moment in time to you, but I will remember it perfectly, just like a memory witch.

ABOUT THE AUTHOR

THE MEMORY CURSE is Sheila Masterson's second novel. When she's not writing fantasy romance novels, you can find Sheila practicing yoga, or curled up reading tarot or a book. She lives outside of Philadelphia with her fiancé and way too many houseplants.

 instagram.com/sheilareadsandwrites

ALSO BY SHEILA MASTERSON

The Lost God